Letters From [illegible]m

Dear Toria, Matt, & Leo too!

Enjoy with all my very best wishes!

[illegible]

A. C. McKnight

with an Introduction by Susanna Denniston

ISBN 978-0-957646193

A catalogue record for this book is available from the British Library

Published in Great Britain
in 2017 by
Polperro Heritage Press
Clifton-upon-Teme, Worcestershire WR6 6DH
United Kingdom
www.polperropress.co.uk

Printed by 4edge Limited, UK

Introduction

All doctors, according to Hippocrates, need a mixture of science and art. This combination is crucial for the speciality of a general practitioner. The science begins at medical school, but the art develops over the years. It includes expert diagnosis and an intuitive understanding of the patient's needs: physical, mental, and spiritual. Being a good listener is crucial; being alongside the patient, just being there.

James Denniston was my great-grandfather. He was born at Greenock on 5th June 1854. In Glasgow he studied the science of medicine, but it was in Turkey that he learnt the art of it. His experiences in that war-torn country are the subject of this book.

Unable to set up in general practice on graduating, due to nepotism and the resistance modern ideas faced in the medical profession at the time, James Denniston joined the staff of the Stafford House Committee for the relief of sick and wounded Turkish soldiers and was one of the surgeons sent out to be attached to the Ottoman army in Asia during the Russo-Turkish war (1877-78).

A word of explanation about the course and cause of this war may help to illustrate James Denniston's courage and resourcefulness in working so far from home, in an alien environment, amid appalling conditions.

For centuries the Ottoman empire was the most powerful imperial power throughout central Europe, the Middle East and North Africa. Its power only began to wane in 1699, but thereafter its decline was swift due to increasingly militant opposition and the rise of nationalist movements throughout its territory. Though the Ottoman caliphs made repeated attempts to recover lost ground by internal reform and modernisation, Turkey's grasp on its holdings steadily weakened down the years.

During the nineteenth century, Turkey enjoyed strong support from Britain, which sought to maintain Ottoman supremacy for fear of Russian encroachment on Constantinople and the Dardanelles. In 1854 the Crimean war was fought by the British against the Russians, whose imperialistic ambitions threatened Britain's own. In turn, Russia was aided by Britain's traditional enemy, France, who shared with Serbia and Russia a strong Christian tradition instinctively opposed to Ottoman rule and Islamic law.

As a result of these sympathies, the suffering of the Turkish soldiery became a matter of great concern to the British public quickly after the outbreak of hostilities. In the Balkans and in Asia they were subject not only to the more obvious ravages of war, but also plagued by cholera and typhus, frostbite and famine. To reports of this, the British public responded with characteristic cosmopolitan charity. A large sum of money was raised, chiefly through the agency of the Stafford House Committee and the National Aid Society. This sum paid for the travel and wages of 40 surgeons and dressers, to be sent along with large quantities of stores and supplies to the various fronts of this war for the relief of Turkey's soldiers and civilians.

Russia invaded Eastern Anatolia in 1877, first attacking Kars, then laying siege to the fortress-city of Erzurum during the winter of that year. Of the doctors mustered by the Stafford House Committee, only a few were sent so far east as Erzurum. Amongst these was Dr James Denniston, then 23 years old.

The letters he wrote from Erzurum reveal a prickly young man, unresponsive to flattery or the patronage of his elders, but affectionate towards his siblings, and loyal once his respect was earned. They also reveal much of Agnes Guthrie, the woman to whom he wrote. It is clear from his first letters that, although they had known each other only briefly, she had impressed him with her strong will and stronger opinions. She was also a devout and committed Presbyterian, in contrast to the agnosticism and scepticism that come through in Denniston's letters. It is interesting, then, that through their differences, they struck up such a rapport.

It is more interesting still, that their relationship should have blossomed while Denniston was supporting the Turks – that is, the side in the war to whom Agnes was at first so opposed, on religious grounds. The letters they shared, however, and the relationship they cultivated, were a lifeline for Denniston in these hazardous conditions and trying times.

Susanna Everitt,
(née Denniston)

Author's Note

The letters James Denniston sent from Erzurum have been preserved by the Denniston family, down the generations. For this novel I have taken them as my primary source, alongside Charles Ryan's memoir, Under the Red Crescent. I have also referenced Denniston's later MD thesis for a sense of the medical challenges he faced in Erzurum.

Sadly, Agnes Guthrie's letters did not survive James's travels, or the trials of time. In his letters to her, however, he is good enough to paint a vivid picture of a woman for whom his esteem is very clear. It's from the impression he gives of Agnes, and the content of her letters, that I've constructed my own impression of her, and tried to give her life as a character in this novel.

While I've tried not to contradict history, and kept to it as closely as the known facts would allow me, it must be stressed that this is not an essay or a biography, but a work of narrative fiction. As such, I've permitted myself some invention here and there. Of these inventions, the characters themselves are the greatest.

September 1877

Chapter 1

The day dawned grey as Doctor James Denniston left Edinburgh, beneath a sky sharp and grey as new-pressed linens. The previous day had been much the same, as had the weeks before.

It hadn't taken Denniston long to pack his few belongings. The process, however, was a ritual one, sombre and focused. It was contemplative in the way that very early mornings make trancelike even the simplest actions.

As he packed, he tested himself – how steady could he keep his hands while he folded his spare shirt small as he could, or as he prepared a basin of hot water, stropped his razor, and shaved? In the mirror he watched his clean pale hands, appraising each slow and deliberate movement. The razor dragged a swathe smooth down his cheek. Firm and assured, steady and reassuring, he told himself – as if that was any way to gauge his readiness for what lay ahead.

As with all things, he found, the key to success was found in practice. So it had been as a student once, when training his Scotsman's tongue to handle words of unwieldy French – carving compartments in his mind for the new language to nestle in. With time it grew easier. Now he practiced conviction in the same way. As if by solidity and will alone he could convince himself of his eligibility: that he was a surgeon – a war surgeon at that – and not only a doctor from Greenock. As if by keeping faith, his body would earn the trust he placed in it, and in the skill of his hands, and the resolution of his nerves.

Shirt folded, Denniston fit it neatly into his case. Other rudiments followed, packed in on top: a tin mug and towel; soap for shaving and soap for washing; razor and lather-brush and horsehair brush for his teeth; socks and blanket. Then side by side he laid a slim stack of medical texts and a stubby little Bible, each page within alarmingly delicate and thin as the sheets of rice-paper he had seen in sweet-shops. What other clothes he owned, he reckoned he could comfortably wear, and so waive the need to cram them into his luggage.

He left the room he had taken at the Lauriston Hotel with the sun still lazy in rising. In charcoal grey, his wool suit matched the weather. Over it he wore a high-buttoned morning coat, a slim shade darker than his jacket and trousers. Neither would be enough for the winter he was soon to travel through, but for the damp aired day beginning around him, the clothes were swelteringly warm.

His left breast pocket held the crisp shape of a letter: his commendation from the infirmary at Greenock. He had carried it so far to Edinburgh, and in turn it had carried him into one embassy, and through the doors and past the doormen of two smoke-stifling gentlemen's clubs, seeking out advice and investment for his proposed venture. He had found, at least, plenty of the former. The latter's lack had left his funds sparse after travel had been arranged. But travel had been arranged and that, he reflected, was what mattered.

The letter would soon take him further still. In a lower pocket, inside his grey waistcoat, he could feel the weight of his watch, ticking.

At ten o'clock he boarded a train to Newcastle and then on to York. Another train carried him overnight to London. His was a sleeper carriage but he slept little, kept awake by the train's loud motion and his small trunk rattling in the rack overhead.

Dawn came, and Denniston woke to a stiff tired face, rough and in need of a shave as he tried in vain to rub some semblance of life back into his cheeks and the muscles of his jaw. The sleepless night he'd spent made the waking world surreal. Nonsensical though he knew it to be, Denniston couldn't help the feeling that, as he travelled south, he was also moving downhill.

The grey of the sky broke often into rain. He spent hours watching the worsening weather from inside the shelter of his compartment: the rain as it streaked the windows; the thick clouds as they swallowed every puff of steam the train's engine panted out. It was soothing, in its way. He supposed he would feel quite differently outside the carriage. But in either case it was satisfying too, seeing England's fields and hills in this drab daylight. It seemed no more 'green and pleasant' a land than the Lowlands round Greenock, no matter what the hymns or the English themselves might say.

In the midst of the Midlands, at Peterborough and beyond, the second class carriage began to fill with suited men. It was slow at first, but the trickle became a steady flow that filled the whole train as it drew closer to the city.

Twenty-one years of life and this was the furthest south he had been. Manchester, before, marked the limits of his travels and, by comparison, London bustled and heaved like nothing he had ever seen, and nothing showed this difference as starkly as its railway stations.

The morning light as he arrived was still the colour of tin but entirely lacking its lustre. Denniston knew days like this well enough from Greenock, Glasgow, and Edinburgh. This was the kind of weather that found its way into every fold of one's clothing; that turned each crevice in the streets into a puddle and every gutter into a channel of surging mud to be leapt across or, at frustrating length, circumvented. Denniston's previous supposition turned out correct; any will he had to romanticise such a day was sapped by the damp air as soon as he stepped from the train.

The platform at King's Cross boiled with motion, catching him up in the comings and goings of other travellers, buffeting him onwards, then back the way he'd come. In waves they hurried about him - top-hatted men, feverishly checking and rechecking their pocket watches; workers in brown with caps on their heads and maids in black and starched white - and he struggled against and between them, head already spinning with the riot and tumble of London.

He later remembered the city like a whirling carousel of grey that would not stop for him as he elbowed out from the station. From there he walked an hour towards the river and onto the Strand. In squares and street corners the stalls of fruit markets dashed colour into the midst of a city built from austere marble and soot-stained brick, just as the wheels of passing cabs dashed mud onto every pavement. Insignificant and overwhelmed, Denniston felt himself always half-lost - adrift on streets chaotic with bankers and sellers of newspapers, and begging children he tried not to see.

He reached Charing Cross starving for stillness, peace, and quiet. In a room at the station, he found a scant share of all three. He pulled an enveloped photograph from his jacket's breast pocket and allowed himself to think back.

The fevered beat of his heart as he fought to sit still for the camera; the photographer huddled beneath the contraption's black cape, leaving Denniston to stare, confident as he could, into the machine's dark glass eye. That had been in Edinburgh, on the eve of his journey south. The resulting photograph had been intended as a memento. Wasn't that the done thing, between young men and women on the edge of some long separation? He had hoped so, but now he looked at the photograph, it seemed far from how he'd like to be remembered.

It was of a hazy quality and washed with a green-grey tint. Denniston's charcoal suit had been recoloured by the albumen print while his cuffs and hands glowed white. He tried to see himself as someone else might - as *she* might - and the headiness of it almost overcame him.

In the picture sat a slim man with folded arms. His face was long, almost hawkish at the nose, and his hair was a problem all its own. Darker than its usual bronze, it curled fiercely about his temples, then down into sideburns on either side of his jaw. Try as he had to tame it, furiously combing it across his crown and into an even parting, it still found new ways towards wildness, refusing to behave.

But worst perhaps was his expression. He had intended it to be a serious one – another exercise in the firmness and conviction he would soon need – and yet there seemed now to be something quizzical about his eyes and his brow's down-folding furrow. Instead of a man decided, the photograph showed him asking for approval. Fitting as that might be, he'd have preferred a picture that showed him more and exposed him less.

Despite this, Denniston slid the print into an envelope, nestled alongside a small letter, and sent them from the station. He hoped that sending neither would presume too much.

James

Dear Miss Guthrie,
I do hope you arrived safely in Manchester after your long visit to Scotland, and that this letter finds you quite well. I hope for your benefit, and that of Scottish society as a whole, that your stay proves to be an annual affair. I fancy it would improve the atmosphere of Glasgow and Greenock immeasurably.

I'm afraid you must have thought me rude the other night in asking for your photograph. You voiced concerns as to whether or not it would be proper, and I feel quite bashful for how I pressed you. I assure you, however, I was very glad to get it and value it highly. I shall of course keep faith with you on the matter, if you desire it.

I enclose a photograph of myself in return. It's no fair recompense, I'm sure – our looks are not currencies struck to the same value – but I do still hope you will be pleased with it, if only in some small way, or else as a gesture of my gratitude.

You'll perhaps not be surprised to hear it, but I am going out to Turkey, where my intention is to help the wounded and the sick. I've always thought that it is the duty of a young man, not bound by any ties at home, to go out as he can and help how he may. Whether Russian or Turk, Jew or Gentile, my concern and sense of duty is impartial, and owed rather to poor suffering humanity than any one creed or race.

I say it ought not to surprise you, for I think I recall we have discussed as much. You may also recall and deduce though that humanity cannot be my sole object in this undertaking. Sad to say, my prospects at home are not very bright, being without money, fame, or an established name by which to get on in the world. Put shortly, this is a venture and may be the first step to something higher. I only hope it is, and that I might have your sympathy, even though I am allied to non-Christian people, born to a foreign land.

Our friendship has been a short one so far, but to me it has been very pleasant. That is to say, it has been a bright spot on what has been hitherto rather a gloomy existence. I hope if I come back it may last.

For now, I expect to be out of England tonight, and thence to Paris,

Marseilles, Constantinople, and perhaps thereafter to Trabzon, to gain the Turkish interior. Might I ask you to write me in Constantinople – or Istanbul as I ought to practice calling it? I am a bad correspondent I'm sure, but your letters are full of interest, and I shall enjoy them doubly in a strange land, where English conversation will be rare.

I must stop now, though I need not say that I wish you and your family all the good that can possible be.

Believe me, Miss Guthrie, in the meantime I remain

Yours very sincerely,

James Denniston

Chapter 2

Only in Paris did Denniston have time to stop. The city all but demanded it. Like an idol, impossible to pass without genuflection, Paris asked a day of him. He gave it willingly. After a week's long and ceaseless travel – down from Scotland, and now across his journey's first stretch of sea aboard a ponderous flat-bottomed ferry – he admitted that even the staunchest convictions have to rest and recoup.

He stepped from the side of the steaming, seething train and onto the platform at the northernmost station in Paris. Toting his luggage with him, Denniston passed through the station and the disparate flocks of waiting travellers that lined the platforms and then through the stationhouse's echoing interior. It was midday and an unseasonal sunlight streamed through the windows, drawing diagrams on its floor.

It seemed to Denniston as though the station and the street outside could not make up their minds if they were close to empty or bordering on full, the crowds hollowed and refilled them both at such a rate. Perhaps the time of day was to blame. Lunch called some to table, while noon called others to commitments, and departures by rail to far-flung places. Most would be bound for other corners of France. Few, he imagined, would have so far as he still left to travel.

Only one small family seemed a likely exception. Two tired parents herded and guarded four children in a sliding scale of sizes. The smaller ones sat on trunks that looked too big to lift, let alone journey with, while the father stood careful guard over a wheelbarrow piled chest-high with bulky shapes partially obscured under dust-sheets.

As Denniston watched, a woman he presumed must have been their mother crouched down to the height of the smallest child, listening. The girl wore a straw hat so large it all but overshadowed any features save for tumbles of glossy brown curls. Face fighting the urge to frown, the girl spoke to her mother in French, a stream of words so rapid that the words milled together, impossible to overhear or understand.

Denniston turned away from their conversation and eyed their luggage in passing. Like snails, he thought, they seemed to carry their whole lives, home and all, along with them. For it, they would be fated to a slow going – a snail's pace.

When he exited the station, Denniston found himself on a wide street. 'Boulevard de la Chapelle,' a nearby sign declared.

The wind was high that day. The whole street stormed with fierce currents of air, forced down its length. Denniston stood for a moment in the shadow of a cast-iron railway bridge. Its shelter from the breeze gave him room to think.

In his pocket, he felt again the weight of his watch. He could almost convince himself he felt its very ticking, each click of its machinery taking from him a moment of time he would never get back. But his time was his own until evening, he thought, and after that a new train and another leg of the journey awaited him. That was an appointment it would not do to miss but, until then, he had time spare for the spending.

From what he knew previously of Paris, and what he'd seen through the train carriage's windows, the city was vast. London sprawled in a haphazard fashion, growing outward every year, building suburbs on its edges and then absorbing them. Paris, however, amassed to itself another kind of grandeur: tall buildings in faded white, blocked together, in a contradictory kind of regimented disarray. Its buildings grew against each other, organic and architectural, like honeycomb.

To Denniston's left the boulevard widened, coming to a juncture. Above that crossroads, the buildings began to rise, tending upward in rows. It was the start of a hill, he saw, through the junction's mouth.

Nearer by the structures were built so tall that it was hard to get a sense of Paris – the city itself was blinkered off by the buildings that comprised it. Denniston turned towards the crossroads and the hill, in search of a higher vantage.

He walked the Boulevard de la Chapelle until it went by another name and narrowed down, concentrating the wind. Off the way he found and turned onto a sharp, thin, cobbled street, barely wide enough for two walking abreast and too rough and steep for anything with wheels. Denniston was put in mind once again of Monsieur Wheelbarrow and his family back in the station. At least his own lighter luggage would not impede him as much as theirs. He began to climb.

The air was cool but still now, cut off from the buffeting wind. It was not long before Denniston's thighs and calves began to ache, a dull burn forming in the muscle. A breeze, he quickly thought, would not have gone amiss. Already sweat was beading on his forehead and his arm strained at hoisting the handle on his case.

When finally the alleyway ended and the footing evened out, it was not onto a hilltop that it opened, but a square: a small plateau, lined with short squat buildings and cafes with canvassed awnings. Past the buildings on one side, he was disappointed to find nothing but cloud-streaked sky. On the other the buildings continued to rise, further up the hillside. He might climb further, he thought – ascend to somewhere with a less disappointing view – but he was hungry now, suffering for it, and worn from just this short uphill walk. There was also the matter of time.

Spilling from the cafes, tables studded the cobbles, dotted with couples sipping wine from bottles couched in steel coolers, old men silently playing chess and games of cards. Denniston looked over the cafes and picked the nearest doorway.

The interior was shaded and warm, a thin room, much like a broad hallway. Half of its tables must have been outside by necessity – in here there would be no room for them.

A man stood in the welcoming gloom behind a low bar of smooth wood. Behind him stood rank on rank of bottles, their contents golden brown, reddish amber, clear as water, lurid green. He wiped an endless succession of glasses on the edge of his apron and set them back shining, all without taking his eyes from Denniston.

The seats before the bartender were almost like grammar school chairs, low and stable, chosen to match the bar's height. Denniston eyed them, pulled one out, and setting his trunk beside it, he set and caught his breath.

'Something to quench your thirst, *monsieur*?' the man asked in French, from behind a quivering moustache.

'Yes!' Denniston responded, perhaps too enthusiastically than was quite proper. 'Yes, if you please.'

'I have wine on ice, beers too . . . Or something more fey perhaps?' The bartender offered a conspiratorial wink.

'Coffee?' said Denniston, cuffing the last dust of disuse from his grasp of the language. 'Yes, a coffee please, if you have it.'

He received a quizzical look from the bartender, but the man tweaked at a corner of his moustache, turned, and brewed a small dark cup of coffee nonetheless. Another similar look followed when Denniston asked for a little milk, as one would take with tea.

With his coffee pale brown from a splash of milk, Denniston sat and absorbed the cafe's atmosphere: the quiet murmur of conversations from its corners; the crisp sound of the bread he ordered, broke, and ate there with good salted butter; and the stubbled faces of men and the made-up faces of women, animated in discussion outside in the sun, or inside with him in the shade.

The owner had seemed so disappointed in his choice of drink that Denniston felt obliged to order again. A glass of wine followed his coffee, and another after that.

He never reached the top of the hill or the vantage point he'd hoped to find there. Instead he whiled away the afternoon, guiltily ordering and drinking. The cafe filled. Between sips, he watched the bartender polish glass after tiny glass, to hold drams of aqua vita, bright brown brandy, and fascinating emerald liquors that the clientele drank with sugar. This seemed a hypocrisy to Denniston: why should those who took their spirits with sugar have grounds to mock anyone who took milk in their coffee?

Soon the light began to fade. Day turned to evening before Denniston knew it. Under the last slanting rays of a setting sun, he rushed south through Paris as fast as he might, striding quickly to beat away the half-drunken drowsiness that still clung to him from the dark cafe.

With but a few minutes to spare, he boarded a train that would take him to Marseilles. For what seemed the first hour of its journey, Denniston panted along with the train's steaming engine, quite unable to catch his breath.

The stop in Marseilles was a short one, lasting only the interim between his train's arrival and the hour his boat began to board. It seemed shorter still when compared with the sixteen tedious, listless hours spent speeding through France towards the coast. There was time enough to see only a little of Marseilles – from the railway station, down to the docks – but that was sufficient to convince Denniston that he'd seen quite enough.

He thought it a charming if ordinary seaside city. Flat-faced buildings bordered onto a coast of ragged cliffs, both bleached white as if by the bright Mediterranean sun that shone despite the autumn cool.

It had, however, an air quite different from the grand corona of Paris, or London's great grim dignity. "*Liberté, Egalité, Fraternité,*" was proclaimed from every corner and by every possible medium: lines of celebratory bunting, banners, roughly daubed graffiti.

There was almost, Denniston decided, a petulance to the slogan – something defiant and alien to the heart of a Briton, raised to the reign of a queen. It seemed to follow him through town, leering in again at every turn he took, until with time he grew nervous of it.

The stay's brevity, he concluded, was a mercy.

It was only Marseilles' view of the vast sea that saved it from Denniston's earnest dislike. This was his first sight of the Mediterranean: bluer than ever he'd seen the sea and practically blurring into the clear sky where, he supposed, it must reach the horizon.

On the edge of that sea he left France behind, and more besides, when he thought on it. The gangplank of the steamer, as he crossed, became his rubicon, with Europe left ashore.

October 1877

SERAGLIO POINT, CONSTANTINOPLE.

Chapter 3

James

Dear Miss Guthrie,

While I greatly admire your perfect confidence and faith, I'm sorry to say that I have little of either to call my own. It must be a most comfortable feeling to know and to believe that whatever is must be so because it's right – and vice-versa too, I suppose. The world, I imagine, must seem very well put together from such a perspective

It must, however, also be a very great trial of faith to see things go against you in every way, and yet cling to this point of view. That is to say, to believe the world to be, by its nature, good, while seeing at every turn quite how much evil it contains.

Admire this faith as I might, I cannot for myself participate in it. For what I'm to undertake, I only wish I could.

Perhaps you might have faith on my behalf? I hope your confidence and belief in the goodness of things extend to me, and consequently you'll forgive the time between this letter and my last.

I had intended writing from the steamer I boarded at Marseilles, but I found so much to do in the way of amusement that I had no time for letter-writing. Passing between Corsica and Sardinia, and then through the Straits of Messina, and afterwards all among the Grecian Isles, it blew very hard all the way. I am, if I might admit it, an excellent sailor though, and enjoyed our hearty pace very much.

There were several English on board and a lot of French, all bound for Constantinople. I was obliged to brush up on the language of the latter group quite a bit, not only for their benefit, but because I have no Turkish at all and imagine I shall have to make do with English and French for linguae francae – at least so far as I can. I intend to get better by practice and effort, but for now I fancy you would have been amused by my accent and desperate attempts to get people to understand what I meant to say…

We called at Syra and Smyrna and at both places I had four or five hours ashore. They were both very oriental in varying degrees, in some ways readying me for the lands beyond the Bosporus. In this sense they were very interesting to me, but they cannot, however, compare with Constantinople – or rather,

Istanbul. I feel the Turkish name is well-earnt, for though it might be the gateway between Europe and Asia, I have found it oriental and unusual in the extreme. I think I shall only find it more so as it and I become more acquainted. In the meantime I am

Yours very sincerely,

James Denniston

Denniston laid down his pen and looked sideways out of the window. The gesture was mere instinct, there being little enough to see: a sharp rise of plaster facades on Western-styled buildings; tiers of russet-tiled roofs, then the distant peak of a dome in Istanbul's blur and bird-chased sky.

He had been guided here the night before, by a lad he'd found at the harbour, only moments after disembarking from the steamer. In hesitant French he had made his request of the boy, who latched only, it seemed, onto two of them: '*hôtel*' and '*Anglais*'.

The boy had replied at speed in Turkish before taking off, walking as fast as he spoke and toting along Denniston's trunk with one hand. As they went, he flung the other hand out at each dimly lit street corner they passed.

They were directions, Denniston presumed, and demonstrations of any local landmark the boy could spot. All Denniston saw, however, at the end of each gesture, was an alleyway or narrow crevice, darker still than the route they took.

'*Hôtel Anglais*!' the lad had announced proudly, setting down the trunk outside a flat-faced brick building.

Where before he'd chattered with an exhausting enthusiasm, his Turkish now turned almost to argument. He had held out an open hand as Denniston tried to pick up his trunk and venture inside, then scowled and held out again, more emphatically, when Denniston thanked him in French and tried a second time.

Denniston tried to explain slowly and in English, then in careful French, that he had neither Turkish money nor any grasp on the Turkish language to offer or interpret what the boy wanted.

It seemed, though, that nothing would shake the boy. Like a stray dog, he would not let go once his teeth were sunk in.

Feeling into his pockets, Denniston had brought out a pair of pennies, both far from their home by then.

The lad inspected them, objected, then eventually gave his grudging assent. With that and his two foreign pennies, he strolled off into the night with not a word of gratitude – at least none that Denniston could understand.

He begrudged the money for only a minute. What other reason had he to be among the Turks in the first place, he reflected, save that of charity?

Inside, the hotel's heavy-eyed mistress had seemed half-mute. Mostly she gestured, with a hand that trailed smoke endlessly behind it, from a cigarette that appeared never to go out or burn any shorter. She took her own share of Denniston's currency – francs, this time – and led him to his room.

It was small. That had been his first and only impression of the place, before he collapsed onto its narrow couch-like bed and into a heavy wood kind of sleep, too exhausted to be dogged by dreams.

Now morning was breaking across the city, in a cool fog that pooled in the streets. Denniston had woken not long after dawn, hoping to steal some time for letter-writing, but now it seemed more that the letter he'd started had stolen time from him, leaving but little left over in which to shave, dress, and take breakfast. He would have to work quickly if he was to set his plan into action. But he was close, now, to what he'd come for. That thought, at least, filled him with purpose.

Around the hotel, Istanbul woke early. The Call to Prayer sounded out in words that seemed wordless to the point of music, rising up from the city and skyward.

Denniston readied himself with basin, brush, and razor, and put on the single suit he owned. In the hotel's shady atrium a youth in a red cap with a fuzz of aspiring moustache on his upper lip had replaced the matron from the night before. A nod of greeting passed between them, then Denniston was through and into the street.

By daylight, the sign outside was faded but easy to read. "Hotel d'Angleterre." Denniston smiled. The lad who'd led him here at least had earned his pennies, interpreting the request of his foreign charge with commendable if literal exactitude. All the same, Denniston found himself hoping that today no guide would be needed.

The night before, these same streets had seemed alien in the extreme. Prowled by cats and the occasional lone and wiry man, hurrying on their own obscure way, every road seemed an alley, deep in uncertain shade. Now the light of day made Istanbul seem more akin to Marseilles: Mediterranean, yes, but European all the same. There was, however, a concentration to the place. The buildings themselves crowded together, clambering into and over each other as they loomed above each narrow street. It put a tension in the air.

On this side of the Golden Horn, amongst the diplomats and Christians of the Pera and Galata district, they still called the city Constantinople: the ancient edge of Europe. Cross, however, into the Fatih and it would become Istanbul. No doubt it was the same across the Bosporus, on the city's Asiatic side, though Denniston had not yet seen for himself.

In Edinburgh he had spoken to an old military gentleman at the New

Club: a former colonel, at leisure in his twilight years, and equally full of advice and of port. From their discussion, Denniston had managed to glean a sense of the city. It was the old colonel's directions he followed now, pencilled onto a leaf of loose paper and folded into his jacket.

From the hotel, he found and followed the Grande Rue de Pera. From its name he had expected, if not a broad causeway, at least something wider than the main street in Greenock. Instead it was needle-thin and ill-paved, and whatever grandeur had earned its title seemed to come most of all from its length.

It led him endless between rows of looming townhouses, flying embassy flags and built in loose interpretations of the Western style. He passed a bank, making a mental note to return and go about changing his francs and sterling into something more local. The occasional ill-kept church sprung up along his path, in a dozen different modes of architecture, a handful of denominations.

Eventually the great cone-capped column of the Galata Tower rose before him: the landmark he'd been waiting for. Seeing it, he turned left and starkly south, and held his course until he reached the waters of the Golden Horn, and the bridge that traversed it.

The Galata Bridge spanned the mouth of the Golden Horn in planks of wood, wide and sturdy. It bobbed, however, with the water below, buoyed up on a series of pontoons rather than set on solid stacks. Denniston noted more than twenty of them before he ceased to count.

It was the view from the bridge which distracted him. Here was the view of the city his hotel-room window had denied him, open outward in every direction. The day was cold but the fog that flowed in the streets at dawn had since cleared. A yolk-coloured sun shone out from a cloudless blue sky and set the sea to glittering. To the east and over the Bosporus rose Istanbul's far side. And beyond that, he thought, was Asia itself: Anatolia spreading vast towards the Russians and the warfront.

A glaring difference took hold of the city as soon as he stopped from the bridge and into the older Fatih district. The streets here were unpaved and every step that Denniston took roused scuffs of dust in his wake. The same applied to every other pedestrian. The fog had gone, but in its place now was a haze of rising dust that hung in the air: a curtain of gauze, spun from grit.

The causeways now were barely wider than the narrowest alleys he'd seen across the Horn. Even the broadest seemed so only to let pedestrians teem through with greater force, packed together like steam in the cylinders of an engine.

Denniston was surrounded and swallowed in the crowd.

Heavy-moustached men in sun-faded fezzes; broad-legged trousers and bright turbans; the rare glimpse of a woman, veiled in white – all rushed headlong in every direction. Some led mules who in turn led carts, weighed down with lemons, sacks of rice, thin purple vegetables stacked in baskets like sausages in a butcher's window.

New sight after new sound bombarded Denniston, against a backdrop of scents and sunlight – both refuse in the gutters and the perfume of street-sellers hawking pastries, or the whisper of a passing veil or cape – until the city had quite suffused him with strange impressions.

He had walked into a confusion beyond that of any railway station in London or Paris. Footfall surged between ramshackle wooden houses, shopfronts and stalls, set alongside scarce juts of buildings in brick and concrete, positioned like bones amongst the changeable flesh of this timbered district.

Earlier, from the heights of Galata, or else from its bridge, Istanbul had looked quite beautiful in its own unfamiliar way. It was as serried and multi-hued as a great forest's canopy in autumn. From there he had seen a city both united and disparate.

Now, deep in the maze of the Fatih, he saw the streets were filthy, the gutters strewn with waste, small bones, trimmed fat and offal, haunted over by cats and the quick shadows of mice, picking over the refuse with leisurely greed. The Turks, by contrast, seemed hurried and haggard, striking their mules or shouting to each other in their mother-tongue, all sounding angry as the last.

Dust and dirt, a tight cram of wooden buildings, minarets reaching occasionally skyward above the mess and grit of it all. This, he thought, is the true Istanbul – or at least the truest face it had shown him thus far. It was a dizzying place, a nonsensical city, and in it he felt lost, even when his surroundings matched the directions he'd been given.

The day was passing swiftly, as if hurried along by the crowds around him. In the rush of people, Denniston found himself growing impatient.

The sun had passed its zenith and the Call to Prayer went up once more. Here in the Fatih it was louder, rising from every direction as it rippled through the district. In Galata this morning it had been drab by comparison, nothing but a chant, but from one nearby minaret it sounded close to song.

At last Denniston found his destination, on the edge of a bustling square: the war office for this district, the *seraskeriat*. Bristling with harried people, the square was thick with the tension he had felt in other parts of the city. Like a string, drawn out and humming its long low note, it was a kind of stress and a kind of sorrow, in the faces and voices of everyone present. Here, so close to the *seraskeriat*, perhaps it was the shadow of war.

Built bleak from concrete and tacked onto the edge of an old tower, the war office was, at ground level, one of the newer buildings on the square. Its turret, however, rose up from the crowds and the dust like a reaching hand to heaven.

Packs of men were drawn round its doors, some in plainclothes, others in the blue and olive jackets of uniform. Between them they sported a constellation of stars and crescents on sleeves, caps, and sashes. There were those who stood at guarded attention, rifles shouldered. Many more slouched in what shade they could find, smoking, talking, watching the crowds as they waited for some unknown signal.

Denniston decided he would not wait. There was nothing to be gained by that. He ventured in. The guards by the doors eyed him as he passed between them, but said nothing. A Westerner striding with purpose into an Ottoman war office – such a man, Denniston thought, must be assumed either very lost, or so far from it as to go unquestioned.

The inside of the *seraskeriat* was a corridor cast in shade. Lingering smoke clung to the high reaches of the dark ceiling. At intervals a door led off to left or right, through closed and arch-framed doorways. At intervals a shaft of skinny light fell, thick with dancing dust, from an occasional high-set window.

Mingling with the shuffle of booted feet in other rooms, and the stifled conversation of hidden voices, Denniston's footsteps echoed against the plaster walls. Here and there a string of words rung out in a raised voice, hoarse with hard use. He had no hope of understanding the language but it took no knowledge of Turkish to comprehend their tone.

A final doorway stood at the corridor's end. A man exited from the room beyond, in a brief glimpse of a desk and blue uniform, before the door moved closed. This man was jacketed in green, his rugged face framed by beard and head of matted hair. A wooden crutch butted into the pit of his right shoulder.

On instinct, Denniston shuffled to one side, his back against the wall. The other man hobbled past, working not to meet Denniston's eye. The doctor's gaze, however, drew too low to catch. The surgeon he hoped to become had already demanded a look at the soldier's injury. The Turk had lost a leg below the knee. No doubt he had recently returned from the front. A tendon in Denniston's neck hardened. He scolded himself for it. He would see more of this soon enough, and worse besides. The sooner he might inure himself to it, the better. Yet for all the small twinge of distaste that went through him, it was hard to look away.

'Excuse me,' Denniston ventured in French, as much to ride over his urge to recoil as to ask in earnest: 'Would that be the office of Reshid Pasha?'

The injured man swung to an awkward halt, half-turned, and fixed Denniston with a difficult stare.

'I'd hoped I might speak with him,' Denniston tried. 'I was told I'd find him here…'

The soldier scowled and jutted his chin over one shoulder towards the door he'd come from. 'Reshid Pasha,' he growled and resumed hobbling away. It was an affirmation, but spoken like an oath. Denniston half expected him to spit after speaking it.

'Sir?' Denniston's conscience prickled at him, demanding that he ask. 'Your leg. My deepest condolences, but I'm a doctor. Do you understand? A doctor, me, so if you should… If you should wish for someone to…'

But the soldier had gone.

Sighing, Denniston moved to the large door. Steeling himself, he knocked once and entered.

Immediately he faced a barrage of Turkish. A small man sat behind a paper-strewn desk, still speaking, stabbing gestures at Denniston as he let himself in. His glorious moustache twitched with each word, full and sleek, oiled and waxed. But the hair on his head was sparse, hedged to tufts around his ears, and his bald crown was pale from hiding beneath the round red fez that rested on the desktop. Next to it was an officer's swordbelt and a long curved blade, sheathed in its filigreed scabbard. His was the deep blue jacket that Denniston had spied through the doorway. A red panel buttoned to the jacket's front and crescents decorated his sash. Embroidery detailed the cuff of one sleeve. The other was folded in on itself, round an arm lost at the elbow.

For all this finery, certainly he looked every part the *pasha*. Despite their shared injuries, oceans of difference stood between this man and the soldier Denniston had met outside.

Beside him stood a tanned man, younger, with a neat beard. He was not dressed in uniform but still with uniformed precision, his suit not quite European nor fully oriental, but occupying some impasse between the two, like Istanbul itself. He inclined his head, speaking measuredly over the officer behind the desk. He was interpreting.

'*Monsieur,*' he began in clipped French. Clearly he had heard Denniston through the door. Perhaps that also explained his cordiality. 'Kara Reshid Pasha welcomes you, but asks that you please wait your turn. These are difficult times, and he is hard-pressed to—'

'I understand completely,' Denniston cut in, also in French. If he did not assert himself now, then when? Here where he was needed, valuable, and speaking to a man who perhaps already knew it. 'I'll try not to take up too much of the *pasha*'s time.'

'Your accent… Might I presume that French is not your preferred language, *monsieur*?'

'I'm a Scotsman.' Colour rose hot in Denniston's face. He had not thought his French so bad. 'But with respect, *messieurs*, my reason for being here is more important than where I've come from.' He was hurrying now, the words falling clumsy. 'I'm a medic, of good training, come to give help, any help I can to—'

The attendant turned to Reshid Pasha, making spark-fast gestures and speaking in Turkish as clipped as his French. Talking over him together in hurried tones, they acted as though Denniston had already left the room. Only the occasional sidelong glance suggested that they still paid him any mind. In their conversation he heard two words emphasised over any others: *İngiliz* and *hekim.*

Finally the *pasha*'s hard-lined face broke into a smile. He raised his left arm and uttered a short phrase in reverent tones.

The attendant moved the conversation into English. Denniston felt the change like a reproach: gentle but patronising. The heat of his blush rose up to his temples and down beneath his collar. In clear and formal English, the attendant played interpreter between Denniston and the *pasha*. Regardless of the language spoken, Denniston felt like a dull schoolboy, stumbling behind a cleverer boy stood at the front of the class.

'The *pasha* bids you good health and gives praise to God for your arrival. We have had several English come as doctors already. The results of their work, I am pleased to say, are very fine indeed. The *pasha* counts himself blessed that you should come to us now, and offer us your skills as well.'

A pause as the *pasha* spoke to his interpreter, smiling.

'The *pasha* would be pleased, sir, to learn your name.'

'My name is Doctor James Denniston,' he said, and thought to say more – *And I am not an English doctor* – but he held his tongue. It wouldn't do to be flippant, just as the conversation was starting to show promise.

'Then, doctor James Denniston, Kara Reshid Pasha would be pleased to count you as a friend. He already has many friends among the English doctors of this city. Indeed—'

'This city...' Denniston chewed the inside of his cheek. 'In truth, sirs, I'd had hopes for the front. To get to where the fighting is thickest, your men's suffering greatest – the *need* for men such as me, greatest. I've heard, for instance, that Mukhtar Pasha in particular is in a bad way with the Russians at Kars. Perhaps I might...'

The interpreter blinked and raised a hand to smooth his small neat beard. The *pasha* and he exchanged words: a searching question and sharp answer.

'Doctor Denniston,' the attendant finally said. There was an apology in his expression. 'The Sultan – his Imperial Majesty, Caliph of the Faithful – the Sultan's empire is *substantial*, doctor. In Asia alone – Anatolia alone – the distances are *not inconsequential.*' Once more a hand fretted at his beard. 'Kars, for instance, is more than a month's travel from Istanbul. With winter coming, there is no way of knowing whether the army of Mukhtar Pasha will last out the next two weeks, let alone as long as it may take you to reach him. Kara Reshid Pasha...*humbly* suggests that I guide you to one of Istanbul's fine soldiers' hospitals. Indeed, there is one nearby, no more than a short walk from here, and among the best in the city, I assure you!'

The red that had risen in Denniston's face washed quickly away. A tendon pulled taut in his neck. 'I have not come so far to give help to those already safe. Already being helped, given hope. Not when others are so far removed from both.'

His brows knitted. His voice had come out more vulnerable than he had hoped, cracking as he spoke. The *pasha* wanted to keep Denniston's care and skill for himself, his fellow *pashas*, and as a gift to give out, a favour to pay. And to whom but men already clean, comfortable, warm for the winter? A dry grim taste filled Denniston's mouth, as if the curses he longed to sling at this man were gathering there, acrid around his tongue and gums. He drew in a pointed breath through his nose and proceeded:

'My apologies, sirs, but to help where I'm most needed is still my firm intent. If you'll not help me, rest assured I shall find my own way...' He let the moment hang. 'In which case, I'll wish you good day, sirs.'

Denniston turned, shoulders suddenly aching as if from some new burden, and began his return down the corridor. Behind him the two men spoke heatedly in Turkish until the attendant broke away.

'Wait! Sir, please? Allow me – allow me to show you out.' His footsteps rushed in pursuit.

Denniston strode out into the sun, shielding his eyes against the cool white glare. The scuffle of soft-soled shoes came to a halt beside him. The attendant stood in the *seraskeriat*'s shaded doorway, needlessly neatening his beard.

'Doctor Denniston, I apologise on behalf of Reshid Pasha. He has his reasons in wishing you and others like you kept close and out of harm's way. The *pashas* are right to value you, but...their esteem may be unhelpful at times.' He gave a weak smile.

'Esteem?' Denniston grimaced, despite himself. 'I've done nothing as of yet to deserve any esteem, neither from them nor anyone else. I never shall if the *pashas* keep me so preciously. What good am I then, untested?' He paused, checked his rising voice. 'Esteem – I want only a chance to earn it. There are better men than me in your service, I'm sure of it. Keep *them* from harm's way, tending to the *pasha*s' coughs and nightsweats. Let me go where I'm needed.'

'Peace, doctor. As I said, the *pashas* have their reasons. I myself have my own.' The attendant's thin lips quivered. A small change, but his polite smile became genuine, shining now in his dark eyes. 'It was Kars that you mentioned, yes?'

'The front, yes.'

'Will you walk with me, doctor? There are other ways to find oneself under the Red Crescent.'

In silence at first they headed back through the Fatih and returned by bridge across the Golden Horn, tending northward to Galata. It was easy to be sure of one's bearings, Denniston reflected, with a local for a guide. Or a man he presumed to be a local, by the shortcuts they veered down, and the confidence of his stride. But beyond that, he knew almost nothing of this man – not even his name.

The Turk left no room for questions. The juncture of every alley and every streetcorner reminded him of some new story to tell; some new secret to reveal, with that same slight smile he'd shown outside the *seraskeriat*.

'You know, this is the third bridge to be built at this point? No disaster prompts the tearing down of each old bridge and the building of a new. Only a desire for something better, larger, more modern. This one? Young, as you can see by the wood. Only a matter of years since it was built. By your people, I believe! Turkish ingenuity and effort, in cooperation with English engineering. Truly, a testament to the things two great peoples can achieve when working together…

'And there, you see that shop with the red ring-shaped sign? There is *the* place to buy *börek*, should you have the fancy. And why should you not? You are in Istanbul! Only a fool would spend his time here longing only for the comforts of home while refusing the pleasures native to where he finds himself. But these *börek*, Denniston *effendi*… The best. Truly, by God, the best around. There are those who travel over from the Anatolian shore, across the Bosporus, only for a taste! From as far as Üsküdar, it is a pilgrimage worth making barefoot!'

There was barely a pause before he continued, leading them off along another Galata street.

'Do not feed the cats, doctor, whatever you do. They will follow you home and beg for more. For the rest of your life they will haunt you, mewing and purring. In winter, by God, they got like wolves, if not in size then in sheer tenacity.'

By the way he spoke, in at least three languages, this attendant was a man of the world. But for all he seemed well-travelled, he knew Istanbul like an old friend, familiarity undimmed by any distance or time spent apart.

His English was confident and natural, peppered only by the occasional emphatic oath or honorific in Turkish. The busyness of his talk, his gestures, his tales of the city left Denniston feeling more a part of his surroundings.

Despite their hurried travel, he thought he might have a sense of their position. They had arrived once more in the neighbourhood of Pera, close to the hotel where Denniston had spent the night, though how close exactly he could not say.

'Won't Reshid Pasha notice you're gone?' he asked as they walked. 'Whatever will he do without you?'

'You mean, if a troupe of more *obliging* English doctors should appear, all at once? Begging him to enlist their services as he sees fit?' The interpreter's eyes glinted with a smile. 'Perhaps he will speak to them through dance, as bees do… I would be almost sad to miss it.'

'Then why is it you're assisting me instead? As much as I appreciate your help, sir…'

'You may call me Aydin, doctor, if you would prefer.'

'Then I'd have to insist you call me James.'

'Doctor,' Aydin nodded. 'What do you know of the Stafford House Committee?'

'They are some sort of…charitable organisation, are they not? English. Advertised in the Sunday papers, on behalf of one duke or another.'

'You think little of them, then.'

'A diversion, I always thought, for those more moneyed than me.'

'Doctor Denniston… The Stafford House Committee is an organisation founded by your English Duke of Sutherland, in that you are correct. But it also endorsed by His Imperial Majesty the Sultan – through his first secretary, of course.'

'A charity at work in Turkey, then.' Denniston began to understand.

'It is, at present, committed to taking whatever steps funds will permit towards relieving the Turkish soldiery in this war. Medical aid, doctor, is its priority. Namely the mustering and sending out of surgeons to war hospitals throughout the front.'

Aydin examined the nails of one hand as he walked. He cultivated a casual air, but an edge of intensity had crept now into his voice – a passion more raw than Denniston had seen in him before now.

'How is it,' Denniston asked, 'that you know so much about this committee?'

'My business is in knowing these things. A man of your goals and ambitions, doctor – I am more surprised that you know so little about them!'

Denniston flushed. Pride, it seemed – a sense that Turkey should be so grateful for his assistance that he need only ask for what he wanted, and surely receive – had blinded him to the simplest way east. He hurried the conversation from his shortcoming:

'And why do you – an assistant to a *pasha* – feel any differently from the *pashas* themselves about the soldiers beyond this city? In Kars, or elsewhere?'

'Do not presume that all *pashas* are of a like mind. Every man has his reasons to do as he does. One cannot understand them all at a glance...' Aydin stopped, turned a neat half-circle to face Denniston. 'In any case, we have arrived, doctor. Your destination!' He gestured at the unassuming building outside of which they stood. 'As you say, I ought to return to my duties. If Reshid Pasha has resorted to dance without me, well, perhaps I shall be back in time to see the last desperate steps.'

Certainly, nothing would announce this building as particular from any others in the area – not such as one might note while walking by in a rush. It might once have been an embassy. A flagless flagpole jutted out above its whitewashed portico. But whatever it once had been, now it seemed only another Western building in red brick and white plaster, tall and narrow on a hasty-paved street. A small brass plaque quietly stated its purpose:

Headquarters to the Honourable Stafford House Committee,
Care of Mr. Vincent B. Barrington Kennet,
Commissioner General by appointment of
His Grace the Duke of Sutherland

Aydin, meantime, had already disappeared, melting into the crowds that led back towards the Grande Rue de Pera.

The sound of prayer rose up, all through the city once more. With time, Denniston thought, he might find it soothing, to have the day so portioned and orderly, between those waves of sound.

Outside, the day was darkening into night. Still Denniston waited. The luck he'd had at the *seraskeriat*, strolling in unannounced and meeting one of the few men in Istanbul inclined to help him, seemed now to have run out. He was in an antechamber, patience pulled to the pleasure of a Mr. Barrington-Kennet.

Commissioner General of the Stafford House Committee – that was the office Barrington-Kennet held now, but he had begun his professional life inauspiciously, as a lawyer with no talent for the bar.

A Committee aide – a pale young man with thin red hair and an unwise attempt at a beard – had confided as much to Denniston, when he asked what manner of man he was waiting to see. The aide spoke of Barrington-Kennet's background with all the hush and fervour of legend. It was only by tireless work, ravenous compassion, and a deep respect for improvisation in himself and in others, that the world had turned and put Barrington-Kennet in his present place.

It was hard to tell how much of this reputation was deserved and much was the mere myth that Barrington-Kennet had built for himself. However, Denniston reflected, if he was to pin his hopes on any kind of man sending him off to work as he hoped to work, it did not seem unwise to place his faith in a man such as this.

Denniston sighed and looked around him, studying the room for the umpteenth time, by now more from boredom than from true curiosity.

The wallpaper wrapped the room in a fading print of blue plums and yellow leaves. The red armchairs too were faded, three of them, coughing dust from their cushions as one sat or rose. He could only hope the shabbiness of the Committee's Istanbul headquarters were evidence of their priorities – that they would rather divert their funds to places in need of more than a coat of new paint or paper.

Apart from a tall ticking cabinet clock, and the distant call to prayer, Denniston sat in solitude, wishing he had the foresight to have brought something to read. Which would provide the better impression? The Bible Miss Guthrie had sent him, or one of his medical manuals? The former might mark him the bearer of a charitable heart, or else a sentimental one, and naive. The latter would show him capable, or perhaps unveil his inexperience: a boy before an examination, trying to cram his brain to bursting with all he did not know. Left to their own devices, Denniston's thoughts ran off with him.

'Have you dined?'

The voice was sudden. Its English accent broke through the background noise like the ringing of a glass across a crowded room, demanding attention.

Denniston looked up. The man who stood before him was well-dressed, though in tan clothes, more for country than town. The jacket and trousers were seamed for sport, fitted to broad shoulders, a robust body. His face was on the waning edge of what Denniston would still call young. His hair was thick and full, combed back but curling near the collar of his shirt, and showing dark blond from its tips to the blunt fullness of his beard.

'Mister Barrington-Kennet?' Denniston half rose from his chair.

'None other, Doctor Denniston, none other!'

Denniston squinted. He had expected someone older, or else someone who seemed more aged, whether by tiredness, travel, or travails. Istanbul, however, had startled him so many times already that he was growing quite used to surprises.

'Now, answer my question, man! Are you yet to dine tonight?'

Denniston frowned, trying to reason out the import of the question. 'It won't be any trouble to wait longer, sir,' he said carefully. 'If that's what you're asking?' In truth he had not eaten since breakfast. The growling of his belly had begun to sound louder than the ticking clock.

'Well I certainly shan't wait any longer for my own supper! If you'd sooner wait out the whole war in here then that's all very well for you, but I'd rather you joined me – always an unfortunate thing, to eat alone.'

Denniston rose fully now. 'I couldn't agree more.'

'Supper it is then! Quickly now. I rarely have any clue what it might have in store for me here, but dashed if I'm to let it go cold!'

Barrington-Kennet led Denniston through a narrow corridor and into a small parlour. It was similar to the antechamber in size and decor and all but the round table at its centre, laid optimistically for two. Hardly more than a parlour, it seemed to Denniston otherwise to be a room meant for a gentleman eating alone.

Drab though the room might have been, the table itself was clothed in white yet scarcely visible under the particoloured array of different dishes already heaped upon it. Denniston's stomach began growling again. Heady scents rose with the steam from each plate and bowl. His mouth, he could swear, had begun to water.

'Please, doctor, do sit.'

There were plates of dark vine-leaves, wrapped into cigars and filled with rice and sweetmeats. What seemed to be a melon, opened at its top like a teapot, concealed a stuffing of spiced lamb mince. Beside that were potatoes folded into a sauce of yogurt with a sprinkling of a spice that stood out red against the wax-yellow and milk-white. A pair of eggs lay broken and baked over a bed of wilted spinach. In an earthenware dish lay pulses, covered with a silken layer of what might have been baked tomatoes.

'I must say, you look quite dumbfounded, doctor,' the commissioner said, sitting down as a Turk in western butler's black pulled out his chair and adjusted the lamps to a dimmer glow. 'I promise one develops a taste for it. So long as one always has proper silverware, it's easy enough to feel very civilised. Quite the race of wizards in their pantries and kitchens, the Ottomans, I assure you. Though one does start to have dreams about British beef after a time...'

They ate. Denniston fed more ravenously than he'd intended, but he was at least in good company: Barrington-Kennet's appetite put away more than enough of the meal for one man.

To Denniston it seemed a feast. His jaw all but ached with overstimulation. He savoured each mouthful, though the sharp spice of some brought tears to his eyes. Faced with such luxury, he felt suddenly as if he had been hungry ever since leaving Edinburgh.

'I hear you've had a run-in with that old beast, Reshid Pasha,' Barrington-Kennet said, between one *dolma* of vine leaves and the next.

'I'm glad to hear you call him as much. I must confess, I found him...a difficult man.'

'Oh, quite insufferable!' Barrington-Kennet grinned. 'He's been collecting good *Hekims* like butterflies ever since he lost that arm. One can't quite blame the man, of course, but...you understand, James – may I call you James? – an old soldier like that? One sees too much of the front and simply cannot imagine why any other man should want to go there. He's known difficulties and they have made him difficult.'

Denniston paused, remembering the *pasha*'s empty right sleeve. He suppressed a shiver. 'I found his assistant quite a help,' he ventured, braving a spoonful of bone-white turnips in richly red sauced stew.

'Assistant?' Barrington-Kennet murmured, thoughtful, then broke into a bark of laughter. 'The man who brought you here? Who wrote me this afternoon, telling me he'd just met a most stubborn and driven young doctor, for whom he could personally vouch? Ha!'

Denniston's skin prickled with the beginning of a blush as Barrington-Kennet continued:

'That was no *aide-de-camp* or lowly official, man! That was Aydin Vefyk Pashazada, and the bearer of plenty more titles than that besides.' He made a show of dabbing at his dry eyes. 'I apologise, James, my intention is not to tease. I'd explain if I had a better sense of his precise office but, so far as I see it, and so far as his influence affects men like us, why...if Reshid Pasha is a stubborn old goat then young Aydin is the one tasked with keeping him – and others like him – from the cabbage patch, so to speak.'

Denniston's blush was not merely brought on by his mistake. Now the deference that neat-bearded interpreter had shown him added to the colour round his collar. 'And how does that affect men like you, sir? Men like me?'

'Sometimes – quite rarely you understand – he will tell me of something he believes I might find useful. Of course, he is a part of the Sultan's court, I am under no illusions that he does so for any reason but that, in having these resources at my disposal, I can in turn be useful to him. But no matter. The Stafford House Committee would sooner have good ends than good intentions. By the way he wrote about you, he seems to believe that you have the latter in droves... But tell me, James, in all honesty, what do you know of the situation here in Constantinople?'

'Little enough,' he began defensively, 'but enough.'

'Enough to be of a mind that men such as you are of more use to men like me when placed in the field, yes?'

'Yes.'

'James, as of the last report I received, there are twenty-seven hospitals in Constantinople and its suburbs. Almost all are overcrowded to one degree or another, and ill-adapted to caring for the Turkish military sick and wounded.' Barrington-Kennet had set down his knife and fork. His fist was balled in restrained frustration. 'This number – twenty-seven –

has increased by six, you understand, since the start of this war. Many of these so-called "hospitals" are merely homes and warehouses: buildings converted hastily into makeshift wards.

'And do you know the trouble with this? The trouble is that, just because there's a war out in the east, the good citizens of Constantinople don't simply stop getting sick out of consideration for it. Crowded out of hospital by soldiers, they leave their illness at home, or in the streets. Whatever maladies they might have, they spread the damned things like wildfire. The sick and wounded in the hospitals number in the thousands – the tens of thousands. It isn't only the front that this war is tearing to pieces, but Turkey itself. And Constantinople is her ailing heart.'

Denniston's stomach dropped, feeling suddenly overstuffed, constricted. Here it was once more, he thought: the same rhetoric that would confine him to Istanbul. 'What of Kars in the north-east?' he said quickly. 'The rest of the front?'

'What indeed. Kars and the front are another question all to themselves. Or perhaps they are not... Those are areas that produce the injured and sick, and are so damned busy doing so that they don't produce the food that would otherwise feed Constantinople. They fill Constantinople's hospitals fit to burst, and how many cases grow worse on the long way back west, to those same hospitals, do you think? How many die before the journey is done?

'In truth, a river of the walking wounded is flooding this city. Men like you help to dam it up. Those treated in the field can stay in the field. Our stake may not *officially* be in winning this war for the Turks, but in saving what would otherwise be lost. But defending the front keeps famine from the capital...' Barrington-Kennet let the suggestion hang. 'Do you understand?'

'I think I do,' said Denniston, beginning to smile. Rarely had he been so glad to have his expectations proven wrong. 'You'll send me off, then? To the front?'

'I shall bloody well try.'

James

My dear Miss Guthrie,

For five days now I have gone under the Red Crescent – or rather, have worn it on my sleeve – and though I've done but little to deserve it, I take no small pride in it. Indeed, the manners of the native Turks towards a foreigner wearing such an armband are, in my experience, very different as compared to the way they treated with me before. Reverent murmurs by way of greeting and sometimes a bowing of heads – it is enough to leave me quite humbled in the face of all I have yet to do.

It is to the Stafford House Committee that I owe my thanks for this band of rough cloth, the little red cut-out it bears, and all that comes with it, both in the way of respect and responsibility. I hope that I shall soon be told the time has come to resume my travels and be off on my way towards the front – to Kars or wherever shall have me. For now however the intervening days have been busy and I don't imagine they shall let up before I'm sent on.

Mr. Barrington-Kennet has deemed it important that I get a grounding in the workings of a Stafford House hospital, and the ways of Turkish soldiers. By day I've visited two different hospitals within the city, both quite crowded with civilians and combatants alike.

Crammed together, of course conditions such as flux and fever are rife, proliferating in the poor conditions. Between introductions with patients who have a good level of English or French – enough that I might ask about their experiences – I have spent a great deal of my time in these hospitals cleaning, and enlisting the help of Turkish aides to clean alongside me. If by lessening the squalor of these places I can stem even slightly the worsening of cholera, typhoid, and so on, I will rest easier knowing that the time I spent waiting in Istanbul was not time spent all in vain.

Come evening I am often found at supper with Barrington-Kennet, and at table with other notables within the Committee. Useful bureaucrats like Barrington-Kennet himself, most of them, but I've had the luck so far of meeting a few of my peers also: doctors, whether assigned within Istanbul, or else in my position, still waiting to be sent east. There are eight at least in the city at present, though some have passed from being carers to cared-for, and are recovering from the same conditions that plague the hospitals. I even heard of a ninth poor fellow who sadly died of the same symptoms that he, himself, was working to treat.

There is one I might call a companion by now. Certainly we have chanced upon one another often enough, at work, or else in endless journeys to and from the British embassy to arrange the 'possibility' and 'eventualities' of our journey, yet frustratingly never helping us settle a date, route, or destination. Most often it is at supper though, for he is a house-guest of Barrington-Kennet himself, having I think some family connection with him. Casson is his name, a decent English fellow, and with an invaluable knack for languages: very fine French, and a fast-growing aptitude for Turkish, alongside, he says, 'a schoolboy's share' of Latin and Greek.

As much as I appreciate having leave to write to you, and open out my thoughts like this, I am glad to have made the acquaintance of another man in my position. Between yourself and Mr. Casson, I am in good spirits. All things are a good deal easier to bear when one has friends, I think.

At present, it rather turns my daily trials into something quite exciting, if far from pleasant. The hospitals are one thing, but do you know, the streets I walk to and from them, the Committee headquarters, and the hotel where I am lodged, are another thing entirely.

Packed with wounded and sick, and strained I suppose by war, Istanbul is rich in all kinds of wretchedness. Of chief concern are the thieves and scoundrels that roam the streets, and would sooner take robbery and assassination as their professions than 'stoop' to honest work.

I think of myself as cautious in such matters, but Barrington-Kennet has insisted on a gift for all Committee representatives, to supplement our caution. Mine is a snub-nosed revolver, surprisingly heavy, dark and greasy to the touch. I must say that if it eases Barrington-Kennet's mind that I have it, it does nothing at all to ease mine, whether sitting on my desk while I write, as it does now, or hanging awkwardly in my pocket. A proverb comes ominous to mind, does it not? Those who live by the sword will die by the sword.

However, I do not fail to see its necessity, here or on the journey ahead. News and rumours pass easy about the supper table at headquarters. At my hotel they come in a muddle of European languages, plentiful as matches for pipes, papers for cigarettes, sugar for coffee. I heard an Englishman had been robbed and badly wounded by a pistol shot recently, in this very area. Indeed, strange how such things plant ideas in the mind, but I could swear that since I heard this news I remembered hearing a sound too, only the night before: gunfire, loud as a whipcrack across the district.

For now I should stop. It's getting late, and I'm afraid this letter – already looking a state for the poor pens and rough paper – will only get worse, more tiresome and rambling if I continue. Having no desire to subject you to receiving such a letter, I shall sign off.

I hope you will send any letters with which you might honour me to 'The Stafford House Committee, under care of Barrington-Kennett Esq'r, Constantinople.' He will know where I am and, if I have any luck and am already away by the time you read this, he will forward them.

In the meantime

I am yours very sincerely,

James Denniston

Agnes

Dear Doctor Denniston,

I fancy you have never felt yourself so popular, and with so many friends to speak of, as you do now that you have left them behind. Whether from those with whom you studied in Glasgow, met in Edinburgh, or society such as myself in Manchester, I am sure you receive many such panegyric letters from these friends. You say, however, that you will not mind that I add my own more sober correspondence to the multitudes; after all, have you not already praised me before, in saying how fine a correspondent I am? I think my writing scarce matches your compliments, but I shall do what I can to live up to them, from time to time.

Indeed, I think it might be, to some small extent, my duty to do so, being that I offer not only news and kind words from places close to your distant home. You are self-professedly a young man in neglect of his Bible – one among many in our generation, I think – and, being in foreign lands and amongst unchristian creeds, would it not be easy for you to slip unknowing into unchristian ways as well? Given time, any man will change to suit his surroundings, or else find that he is changed by them.

My duty, as I put it, shall be to allay this moral decline. Should you feel you have doubts or fears, I hope you shall open them out to me, and let me help you to consolation. It gives me a deal of solace to hear you have taken with you the presents I gave, the Bible and Psalter both; I think in turn they shall give you great solace in turn. For my part, the verses of Shakespeare you sent are very fine gifts themselves; no-one, I think, has written such truth with better grace since: 'For we which now behold these presents days have eyes to wonder, but lack tongues to praise.' etc. So, for them and for your photograph, I thank you.

But how exciting your journey already seems! Certainly it is – and, I am sure, will prove – quite enough to fill a novel of the better sort; perhaps not in three volumes, as is the fashion, but this will depend upon the depth and degree of your adventures, will it not? Indeed, perhaps it is best that, if ever anyone should write of your exploits in this way, it should be me, to assure you it is of the best sort possible.

Your letters alone, however, will surely provide much material for those who find their hearts are thrilled by thoughts of adventure throughout the Orient. Indeed, they already have. I recall that you mentioned, when we met, an admiration for the Reverend Charles Kingsley; while I might find his support for Mister Darwin to be unbecoming in a man of Faith, I will admire that the Reverend Kingsley's writing is of the kind I like very much, and I find myself wondering now: have you read his novel, Westward Ho!? Reading it as a girl, it put quite the fancy in me to see the Americas. While I do not know if I ever shall, or if I shall ever travel so widely as you already have, I think that if any other writing were to inspire in me the same ardency, yet directed now towards Constantinople and the further Orient, it should be the content of your letters.

What occurs in my own life is somewhat less dramatic. You will recall Mr. David and Mrs. Sarah Carmichael of Edinburgh, perhaps, from their attendance in Greenock; we are to visit with them once more within the month, that we might assist with their most recent passion project: a dance by which to raise funds for Edinburgh's Christian working poor. I do not doubt, of course, that your own work is for good, but I feel that it is, nonetheless, a pity you should not be in attendance.

Toward the ends of your good work, you seem quite taken with the cause of the Turkish soldiery; I only hope it is not beyond the call of compassion. You will note, and doubtless already know, that I cannot hope for a Turkish victory in all this, for the unconscionable cost at which it would come to Christians and Christianity in the East. The tales I have heard of the Ottoman bashibazouks and their reputation for savagery tells me enough of that cost that I do not wish to think on it further. But I do not wish the Turks ill, no more than I could wish any soul ill, whatever God to which they have given themselves over. Through you I wonder if I shall begin to sympathise more than, at first, I thought I might. For now, my sympathies are with you too.

I have enclosed with this letter a copy of The Times and hope it will reach you at a fair rate, such that the news within will still be new. You mention that news from the West is hard for you to come by, however, so perhaps even late news is preferable to no news whatever.

Until then

Very sincerely,

Miss Guthrie

He was packing again. It was what he'd wanted ever since his arrival in Istanbul – to be sent out to the front, not only to wear the Red Crescent but work under it – and yet now that the time had come, it found him conflicted.

The news had come that morning by courier and had been waiting for him with his breakfast. Slotted into the tin rack with his toast, written on Stafford House Committee notepaper and packaged up in a monogrammed envelope, the missive padded its meaning, but the message itself was clear.

Doctor Denniston.

As commissioner general of The Stafford House Committee, it pleases me greatly to inform you that the SHC has chosen to take you on as a fully salaried field doctor and surgeon, under the Red Crescent, and assigned to the orta of Sadik Pasha in Erzurum Province, or whosoever commands the garrison at Erzurum upon your arrival.

Your salary will stand at £1 sterling per day, and shall be deposited monthly into an account kept by the SHC until such time as your employment with us is terminated. An allowance of £10 sterling, rendered in Lira and Kuruş, shall be with drawn from this pay and made available to you monthly, if your whereabouts are known and reachable; this shall do for your maintenance.

As to travel, transport by boat from Istanbul to Trabzon has been arranged for yourself and all soon-to-be colleagues assigned with you to Erzurum. An agent of the SHC shall brief you there as to the remainder of your journey. Enclosed is a cheque for a sum of £50 sterling to pay for further travel to Erzurum and back, and to be cashed in Trabzon. In the changing of this cheque you accept a contract of six months' service to the SHC, renewable at your discretion after such time as this duration has elapsed.

The Liakáda will depart no later than 8 o'clock sharp from berth 16 of the Bahçekapı harbour in the Fatih, tomorrow morning.

Godspeed and good luck,

Vincent M. Barrington-Kennet

P.S. – I advise you as a friend to see to the disposition of your salary fund. In the event that you should be unable to claim it, I will personally see that it is dispensed with according to your wishes. In any case, I've always found it to be true that the best way to ensure a thing will not happen is to diligently prepare for its occurrence.

Denniston had bought an atlas of Anatolian Turkey days before, at a bookshop in Galata. It lay open now on his desk, propped wide with a shoe, and showing the hundred or so miles that separated Kars and this city of which he had never before heard: Erzurum. So far as he knew, those hundred miles lay between his destination and the war's true front.

Once again, he thought, he was being coddled, kept back – saved for best like the good china at home that he'd always thought to be useless for how little use it saw. At first he had fumed over it, shaving himself viciously, badly, but like any fire his anger burnt out all the faster for how bright it once had blazed.

Stewing now, Denniston closed his shaving kit and stowed it in his case, between books, thick socks he'd bought for the winter, a new shirt he'd bought in reserve. He would evaluate the situation logically, he thought. What other option did he have? Careful and calm as he could make himself, he turned it over in his mind as if chewing it: shaping it through unpleasant process into something that, finally, he might be able to swallow.

In a war being lost so swiftly as this war the Turks were fighting, one-hundred miles behind friendly lines was little when so much might be lost so soon. Since arriving he had heard nothing but ill spoken of Mukhtar Pasha's prospects in holding out at Kars. Indeed, any news from east or west was already old by the time it reached Istanbul. Kars may already have fallen, whether overrun or surrendered. For an army gaining ground so swiftly as that of the Russians, one-hundred miles would bring Erzurum next in line.

That realisation brought a moment of excitement as he closed his atlas, cleaned and buffed his shoes. Another came moments later, seeing his own face in the black shine of his brogue's toecap. It sunk his stomach and filled it with lead.

This excitement – his hunger for danger, exploits, adversity to overcome – was vanity. He had given no thought at all to the suffering of men, whether in Kars, Eruzurum, or Istanbul, for all his words, and all the passion that Reshid Pasha, Aydin Vefyk, or Barrington-Kennet had seen in him. It had all been for himself: a need to save lives not for their sakes but for his, to prove his mettle and show his skill.

When he thought of the front, he had glorified it, just as he had in boyhood, fencing with sticks that imagination made into sabres. It had been, at the time, a way to make sense of the shadow that hung over their childhood. He and his siblings, through play, had pretended to understand what those older than them meant when they spoke of the war just concluded in the Crimea. Just as the adults offered tea and shortbread and conversation to turn grief over lost cousins, lost sons, into consolation, Denniston and the other children play-fought til every soldier – living or dead – was a hero, and all war looked like justice.

But he had become a healer, not a soldier. Any glory he might win would be in soothing suffering, saving lives, and no doubt Erzurum suffered as Kars did – plenty more than its share. If he learnt anything from Erzurum, he told himself the first lesson would have to be in humility.

Ashamed of himself and his ambitions, Denniston finally wrote to his mother: a short note, but with more words in it than they'd shared since he'd left Greenock.

James

My dear Mother,
I do not know if you had expected to hear from me before my return. You said, after all, that you feared I wouldn't return at all. And I do not know if you can remedy the damage I did in going against your wishes and worries, and on such poor terms, but if this is a thing that can be healed, I think I'd best start now.

I'm writing from Istanbul. Fancy that! But I shall be gone by morning, and on my east by boat to Trabzon, and then to a city called Erzurum. And at first I was disappointed to the point of anger.

I fancy my reasons were much the same then as they were for my anger at you when you told me I ought not to go out as I have. That is to say, pride and pig-headedness, on my own foolish part. But I've since seen my error in both suits.

I'm certain there's good work to be done in Erzurum, and I'm as good a man to do it as any. Perhaps I shall even be safer there, and so ease some of your fretting. But already, in being assigned there rather than the chaos and supposed glory of the front, Erzurum has already taught me one lesson, and that has been in humility.

Ma, I'd apologise if I only had the words for it. But whatever words I write could never take back those I said before.

As such, all I'll say now is that I'm sorry for them all, and shamed by myself, and that I'll try to keep well, and return a better man. I only hope that, when I do, you'll still greet me as a son as I hope to greet you again as a mother.

Until then I'm yours
Very sincerely,
James

Chapter 4

The *Liakáda* purred slowly along the coast of Turkey. Compared with the ship that had carried Denniston from Marseilles across the Mediterranean, this boat was smaller by far. The weather had been windless since leaving Istanbul, and there was nowhere on board where the chug of the *Liakáda*'s little engine-room could not be heard, rambling along always like the beat of an ailing heart.

Useless sails furled, they had carried on at this pace for almost two days. The going was gentle, the view of the coast pleasant as they skirted it, but Denniston found it frustrating above all else.

A book of anatomy lay open on his lap as he sat on deck, back to the rail and facing the open blue sea. Impatience, it seemed, could cloud the faculties as much as distraction or worry. He must have read the same paragraph countless times now and still learnt nothing from it. The pages had shown the same layered diagram – muscles, ribs, lungs, the heart nestled lopsided between – so long that he swore the print must have faded, at least a little, beneath the cold pale sun.

Company, perhaps, was as much to blame as short patience, however. The little *Liakáda* had but one cabin for passengers. Every night aboard was spent cooped up inside it with six more fellow surgeons, crated up like goods for transit, below deck with the supplies in the hold, en route to Erzurum as much as they were. By day they strewed the deck, talking, stretching their legs as space allowed, studying – or in the case of Guppie, doubled over the balustrade, vomiting, or waiting to retch once more.

Guppie, of all the surgeons, had taken worst to travel by water. In Istanbul some flux had laid him low and forced him into one of the hospitals he was meant to be offering help. Weeks of illness there had left him pale and drawn, all waxy eyelids and a clammy amphibian cast to his face – and this despite the fact that he, supposedly, was recovered. He had barely come back to health by the time the Committee had sent them eastward, before the sea – even so gentle as it was – threw him headlong into relapse.

Between the noise and dramatics of his seasickness, Denniston had found Guppie's acquaintance pleasant enough. He was the owner of a weak but easy smile, a cautiously optimistic manner scarce found among any but lifelong invalids. There was, however, a translucency to him, his complexion, his whole character. He looked now so thin and fragile that if they were granted any wind at all, the faintest breeze might carry him overboard and away. And that, only if some new malady did not carry him off first – or so went the whispers among the other surgeons, grim as an omen, exchanged in secret.

Denniston watched now as Guppie's back convulsed and heaved, hunched over the *Liakáda*'s side. No doubt the trousers the other man wore had once been made for a sturdier man. Perhaps Guppie once had even been such a man himself. If this was true, of late it showed only in the way his flesh hung on him. Illness had left him with a thin man's shape and a plump man's skin draped over it, ill-fitting as his clothes.

There was an awful fascination in seeing it, and Denniston found he couldn't stop looking. He'd felt it before, in the hallway of the *seraskeriat*, confronted by the one-legged soldier. Before that, too, in his younger years as he saw a young horse take fright in the bolt and press of Edinburgh's streets. Careering amongst the panicked crowds, upsetting the stalls of traders, it had set the whole street to chaos, while Denniston stood frozen. Torn between helping those who were hurt and stopping the poor beast, he had done nothing but watch, transfixed.

He closed his book and slipped the slim text into a pocket as he rose. A moment passed and he balanced himself, setting his feet with the boat's lazy sway, then crossed the deck, over to Guppie's side.

The other doctor had since stopped vomiting. Still he was bent over the balustrade, queasily watching the sea as their progress ploughed it into eddies of white. His shoulders trembled. Between them, sweat had made a dark triangle on his shirt's back.

A twitch of instinct warned Denniston away; told him not to touch a sick man. It was the same feeling that rears the eye back from taking notice of beggars, or of things not right in the face or body of another human being: something like embarrassment, so acute it feels for a second like a kind of horror. But Denniston had felt it before and long since cursed it away. All the remained was vestigial. What kind of doctor would he be, after all, if he feared to be near the sick, the hurt?

'Even the best sailors get seasick,' he said, standing a few feet now from the balustrade, arms across his chest and wearing a smile that didn't quite reach his eyes. 'I think that's often how they get to be good sailors in the first place.'

'Is that true? Then I imagine I shall be the best sailor of us all by the time we get to dry land once more.' Guppie straightened and turned to face Denniston, voice weak but not without humour. Still he leaned against the rail in his baggy trousers and shirt-sleeves, as if he were a tent that would fall if it weren't pitched. His eyes were watery and his lids a damp pale pink.

The two men shared a look, and then a snort of laughter.

'It's all in the practice – everything is – I promise,' said Denniston. 'Once you're used to the yaw of the boat the sea air'll start to do you good. Truly. You'll be right as rain for the way on to Erzurum.'

'I hope so. I certainly do. What kind of an example would I set my patients if I seem as much an invalid as them?'

That evening a cold wind encouraged the bright-eyed Greek captain and his two-man crew into their pilot's enclosure, and the doctors all into their cabin.

Guppie was curled foetal on his narrow bunk. He shivered sometimes, but otherwise Denniston hoped this was the first step towards the health that he'd promised. It looked at least like peace.

The rest sat on the cabin floor like boys telling ghost-stories round a lantern. In the middle of their circle was a small spirit burner, ticking away with its little blue flame to brew a pot of tea. Over their heads, and from their pipes and cigarettes, pale smoke crawled towards the ceiling.

This was the second night Denniston had spent in their company, but time at sea had a strange way of distorting itself, he reflected. Close quarters and a shared goal made their camaraderie feel like something they had worked at much longer. Though certainly, Denniston wondered how much of this was the doing of the brandy they added to their tea.

"Gentlemen?" Kincaid leaned towards the pot, bottle in hand. "It's a cold night, after all…"

His suggestion found no solid objection. A half-guilty feeling uncurled in Denniston's stomach – what might Miss Guthrie say to all this? – but the promise of hot tea and the warmth of brandy quickly silenced it.

Featherston's refusal was quiet, shy and small, much like everything else about him. He was a midlander; a non-drinker with a youth in his face that made his true age hard to place. Though his eyes were round, brown, and expressive, Denniston had heard him speak little more than to graciously decline tobacco and brandy, or give thanks for tea. Now he simply hugged his cup with one hand, and slipped the other over its mouth like a lid.

At varying speeds the others drained their own cups, and refilled them from the newly doctored pot. It put them at ease, made them dreamy and fond, and filled the cabin with a sentimental kind of silence. There was only the occasional comfortable sigh; the even whisper of Guppie's breath; the scratch of a pen as it turned out a letter, or the sound of Pinkerton's teeth as he chewed the stem of his empty pipe.

That was one of his two affectations, without which Denniston had yet to see him: a stubby pipe in hand or between his teeth, and a little black Bible in his jacket pocket.

“Trouble you for a pinch, could I?” Pinkerton smiled a tan-toothed smile. He was from Devonshire and the town he came from had rounded his accent. Perhaps it had also left him his easy manner and oft-shown smile. “Thank you,” he said, and began once again to pack the bowl of his pipe.

It was Walker that had obliged, reaching now into his tobacco pouch to roll himself another cigarette. His hands moved, small and clever and sun-browned, though Denniston remembered from his firm handshake that their palms were rough as a workman’s. But he was a Londoner, short and slight-built, dark eyed and darkly complected; there was no telling what Walker had been before he had made himself a doctor.

Casson’s was the scratching pen, writing letters as ever in neat copperplate, with a pair of round spectacles perched on the slight-crooked bridge of his nose. He was the only one among their number who Denniston had known in Istanbul: Barrington-Kennet’s guest, and a friend perhaps before even they’d boarded the boat.

Up from the quiet there lilted a note. It was Kincaid’s voice, raised in song: *‘Oooohhh-a-as I roved out of a bright May morning…’*

For a fierce-faced man of Liverpool, haloed with wiry red hair and combed copper beard, his voice was pleasant, its melodies sweet and almost Irish. His song continued amongst the smoke and fumey scent of hot brandy.

Denniston rose as the last note’s faded. ‘My God, but it’s a fine set of lungs you’ve got on you, Kincaid!’

Kincaid raised his steaming cup in response. ‘Do them a turn would you?’ He pointed with his cup through the smoke to the porthole nearby. Obliging, Denniston opened it, eyes suddenly stinging, to vent out the smoke and let in the cold night air.

If brandy made Kincaid tuneful, then it seemed that it made Denniston honest – or rather, half-honest, for in truth he’d meant to say more. Kincaid’s voice had been beautiful, his song strangely sad. Only, Denniston had been too shy to say as much and to admit to so much sentiment.

A warm wind blew in from the west come morning. It creased the sea like hands over blue-grey cloth, testing the quality, feeling the texture. While at night the breeze rushed in from the blackness beyond the boat-lamps’ light, and spoke of a coming winter, that morning remembered summer still, and the eastern sky was pink with the dawn.

In the breeze at last the *Liakáda* had opened her sails and the little boat’s speed picked up for the final stretch of her voyage.

Denniston stood on deck. He had always favoured the feeling of travelling by sea, and always preferred the sensation of going under sail rather than steam. Rather than trying to work or study, he allowed himself this simple pleasure, and watched the coast scroll by.

On a swell of shore in the distance, he watched Trabzon grow. At first it was a blur of white and red, catching the sun against green and grey hills. Quick though, it became a bristling of piers and a cram of buildings beyond them.

First he saw the other steamers, some at rest, but others puffing plumes of vapour dark into the sky. They were stoking their engines, he supposed: like men smoking cigarettes in the shade before heading to work once more. But between them and out on the ocean beyond, there were older sailboats all in motion. Fishermen, Denniston thought with certainty. Small and wedge-shaped, with tall triangles of sail, they were already at work on the Pontic waters and by noon would be laden with their catch. It was familiar to Denniston; comforting for it. Wherever you are in the world, fishermen rise before the sun.

The city spanned the shallow headland and, after, clambered up the hillsides, buildings perched like flocks of goats. By now they were near enough to make out individual roofs, the colour of rust or sun-baked leather.

The *Liakáda* had been the floor beneath their feet and the roof above their heads for two days and two nights' constant travel. Now, on the third morning, it pulled into port, hull skudding against the pier as its skeleton crew made it fast.

On board, the seven British doctors collected their belongings and hauled them above deck. Casson had brought more weight and bulk almost than the others combined, Denniston observed: a heavy steamer trunk and two cases, each larger than his own. Paying a stevedore at the docks to help heft his luggage, Casson watched from the pier as the stevedore worked, stripped to the waist, straining to haul the metal-bound trunk down the gangplank. Denniston waited with the rest, smaller cases in hand, sun unseasonally hot on their backs.

There was no reception to welcome them; no other passengers to disembark. The *Liakáda* had sailed to the commission of Stafford House alone, and yet all that showed of the Committee's influence now was an address in Barrington-Kennet's scratchy hand, scrawled upon an index card, safe in Guppie's pocket.

The upstairs apartment had not even so much as the small plaque of the Istanbul headquarters to mark it out for the Stafford House Committee. Only by recommendation – the scribbled address in Guppie's possession – would an outsider think it any different from the other apartments, stacked each upon the other, either side of a narrow street leading off the harbour of Trabzon.

Through a half-open window the chipping sound of horses' hooves and the padfoot sound of human traffic crept in. Occasionally there would come the wheeze of a coastal wind picking up, forcing itself through the gap between window and sill.

Inside, the seven doctors sat around a low circular table, oriental in style, taking breakfast with a stranger. He had heard much about them, it seemed. Denniston only found himself nervous that they knew so little in return.

'In Turkish, the word *kahvalti* does not mean 'breakfast,'' the stranger said in accented English. 'Not perhaps as you might understand it, gentlemen. Rather, it means something closer to 'what comes before coffee.''

He was a small Anatolian Greek, dark-haired, with bruise-coloured eyelids and the peach-like cheeks of a cherub in a tasteless painting. This was their administrator on behalf of the Stafford House Committee: their agent in Trabzon, and this room his agency.

At least for all the informality of his manner and surroundings, there was an air about him that inspired confidence – or rather bespoke a surplus of it on his part. He conducted speeches, breakfast, and bureaucracy all with the same air of ritual and efficacy. Soothing, Denniston thought, to be taken in hand: swept along on the tide of someone else's competence, until Denniston's own could be put to use.

'The start of the day has its own beginning and its own end,' the administrator said. 'That is, if one is to do it right. Fortunate for you, I have started it all quite wrong – quite late – this morning. You, doctors, are exactly on time.'

He gestured with a soft thick hand to a pair of teapots, each stacked on top of the other over a small black iron brazier, hot with coals.

'*Kahvalti* has its proper end in tea, but the beginning – and the middle, yes, also the middle – are a matter of proper *nourishment*. I suggest you eat well, my friends. Provisions will be scarce for God only knows how long after you leave Trabzon. *Hekims* you might be, but still there is much you might learn from the soldiers you tend to. The chiefest of lessons they will teach: eat whenever you can, whatever you can. I fear for you, my friends. I fear there might only be coffee ahead of you, for a long, sad while.'

Dishes covered the low table, more than enough for eight men. There were baskets stacked full of bread, some dry as if deliberately staled, others soft, freshly baked, steaming as they broke open. Dense and almost flat, the loaves ranged from the dark sour colours of whole wheat to the lurid yellow of ground corn glazed with beaten egg. There were dishes of wrinkled black olives, cured in salt, and dishes of their fatter green counterparts whose soft tart flesh fell lushly away from their pits with one careful bite. Plated beside them were two kinds of cheese. One was soft and crumbling – delicious, Denniston found, crushed onto a shred of flat bread – and the other was hard and smooth, its rind tough, its flavour nutty and lingering.

'My apologies, my friends, for the meal,' said the administrator. 'It's sparse fare, all told, but these are scarce times, and we must all forgo what we can for the sake of our fighting men, a short journey east.'

'My friend, there is nothing whatever to apologise for,' said Casson, effortless, gracious. 'For dry times you've put on quite the spread for us!'

Denniston wondered at the easy words they all spoke: "my friend," "my good man." They had become fast friends too fast for his comfort, it seemed.

'A short journey, you said,' Denniston cut in, feeling graceless by comparison. 'How short? I've looked over maps, but journeys are always easier on paper...'

'Oh!' The Greek gave a boyish grin. 'Why, a matter perhaps of...well, more than one-hundred miles and fewer than two-hundred.'

'And how much of that over hills and between mountains? How much on poor roads? We'll have guides?'

Denniston lowered his eyes, realising his voice had grown hard, insistent, shattering the spell of calm the others had woven over breakfast. They were looking at him now. He could not see it for a fact, but felt their eyes hot as a blush upon him.

'You shall have a guide, of course you shall have a guide, my friends, I have seen to that thoroughly. The journey is a matter of days. Four or five, no more. It only pains me that you should have so short a time in which to enjoy Trabzon..!'

Both guests and host moved inward across the table's array of dishes. With red-faced relish, Kincaid finished a cast-iron pan of baked eggs and fried spiced sausage, pale blue eyes watering. A forbidding and pungent paste of crushed anchovies and spices sat in an earthenware bowl, which only Casson and the administrator finished. How the latter found time to eat so much and talk so much in tandem amazed Denniston more and more as the meal went on.

'All things that this city is or has been,' the administrator said, 'are things left to the Turks by the Greeks. You sit and drop crumbs on what remains of an empire, my friends. More than one, perhaps!'

Sooner than later, Denniston thought, another fallen empire might be added to Trabzon's heritage. That hung in the balance of this war.

'Istanbul was Byzantium and Constantinople,' smiled Pinkerton, with the tone of a man pleased to talk of his particular interests. 'But Trabzon has been Trapezous, Tribisonde, Tara Bozan, Ozinis, and Trebizond.'

'A scholar of history as much as medicine!' The administrator beamed.

'Only a dabbler, I assure you, a mere dabbler,' said Pinkerton. 'Just an old man more curious about what's gone before than whatever lies ahead.'

'Let it not be forgot,' said Casson, 'those who do not know their history are doomed to repeat it.'

'And those who do know it are due a deeper sense of the present day,' said the administrator, tapping his nose with a finger. 'Why, only a matter of weeks ago, a veritable hoard of *drachmae* was unearthed not a mile from here! Silver – can you imagine it, and all steeped in history! A man acquainted with the past knows that everywhere in the world, one walks on buried treasure. Knowledge or wealth, it makes little difference…'

The tea, when ready to drink, was served in glasses so small that Denniston would have mistaken each for drams of whisky if he had not seen the administrator pour them. Its perfume was strong and its colour stronger: the rusty red-brown of rabbit's blood. As to the food, only crumbs remained.

'Now,' said the administrator, casually licking his fingers. 'You have taken your first steps, and as to what must be seen to…' He looked at Denniston with a glint in his eye that could either have been amusement or quiet cold threat. 'You may rest assured I have seen to it. Why, I know a man in the market who is brother by marriage to the most honest mule-driver in all the province! For a reasonable price I can see you supplied not only with beasts to carry your burdens, but carts, mattocks with which to dig latrines and shovel the coming snow, beef tea, hard tack, dried meat, and coffee, of course you shall have coffee. Winter coats? Tell me, how many of you have proper winter coats? Come now, I speak of *fur*, my friends, thick as your forearm. You shall need it! There's snow already in the mountains. Tell me, my friends, tell me, how many of you are versed in the use of firearms? Dry times, my friends, as I said, and in the countryside I am sorry to say, dry times make for a drying up of the moral fibres. The roads are quite *swarming* with bandits, robbers, and the like. Tell me, my friends – have any of you ever shot a wolf?'

James

My dear Miss Guthrie,

Two days now we have been in Trabzon and I think the winter has well caught up to us, or rather it has come early. It already hangs cold in the air, even here by the Black Sea coast. There are films of ice on the stable troughs and set in every street-gutter. I daren't imagine what it shall be like in the mountains we're to pass through, yet I think it's inevitable that we shall soon find out.

I cannot write a long letter, or I think a very good one, for we're to leave early in the morning tomorrow – a Sunday – and I should like to get a good start on, and a good night's sleep before that. I don't think I can hope for another chance at such a sleep for quite some time.

I rely, as ever, on your forgiveness for the time since my last letter. These last two days have been a blur of preparations. Lodged all at the same hotel –

quite dingy, and three to one room, four to another, of which I am fortunate in being one among the three – we pass our days looking at horses, hats, barbaric second-hand coats of greasy fur. An adventure, you have called my intended exploits, but such drudgery and administration we must go through before the adventure can begin!

Still, I have cashed the cheque given me by the Stafford House Committee, and contractually speaking this means that there is no going back now. Nor should I wish there to be. In particular as I would have to return all that part of its sum has bought me:

That is to say, my share in all the rabble of crates, cloth bundles of burlap, and stacked baskets that weigh down our waiting cart. Much is supplies for Erzurum, so that we might set up a hospital and aid stations there: linen for bandages and the means to launder it; silk for sutures; strange-shaped blades for the enacting of various kinds of surgery; chests of Epsom Salts and sterner medicines besides; purgatives and stimulants; alcohol for rubbing and ether for numbing. But as to our personal affects we have luxuries – eggs, tins of ground coffee and of beef tea – and necessities: blankets, harsh little loaves of dense black bread, tobacco; and of course, beasts to carry us and pull our cart, and a kind of muledriver-guard-guide character, Turkish and with no other language known to him, but a knowledge of the tracks through the mountains and inland that is, apparently, unsurpassed.

Much as I complain – I think quite tiresomely, for which I apologise – I am eager to get underway. This 'adventure', if you insist on calling it such, has been put off quite long enough.

I shall certainly write you when I reach Erzurum, and hope you shall write me there too. Perhaps though, I will have some chance, by the roadside or at some coaching-house along the way, to write to you before. If so, we'll be making very good progress indeed to warrant such a pause…

Until then I am yours,

Very sincerely,

James Denniston

Chapter 5

Day broke across Trabzon as they departed.

For two days and nights it had rained, making the sun that shone on their arrival seem a rare and teasing accident: the last they would see in some time. Regular and slack like the rains of Glasgow and Edinburgh, it had come down like a wet mist from the sky, invisible but felt to the bone. Such rains make walking out of doors a daunting prospect, let alone beginning a journey one-hundred-and-eighty-seven miles inland, by mule-cart, on roads of downtrodden dirt.

As such, the air on that Sunday morning was a small miracle: clean and clear, mercifully without rain. But the wet days gone by had left the roads a-churn with mud. Half-tempered by cold nights, the ruts and potholes in the black dirt had stiffened, but gave way when least expected, to thin-skinned puddles of muck, and boggy morasses, and then spiny rough stretches that sent the wheels of their cart rattling.

The cart's bed was weighed down with Casson's ironshod trunk. The rest of their luggage and supplies were arrayed around it, or else hitched to the saddles of the beasts loaned to them in Trabzon.

Two mules and an indifferently coloured horse, they took turns to pull the cart, one at a time, as the men took their turns in riding the remaining two. Denniston could not help but be unnerved by them. They gave off a mood that affected his own, as surely as that of any man among them. Their docility was glum rather than meek, and somehow every mile they covered made the sound of their disk-shaped shoes on the road seem more of a reluctant trudge.

Their journey began out from the city's edges, walking, riding, driving. The road moved between houses, fewer and fewer as they went. Then there were farms, pens of sheep or a few slack-bodied cattle, between two huge gradual-sloping hills to left and right. But the hills closed in, dark green with scrub, and became the sides of a valley. They were in the city no longer, Denniston thought. Here the wilds began.

A few hours passed before they paused. Casson rode, insisting that he had put on the boots for it that morning – fine black leather, shining, and fitted to his calves – but they had quickly become piebald with mud.

'Breakfast?' asked Guppie, looking longingly at a flat spot by the steep-sided road.

'*Kahvalti*,' corrected Walker, in a fair approximation of the Trabzon administrator's manner and accent.

A small ripple of good-natured laughter went among the doctors. The guide sat silent on the seat of the cart. The mounts twitched their sides and fluttered their tails.

'That,' said Pinkerton, walking to the flat area, 'would imply we had tea.'

'Or food half as good as our last *kahvalti*,' said Casson.

'I'd settle for half as much,' said Kincaid, combing his fingers wistfully through his red beard.

'Nothing but coffee from here,' said Walker squatting by the roadside to set up their spirit-burner and a little Turkish copper pot above its small blue fame. He opened a tin of coffee and sniffed the contents. 'None too good, either. You certain someone didn't pull one over on us? Sell us cigar ash instead?'

'Ah…' said Casson, raising a mock-guilty hand. 'You see, I would've insisted on the best, but I thought it prudent that we not get too used to luxury out here. It would only make us bitter.'

'Bitter coffee for bitter times,' said Pinkerton.

Spirits stayed high as each man took his share of sour black bread and bitter black coffee. Even meagre as it was, hot coffee warmed and woke them, unpleasant as the taste might be.

'What a barbaric dash we must cut,' said Casson. 'Seven Englishmen in a dozen pelts a piece from who knows what manner of beast. Drinking coffee with neither milk nor sugar to speak of, and decked out in pistols and mud!'

'Englishmen..?' Denniston echoed with an upward twitch of an eyebrow. He smiled as an afterthought, but was only half-joking.

'Britons, then!' Casson corrected himself. 'Subjects of the Queen.'

'God save,' said Featherston, softly, raising his little tin cup.

'Perhaps…' mused Pinkerton, 'Perhaps all this talk of bandits and robbers was a mistake. Perhaps it's this road – this country – that makes bandits of every man.'

Casson gave a snort of laughter through his crooked nose, soon picked up by the other men in chuckles and huffs of amusement. 'Certainly we look the part!'

'I'd sooner look a bandit but keep warm for it than go off in tails and spats and freeze,' said Denniston. 'I know what I am, grime and furs or no.'

'Here here,' grinned Casson, raising his own cup.

The others followed; the first toast of their journey.

Much as they joked of bandits, wolves, and frostbite, the laughter they shared grew thin and nervous. Against each of these worries they had taken fair precaution, happy to tease the administrator in Trabzon behind his back for being over-dramatic, over-cautious. On the road, between the hills, and under the open sky, however, it was hard not to fear that all the dramatic Greek's advice had been sager by far than he seemed.

Like shepherds, each man was soon clothed in dirt, fleece and fur. Each man had a pistol nestled heavy and snug inside his coat or on his hip: ugly things the colour of soot that none could reload in less than two minutes.

Like ill-shod soldiers, ill-supplied and forgotten, the seven men shared one new rifle, half-hidden inside the cart: a Martini-Peabody, with a well-oiled lever-action, as untried and unused as its owners.

'You know,' said Kincaid, 'we ought to try shooting it. I'd rather not be caught short when the times comes to try it in earnest.'

Denniston looked over at Guppie, saddled now on one of the mules. He seemed to have grown suddenly paler.

'And deprive poor Cebrael of his prize?' scoffed Casson, gesturing at the guide.

For all the doctors seemed nervous of the rifle, their guide seemed covetous and comfortable. He was a tan and worn-faced man with an ill-kept black moustache and days of iron-grey stubble on his sunken cheeks. Sat on the cart, he kept the Martini-Peabody always precious and close, bedded down like a babe beneath a blanket, to keep it from the damp.

'He *does* seem fond of it,' said Denniston, 'I'll give you that.'

'It's British design,' said Casson. 'A fine thing out here! Why shouldn't he be?' He looked over to Cebrael and said something convivial in Turkish; a question, Denniston thought, by the sound of it.

'*Lanet sağ,*' Cebrael grunted with a nodding lift of his chin. He reached into his fur coat – thicker than any of the doctors', and greased with something to keep off the rain – brought out a little steel flask, and drank.

Denniston frowned. 'Should he be..?'

Cebrael looked over, gave another nod, and this time a gap-toothed grin as he gestured at them with his flask. '*Hristiyan.*' He then pointed at his own breast. '*Hristiyan da.*'

The doctors looked expectant at Casson, waiting for a translation.

'He says he's Christian,' Casson said. 'I suppose that means he can apologise for it later.'

'Cebrael…' said Pinkerton. 'From 'Gabriel', I suppose. Hm. Our guiding light!'

'So one would hope…' said Casson.

By afternoon they were all soaked to the skin. Their limbs were heavy, the soles of their feet tender as they walked the length of a narrow valley. From off its scrub and stone walls, the sound echoed as Kincaid began to sing.

'Ohhh the king has been a puir prisoner
And a prisoner lang in Spain.'

It was louder than before in the cabin, more confident for the open space, though the echo made the English words foreign in the ears. Or rather, not quite English, Denniston noted with pleasure. The song was a familiar one, half-remembered: a ballad in Scots.

'And Willie, oh he o' the Winsbury
Has lain lang wi' his daughter at hame...'

Whether for Denniston's benefit or not, it was a comfort amid the rain, the cold, the clammy sweat that had formed on his skin despite the chill. The humidity perhaps was to blame, but no less than his own constitution, unused to such long walking on such bad ground.

The song fell off abruptly. Cebrael let loose a tirade of what could only have been curses in Turkish, setting the doctors off in English too.

'You bastard! Oh, you bloody bastard!'

A wheel of the cart had tumbled and stuck into a rut already carved in the mud. Denniston was close enough to see as much, and stepped closer, surveying the damage. There was no harm done to the spokes or structure of the wheel. That, at least, was a mercy.

'It's stuck,' said Casson from his horse.

'Then we'd best bloody well unstick it now, hadn't we?' said Kincaid, ruddy-cheeked, brows stormily fierce.

'Suppose we ought to push,' said Walker.

'Better still if we can push as well,' said Casson, dismounting from the horse. 'You too, Guppie, on your feet and hitch her to the cart now.'

They set about with ropes, fashioning makeshift harnesses for the mule and horse they had formerly ridden, attaching them to the same yoke that pulled the cart.

'Rest of us,' said Denniston, 'behind.'

'Like ploughing a field,' laughed Pinkerton. 'Some days it won't plough itself, and needs must. You get behind the draught and push.'

'And...Push!'

'And...Plough!'

The beasts squawked. The men heaved, doctors, Cebrael and all. Their boots skidded, digging at the mud. With a sucking grit-grating sound the wheel came free. The cart lurched a half-dozen paces suddenly forward, free of the men behind it, and left them laughing, bent almost double and breathless.

Featherston had fallen, knees and hands, into the muddy road. Between giggles, the quiet midlander was letting loose with a stream of curses more colourful than any had dared to utter so far.

In fits and gasps of laughter, they caught up to the cart, unhitched the horse from it, and carried on, pink-cheeked through the wet, eyes bright for smiling.

Amazing, thought Denniston as they walked on, how soon they all began to swear and joke like sailors. Whether raised as gentlemen or anything less, here in the absence of women, they were rude, and rustic, and roughly equal.

'Crafty bastard,' said Pinkerton, 'this thin, drippy rain. Knows just how to run into your collar and down your back.'

'Gets bloody everywhere,' Kincaid agreed.

'Like bloody fleas,' said Walker.

'Or typhus,' said Denniston.

'Or low spirits,' Guppie sighed.

'Well, we shall have none of those,' said Casson. 'Not in present company!'

The sky turned black, first with clouds and rain combined, and the shadows of the valley sides, but soon with the incoming evening. The travellers scarcely noticed when night itself had fallen. It had crept up and over them, dressed in the darkening weather.

Denniston's turn had come to ride the horse. His feet felt broken from the miles of black sucking mud they had churned through before now. For that, even a bruising hour of wincing at every roll and bump of the mare's scrawny back was preferable to walking. He was thankful for the rest.

They lit storm-lamps against the gathering gloom. In the small pool of light they cast, they travelled through the dark while the world contracted around them, like the pupil in an eye – or the artificial equivalent, in the beady black lens of a camera.

'See that?' said Pinkerton, pointing beyond the edge of their dim little world.

'Hm?' Denniston followed his finger.

Hanging in the air there were lines and rows of lights. The space around them was black, blotting out the stars as they began to come out. It must, Denniston reasoned, have been a cliff-face then; one of the crags ahead, but studded with what seemed to be windows, lit from within.

'It's a monastery,' Pinkerton said. 'Or rather, I think it's a monastery. A church before that. One I've read about. Apparently it's quite stunning on a clear day.'

'Pity we had to pass it on the wrong side of dusk, then.'

'A pity,' Pinkerton agreed. 'I would've liked to see it. Built into the cliff, I hear. Stunning. I'd been hoping, you know...'

'Cebrael, and now this monastery,' Denniston began. 'There's a lot more Christianity in these parts than I'd been led to expect.'

'And who told you what to expect, Doctor Denniston? Eh?'

'Oh...' He chewed for a moment over how to refer to Miss Guthrie. 'A friend. Knowledgeable in all kinds of ways. Though maybe not all, I suppose.'

'No-one can be.'

'It only surprises me. That's all.'

'I think – I *think* – a fair deal of this province is. Christian, that is. You heard our friend in Trabzon, after all. It was Greek – many still are, I suppose – and then Byzantine, and now..? Well, I suppose that deep roots don't mean others won't try to pull them up. That monastery has been ruined and repaired five times in as many centuries.'

'Something else you read, is that?'

'Something else I've read. I've had near three times longer than you young ones to read in, now haven't I? Funny though – at least if the Russians came this far, the monastery might be in better hands...'

'Or just more hands,' said Denniston. 'Christians pillage too.'

'This monastery of yours,' Walker chimed in. 'Suppose they're the charitable sort... Reckon they'd let us in, would they? A stable to sleep in? Maybe a comfy cell?'

Tiredness, and the breaking down of barriers throughout the day had caused his accent to slip, much as Pinkerton's had. But whereas Pinkerton's vowels stretched and his consonants grew rounded, many of Walker's disappeared entirely, the 't's vanishing south of the Thames.

'That they might,' said Pinkerton. 'It's in our climbing up there that the problem lies...'

Denniston by then had stopped listening, distracted by the complaints of his thighs and hips against the saddle. He was not a natural rider, nor a well-practiced one. In all his life he'd spent only a stunted handful of hours in any saddle, and only ever at a gentle walk. The first time was as a child by the sea at St. Andrews. He'd sat on the back of a donkey whose hoofs sunk debilitating into the sand and the stones – half an hour bought for half a penny. The second time was on the back of a carthorse, after the cart's wheel broke and he was sent ahead to fetch help. And finally, on the way to a gathering on the outskirts of Greenock – a distance he insisted he'd prefer to walk – and at which he'd spent the evening's entirety feeling bow-legged and unsteady, then giddy from once more meeting a woman he had expected never to see again...

Bow-legged and unsteady he might have been now – certainly more than would let him scale a cliff-face towards any lofty monastery – but that only made him dread walking more. All the same, the time soon came to dismount. He loosed one boot from its stirrup and tried to clamber down. Something slipped; one foot or the other, it was hard to tell. The boot he'd lowered twisted awkward into the mud. Like a wire drawn taut from ankle to hip, pain burst along the length of his leg.

Denniston's knuckles gripped the saddle's peak, wet and white, as he grit his teeth to bite back a groan. It was hard to say what was worse: the pain, or the fear of showing it in front of the others. With grating care he let down his other leg and balanced his weight on the hip that hurt least.

'Whose turn now?' he asked, voice more cracked than he'd hoped.

No-one spoke. The wind rushed in to fill the silence between them with a saw-toothed moan. The doctors only looked at each other with sidelong glances — like wolves eyeing up the last scraps of their catch; or spinsters around the last slice of cake.

'Gentlemen?' Denniston asked again, as the flash of pain dissipated.

The question was aired to all of them, but he fixed his eyes on Guppie. Slowly, the other doctors' gazes slid over him too.

He was shivering, waxen-skinned, pale hair flat and thin against his soaking scalp. With every step he attempted, he faltered and almost stumbled. He had his turn riding that morning, but travel, it seemed, wore at him worse. The rain weighed heavier on him than the rest; the mud grasped his boots tighter.

'Guppie,' Casson said, affable even through chattering teeth. 'Be a good chap and get on the bloody horse.'

Guppie was silent. When he looked around, his eyes had the glassy unfocused stare of fish brought up fresh from the sea: not shocked anymore, but resigned. It was the same look the two mules wore.

'Here,' said Featherston, breaking the silence he wore so constantly, like a frugal man might over-wear his only suit. He knelt in the dirt beside the horse and wove his hands together to make a step below the nearest stirrup.

'Not long now,' said Pinkerton gently. He lay his head on Guppie's shoulder and led him over to Featherston.

'Only a little farther,' said Casson. 'Cebrael says he knows a place up ahead. A little farther and then we'll stop. Night's come in, see? Rest, shelter, and something warm to drink.'

'Night?' asked Guppie, blearily. 'I'd hardly noticed…'

They spent the night poorly. The shelter their guide had promised earnt that meagre descriptor but no further praise. It was a little mud hut, a short and filthy scramble up a hillside. The floor was packed dirt and the darkness filled with biting things: fleas and midges, itching and insinuating themselves into the men's damp clothes.

There was little conversation. The day had taken it out of them. In wet heaps around the spirit-burner they ate hunks of sour black bread and mugs of beef tea. Denniston drank his so hot his tongue and mouth were burnt, but was only glad for the warmth. He felt he'd never before spent such a miserable night, but no doubt he'd soon spend plenty worse.

It was before dawn when they woke. Cebrael was up before anyone else, toeing the others into action with words in Turkish, jabs from his boots. Breakfast passed much the same as dinner, in black bread and tin cups of coffee.

The way ahead led through trees, dripping with the night's long rain, before they could rejoin the main road. At least it led downhill, where before they'd clambered up. They began the journey once more, trudging, glumly talking.

'Black bread, black coffee…' muttered Walker.

'Both bitter as sin,' said Pinkerton.

'Can't tell where one ends and the other starts,' said Kincaid.

'Only difference I could tell,' said Denniston, nursing his burnt mouth and cooling his coffee before sipping it, 'is that one came in solid form, the other liquid.'

Kincaid grunted. 'A Christian man wouldn't feed pigs what we just breakfasted on.'

'A Christian man wouldn't get his dogs up before dawn two days running,' Casson agreed.

'Still,' said Denniston, thinking aloud, 'we made poor progress yesterday.'

'Poor progress?' said Kincaid. 'We walked from dawn til after dusk!'

'And covered thirty miles,' Denniston said, briskly defensive. 'And that if we're lucky!'

'Beg your pardon if I was too busy walking the miles to be counting them too,' grumbled Walker.

'I've checked my maps,' said Denniston. 'I know. I've seen where I reckon we are, and it's not so far on as we ought to be. For all we know the Russians could be at Erzurum before we are!'

'And yet here we waste strength on squabbling,' said Casson, diplomatically.

They carried on, but in a grim and sullen silence for which Denniston felt himself responsible. He had not meant to be so imperious with the others. He had not the gift that Casson did of making any order seem a good-natured request; of making others want to please him. It came down, he supposed, to Casson's surfeit of charm, and his own lack, that even when Denniston spoke sense, it seemed too much to ask. Still, he regretted his tone, but not the words he'd said.

Casson set to encouraging the mules and horse as much as the men, speaking to them, soft but firm to urge them on.

Internally, Denniston attempted the same with himself, just to put one aching foot in front of the other. One stride at a time, he told himself, is how all journeys are made.

Finally Casson spoke up. 'Our Scots friend has the right of it, gentlemen, though his tone could be more mannered...' He turned and offered a weak smile that flooded Denniston's chest with relief. 'The pace, gentlemen! Let's pick it up while there's yet daylight.'

'Is there?' Walker said in a mock-grumble. 'I hadn't noticed.'

Around them was still only twilight: the grey dawn of an overcast day.

'All the better then,' said Casson. 'Back to the road before the sun's up, how about it? Let's see if we can't race the morning!'

'And win!' said Featherston, louder than any had expected from him.

For a moment, his was the determined voice that spoke for them all. And yet, Denniston realised, it remained Casson that they were all following. Even in his uncouth coat of pelts and no uniform besides, he looked every bit the young officer rather than a doctor. He led the horse on by its reins – Pinkerton on its back – and the men on by his bearing, speaking with the ease of a man who had spent his life being listened to.

Denniston would have expected little else from him, however. Casson was handsome, educated even for a doctor. With his boots, his way with horses and with his fellow man, his clipped efficient English and skill as a linguist, what could Casson be but a man raised to wealth – to leadership? Next to breeding and lifelong practice, how could Denniston compare?

They broke out of the woods a time after sun-up. The land they found beyond the trees was harsh. Denniston wondered if the forest only faltered and fell off where it did because the soil was too poor and the ground too rocky for any decent roots to take. Its colours were dark and the chill air set the earth hard and cruel under their feet. Like a landscape hewn from pig iron: raw and black, unforgiving and ugly.

Conversation flared up and petered out, like lucifer-matches, blazing bright then burning down. But the doctors shared silence companionably as they shared coffee, tobacco, or beef tea. Even Cebrael's own silence seemed a part of theirs now.

There was no rain, but the changing landscape brought new challenges. The road sloped up through the morning. Past noon it led them onto hilltops, between rough crags, out of the valley and into open air. With neither woods nor valley to shelter them, the wind attacked them viciously, fighting their progress every step of the way. Soon Denniston's cheeks and knuckles stung, and his fingers were stiffly cold.

'First for the rain, then for the damp, and now for this endless wind!' Pinkerton groaned. 'A chance to light my pipe, God – that's all I ask!'

When night came, it raced in quickly, early, hard to predict. With no hut for shelter, they hashed together a tent: mats on the ground to sleep on, a canvas tarpaulin overhead, fly-pitched against the side of the cart while the horse and mules slept standing outside.

Next day the road disappeared. All that remained was a flattish stretch of track, seldom trodden and seldom travelled, clinging to the edge of a hillside that had fast become a mountain.

Behind them they saw the craggy climb of yesterday, arrayed now in the distance. Walker reckoned, through the thin and brittle air, he could see the snarl of forest they'd left behind, murmurous with fog.

'Raining down there, back where we came from,' he observed. 'Can see it in the valley. Sheeting down!'

'And up ahead, all blue skies,' said Denniston.

He had meant it as sarcasm but it played like prophecy. Sometimes there would come a howling gale to slow them, but each time it soon blew itself out. The sky was huge and clear. The land below shaded to croppings of brown and grey rock, yellowish grass clinging to the slopes, and occasionally a deep green verdance of scrub, evergreen despite the coming months of cold.

The cart wheels rattled over dry ground, raising dust now more than wet and spattering dirt. Ahead the road remained hard, but at least now it ran downhill.

Like a long-distance runner who stretches before his race, and thinks about it with mixed apprehension and hope; who begins to run and, beginning, starts to suffer. No training and no readiness can stop his muscles from screaming. By the race's middle, his whole body aches. But towards its end, the brawn he's made from ceases its strain. It no longer shrieks but falls into silence. Then, instead, it sings. His limbs are light now, as if purified by the pain of this. The run becomes effortless as he crosses the line. And the ease is bliss.

Like that runner, Denniston started the following day in good spirits. By the pace and manner of the others, they felt much the same. His feet had been tender before, so that every footfall stung. Now his whole person felt hardened, his face tanned and lined from the cold sunlight, and covered with the beginnings of a beard.

All of them walked now like natural men, not like gentlemen or whatever they had been in Britain. Lurching where lurching was needed, lax where laxness would help, they walked instead like men used to walking.

We've hit our stride, Denniston thought, as the sun grew towards noon.

The mountains they'd crossed became hills once more, wide and rolling, in rises of sun-bleached grass.

Cebrael spoke, and Casson translated:

'He says we're making good progress. That our pace is good. We could divert, if we chose. There's a city ahead.'

'Bayburt,' Cebrael put in, followed by a few words in Turkish.

'Bayburt,' Casson nodded. 'We should reach it before nightfall. To beds, gentlemen!'

'And roofs over our heads!'

'Hot food!'

'Walls to keep the wind off!'

'And a chance to restock,' said Denniston. 'Resupply.'

'Right you are once more!' said Casson, slapping Denniston on his fur-coated shoulder. 'We're running quite short on tobacco!'

In truth, Denniston had smoked little since beginning their journey. He found that he'd scarce had the time. In the line of supplies he'd had a mind more to practical things: food, fuel, feed for their three mounts. As for luxuries, he looked forward to nothing so much as a desk or table, and a chance to write.

James

My dear Miss Guthrie,
I must confess I am hopeful, and filled with confidence, at this point more than halfway through our journey. I had scarce hoped for even a village to stop and resupply in, and yet here we find ourselves in quite a charming little city, and with many of the trappings that men think of as 'civilisation'.

Bayburt is picturesque, situated on the bend of a river, bridged in a couple of places, and in the shadow of a bleak old hill-fort. Pinkerton tells me – learned man as he is, in matters of history – that the whole city had walls once, as Erzurum does, but that they were torn down, not fifty years ago. And who should turn out responsible, when I asked? None but the Russians, who pushed as far as this when last they tried to take Turkey. Hearing that, I admit, a part of me will not be surprised to find their army encamped on the outskirts come morning!

In the little tavern we have found to lodge in, I suppose we have set up what you might call a clinic. Our intentions are good, but we have little in the way of supplies to spare for Bayburt, and I think it quickly became a way for us to get something for nothing. That is to say, drinks of ghastly clear spirit and bowls of mutton stew in return for having Casson listen to a line of locals as they recited their woes, while we passed among them, asking over and over 'dilly nigoster' – 'put your tongue out' – before staring into their mouths and nodding sagely. I think I should feel quite guilty in all this, if I had found any true signs of ill-health. Instead the results of our antics only put healthy Turks in confidence as to their own good health. What damage, then, was done?

We have so far struck a good pace cross-country: down valleys, across hillsides, and along the side of a mountain. The landscape is, I think, quite sublime, though often bleak. What I note most of all, compared with England or Scotland, is that there is quite so much sky, and quite a beautiful one this past day or so – blue and enormous, and most mercifully of all, dry, for we had such rains and miserable nights as you would not believe at first.

Trekking in such a way, I almost feel as intrepid as you would make me out to be. I wonder if adventure is the right word for this business after all. It is all helped – my spirits and my progress – of course by the fact that I feel I'm among friends.

Comparison, however, to my new friends has made me feel all manner of ways. A conversation we had over our stew, for instance, has made me examine my motivations for this journey more carefully than I had before. Most among us seem to have inspired themselves along just the kind of lines you would approve of: to give aid and use their skills to lessen human suffering, nothing less and nothing more. Pinkerton, I think, is only accepting a retainer from the SHC, with all the rest of his pay going towards supplies and suchlike! But he is, it seems, a religious man. More than that, he is an older gentleman, with a lifetime of safe general practice in a Devonshire village behind him, and a pension ahead. And Casson's family, I think, are quite well-off and will support him all he needs, if need ever arises. Such motivations as theirs are the kind that financial comfort and good prospects can afford. In my own case, I hope to help as much as I'm able, truly I do, but I attracted such glances as you would not believe for my honesty in this discussion: that a salary and perhaps a name to trade on in future would not go amiss from this venture, either.

I hope I might find some word of yours awaiting me at Erzurum. I do not presume to be certain of it, yet still it feels the surest thing in the circumstances of our arrival. The rest is all quite unknown. We may find ourselves enjoying the hospitality of the Russians already, if their generals have pushed them west from Kars as they have before. Or perhaps we shall still be quite behind friendly lines, and have an easier time of it than at first I'd hoped for. I say 'at first', for now I think a short rest of unchallenging work would be welcome and well-deserved...

Until then I remain

Yours very sincerely,

James Denniston

November 1877

RED CRESCENT AMBULANCE No. 3 ON THE ROAD TO THE FRONT.

Chapter 6

The country after Bayburt was all dust, cold winds, cruel sunshine. The sky was a steel-blue omen: flat and promising snow.

The first fell that night, as the doctors took shelter in a brief thick patch of forest between two hills – the better to keep from the wind, Cebrael had reckoned, and the better yet to hide in. They were in uncertain territory now. Though the front of the Russian forces lay somewhere uncertain, between here and Kars, their closeness would only mean unrest, desperation, refugees and bandits.

'We ought to keep watches,' Kincaid suggested.

'I'll take the first,' Denniston volunteered. 'Someone has to.'

He met no resistance from the others. After a day of long walking, he understood their reluctance, but he also understood necessity.

They huddled under their tarpaulin as the snow began to fall. Denniston sat at the lean-to's mouth, legs akimbo round the small sputtering fire they'd allowed themselves amongst the trees. Outside its shaky glow he saw nothing of the snow. But as he listened, the woods groaned, all its limbs weighed down more heavily with each passing hour until Kincaid relieved his watch, and Denniston, too, slept.

Morning found him bleary-eyed, unable to feel his toes. In the daylight, he saw the snow had settled, but beneath the eaves of the copse it lay light upon the ground. Beyond, however, as they set off, and struck a path out from the wood, it seemed to have fallen more thickly. The world was buried in dishwater-grey and drifts of grubby white as the land sloped up once more.

'Hills…' Kincaid grumbled. 'The bloody backs of my bloody calves…'

'Lucky you can feel your legs at all,' said Walker. 'Mine feel like stumps.'

'If there was ever a sign you've been knee-deep in snow too bloody long,' said Casson. 'I think Doctor Walker has found it. My poor girl's none too fond of it either. Are you girl?'

He'd taken to speaking to the greyish mare, sweet as he could and constant, since the snow forced them all to drag her and the mules on by their reins.

To Denniston's mind they were all but dead weight now – the horse and mules – all three hitched to the cart but barely pulling as the men took turns behind, pushing it, as they had through the mud before. Wading ahead through the thick pall of snow, he heard a stumbling behind him – a snorting and then the mute crunch of compacted snow. There was dread in the sound, though he couldn't at first say why. He stopped. The others too had fallen silent. He glanced over one shoulder, then fully turned round.

The mare lay in the blanket of white. Her indifferent coat almost melted almost into it,. She had stumbled onto her side, three legs folded a little under her. One of her eyes was wide, looking skyward and puffs of hurried steam came quick and heavy from her nostrils and from between her bared flat teeth.

Casson knelt beside her. 'Oh no,' he cooed. 'Oh no no no, this won't do. Up with you. Come on, girl, up and onwards.' He spoke, on and on, in reassuring circles with his hands on her flank, talking like a midwife might to a woman in labour. 'You're stronger than this, girl. You can, I know you can…'

The other doctors stood about them both, stunned into a hollow solemn stillness. The mare's legs thrashed at the snow, scrambling troughs into the white as she once more tried to stand. In an unsteady clamber, she got up once more, head bobbing like a broken puppet's.

'Good girl. There's my girl. There you go…'

She made it only four or five limping steps. Her front legs buckled. She plunged again into the white.

'No!' Casson groaned. 'No, no, no. You're a strong old girl – stronger than this – get up.' He slumped next to the mare, onto his knees once more. 'Only a little farther. Just a little more's all I ask. Then you can rest where it's warm and dry. Just get up and go on a little farther for me now.'

Denniston's thoughts stirred and began to simmer. The other men had not moved, thinking no doubt as he was. There was no helping the horse; not in these hills, in this snow, and not when night came once more. They were wasting time on sentiment.

'Casson…' he murmured.

'Wait!' the other doctor snapped, not looking up. 'Wait a minute, she only needs a minute, that's all!'

The fire in Casson's voice cauterised them all, stemming what words they might otherwise have said. They waited a minute that stretched long and awful. The horse shivered, legs no longer moving. The lather on her flanks glittered, beginning to freeze, as their breath hung foggy on the air. The horse huffed and snorted in useless panic.

Denniston's footsteps creaked loud as he moved to crouch beside his friend. 'Think clearly about this. Please, Casson.'

Casson only closed his eyes and took in a deep breath, as if trying to hold something down, low and thick in his throat.

'I don't think she's getting up,' said Walker, softly. 'I don't know the first thing about horses, but… I don't think…'

Casson's shoulders rose and fell, uneven. The mare's skinny ribs fluttered.

'She'll get up,' he said, slow and deliberate and darkly forceful. 'She only needs time. A little rest.'

'Think clearly,' Denniston repeated. 'Do we have time to spare?' His calves were already damp and cold from squatting close to the ground. Snow had melted into his boots and soaked the hem of his coat. 'We can't stop here.' He reached out to touch Casson's shuddering shoulder.

Casson flinched. 'We can't!' He gripped Denniston's wrist, rethought, pushed his hand away. 'Those mules will be dead lame in a day if the snow keeps on, pulling the cart on their own! What then? We'll be going nowhere! And how long before the cold kills us too, with Erzurum still God knows how far away!'

'That's why we need to get on,' said Denniston, carefully, trying to catch Casson's wild eyes. 'We can't have a lamed horse slowing us down.'

'Lame? What do you know about horses! You? Any of you! What does a Scotsman know about anything but hurrying on to half-arse the next job? Leech out whatever money you can, then throw it all away and move on!'

Casson pushed Denniston full in the chest with both hands. He rose as Denniston fell, sinking into the snow. The air wheezed out of his lungs, but something inside Denniston had caught ablaze.

'Think!' he shouted, struggling to get up. 'Think damn you! For just one moment! She's good as dead already? What can we do! What! What can we do for her?' His fists were balled by his sides now, and he scrambled to his feet, caked white with snow.

'Be reasonable,' someone urged, almost whining.

'Be reasonable! We're all of us tired, cold, wet. Hold on. Hold on just a moment and—'

'Damned bloody mercenaries, all of you!' growled Casson. He stood shorter than Denniston, close and face to face, every inch of his posture iron-straight with a shuddering strength. 'Rushing on! Rushing on so you can get the job done!'

Denniston's eyes flickered downward. There was a piece of grey metal in Casson's fist: a revolver.

'Go on then!' Casson spat.

He pushed the revolver into Denniston's chest. The blunt butt of it jarred against his sternum. On instinct, his fingers closed round numb and stiff round it, but fumbled, failing to find the trigger.

'Get it over with,' Casson said. 'Bloody shoot her so you can get on, get paid, and go home. Damn it. Damn it!'

Motion and a surging rage.

Suddenly Kincaid was pushing them apart. The others were jostling in. All were shouting then, till the hills echoed with alarm. The moment fractured and blurred. Casson was shouting loudest of all, cursing bright and harsh. Someone wrenched the gun from Denniston's hand and held him down. His body prickled with the heat of the moment and cold of ice.

A gunshot rang out. The shouting ceased. Guppie had shot the horse and blood flecked the snow.

The matter of the horse had divided them. The argument deflated the men's good humour and, it seemed to Denniston, had dented their camaraderie. Squabbles broke out over the smallest things for the rest of the day.

First of all was in how to proceed. The snow that surrounded them was deep. With now only two mules to pull the cart, they would have to lighten it. Before they could continue, they abandoned heavy goods behind them by the road: mattocks, shovels, and hammers; the crates leftover as they crammed supplies together, loose.

'A present,' said Pinkerton. 'For whoever next comes this way. Think of it as charity.'

No-one laughed. The laughter had gone from them all, for now, and showed no signs of returning. Casson was silent, glassy eyed. Denniston seethed in exhausted silence, humiliated by his own hot-headedness, and by the words of a man he'd counted as a friend.

Progress suffered. They scarce travelled any farther before nightfall; only enough that they started downhill again, and found that ahead the snow was lighter, or else had already begun to melt. Drifts remained, slowly shrinking between crags and cracks of rock, or frozen in the bark of the occasional old tree. Otherwise, what snow covered the ground was thin, restricted to smatterings that soon would sink into the soil.

That night, more fell. The snow, however, was thinner, more wet. What little settled was gone by morning.

The land grew harsher as they carried on. The headlands were higher, their angles crueler. In the distance, plateaus reached skywards and then stopped flat, capped with lingering snow, like kitchen tables flour-dusted for the kneading of bread.

The road worked through crevices so narrow they seemed chiselled from the tough craggy land the doctors found themselves in. More than once, the cart proved almost too wide for these paths. The tight rock walls planed splinters from the cart's sides and all of them walked, either ahead or behind.

A trickle of other travellers passed them, when the road broadened once more. Some were well-dressed in winter coats and boots, while others shivered in what Denniston could only call rags. A scanty few had carts.

Many had only baskets on their backs and a sack or two. Infants too young to walk with their parents slept or cried, swaddled and tied to the fronts of their older kin.

All among the refugees, whether they seemed rich or poor, had the same wide-open eyes; the same sore lids and wind-chapped lips. In their faces were written the silent signs of those who had been awake and on the road too long. Denniston recognised them well by now; he and the doctors wore them too.

Every one of them was travelling in the opposite direction from Denniston and the others. Once, a shepherd went by, face etched with age-lines and and driving a river of dun-fleeced sheep down the narrow road.

The doctors were forced to stop and let him pass. Little as Denniston would admit it, he was thankful for the pause.

Where the previous travellers had kept down their gazes and all but avoided the doctors, the shepherd spoke as his herd coursed by. Casson had greeted him in polite Turkish, and they stood together after that, in conversation.

So far as Denniston could tell, much of the conversation flowed slow and easy as neighbours sharing news. Often though, it picked up, hurrying to a quicker higher pitch as the shepherd's voice grew passionate.

The last sheep passed, black-coated, and as it trotted by, the shepherd said his farewells and moved on.

'What was he about?' Kincaid asked.

'He says we're going the right way,' Casson said, flatly, as if the conversation had exhausted him.

'You sure?' Walker asked. 'Seems to me we're headed in exact opposition to everyone else. Maybe they all have the better idea…'

'They weren't going the right way,' Guppie said softly. 'Only going. Away.'

'That's the way with refugees,' said Pinkerton. 'Where was it they were running from?'

'Erzurum,' Casson answered. 'Or near it.'

'Then we're close,' Denniston said.

'Us and the Russians both.'

When the morning came on the following day, it was full of birdsong. Close to Erzurum now, with less than a day between the doctors and their destination, a mixed feeling went among them. For Denniston, it was apprehension, relief, and hope. They were almost there.

The close and craggy country they'd come through opened out into broader valleys and defiles between gentle slopes, all smoothing out like creases in cloth into what Denniston's maps suggested ought to be a wide plain.

Listening to the birds, he tried to pick out the tunes and remember the names of the singers. They were strange to him. Whether from distance in time, or distance from home, he remembered none of them from boyhood, though he'd once been an enthusiast. He'd spent mornings upon mornings, sitting in the shade of a tree outside their house in Greenock, with a dog-eared book of avifauna on his lap, listening. But none of those mornings had been like this.

The birdsong didn't last. The valley they walked was silent, save for the sound of their boots against the dust — a night past, it might have been mud, thought Denniston. He found a small mote of relief in that. But he missed the music he'd heard in the mountains that morning.

He raised a hand to shield his eyes from the sun. Silhouetted against the bright sky, Denniston made out a pair of wide wings. The bird might have been a buzzard by the way it glided, wings motionless, but it was hard to be sure. That sight at least was familiar, reminding him of Scotland.

As they continued, the quiet seemed only to grow. The hush became uncomfortable, in a way Denniston couldn't explain, as if he knew something was wrong, but didn't know how he knew it. The knowing belonged to some wordless backwater of his brain, wise without knowledge and strange with instinct.

The gliding shapes set against the sky only seemed to multiply. Denniston tried and failed to count them.

'Do you smell that?' Walker asked, from the back of their procession.

His were the first words any of them had spoken in what may have been an hour. They hung anxious on the air. Denniston had barely begun to process them when their path led to the edge of a flattish pass, then sloped down. One by one, the doctors all came to a halt.

'Like a meat market at the end of a midsummer day!' Walker said.

The others gave no answer. There was no need. In a moment, even Walker saw for himself.

It was a mass: the same chaotic form that a thicket of brambles takes when it has the time to spread, and grow old and cruel. A tangle, then, thick on the floor of the valley. Dozens of men, cramped together, close and vile and covered in dust. Corpses, and the reek that came with them.

The doctors stood all on the edge of the rise, looking down in stunned silence. Casson raised a handkerchief to his mouth and nose.

'My God...' someone muttered. It didn't matter who; the voice spoke for them all. It was the one thought that filled Denniston's mind: My God...

Below, glimpses of colour throbbed dull amidst the tangle. Most of the bodies were in uniform but the uniforms were mixed. Here was a patch of dark pine green and there was a flare of officer's white. But for the most part, they were dressed in another green: the olive and deep blue colours of a Turkish regiment, stained throughout with darkness.

'An ambush..?' Denniston spoke up, but his throat was sore and dry.

'It looks more like a landslide victory,' said Casson, voice muffled by his handkerchief.

'A defeat then,' said Denniston. 'At least as far as we're concerned.

A strange and bitter part of himself compared his voice to Casson's and took pride in its cold calm. The Englishman was obviously shaken. Steady as his voice might be, however, Denniston felt all his thoughts were covered in a film of oil. Something was trying to well up and through but it was still too murky and weak a thing to make out.

It was like the grief that had hung over his sister's small funeral. The feeling had hung in the eaves of the chapel, and gathered between the pews, but failed to take root inside him, as if his heart was too withered by loss to fill up with anything at all. It had taken weeks to finally germinate. The patient grief took him, then, but found him no more ready than he had been at his sister's deathbed.

Slowly, a thought broke like a bubble through the oily surface. 'We should check for wounded,' Denniston said thickly. Survivors.'

'How could there be any?' murmured Kincaid.

'It's why we're here,' said Denniston. 'It's what we're meant to do.'

He started down the slope. Someone – Casson – grabbed him by the shoulder, halting him.

'James...' he said, using Denniston's Christian name for the first time.

Denniston struggled free and wouldn't stop.

'Damn it James, they're dead! There's nothing we can do!'

But Denniston was like a sleepwalker. His thoughts were empty, his purpose clear.

'James, listen to me. There are living men in Erzurum. They're waiting for us. You said yourself, we can't stop! We need to get on – for them! James!'

Kincaid caught up with Denniston, skidding down the rise. He was strong. He seized Denniston by the shoulders. The pressing, gentle, conclusive force of a hospital orderly; the same patient authority. He looked into Denniston's glassy eyes and told him, firmly:

'There's nothing we can do. Time is short, now more than ever.'

Denniston's shoulders heaved. Strangely distant, he was aware of the urge to vomit more than he truly felt it.

The next moment the other doctors stood round him.

'There's no one alive down there,' he heard Walker say. 'Even those who survived the fighting will be gone. Nothing smells like that til a few days have gone by. Not when the weather's cool.'

'If we ever had a chance,' said another – Pinkerton, 'we've missed it.'

'Days back.'

'Still something we can do,' Walker said, lips set tight in distaste. 'There might be things the Russians didn't take. Jewellery, money, rations, playing cards – I'll bet you that's all gone. But medical supplies? Maybe they wouldn't know what they were looking for.' He paused. 'I'm going down.'

'And we can spare time for this, can we?' Casson said, doubtful.

'If it'll spare lives later on? Hell yes!'

Walker reached the bottom of the slope. Beneath him, birds picked amongst the corpses. Only when he got close, and they took flight, could Denniston make out how many there'd been. A dark cloud of them lifted skywards, to circle above and fall to feasting again when the pass was quiet and empty once more.

Denniston's shoulders shook still. The others spoke, but he couldn't make himself listen. Behind, hitched to the cart, the mules stared on blankly. With flicks of their tails, they swept the last old and hopeless flies of autumn from their skinny flanks. And into the bottom of the defile, Denniston stared without seeing or understanding. Regardless, the image had already stamped itself on his mind's eye: not the dead men's faces or the wounds, but the shape of those bodies, tangled together. That was what was left over, when the fighting was all done. That was the leavings that always came from what other men might term glory.

The first feeling that came over him after, when he felt anything again, was a kind of nauseous shame. He had been too much of late; shown too much of himself to men who might as well have been strangers for the brief time he'd known them.

Yet still they carried on. That was the way with a pack or a herd, and perhaps that's what they'd become. When one was too weak or absent from themselves and the others to push on for themselves, the rest still continue, and the weak are hurried along so as not to be left behind.

Strangers they might have been, but they'd put Denniston in the cart and pulled it downhill as the country opened around them. An hour passed; two perhaps. The sun swam towards noon. Without a word, Denniston slipped from the cart, boots to the ground, which melting snow had turned to cold black mud. Once again, he walked.

They were close now, and drawing closer. The leavings of the skirmish, the refugees – all those had been indicators. But as they walked through the widening basin, Denniston saw Erzurum itself: a raised shadow in the center of the sunken plain, surrounded by a straggle of uncertain shapes, low forms, blurs of colour.

'The outskirts?' Casson said.

'Farms and pastures and fields,' Guppie said. 'They left all this behind? I mean to say, the ones we saw before, on the road?'

The mud road went between fields. Heads of wheat hung ready and ripe, waiting for an Autumn harvest that would never come.

'Either it'll rot out here,' said Pinkerton. 'Or more likely, it'll feed the Russians while Erzurum starves for lacking it.'

Every splashing step and rolling wheel dug pockmarks and trenches into the face of the road. Already the plain was pitted and striped with darkness and damp, between the farms, fields, and fortified suburbs. A fierce greyness surged all around and called itself day. Somewhere inside it, at the storm's boiling centre, a battle raged to the city's north. Helpless, from the west, they saw it and struggled on.

It began to rain. The cart came to a halt. Cebrael had reined in the mules. Wearily, Casson turned to talk to him, with a sharp question, then a steady-rising voice.

The other doctors huddled miserably about the cart, already weighed down by the rain. Thunder rolled in the distance – or perhaps it was the din of cannons.

The tangle of bodies in the valley had been a warning. But the fighting that thrashed so close to the city was the truth of what they'd come for. For the first time on their journey, Denniston was afraid of their purpose, and afraid to carry on. They would have to pass close by the fray or else turn fully back.

Casson, all the while, had been fighting his own battle. Denniston saw him tilt his head skyward, eyes closed against the rain. His lips shaped words that might have been "thank God". He struggled through the mud towards where his comrades clutched together.

'The bastard will do it,' he said, with a wild look in his eyes. 'He'll do it, but he wants paying more.'

A flash of lightning scored the grey. At least one of the great drumrolls had been true thunder then, and not just the kind man made.

'What other option do we have?' said Guppie.

'None at all.'

'Then how much does he want, and how much do we have?' Walker asked.

Denniston squinted against the rain as the others spoke amongst themselves in a confusion of counting: kuruş, akçe and who knew what else. Watching the battle was like watching a forest move. Some distant part of Denniston's mind thought briefly of Macbeth. Here was Birnam Wood before Dunsinane Hill; the shapes of men and muskets and bayonets, fogged in smoke, surging about earthworks and barricades. They moved against and over each other, shifting like stormfronts at sea.

'Thank God for Barrington-Kennet!' said Casson. 'He fairly loaded us with cash for the journey, after all...'

'Now we know why,' Walker said. 'No wonder...'

As Denniston watched, the battle moved, gaining momentum, moving faster. For smoke and mist and distance, it was impossible to make out figures, but he saw trajectories, directions – sometimes the fountain of dirt that came when cannonfire struck. The bristling darkness gave ground, flowing towards the city's northern outskirts. Soon it began to lose itself in the shapes of buildings, and things that were buildings no longer. A flank circled round towards the west.

'The Turks,' Denniston put in, bluntly. 'I think the Turks are routed.'

At first the men fell silent. It was Guppie that finally spoke, thin-voiced but steadfast against the rain and thunder: 'They'll need us, then.'

'That they will,' Pinkerton murmured.

Agreement rose up amongst them: a growing mumble that became something breathless, fearful, hopeful. It was almost an excitement. Where fear had pooled cold in Denniston's gut, now his insides were writhing with energy, anticipation.

Casson leapt up onto the cart beside Cebrael and took up the rifle from near the driver's seat. He raised it over his head and rallied them. 'Gentlemen! We have our colours!'

Denniston was on the cart too before he quite knew what he was doing. He rummaged amongst boxes and baskets and lain tarpaulins til he found what he was looking for: a white flag stitched with a red star and sickle-moon. 'The Crescent?'

'The Crescent,' Casson agreed.

It went through them, another wave of murmurs. 'The Crescent … The Red Crescent … We'll raise the Crescent…'

'They're moving around,' said Walker, pointing as one front of the battle churned to encircle the city. 'If they catch us before we make the walls…'

'Will the Crescent help?' Guppie asked.

'We're non-combatants. Medics. If they have any honour in them, it will,' Casson said fiercely. 'And if they don't, we'd best be fast.'

In a fumbling of wet hands, fingers gingerly touching, Casson and Denniston fastened the flag to the butt of the rifle and held it high.

'Ready?'

'Ready!'

'Gentlemen!' Casson shouted above the growing din. 'Under the Red Crescent, I say: Erzurum by sundown!'

'Erzurum!' It went up like a battlecry. 'Erzurum by sundown!'

And that was it, thought Denniston. That was the Casson he'd hoped to call a friend – who if he could not be like, then at least he could be near.

'Hyah! Hhhyah!'

Cebrael whipped the mules into a wild-eyed run. The doctors pushed, kicking and loping against the mud as they hurried behind and besides.

Above them, tied to the unused rifle, a howling wind unfurled their flag.

In what seemed like moments, but covered strange stretches of cannon-cratered ground, Denniston's voice was raw with shouting. He didn't remember raising it. Instead, the distance was chewed up by panic and spat out in blurred pieces.

Trenches, as yet unused by the defenders, dug difficult into the ground. The road broke amongst them and they were forced to swerve between. The wet rattle of the cart's motion, and all the cargo it carried, joined the deafening sound.

A many-bodied straggle of men manoeuvred around. Russians, a wall of infantry, cavalry wheeling about against the darkening sky. The line had got behind them now, and ahead there raged a sea.

Like waves crashing at the lip of a sea-wall, or dashing against a shore, the beaten Turks teemed against the walls of the city itself. Brown irregular stone, grey mortar, slope-sided stacks for support, and hexagonal outcrops, jutting like headlands from a sea-cliff, bristling and flashing and smoking with cannons. Above the clot of fleeing Turks were others; shapes on the walls, waving and aiming muskets and rifles at the Russian pursuit.

Denniston didn't dare look behind, but he heard the crack and echo of guns, shouting voices. And then the shouting was all around them. They joined the seething mass and their little cart became an island in the midst of it: Turks, faces seen and forgotten in moments, wounds seen and forgotten, all pushing for the walled city's open western gate.

There were too many sights, too many voices. Denniston could do nothing but block it out and detach himself. He concentrated on pushing, striving with his feet through the mud, the strange soft lumps that heaped the ground and might have been other than dirt, struggling with his elbows against the crowd that tried to swallow them.

Dimly, he was aware that he might have been crying. His eyes were sore and stinging. The cannons argued on, deafening overhead. The sky went out, blocked off, as they passed under the gatehouse, and piled into the citadel's streets.

James

My dear Miss Guthrie,

We have arrived and not a moment too soon. Already embattled in Erzurum's first assault, the Russians had us beaten to the city by a matter of hours. What crucial hours they proved to be!

With the Turks in full rout, and the Russians mustering for pursuit, we scarce outran the latter's efforts to round up those who fled. Pushing the last few miles to the city, alongside the Turks for the final stretch, I don't exaggerate to impress you or to win your pity when I say: those last few miles were the hardest of our entire journey. But it felt like wading through a dream. I don't quite feel like I've yet woken up.

Tired as we were, we put it all aside, and made ourselves of use. In the filthy rain-drenched streets we ministered to filthy rain-drenched men, dressing more minor wounds, checking injuries for severity. All the while Casson tried to ascertain from the soldiers where we ought to head. Our hospital, in the end, was not hard to find. We needed only to join the lines of walking wounded, and follow the stretchers uphill, through the winding streets of the citadel.

In the walled city's upper reaches, we found it – not much more, at the time, than a building emptied out in waiting for us, but quickly filling with injured. It was staffed with jara bashis – Turks trained to give rudimentary aid and assist professional doctors – and we found they had been waiting for us too. Longing for our arrival, in fact, for they were quite overtasked before our arrival.

Now we are overtasked as well, but at least the work is shared. For of course the battle has left us with a tremendous amount of work. Two days now, and I still don't feel I've slept. Perhaps a few snatched hours on the hospital floor, but a sleep deep as the grave for my sheer exhaustion.

An orderly passed me a letter of yours this morning, before I could get to work. I gather that it had been waiting for me, and I'm very grateful for it. Now I snatch not sleep but a few minutes, here and there, to write you back when I can. But I fear that this makes for a very bad and broken sort of letter, for I'm called off so regularly.

I only half wish you might see the place and the circumstances from which I am writing. Just now I think I can hear some awful row kicking up. Soldiers still stricken by panic and inhabitants with a battle on their doorstep. Defeat has put in everyone a kind of madness.

I say it's only half a wish for I wouldn't want to worry you, showing you the scenes that surround me. Or am I only flattering myself to think you'd feel some anxiety on my behalf? My apologies if I assume or say too much.

For now I will only say that there are three wards in this hospital, and a number of smaller rooms for individual patients and for operations. All were in quite a sorry state when we found them, crammed with soldiers from the battle. And I must say that now they are little better. But 'little better' is still a little better, I think. Things at least are a fair bit cleaner.

Casson, who of course can understand the soldiers' talk – or the talk of those still able to form words – and it's rumoured the Russians have advanced their lines in the wake of the battle they won. They've established camps and are getting dug in. No doubt they will be asking whoever is in charge here for their surrender soon. I say, 'whoever is in charge' for in all the chaos and for all our work I still don't know.

I don't think the Turks will give up even then. Whether in battle or defeat or in rout, or under the hands of strange foreign surgeons – your humble servant, and his comrades beneath the Red Crescent – they are a startlingly brave lot, and already I admire them very much.

So, the Russians I think will try to encircle us, though there's no telling how long this might take, or whether they will be successful, but already they have the north and east of the citadel. If they do, it will be a siege, and you might not hear from me for quite a time…

Onto matters brighter, though! Your idea of a novel is novel to me, though it finds me quite bashful! I don't doubt your ability to carry it out, but I only regret that I'd fall very short of what it ought to require in a hero. Diligence, charm, a certain magnetism; a man whom other men, and the reader themself might follow and wish towards success. I am not that man, and my list of shortcomings besides is rather too long.

Still, your letters are of splendid great interest to me, though mine are poor by comparison. This one, I think, in particular is quite awful. I only hope you'll be able to make out the writing, and will forgive any errors and blots.

I am only partly to blame though. The rest is down to a bad pen and very little ink, for I quite forgot to mention that we lost no small amount of baggage in the rush towards the city and through the citadel's streets. My good writing materials were among them, and your photograph also – as such, I'm shamed to admit, I shall have to beg you for another.

Until then I remain

Yours very sincerely,

James Denniston

Chapter 7

The messenger came at noon. Overhead the sun shone broad and bright after days of rain. But the ground beneath his horse's hooves was still soft, uneasy, cut up with feet.

The Russian lines were hasty made and shoddy: a forest of tents, struggling not to sink into what was fast becoming a swamp. Puddles the size of ponds stood, reflecting the wide cold sky.

Outside a tent, a man with fine moustaches and good boots half-ruined with mud spoke to the mesenger in Russian, expecting him to understand. He did not. But he took the missive that the officer – for he reckoned the moustached man was an officer – gave him. A folded square of good paper, stamped and sealed with a two-headed eagle. Turkish or not, he'd have no use for the writing inside. He'd never learnt to read, but all the same, he was no fool. And only a fool could fail to guess what the letter meant, or what its message might be.

Surrender, it would say. Or don't, and see what happens.

The officer gave him an escort. Five Muscovites, thickly bearded, dressed in coats of deep green. They looked more ready for the winter than their officer by far. Even in his own black coat, the messenger envied them that. Still, he told himself, the wages they paid for this work would help him and his family through the cold all the same. It was more than the Turks would pay him, hiding behind their walls. In truth, it was more than he'd ever want to accept from them.

They mounted up, he and his escorts, and struck out across the plain. The ground was treacherous and the going slow. Fighting had torn the earth to pieces here. In places the rain had smoothed the damage over. In others the water had only worsened it, carving away great pits like a river swallowing chunks of its bank when in springtime the floods come in.

The messenger saw it all with strange sorrow in his heart. No doubt it was different for the Muscovites. No doubt that even the Turks would not feel the same. They'd taken this land by conquest. So had the Russians before, and most likely they would again. And before them had come Persians, Seljuks, Greeks, and Arabs, down through the ages, and through the stories his grandmother told him. But all those stories ended the same way. She would tell him: You are Hay, and this land is yours, in both your blood and bones; it belonged to our people once, and though the conquerors come and go, it will be ours still when they are gone.

So then, he had no loyalty to the Turks. What loyalty he owed to the Russians came with the money they paid, and how likely it seemed that they would be the winning side in this most recent war. But the country had seen wars beyond counting and the city had watched from its hill. Wars had come and gone; his family had remained. His loyalty was to them, to the land. Perhaps that was why it tightened his heart to see how this fighting tore at it?

Erzurum loomed ahead. The city's outskirts, cracked and hollowed by battle, and then the citadel, the outer ring of walls that surrounded the foot of its hill. They were irregular, clinging to the slopes like a mountain path cleaves to the mountainside. Forts and towers stuck out, cone-roofed like beehives. And from the outer walls, and from the inner walls, the city was watching.

The gates of a fort opened a crack and let the messenger ride through, flanked by Russians with flags that meant, for now, they came in peace.

Inside, the buildings were the colour of wet sand. Flashes of colour burst out and then were left behind. Blue tiles, women veiled in green, skirts and Turkish trousers of burnt orange, hats of red with black tassels. Erzurum's people looked down as the messenger climbed the sloping boulevard at a walk. They looked from flat rooftops and out from patchy vegetable gardens. They looked with soldiers' eyes from skeleton postings on the tops of the inner walls.

It was at those walls that the messenger stopped and gave his message. A Turk with a curved sword and decorated jacket accepted it, opened the letter, and told him:

'No. General Heimann says he will take the city peacefully? I say, peace will not gain him these walls. Peace will not gain him Erzurum.'

The soldiers looked down. There were no cheers from the walls or roofs. Only grim acceptance. The messenger took a moment to look. Some had rifles or muskets shouldered, others had no weapons at all, but even so it was hard to draw a line between soldiers and townsfolk. If the Russians broke through the walls, that line would disappear without a trace. These were determined faces and fierce eyes; men and women who would fight for their homes, as his own parents and their forefathers had fought before.

In another war, he thought, he might have been among those men and women. He might have ridden for them, delivered their messages. But today he had come to deliver Russian terms to Erzurum. And what the Russians did with the Turks' refusal was Russian business, not his.

As they rode back, the sky gaped open, flat and cold; growing colder every day.

Chapter 8

Agnes

Dear Doctor Denniston,
In my last letter, I made mention that I would soon be a guest of the Carmichaels in Edinburgh, and it is from their home that I write to you now. It has been, however, quite a struggle to find the time and peace to do so: we are all kept very busy indeed by preparations for the charity dance, of which I also told you in my previous letter. Being judged a great lover of music by Mr David Carmichael – for I cannot deny that I appreciate it greatly – I have been set to purpose in finding suitable musicians for the event. While in Manchester I could enlist the talents of a very fine string quartet with almost no trouble at all. In Edinburgh I am at a disadvantage. Do you enjoy music, Dr. Denniston? I wonder if perhaps you might have better luck in finding four sets of strings and four pairs of hands with the skill to make them sing.

There is also the matter of invitations that must be written and sent, refreshments that must be considered, etcetera. However, I will not tease you with too much mention of the latter, for mercy's sweet sakes. On the road to Erzurum, hunger seemed to be one of your chiefest miseries – not perhaps the hunger that comes of lacking food, but of lacking anything good or wholesome to eat in quite some time. Has this relented somewhat at least since, I presume, your arrival by now in Erzurum?

In any case, I fear that despite your protestations, all the content of my letters must seem frightfully dull, or else of little consequence, when compared with what keeps you occupied. And yet, for whatever reason, you continue to praise my letters beyond their dessert; so, for as long as you take comfort in them, I will continue to write them. Perhaps,then, in some small way, I will have added my own help to your cause?

To this end I will endeavour to bypass my reservations, or any dents my humbleness might take in speaking of myself at such length. For your sake, I shall spin the fabric of my life into tales, poor as the material might be, and tell them as well as I may. I only hope that you will find them of some interest. Perhaps it will inspire you toward offering me greater detail of your life and exploits as well?

Mr. David and Mrs. Sarah Carmichael, my hosts, you have already met. But news of this dance has gone out like a clarion call, and we are gathering arrivals from all branches of the Carmichael clan each day, as the dance draws nearer. Of course, the house is fine and modest, but narrowly tall, as many of the stony homes in this part of Southside tend to be. So, even with such a house at their disposal, and a good number of rooms for the use of guests, our two mutual friends the Carmichaels cannot hope to take on the remaining accumulation of Carmichaels – quietly, I am only glad that I got in before the deluge!

Among their guests they have taken in both myself and a Miss Evelyn Carmichael, whose acquaintance I do not think you have made. She is Mr. David Carmichael's sister, unmarried, and much like me in age, and perhaps in temperament. We are lodged together in rooms that nestle side by side, and so I think we have both considered it meet that we become quite well acquainted. Thinking myself a fair judge of character – though tending towards simply judgemental, at times, as you will recall from the night in Glasgow when we met – I predict we might soon think of one another as friends.

Miss Carmichael is a welcome aid in our rush to make ready, in particular with matters of the kitchen. Servants, she says, may come and go with times of plenty and paucity, and though it might not be seemly for a woman of birth and upbringing to be well able to bake her own bread etcetera, seemliness – Miss Carmichael says – will feed no-one. She espouses and displays such practical ability in all things, I find myself both ashamedly envious, and, to no small degree, inspired. If I were to say that she is a woman of radical mindset on any number of issues, I think you, of the few gentlemen I know, will not take it as a show of spite towards her, nor would you hold any spite of your own. Indeed, I think you might admire her for it, whether others would not.

Quite aside from all this, I must admit that the business of this gathering brings not only hard toil but also reward. I have funds that will stretch, I think, to a new gown for the occasion, if the gown is but a modest one. However, I have set upon a prize that would leave me happy to forgo the new gown entirely if that were the only way to gain it: a pair of bright blue slippers. They should be quite useless out of doors, but they are beautiful things and, I fancy, almost oriental in style. I think they would be too good for anything but dancing.

Good health and good fortune, until I hear from you again

Sincerely yours,

Miss Guthrie

The letter had been waiting for him at Erzurum. Denniston read and re-read it, clutching at the words that so steadied his nerves. Then, in a frenzy of thoroughness, he washed his hands.

The leathery scent of carbolic soap led his mind back to Glasgow. Back to textbooks and lectures; rituals of cleanliness; patients and cadavers, neat as diagrams. Not so here. In the Erzurum SHC Hospital, the carbolic took a new form, and a newer more biting aroma.

The scent became a stench in surgery. Carbolic soap was saved for the doctors. It was carbolic acid that was left for patients, to scourge their wounds and dressings. It reeked and burnt like vinegar, searing the inside of Denniston's nose and filling his lungs. Even then he was thankful. It masked the smell of fearful men, and blood, the sharp tang of bodies crowded too close together. But for how it stung at him, he could only imagine how sore it affected the men.

Cleanliness, though – it was all in the name of cleanliness. And in modern medicine, cleanliness is key, much as the old guard within the profession might fail to admit it. There were those among general practitioners, the English in particular, who subscribed still to superstition over science: miasmas, spontaneous generation of corrupting agents, cholera hospitals that emphasised sunlight and roundly cornerless wards over any earnest attempts to treat the disease. By comparison, his time studying in Glasgow had flung him towards enlightenment. The university had lost Professor Lister to Edinburgh, but his legacy remained in how many were convinced by the new "Germ Theory of Disease"; how many among the professors, indeed, taught his work, referencing Pasteur and Koch and Snow. Denniston had learnt that it is always better to keep infection out of wounds and prevent illness before it can take root than to find oneself treating either later on, when infection or illness has become full-fledged. So, he reminded himself: sanitation and cleanliness, always, even here amidst the chaos and squalor.

Denniston slipped from the corner where he had set up a wash-station and returned to work.

Voices rang out in bedlam, and more he allowed himself to hear them. It was hard to differentiate between groans and screams. Words and empty noise mingled, as if the whole hospital spoke not Turkish or English, or any variants of either, but in tongues. Sometimes they were all too clear, like the wide-ranging tongues of apostles, so that Denniston almost understood. Mostly they were fractured: the broken tongues of Babel. He had lost count of the patients he'd seen already.

The windows in this ward were high, round eyelets, set in the flat ceiling at regular intervals — twenty perhaps across its whole length. They were lidded with slatted wooden shutters, but shutter and glass were both thrown wide open. It was an insistence of Pinkerton's, and though it smacked of Miasmatism to Denniston – a belief in bad and good airs – he had agreed to it, if only because fresh air helped to vent the hospital's stale smell.

The light through those windows was ambiguous, cold, seethingly pale.

Even so, they glared into the hospital's gloom, bright against the fading whitewash of the ceilings and walls, and cast columns of light onto the endless beds: both iron-framed and makeshift; on the floor and raised in barrack-style bunks above it.

Walking between the falls of light put Denniston in mind of paintings: the sort created for churches or vicarages; the gaze of God cast golden through parting clouds. But such thoughts were idleness. He let himself process them only for a moment.

His next patient was broad-chested, moustached, with outgrown mahogany hair. They had stripped him out of an officer's jacket to get at the injury. Strong-armed but gentle, Kincaid held him down, providing nips of ether while Denniston gave his whole mind over to the patient's wound.

To some long-suppressed part of himself it was loathsome, but the doctor in him had learnt to look only with mixed curiosity and sympathy – what chance was there here to aid the man, and what chance did it offer for learning? As bullet-wounds go, it was mild. It had entered near the hip, through a small piercing, and left mercifully straight out the other side. The exit was wider than its entry, with loose flesh ragged at its edges. The procedure, then, was a simple one. Days back, it might have daunted him, but a theoretical knowledge, from observation and study, had fast become something more practical. That is the way with necessity, he thought.

Denniston worked with the exit wound, cutting away what was frayed and ruined, lancing and draining what was logged with fluid. The patient, throughout, was still, removed from himself by the ether. Only the muscles in his neck and jaw strained, cording tightly. After all the madness of recent days, this case was almost close to Glasgow: all but academic in its clarity and ease. No lethal damage to tissues, no shattered bone or lingering lump of bullet – the wound was quick to treat and clean.

'Fates be kind, he'll heal up well,' Denniston said as his own jaw unclenched from concentration.

'They've been kind to him so far,' said Kincaid. 'Easiest bullet I've seen all day.'

'He'll be back to the walls soon. How kind is that really?'

The patient was smiling now, half-drunk on relief.

'*Uzun yaşamak*,' Denniston said to him, clumsy but sincere: may you live long. It was one of a handful of phrases for which he'd braved the scorn that came with asking Casson for anything; words to let their Turkish cases know that they were more than just meat in the hands of foreign butchers.

'*Teşekkürler*,' the Turk said, breathless. '*Teşekkürler, hekim effendi.*'

This, too, Denniston understood as thanks. It weighed thick and sentimental in his throat: a knot he swallowed down to keep his eyes dry and his voice from cracking as he carried on.

The previous patient he'd called on had died under Denniston's first touch. Even as he tried to manage the unfamiliar sounds – 'There now... There now, I'm Doctor Denniston. *İngiliz hekim. Adınız*? Your name? What is your name?' – the patient had let out the last of his breath. A shallow loss of sound, through gritted red-flecked teeth. The words had dried in Denniston's mouth before he could finish saying them. He had moved on, washing death from his pale and shaking hands.

The beginning and end of every day had become routine. Habit, Denniston reflected, is the quickest and most desperate way to turn any shambles into something that one can make sense of. Habit and mere exposure will make anything ordinary, given time.

At sunset prayer-time, lamps would be lit in the hospital, to make up for the failing daylight. By lamplight, the doctors would work, all of them, a while longer – a few hours, perhaps more, depending on the nature of all their cases. Then two would make ready to work through the night, watch over the patients and over each other, and the rest would start the downhill journey home, once more to the sound of the call to prayer.

Come morning it would all start over. Those who had slept the night through would rise at dawn with the first call to prayer. Back at the hospital, they would relieve the two who'd taken the night-shift and they, in turn, would steal what hours of sleep they could before returning to their duties at the time of midday prayers.

It was this cycle that made the madness of all their shifts more manageable. More than day and night, work and sleep now divided their time, and Muslim prayer sounded out their durations.

That evening they left behind Casson and Walker. The rest left the hospital, high on the citadel hill as it was, and took the winding streets home.

A dog barked, skinny sounding just by its voice. Its call mustered up a chorus that spread across the dark city like a clamour, or an alarm. In some windows, light showed warmly golden through the shutters. Through some, voices echoed: arguments and unburdenings of hearts and everything in between. But most houses by now were dark, and most of the streets were silent.

Pinkerton walked with their lamp in hand: a little cylinder of glass and a brass reservoir of oil, shading its wick from the wind. Its light made the world small around them. By day you could see the whole plain on this journey, arrayed on the lowlands surrounding Erzurum. The sights of the morning journey were townsfolk close by, Turkish bills stuck to the walls of alleys, shops, and houses; mountains in the distance, and the blot of the Russian encampment, vast to the north and east. At night the city transformed into something made of shadows below, and an overhead enormity of stars.

'...Fine horses in this part of the world. Very fine, so I always heard,' said Pinkerton, continuing a story to which Denniston had only been half-listening. 'So, it follows that as they hold horses in high regard, they'd hold thieves of horses in particular disdain. Horse thieves – now they'd have a poetic fate ahead of them, in older times. Each limb would be lashed to the harness of a different horse, you see, and then each horse would be driven off hard in a different direction. A few moments – longer for strong men – and then the poor devil's sinews would all give out. Arms and legs, torn off. *Pop*! Like a rabbit for the pot!'

This had become habit too. The doctors would exchange grizzly legends, uplit by lamplight, and then discuss them as they would any other medical curiosity, debating their likelihood.

'Fine horses they may have been,' said Kincaid, stroking his beard. 'But surely now, the sinews, bones, skin and all wouldn't give out so easily?'

'More likely the limbs would just become disjointed,' put in Guppie.

'The shock,' said Featherston. 'They would lose consciousness, wouldn't they?'

'And hemorrhage to death,' Denniston said. 'I expect it'd all be internal. No great drama to speak of.'

'Ah, my mistress Medicine,' Pinkerton sighed. 'And oh, for her sweet sister, Science. Ridding the world of all its wonder, one case at a time...'

'Still...' Denniston muttered. 'I fancy I know how the poor devils felt.'

'Oh?' said Kincaid. 'You look well for a man lately pulled apart by horses.'

'Not quite the whole feeling then. More like a shadow of it. Pulled off so pressingly in every direction at once like that, but you can only be in one place at a time. I fancy we all know what that's like.'

'The hospital?' said Guppie.

'Aye.'

That gave them pause for thought. Denniston imagined their thoughts all were different, but the end of them was the same. The hospital wore on the brain not so much by the things its surgeons were forced to do and see, but for how much of it happened all at once, and for how they were forced to choose between them.

Here there might be a soldier, crying out, at the loss of six fingers to a backfire from the artillery he had been manning. And here there might be the stunned or stoic silence of another, patiently holding ropes of viscera inside his belly with both hands, where a bayonet had emptied them out. And all about, languages would war amongst themselves – Turkish, English, local dialect – but give way to the same cries, the same meanings: '*Hekim*! *Hekim effendi*! *Lütfen*! ... Doctor! Please, a doctor!' On and on, until the cacophony, the din of smells and sights, all blended to become an awful new norm.

The stress of answering each pull, each desperate call – that was what wore on Denniston, til he was so much in need of sleep that no sleep at night would come. All of them worked, working to answer each individual strain, in their own time, in haphazard order, until they could work no more.

Shortly, they found their way home, with the surety of sleepwalkers. It was a barren little two-storey place, plaster-walled inside and out. An external staircase spanned the two floors. Inside there were only chipped blue tiles about the doorways and faded rugs on the floor by way of decoration. Half a dozen sleeping mats, and a small black iron stove nestled against the grubby walls.

It was kept by a bearded Turk – too old to fight, but with room in his house left behind by absent sons – their landlord in every way save payment. As they knocked, he unbarred the ground-floor door from within, and returned to sit on a rug by the stove. That was where they always found him, and where he always sat, gravely silent, before he retired upstairs and to bed.

A few minutes the doctors spent smoking, pensive, long enough only to drain a bowl of barley soup each before the call of their hard lumpen mattresses grew too strong.

Denniston lay in the dark that night, unable to sleep and unable to rise.

Chapter 9

The letter had come to Vashin by accident. It travelled by post-rider, fast, changing horses regularly as it ate up the miles of its journey. It had travelled beneath thick thatches of pine, over mountains, then down onto the plains where Anatolia led slow into Caucasia. It bore messy red stamps for every stop: Törnük, Torul, Arzular, Bayburt…

But it came to Vashin at Aşkale, where the roads from Istanbul and Trabzon joined.

Built along a strip of clean water in the dusty plain, Aşkale was a small and solid little township; a crossroads town, always full beyond what it could hold. Travellers, merchants, post-riders, and at times like this, picketed battalions, and troupes of irregulars. They pitched tents along the water, fouling it with their passing. They threatened or paid their way into beds for the night, or floors to sleep on and roofs to sleep under. It had been this way since before the Ottomans, someone had told Vashin. Aşkale had been a place to water animals, trade goods and news, for a span of time that seemed, to Vashin, like forever. And in it, the Big House was its beating heart.

The Big House was many things to many kinds of people. For travellers it was an inn; a place to drink coffee and raki, play at dice, smoke in the shade in the summer, or else shelter from the winter cold. It was a kind of general shop besides, a grain wholesaler, and for the locals it made up the seat of the landlord.

For Vashin it was a place to listen, drink, smoke. Listening meant news; news meant work. As far as work goes, he'd done worse and known harder than waiting, drinking coffee by the hearth in a smoky room.

He was listening when the horse trotted into the Big House's courtyard. He didn't see it, but of course he heard the news:

'Foaming with sweat..!'

'But no rider, by God, by God! Did it work itself into a lather like that?'

'Must have!'

'Well then, did you ever see the like?'

'Stands to reason, I suppose. A horse rides the same road all its life, and something happens to the rider? It bolts, of course it bolts, but where does it bolt to? Why, down the only road it knows, and on to its destination!'

'But what happened to the rider? That's what I'd like to know – just what happened to its rider?'

'Shot from the saddle, I reckon, God give him peace.'

'Bandits? Soldiers?'

'What's the difference? That's what I'd like to know – just what difference does it really make in these days?'

It was chance, then, but a good enough chance to gamble on. Aşkale was many things to many men, but among those things it was a post-office, and a changing station for post-riders. The post-horse had run on, panic-mad, to where its journey always ended – where it was fed, watered, cleaned, and put to rest. Clever, Vashin thought, in a dumb animal kind of way.

Whatever fate had caught up to its rider, there was no official post-rider to replace him. With interest, Vashin watched the landlord think. He was landlord, true, but post-official too, and innkeeper, shopkeeper, and all-round gossip. The big man of the Big House. His face was still but his shining shaven scalp seemed to twitch. A vein stood out through the skin. Something was about to happen – the kind of thing Vashin spent his time waiting for – a moment of opportunity.

'Good people!' The landlord's voice carried across the smoky common-room, demanding silence. 'Good people, it pains my heart to consider what has befallen your friend, and mine, the good postal-rider, in the line of duty. But the facts remain! His saddle-bags are untouched, good people, and the post…must arrive…on time!'

Saddlebags open on the counter before him, the landlord called out a list of contents. Quickly, the room broke into an auction, every mercenary and desperado bidding and haggling over who would buy the rider's job and take the post to Erzurum.

'Boys, boys! My good, good boys!' the landlord called above the din. 'You can do better than that, surely you can! Letters, my boys, for a city! A city in the possession of a *pasha*! Think, my boys, of the *gratitude*!'

'Gratitude!' someone scoffed. 'The same kind of gratitude as got "your friend and mine" out on the road?'

'A bullet in the back!'

'Only reason Erzurum's got a *pasha* in charge is it's a damned warzone! I heard the cannons!'

'Then… *surely* the risk will come with greater reward!' The landlord pressed on, wringing his hands together. 'See here, I have a package for one Ibrahim Nazif *Effendi*… Another for Mehmed Edib Haji… A letter for one… Hm. Who here reads European?'

Another clamour went up; another smaller scramble of men, offering prices to read the envelope.

'Doctor James Denniston!' the landlord announced, triumphant, slipping coins into the hands of the man who had read it for him. 'A letter for

Doctor James Denniston, care of the Stafford House Committee, Erzurum!'

That was the bait that Vashin had needed. The name was English. From what he knew of Englishmen, he knew what could be gained from their favour. Sometimes, Vashin reckoned, ambition is a bit you must take between your teeth: a plough you must pull if you hope for a harvest.

Calmly, Vashin finished his coffee, smoked the last of his cigarette in three hard sucks, and placed his bid.

Some laughed. What sort of fool would pay so much for two saddlebags without a horse attached? But they were men of short sight and slim ambition, and Vashin was ever an optimist.

The earth was cold and hard as iron. The hooves of Vashin's little brown mare beat on the road like thunder, but left no tracks on the stiff ground.

The sun began to set behind him. For half the horizon ahead, he saw the Russian lines, bristling thick as a forest to Erzurum's north and east. But still they hung back from the city itself. Perhaps they feared cannons, or sallies by night. Perhaps not. Still, they dug in, and pitched their own little city of canvas and earthworks, melting in the rain. This, Vashin knew, was what an impasse looks like: both sides out of range of the other's guns, and waiting for the first move.

With the sun at his back, a lone figure on a plain emptied out by battle, he was conspicuous, riding hard by troughs of frozen black mud and the shallow graves dug by cannon-shot and shells. Though camped along the far two flanks of the city, the Russians would have eyes all around. Unless, that is, they were fools, or undermanned. Vashin was ever an optimist, but hoping for that seemed longer odds than even he would take.

Vashin had been many things: goatherd, traveller's guide, smuggler, irregular soldier, courier once or twice. He would play whatever role gave the right incentive. He was nothing if not resourceful. Back in the Big House, turning blockade-runner seemed a clever gamble, a venture he could be proud in, get rich in. But as night fell, and his horse began to flag, and his ears stung sharp with the cold, even through his thick fur hat, he began to wonder if he had made a mistake. What sort of fool would pay for the privilege of riding through a warzone, after all?

A whipcrack of sound rang out distant across the plain. A buzzing whistling followed, cutting past him with a mosquito's high whine. Gunfire, confirming his fears.

Vashin jolted to his senses in panic. Dug his heels into the sides of his horse.

'Come on… Come on…' He groaned, hunkering down against her neck. 'There'll be time to say sorry later, only give me a mile! Give me a mile or two of speed!'

Low and small, down flush to his horse's saddle and bridle, Vashin braved a glance behind. Riders, trailing him. Russian vedettes – he cursed them, under his ragged breath.

On fresh horses, they pressed their advantage. Like ghosts in the twilight, they glided between the ruined farms and huts of the city's wartorn outskirts. Each moment they pelted closer. As Vashin watched, one of them levelled his carbine to fire.

Another crack, echoing through the dark. No insect whir this time; no break in the air. Better still, no sudden pain. Vashin's heart hammered out his desperate thanks. The vedettes had fresher faster horses, but he had night on his side. The darkness had thrown off their aim.

Vashin fumbled a hand down to his saddle and slipped his finger through the trigger guard of his pistol. Blind and backwards, he fired two shots into the night behind him, and veered off to the right. Neither shot would hit, he knew, but when the vedettes shot again, they'd fire at where his pistol had flared up in the darkness. When they did, Vashin would not be there.

The vedettes gave another volley. One came too close to bear thinking about, screaming in his ear. But a moment later, an answering round came from ahead.

The city lights seemed dim compared with the sudden flashes of powder that glared up in front of them. Behind, Vashin heard the crash of cannonfire striking the ground. He was in range of Erzurum's walls now. Safe, perhaps.

Torches and lamps bobbed on the walls of the city's western redoubt. The dark opened up as he drew closer – close enough to see gates, sloping supports, the dark shapes of rifles levelled at him from above.

He was sweating, cold and profuse as his mare while he reined her into a skidding, circling halt. She brayed and whinnied, teeth bared as he stroked her neck and sighed his shaking relief into her fluttering ears.

'Friend or foe?' a voice shouted down from atop the gate. 'Friend or foe! Say quick or we'll shoot you too, by God!'

'Your foes shot at me! What does that tell you?' Vashin called up, voice almost shrill. He leaned down to calm his horse again; his raised voice had made her start. 'Damn it, I have mail! Letters! Letters for Erzurum!'

Chapter 10

A voice came to Denniston through the general clamour. He was calm, the world concentrated round himself and his patient and the wound he was halfway through cleaning. But the voice came behind him, intruding:

'You are Denniston?'

'One moment,' Denniston muttered, voice strained.

'I have letter,' the courier said, then again, more insistent, when Denniston did not respond. 'For you, Denniston *effendi*. A letter for you.'

Denniston fought to keep his hands steady and careful. He lowered himself into a kind of studied cold efficiency as he worked, yet now his heart began to race and a warmth rushed over and into him. He realised he had gone so deep within himself that was no longer sure if it might be frustration or joy.

'One moment,' Denniston repeated in the same flat tone. He finished his work and turned to the courier, begging to clean his bloody hands.

The courier was pale and blue-eyed, dark-bearded, with dark hair curling out from beneath the brim of his hat: a kind of black-furred fez with flaps to cover the ears. "Letter,' he said again with a small bow of his head, and held out a crumpled envelope in his hand.

Denniston took it. It was still sealed, not yet opened. He looked up at the courier, saw he was smiling a little. Denniston, meanwhile, was beginning to grin. The handwriting was familiar as it spelt out his name: neater than his own, more free, schooled to blear and open. He was blushing. Here in the crowded hospital, it was almost more intimate than seemed right or proper.

'My God…' he murmured. 'You're no postman, are you? How did you get hold of this? Carry it all this way?'

The man's smile broadened, proud as a cat with his kill. He opened his mouth, but hesitated a moment, then poured forth in streams of what Denniston took to be Turkish. He gestured throughout, as if his hands might bridge the gap between the two tongues, one or the other known only vaguely by each man. He tapped at his furred hat. He drew lines across his open palm. He jabbed with his fingers and clicked his tongue like a fusillade firing off. He clapped his hands and raised them.

'Letter,' he said in English, with a kind of final gravity, as he gave another little bow. 'For *hekim İngiliz*, Denniston *effendi*.'

'I...' Denniston began. His face wore a frown, but he was edging now towards laughter. 'I... You'll have to wait. Do you understand? Wait, please. I'm—... I have to work.' He folded the envelope into his shirt and left it there close to his chest. '*Adınız*? What is your name? *Adınız ne*? Denniston,' he pointed to himself, hand shaking a little in excitement. 'And you are..?'

'Vashin,' the courier said, smiling. 'My name is Vashin.'

'Then, Vashin, please be kind enough to wait here. I don't know for how long, but I'll make sure it's worth your while, you have my word...Casson?' Denniston called out. 'Casson! I fancy this fine man here – Vashin – has a hell of a story to tell us.'

'I expect,' Casson called back from across the ward, 'you'd have me extract it from him? My, my – not just bullets we're extracting now, but stories too..!'

And Vashin waited.

In the Stafford House Committee hospital, wounded came and went. Some were released back to the forts and fortifications. Others arrived with injuries they'd thought to be nothing, only to have them worsen since the battle. There had been no new skirmishes since the last defeat, and no new attempts to sally out since the Russian messenger's visit. The fight for Erzurum lingered at a standstill. Even so, the wounded came in numbers – one moment, a torrent; the next a trickle. It had been this way for days as the Russians struggled outside the walls to form a loose blockade.

Denniston worked, transfixed, for an elastic hour or more, removing three pellets of shrapnel from a man's thigh, hip and hand. Casson discovered that not even arguments given in their own tongue could persuade a Turkish soldier to allow an amputation, risking their soul to save their life.

Hours passed and night rushed in. Still Vashin waited, with a watchful look on his face whenever Denniston glanced over. For someone willing to wait so long, Vashin fidgeted impatiently. Furred cap in his hands, he worried at it with his fingers, kneading and stroking the dark hairs of it as one might pet a small animal. He had the wary curious look of a man forever listening, a slight smile on his face, as if everything he saw and heard made him, in their own small way, wiser.

'Testing the poor dog, are you?' Casson asked Denniston, as they cleaned their implements and diluted a batch of carbolic. 'For loyalty?'

'I owe him. That's all.'

'Well then, I'm sure he'll wait til kingdom come and trumpet-sound, if there's money in it for him. But why not give it over and send him on his way?'

'I'd like to hear how he came by it. Pinkerton would too, I imagine.'

'Always hungry for another story to tell his—... Come to think of it, I don't actually know: does the old man have grandchildren?'

Denniston shrugged.

'Must be a damned important letter, then, for you and your new valet to fuss over it so.'

'Important to me, yes,' Denniston answered.

'Hm.' Casson murmured. It was only a small noise, but it suggested he understood, and better than he would admit.

Night had drawn in. The lamps were lit as the call to evening prayer went out across the citadel. Inside, the hospital was humid, heavingly warm with the cram of bodies. Denniston had worked all day so far in his shirtsleeves, and the shirt itself was spattered wine-dark up to the elbows, stiff with sweat at the back and collar. Outside, as he and all but Guppie and Featherston trailed home, the chill was intense by contrast.

Smiling, Vashin followed.

'Man's got the look of a stray about him,' Kincaid observed as they walked. 'Dogging us home like he's expecting scraps.'

'I promised I'd pay him,' said Denniston. 'After all the trouble he went through to get here, and after all his long wait, it seems only fair.'

'You do what you like with your own money, Denniston. But for your sakes I hope it's a damned good story he's got to tell.'

'I suppose we'll find out soon enough.'

At their lodgings, down toward the inner walls, the story came out all at once. Like popping the cork from a bottle of champagne that has waited quite long enough to be drunk, Vashin's story foamed forth as they lit the stove and sat on the floor around it, already like well-practiced Turks.

In surprisingly profuse, if broken English, and Turkish translated through Casson, Vashin told his tale, starting with Aşkale…

Agnes

Dear Doctor Denniston,

Fate always moves on strange tides, and it is strange indeed, for me, to find myself in Scotland again and know that you are not. Call it 'fate', though, as I might, I do think that it has just as much, if not more, to do with the will of God. Of course the calling that has led you east to the far-off Orient is medical more than missionary, but whether you know it or not, intend it or not, I believe you are still doing God's work, and I pray that he will continue to look kindly on it.

You say, doctor, that you have little in the way of what a hero truly needs; yet I think a hero is one who does what must be done, decisively and for the good, when the time comes to do it. If you will permit me to judge by your recent letters, you have proven yourself more than capable in that respect and others. Yours is a good cause; better still, your talents value life, and tend towards the saving and preserving of it, with compassion, knowledge, and skill. It is my opinion that soldiering, and deeds which, essentially, amount to little more than violence, are much overvalorised in our society. For this very reason, I think that the papers of Britain, and the novels read within our shores, would do well for having more stories of men like you. Let us honour the healers and menders among us, and let the would-be warriors stew.

All this, however, is only the opinion of one woman, and of little name or fortune to differentiate her from any other. That is to say, I regret that it is an opinion the editors and authors and publishers with whom I share a world would be unlikely to champion, this being, in part, due to the fact that it would mean competition in their own fields: who among them could stand to knowingly publish a woman, or worse, be outsold by her? Better by far to keep her silent. You have known me but briefly, doctor Denniston, but you will have gathered, in even this short time, that silent in the face of those who would silence me is a thing I never can be.

The editors and pressers of news in this country, though, come in two types, I think. There are those who would remold any new development in any way that they can so that it reeks of decline, heralds the fall of our society, etcetera; and there are those who will tell most eagerly any story that can be turned until it looks like victory for Glorious Britannia, and this even in battles that Britain leaves unfought.

I enclose an issue of the Illustrated News that I think might well demonstrate my point. There is in the mid-pages a paragraph or so given to the Battle of Erzurum. Interesting to me is its difference to your own reports, for it paints the Russians as outmanoeuvred, not victorious, when the Turks retreated to their stronger defences. The Turks were 'successful in falling back'; the Russians 'failed to pursue'. The battle, it says, is still ongoing. Perhaps it will be heartening for you to hear that the watching world looks rather more brightly on events surrounding you than you yourself are able.

You complain constantly of poor writing supplies, and I wonder, had I more foresight, ought I to have enclosed also a J-pen; you say that without one your writing is quite useless. I say, Dr. Denniston, that it is still of fine use to me: trouble yourself over your other, greater troubles, and worry less about your writing. It sounds as if those other troubles will soon begin to multiply. If the Russians begin a proper encirclement of Erzurum, I do wonder how you shall ever receive my letters, or how yours shall ever get through? I suppose, to that end, we are, both of us, trusting our missives to fate and faith.

Until I hear from you again

Sincerely yours,

Miss Guthrie

Post scriptum — You ask in your last letter for another photograph. Well, I do not have another to send you. Indeed, I do not think it quite proper to do so again so soon. Perhaps another will follow with my next letter, and you will keep it more carefully than the last. To have two such pictures find their way into the hands of leering Russians, beyond the walls of Erzurum, would after all be further still from the bounds of propriety – don't you think?

It was like thunder, roaring from the sky but with a sound so deep it shook the earth below. The walls of their house murmured with it. The tin dish, hung up near the ceiling to catch the constant leak of water from their ceiling trembled and rattled a moment. Then it fell, with a crash and a burst of cold spray onto the packed earth floor. In the dark, it clanged like a gong.

Denniston lurched up from his sleeping mat. He was on his feet, fumbling in the night for a match or a lamp, before a single thought had entered his head. There was no telling if his eyes were open or shut; if he was dreaming or awake.

Light broke over their single room: its plaster walls and black stove. All was waxy gold and soft shadow, incomprehensible until Denniston's eyes adjusted.

Guppie stood in the doorway, holding a lamp. His eyes were wide and tired, his hands shaking. Featherstoon was behind him, face blank with shock.

Through the doorway, Denniston saw the night was flickering, strange, like a fire just beginning to spark and burn.

Inside, the doctors sprawled and tumbled, struggling awake amidst the dust of the floor, the mats, the overcoats that littered their room.

'It's a damned bloody cannonade!' Guppie yelped, rushing in, pulling Walker to his feet, taking Kincaid by the shoulders. 'They've come into range! Firing! Get up – cannons! – get up!'

Denniston finally wrung sense from what he was hearing. He was fully-dressed, having gone to bed that way. Miss Guthrie's letter was clutched in his hand, crumpled already – he'd fallen asleep reading it. The happiness and calm of all that seemed suddenly worlds away.

The doctors poured out of the house and up the external stairs. They passed the door to the next floor up, smaller than their ground-level room. From inside, Denniston thought he could hear their landlord in a frenzy of prayer. Clambering onto the flat bare roof terrace, they looked out across the city, and into the black beyond the walls.

Lights raced on the fortifications. Beyond them, smaller lights dashed in the distance. Suddenly, a stuttering series of flashes split the black. There was a hung and quiet moment, and then the sky screamed.

Denniston was on his knees. His head cowered down, hugged between them. The sky had started ringing – or was it only his ears?

'My God… My God…' someone repeated. 'God…'

Then Vashin was amongst them, piecing things together. They'd offered him a place by their fire. He'd stayed the night, and now was here. He touched them all gently on the shoulder, one by one. And like in a fairy-tale, or a play, one by one, the doctors stood up, came to life, brushing dust from their overcoats.

'What time is it?' was all Denniston could manage. Somehow it seemed important. 'Do you have the time? Does anyone — does anyone have the time?'

Somewhere in the night, new fires were burning. Part of the distance was washed in orange light. The whole city echoed with shouting.

'Morning, *effendi*,' Vashin answered, strangely calm. 'Fourth hour.' He shrugged as if to say "more or less."

'Is it — is it wise to be on the roof, waving a lamp in the middle of the night? When the whole damned city is under fire?' That was Casson, breathing heavily, scowling.

'Whole city?' Vashin echoed. 'No. Walls only. Still, *Hekims*, down. You are needed.'

'Right…' Walker muttered, shaking his head. 'Right. Cannons go off, shells hit. People get hurt. Right…'

'Work then, gentlemen.' Casson's voice had regained some of its steadiness, a little of its candour. 'I only wish the damned Russians had chosen a more civilised hour to start this whole business…'

'None of us were forced to come here,' said Guppie, quietly. 'All of us chose, knowing what it would mean.'

'Right,' said Denniston, flatly. 'Guppie's right.'

'The hospital, then?' Casson said.

'No,' said Denniston. 'Later. The walls first. For those who don't have time to spare.'

There were no more words of agreement. Not even Casson broke their silent assent.

Vashin coaxed the doctors down from the roof. A moment to gather their effects – needful things – and then he led them, carrying bags, stretchers, instruments, towards the fortifications.

The streets were crowded with shadows, rushing from shelter to shelter, speaking in hurried Turkish. Like in a storm, every few seconds lit the sky bright, and like the flash of a camera, each instant of light showed frozen images that stayed with Denniston as they rushed through the gloom. Folk huddled in doorways. Boys ran, home maybe, or away, or carrying messages to officers. A dog was backed into a corner, snarling, terrified, as they passed.

'No fear!' Vashin shouted over his shoulder, over the din. 'Those shells not kill. They are for *seeing*. For Russians!'

'Splendid!' Casson growled. 'D'you hear, gentlemen? We need only fear the shells we can't see! Truly, I'm heartened to hear it…'

'No fear,' Vashin repeated, with a white grin that all but leered back at the doctors through the gloom. 'Not far now.'

Their way led into a maze of gates and guard-posts. The tide of civilians melted away, giving rise only to grim-faced men in varying degrees of uniform. Some had only an old pattern musket to mark them out as soldiers. Others were hung with braid and bright with red and blue, barking at one group of men, rushing off to find some new cluster of underlings to howl at.

Only Guppie and Featherston had on their Red Crescents, left on from their night at the hospital. But between their armbands and Vashin's wild gestures, and impassioned chatter in Turkish, any guard that challenged them soon gave way.

The walls turned to earthworks, between the outer fortifications and the inner. Underfoot, they trod half-frozen mud and to their sides were the hoardings of dug-outs and trenches. They travelled in single-file till they emptied into what must have been a redoubt.

Here, the ground shook, not with periodic crashes but in waves. They rolled to a crescendo, almost faded to silence, then surged up once more without cease.

They had separated. They had agreed on it: to split, and do more work across wider ground, they'd said. The same pulls as held sway in the hospital had begun once more, in multitudes. Denniston's attention was dragged off and assailed in a hundred ways at once, moment by moment. Time pulled and twisted too, distorted by hard work and dire focus. Unannounced, the sun had crept up and a chill mist hung in the air.

A gunner had lost three fingers to the fire of his cannon. One man's thigh had been pierced by a shard of artillery shell. The bone was shattered. Denniston hauled the man up when he found that he could not stand by himself. They shared one limping gait, towards the barracks at the redoubt's rear.

A sudden sucking emptiness filled the air. A roaring replaced it for half a moment. Then a silence so deep it clamoured like bells.

Denniston scrambled back. Fell. Was on his knees; was scrambling to his feet. Wet soil, strangely hot, fell like thick black snow. Mud, blood, and singes of powder became impossible to distinguish except by touch — those three dark stains covered everything.

He had lost the man he'd been helping to stand, helping to walk. He searched, fixated, digging in the soft churned dirt for a measureless time and found nothing. The man had disappeared like a dream.

He held down a gurgling laughter, delirious as he carried on to the redoubt, alone.

He all but saw himself, from a strange distance, washing his hands in a basin of dirty water. Denniston watched himself as he tended to three more men, ten more men, struggling in the mess of the redoubt. He felt his own breath, short as the burning down wick of a candle, and delicate as its flame. His hands were clumsy with the dawntime cold, but inside his fur greatcoat he was drenched in sweat.

It was frustrating. He could give the wounded only the most rudimental treatment here. In the earthworks and at the front, there was no true healing; only stabilising suffering or paving the way for recovery. The knowledge of this grew inside him until it became anger.

A shout went up, then again, and again. It became a chant. 'Allah! Allah!' Dawn had come, but the Turks had found no time to pray. It was hard to tell now if this chant was a battle-cry, or else their attempt at observance, even in all this carnage.

The cannons had fallen silent. The sound of small arms fire swarmed across the fortifications. The redoubt boiled with men, the shot of pistols and crack of rifles.

'Allah!'

'Hurrah!'

The two dinned together until they grew indistinct. The redoubt was under attack at its outer edges – not just cannons now, but men with steel and shot.

There were bullet wounds to attend to. That thought focused Denniston. He was still afraid, but who in all this would not be? Still, he worked.

Men slumped against the fortifications or else fought on in dark-stained uniforms. Denniston hurried, making his rounds between them. So much blood from such small punctures. The lucky ones among them had exit wounds too, more ragged than the entry and bigger. They needed only patching up after the blood had been staunched. After that, they'd be sent forward to the fighting, or back to the rear, to the care of *jarra bashi*s and ambulance teams to carry them to hospital. The less fortunate had the cooling ball or bullet still lodged inside them, halfway lost in shattered bone and viscera.

Denniston had no Red Crescent to wear. It was left behind, up the hill and into the city. But whether by dint of his bearing or his doctor's bag, he was greeted with a joy that shone in the storm of battle, unexpected and as out of place as finding a pearl in the mud of a pigsty.

Clusters of soldiers cheered to see him. Wounded men reached out to him, not to beg but just to touch his greatcoat, stained already and further stained by their bloody hands. Denniston felt like a talisman, walking amongst them.

A young Turk caught up beside him, clean-shaven, dark-haired, dark-eyed but calmer than Denniston felt. He tried to speak but knew no English and no French, and instead only tugged at Denniston's sleeve. An armband marked him out as a *jarra bashi*. Denniston remembered him from the hospital, darting about like a humming bird. He'd been doing the same here, giving brandy and water to those who would take it, and patching those who would stay stable, if only they would stop bleeding.

But as he spoke, Denniston caught nothing but a stream of titles. '*Hekim effendi — bey — pasha —* Mukhtar Pasha!'

The young *jarra bashi* halfway hysterical, but begging Denniston, appealing to him to follow him, tend to someone of rank. And yet here were the men doing the actual fighting, braving the actual danger: men ducking up over the battlements to fire, ramming home charge and bullet; men caught in the line of the Russian advance, wounded, perched precariously this side of survival. It was a matter of two pulls, and Denniston judged the greater to be the one that kept him here.

'I don't care if it's Mukhtar Pasha himself you want me to see,' he said, trying to stay calm, clear, as he had been trying for hours now. 'I'll get to your officers soon enough, but there's men here who'll die if I leave them. For now, help as you can, or by God please get out of the way.'

The *jarra bashi* stared for a moment as Denniston surged over to the side of one man bleeding from the belly. Then he nodded again, in that same small show of reverence as before, and passed over the flask of brandy and water to Denniston. 'Anything other, *hekim effendi*?' he asked in careful English.

'Carbolic,' Denniston answered, without looking up. He brought out his forceps and tapped them with a fingernail. 'For these. Carbolic, alcohol – anything you have that will make them sterile. Clean. Understand? *Anlama*? Do you understand?'

The *jarra bashi* nodded again and scampered off. Denniston began with the wounded soldier, speaking as soothing as he could:

'You're a brave one, aren't you? Good, good…' He remembered Casson speaking to the horse and tried to master that same soft tone. 'Easy now. You're fine…' He looked as he spoke, surveying the damage. There was no exit wound. The bullet remained somewhere in the soldier's abdomen. There would be pain. 'You're fine… Easy now, will you take any..?' Denniston offered the flask.

The soldier shook his head, tight-lipped, and staring through half-closed lids at the doctor.

'Very well then. Let's see…'

The next casualty was a colonel. When offered, he accepted the drink; a long draught, throat pulsing as he sucked it down. Denniston couldn't decide whether it was impressive or appalling. Most likely it was a little of both:

The English Hospital at Erzurum, September 1877
Illustrated London News

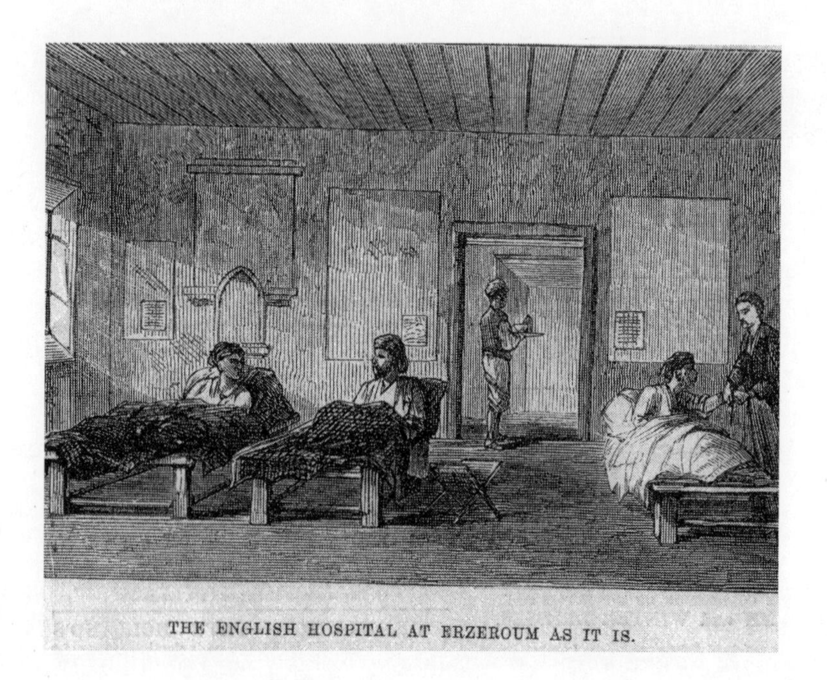

THE ENGLISH HOSPITAL AT ERZEROUM AS IT IS.

a sudden show of vigour and zest for life in the grey-brown fortifications, amid the brown-red hours of blood and bloody work.

'Many thanks, doctor,' the colonel said in French. His voice was smooth, as if stripped by the brandy.

'My pleasure,' Denniston replied likewise, grateful for a lower language barrier than existed between he and most of his patients. 'I am here to help.' He made a small gesture at the colonel's arm, where the bullet had gone in near the elbow. Already the tissue was swollen and dark, even beneath the entry wound's bleeding. 'You can move your fingers?'

The colonel's moustache twitched as he suppressed a wince. The fingers of his injured arm clenched and unclenched in demonstration.

'But you cannot lift your arm?'

This time the grimace came in earnest, the pain overtaking any attempt to hide it. The colonel shook his head.

There was no exit wound in the far side of his arm. Most likely the bullet had struck bone, and at least fractured the humerus where it was thinnest, near to the arm's crook. It was a dangerous injury, though not of the kind that would kill a man outright. If worst came to worst, however – and in conditions like these, it often would – it would still kill him slowly if drastic precautions were not taken.

Denniston might not have had so fine a bedside manner as Casson, but he had become adept at making his face a mask, hiding apprehension behind blank confidence and certainty. He met the colonel's eyes: a dark pine-green in his sun-tanned and wind-roughened face.

'My name is doctor Denniston. Tell me yours, *effendi*.'

'Emin Bey. You helped one of mine before, doctor – sent him back to the walls. Selim Bey, my equal in rank… Tell me, Denniston *hekim*, was he well?'

Denniston remembered the man with the moustache and barrel chest he'd seen to, days back. He had worn a similar jacket to this colonel. 'A bullet,' he said, 'it went in near here?' Denniston gestured to his hip. 'Out at the back, no?'

The colonel nodded.

'Your friend, Selim Bey, was very lucky. It was an easy injury.' Easy to treat, he thought, if not to receive. 'He will be well soon, if he is careful.'

While Denniston spoke, he cleaned his tools for what seemed the hundredth time. The bright cold sun glinted on their metal shapes. It was noon. The sounds of gunfire came more seldom now; no great waves of shouting and shot to signify a new charge.

'And my men?' Emin Bey asked. 'Bastard *jarra bashi* made me leave them… They fought bravely? Without me?'

'I think so, *effendi*.' It was the only honest answer Denniston could give.

In truth, he knew nothing of the battle for someone who had been in the thick of it – nothing save the noise, the wounded, the torturous length of it. 'Do you want something to..?' Denniston groped for the word and came up short. 'Something to put in your teeth?' He gestured to his mouth and bit down on an imaginary strap of leather.

Emin Bey shook his head once more, this time with brows knitted, and forehead furrowed.

After that, Denniston fell silent. He opened the wound to sound the injury, excise shards of bone, and finally the bullet. Held between his fingers, it looked so small. It was the same wicked conical kind he'd taken out of men several times today. It seemed nearly standard issue among the Russians. Small, yet capable of shattering a strong man's upper arm to fragments, such that it would be useless to him, if he kept it all. In war, he could see its utility. In a fair world – the kind overseen by a loving God – he could see no place for it at all.

'It is not only in battle…that men must be brave…' Emin Bey hissed through his gritted teeth as Denniston finished washing the wound. 'A great man is brave…even in defeat, a great man is brave…'

'This isn't defeat, *effendi*. Only a few days at the rear. Back to your men, after.' Denniston only hoped this promise would prove true.

But in his mind already, he was filing the name and the face away for remembrance: Emin Bey. The wound was likely to fester, no matter how well it was treated. It was ragged, loose and pouchy, made worse by shattered bone. In Europe it was the sort of wound that would be best answered with removal of the limb then and there: a gambit sacrificed to save the man. But the Turks were adverse to amputation. Little, as all the doctors had found, could persuade them otherwise.

This colonel had at least accepted a drink to help the pain. Perhaps, then, he was modern-minded enough to accept that perhaps it's better to live and do good deeds in the eyes of your God but be unsure of heaven, than it is to simply die in certainty.

Chapter 11

James

My dear Miss Guthrie,
By some miracle at least we have a moment's time to ourselves. The luckiest among us have been working since about 4 a.m. Those less fortunate – Guppie and Featherston – took the night shift at the hospital, and so have been at work since even before that, until at least 9 p.m. today. As such I imagine they are sleeping like stones now, the former snoring a little, as he does. For myself, I've taken on the duties they had last night: the long watch at the hospital, by lamplight. In any case, it gives me a little time in which to write you.

You see, we've finally had our first cannonades, bombardments, and even assaults, since the initial battle. The Russians mustered themselves sufficiently to make a good attempt on a fort at the citadel's northern flank. Artillery first, to soften their target – and fairly wake up all of Erzurum – and then in earnest charge on the defences. Had they taken the fort, they would have had almost an easy way through to the inner walls, but Turkish mettle is tough, and the Turks have, as the strongest weapon in their arsenal, a sheer and bloody-minded determination not to budge. So, the fort is yet to fall, and the walls yet hold strong.

I might even say that we few volunteers might also be a little to thank. Out before daybreak, in the earthworks and the fort, we tended to the wounded as soon as there began to be wounds for the tending, and worked ceaselessly. We took our work into the field, and carried on at it even while under fire.

Strange, how once I was so keen to get away to the front and distinguish myself, operating in action. Now, a day since the front shifted and I found it raging all round me, I think I could gladly go my whole life never working under such conditions again. Of course I shall have to, though. And as such, there's no use bemoaning or regretting it.

I must say, compared with what you generously term my 'adventures', the content of your letters is a great comfort to me. I like very much to hear of your own adventures, just as much as you seem happy to hear of mine.

I know abominably little of dancing, save what you were kind enough to teach me, and even less of blue slippers, except that I fancy you would look very well in them. Contrast your humble servant, or rather the terrible bear he's already become: sideburns joined by moustache and the beginnings of a beard, for where should I find time to shave, or a barber who'll do me that service; hands ever-grubby, no matter how well and often they're washed; coat just as shabby as my hair, beard, etc., yet acting as sole accessory to constant dirty shirt-sleeves, high boots and so on… I flatter myself by thinking you would not recognise me.

The weather I think is getting colder every day, and tonight I would not be surprised if we were to have snow again. Horrid as it would be – breaking ice before one can get to clean water; the uphill trudge from the fortifications to our lodgings or the hospital, harder than ever before and more perilous – I also have a contrary desire to see this place dressed up in snow. For imagine it, being placed on the highest hill hereabouts, and looking round to see all the scars skirmishes etc. have left on the land, covered up in blinding white!

But I am getting prosy, I think, and should be back to work. It's likely tomorrow will bring more of the same, though in what form I can't be certain. At least, unlike today, it shall end in a decent night's sleep – that is, as decent as any night's sleep I have spent of late, for we have only sleeping mats on the floor of our lodging for comfort. Quite a la turc but not, I feel, very forgiving. Do you know, I'm still unsure under what terms or in whose authority we even hold the house we stay in. For the first two nights after our arrival, we slept in the hospital itself. The next day, some young Turkish ensign came to us, asked us to follow him if you please, and from there marched us downhill and into some poor solitary Turk's home. A number of foot-soldiers brought out luggage along, quite unprompted, and we have been barracked there ever since.

Of course, I thank you for the paper you sent, and for everything else, and shall respect your wishes regarding the photograph – of course I shall. I look forward to hearing from you again, that is if either of our letters can find their way through this blossoming blockade…

Until then I remain

Yours very sincerely,

James Denniston

P.S. — You say that you can be judgemental, but I do not think you are. That is, you are only judgemental towards those deserving of judgement. Certainly, it's no flaw in your character: I'd never venture to say so myself, or even to suggest it, in case I should fall in your jurisdiction and so be judged as well!

Agnes

Dear Doctor Denniston,

I never have been very far from home, such that even Edinburgh seems a little exotic to me, in simply being anywhere other than Manchester. Moreover I never have been out of the company of either my family or its friends. That you should live for any amount of time, in a foreign land, among utter strangers, seems to me a very dire thing, though a brave one also. I suppose it also means that I should not be surprised at how you value my correspondence – thank you for saying so, nonetheless.

I am glad to hear you are in good health, despite all the recent excitement that sounds to have befallen you and your comrades.

I have at least some excitement to report. Foremost among them is the recent dance, which I am glad – and somewhat relieved – went off well, and without undesired incident. For my part, I deigned to forgo a new gown in favour of the aforementioned slippers. Unable to resist them, I attended in the dress of green velvet – one you have already seen – and those blue shoes. In my previous letter I mentioned how fine they might be for dancing – indeed, how they deserved nothing less – and dance we all did, for I was able to find a band of musicians after all, borrowed from a reserve regiment here in Southside. Uniformed and charming, they caused something of a stir amongst the ladies in attendance, though Miss Carmichael and I agreed they were too much in bluster and polish for us, and not enough in substance. Even so, they played well, and long into the night.

Being military men, I worried that our band might tend towards bawdy songs as the evening drew on, in particular if they were permitted some of the punch that myself and Miss Carmichael had mixed for the occasion. I had words with them on the subject, but did not know if they would heed them, my being but young, and a woman, and without my hands directly holding their purse-strings in this matter of employment. But instead they surprised us all, and myself especially, in playing one song that we had not heard before, but that we were told is current in music halls from here to London. For its chorus we too were invited to sing: "The Russians shall not have Constantinople!" repeated to melody. Your struggle, it seems, is felt in the most unexpected places, doctor.

I feel, however, that I might sympathise with it all the better if only I knew with what I was sympathising; and yet you leave your stories all too brief for this purpose, perhaps in the interests of keeping them mild, to spare my gentle character..? To this, I say: nonsense. You said there is much of interest to you in my letters but compared with the things you leave out of yours, I am sure mine fall quite flat in comparison. There is much I would find of interest too, if only you would show me.

Tell me at least of your past, if you won't speak fully of what you're enduring and have yet to endure. When I recall meeting you, I think of a quiet man; one who seemed more timid than brisk or spare in diction. Yet both those men are difficult to reconcile with the one I write to now, who seems for the most part frank and bold – perhaps, by turns, even stern and dour, as I have heard tell you Scotsmen are wont to be. Regardless, you talk little enough of yourself; while your habit of putting others first does you credit, it leaves something wanting in your letters.

In short, doctor Denniston, I hope you will not be offended if I admit: I am curious about you.

For my part, I will not flatter myself to presume you recall perfectly our first meeting, and what I told you of myself — even so, I apologise if I repeat myself in telling you:

That I am the only daughter, and indeed only living child, of my parents, but have not lived my four and twenty years in this world in anything like solitude: our family tree is a sprawling one, at least beyond my most immediate branch, and I have nearly always been surrounded by cousins innumerable – Davids, Janes, Marys, and a good number of Victorias and Georges of course – many of whom have been as sisters and brothers to me, others of whom I might quietly wish were nothing of the sort.

That there are Guthries on both your side of the English-Scotch border, and on my side, for my father is a Scotsman by birth, albeit turned quite English by the long practice of my mother.

That my grandfather on my father's side, was a farmer near Glasgow, and left Scotland only twice in his life: to see his third son – errant yet successful in Manchester – married to an Englishwoman, and to see that his granddaughter was christened, only to die months later, God rest his soul. Yet my mother's father was an officer in Her Majesty's army and fought the Sikh in India, and the Turk in Crimea. How curious, that the sympathies of our nation have turned so completely, in the matter of a generation or so.

Do you see? It's not so hard to talk of oneself, and only a little harder to do so interestingly. I have sat table at enough suppers to know that anyone can be fascinating, if only you help them to ask themselves the right questions…

So please, tell me of your family and your childhood, if you will not tell me of Erzurum. You write fine letters, Doctor Denniston, and I trust that all you tell me, you will tell me with colour and with precision.

Until I hear from you again
Sincerely yours,
Miss Guthrie

James

My dear Miss Guthrie,
If it's colour you wish for in my letters, then it's colour you shall have. Or rather, it's colour I shall try to give you.

Here I am sitting in an unfurnished room, lit up only by a very bad spluttering tallow candle. With the Russians outside our gates, and no forests save up and into the surrounding hills, fuel for fire first became expensive and now simply impossible to come by, except in the form of – excuse my frankness – the dung of various beasts, which is dear as whale oil now, despite its origins.

Outside, there was snow on the ground a few inches deep, just as I predicted, yet now a rain is falling, and our leaking ceiling is doing its best to flood us overnight. I have set up an arrangement of a tin dish and other oddments to catch the falling water, but I think, like many things in Erzurum now, it's to be a losing battle.

If our bare little room had windows I am sure I'd look out to find all the snow turned to grey muck in the streets. But the glimpses I caught of Erzurum blanketed in white were very pretty indeed, for it covered up the tin roofs and the dirt, and instead left the flashes of colour – blue tiles, orange clay, etc. – more vivid for the contrast.

I am told we men don't see colour as a woman does, but being men and only men, never quite find out the truth in our vision's supposed failings. If this is the case, I hope my efforts at 'colour' are vivid enough for your more discerning eyes.

I'll admit to you now, I never have had a friend of the opposite persuasion before. Certainly not one so close as I feel to you, or who bears me quite like you do. So I had always thought there must be some trick or ritual to talking with a woman. Writing to you, and receiving your writing back, feels natural enough now to see that, before, I had misled myself. Or else you yourself are more natural to speak with than most women. You say, in our first meeting, that I seemed timid? Perhaps I am by nature, or perhaps you made me so, it's hard to tell which. But for a lady who quite succeeded in putting the fear of God into me – and in both senses, I assure you – you now set me more at ease than I'm used to lately.

Of course I remember the first time I saw you, and the first time we spoke, at the Glasgow Carmichaels', cousins to those you're with now, I think? I remember your candidness as we spoke; how I mentioned the interest I found in reading Darwin, and you mentioned in turn that you thought it best if you never did, being that consternation and dismay are unbecoming in a lady.

I remember the sudden respect I held you in then – and for contradicting me, outright! And I remember that I thought, as you left, what a pity it was that I should scarcely imagine to meet you again. Fancy the good fortune when chance brought you to Greenock, as a guest of the Reids, at their dance!

I'm ahead of myself of course and may be much mistaken. If there are unspoken rules of conduct for sending letters to a lady, I would be grateful if you were to tell me when I overstep them. As I've said, I'm ill-versed in such things. For the time being, it's comforting to me, to share my innermost thoughts and not fear that you will judge me too harshly for them.

Indeed, you ask me to share a little of myself too, and I will try.

I don't know if you know my age. I don't recall having ever told it you. I'm not bashful of telling you, I have twenty-three years all told, and for the next seven years I'll make about £200 per annum – enough to keep body and soul together, but little more besides. A merry bleak prospect indeed, and worsened by further uncertainty: here and now, halfway across the world, I have no idea where I'll settle when, if I'm lucky, I return in one piece. I like Greenock, but don't know of any openings thereabout, and isn't there something so sad and small about wanting nothing more than to settle in the small town where once you were born – to have no dream larger than that?

The past is more certain, at least. You know the place of my birth. You've seen it with your own eyes so I needn't make you too much of a picture. But I best remember the great broad stretch of water where the Clyde met the sea, and the half-made ships at the yards, and the boats coming and going through the Highlands and beyond. While no sailor myself, I've always felt best at ease by water ever since. Imagine, then, how I feel now: surrounded for miles and miles about by a sea of snow, and beneath that, iron-hard soil!

I had a large family too, but not so large anymore. About seven years ago I had a sister two years younger than myself, and though we were both young – or perhaps because of that – we were everything to each other. Nellie was her name. I always thought of her as perfect, and do think of her the same still, but she died very suddenly in her fourteenth year, with none of us truly knowing she had even taken ill until then. It was very hard at the time, and sometimes proves hard still.

Next I lost my father. He had been a Writer to the Signet – what might be termed, in England, a solicitor – and all told he was a very diligent man. His death, too, was very sudden, though hindsight might let me comfort myself in thinking of that as a mercy, such there was no long term of illness to suffer through. Chiefly though it seems more of an injustice, and all for selfish reasons: I was at school in Edinburgh when he was taken ill, and so was too late returning to see him alive. Furthermore, he was not old when he died, and had put little aside for the maintaining of his family. We were not left well off by his passing, and had scarcely more than our home in Greenock.

I also had a brother, six years older than me, and to all purposes the finest character I ever knew. He caught consumption, and over twenty-eight months went from also being one of the most robust men I've ever heard of, to being quite reduced by illness. As children our family kept to itself, and so he was my particular guide and friend. His loss, too, I felt and still feel keenly.

Please understand though, that I'm not so miserable a coward as to be gloomy or downcast about it. Indeed, I talk and think little of these aspects of my life, so that they might not become part of my character. All told and considered, I hope I can say that life has not been all too hard on me. I look forward to something better yet, despite all this mud and rain, and the bramble-patch of circumstance I've gotten myself into here. It's already been said that we 'English' doctors have already done enough to warrant decoration once this is all over, and I admit that I'm enough of a fool to covet some small medal or other as a keepsake of my time in Erzurum.

For now at least, we've got tobacco to smoke, and we – that is: Dr. Pinkerton and Dr. Kincaid – have brandy and water to drink. Well deserved I think, for we've been working like slaves since eight o'clock this morning, and are only trying to be as comfortable as possible. All this told, I hope you won't be too shocked in our behaviour. Elsewhere in the room, Walker and Featherston are trying their utmost to prepare a pot of tea but without a fire or stove to put one in, it's proving quite laughable. The brandy at least warms us without needing to be warm in itself.

While I write, they all confer in mock-secrecy over whom I might be writing to this time. I never shall tell, but the answer's always the same. Strange to say, but your letters are in fact the only ones I've got since coming to Erzurum. I still write to my mother, but I've got nothing back for some time.

By the bye, my luggage has finally turned up against all reckonings. I had given it up for lost, but fortune smiled on me again. Our man Vashin knows a wily Turkish sergeant plucky enough to have gone scouting into the city's lost and laid-waste outskirts, and who found a trench as deep as a rifle-barrel in the now-frozen mud. And what should he see at the bottom but Casson's great steamer-trunk, emblazoned with his name, and my own small case with – among other less precious effects – two pictures inside: your own and my sister's. I gave the sergeant such a tip for that, I fancy he'll be considered a rich man all his life when he returns home. For my part, I have a little more of home in my possession than I ever thought to get back.

Vashin, who I mentioned above, is another strange tale in himself. I suppose he came to us as a courier of sorts, carrying the second letter of yours that I got since arriving in Erzurum. Since then he has stuck to us like a burr, insisting on making himself so useful that we haven't been able to dispense of him. Indeed, the Turkish command has gotten so used to thinking of him as our man that he's our main line of communication from the pashas to us, while we work. Though Circassian by birth, he came to us with some knowledge of English, and time is improving it greatly. He seems very happy in our employ, as manservant, housekeeper, aide de camp, and whatever else the coming weeks might make of him.

Even with his ministrations, however, I think our conditions are bound to decline. The whole city seems to hold its breath as the Russians tighten their encirclement. Currently, Vashin is daring and clever in the matter of getting us our post, making the hard ride from Erzurum to Aşkale, west of here, every few days. I would not be surprised though if even he was soon unable to make the journey. If I fall silent, then, you will know why.

But for now, tonight finds me in good spirits. I'm tired, yes, but it's a tiredness of a wholesome and satisfying kind, from good, hard, useful work. And that seems as fair a note as any on which to end a letter, does it not? So for now, I'll wish you good night, good bye, and good health too.

I remain yours

Very sincerely,

James Denniston

Denniston got up before dawn. There was no use in wasting a candle while daylight was burning outside so he dressed in darkness, muddling into his overcoat. Once the hospital and the fortifications, and the endless work to be had in each, had all taken take their share, there was little daylight left over. And still the days were getting shorter, more wintry, with every one that passed. He was careful not to wake the others as he cracked open the door to their room, and stole out into the greyish twilight.

The eastern sky glowed dimly pink. What remained above, and in every other direction, was marled and marbled, hued like a mackerel's sides.

Denniston laboured through last night's sullen snow, and last night's sleepless haze, to the trough of water in the yard behind their house. He had spent the evening a guest of Emin Bey, the colonel from whose arm he had extracted a bullet at the redoubt, and who had since taken Denniston under a kind of patronage in exchange for regular visits. Last night this had taken the form of cigars, conversation, and thick black sweet Turkish coffee. It had left Denniston restless, but he regretted it only a little.

Under one arm he had a green-tinged copper basin. His other hand carried the shaving kit he'd thought lost until recently. With the basin's rigid belly, he broke the ice on the trough's surface. Already ragged hairline patterns had formed, orbiting each other where previous mornings had seen the same ice broken, and previous nights had grown it back, like new skin over a wound.

He set up the kit's small mirror and crouched above the snow. Shivering even in his matted fur coat, he stropped the razor on his belt and began to scrape. He'd gotten used to the bearish beard he'd grown recently; all but the constant slight itch of it. But now, patch by patch, it fell away in the razor's wake. In the mirror he saw half the face he'd known before, in every shop-window he'd passed in recent years, and in the picture he'd sent to Miss Guthrie…

In the sky something flashed. It might have been the first stripe of true sunlight over the horizon, and yet its direction was wrong: more north than east. A booming echo came after and a dozen more followed. Nearer by came the familiar answering sprays of sound – rushing soil and snow; splintering timber – as the morning's first shells hit the city's beleaguered earthworks.

Denniston flinched only at hearing the first impact. By now, the rest was familiar: Russian cannonade, and moments later, the Turkish response, fewer guns but louder for their proximity. He'd done more delicate work in the midst of worse. Scowling, with steel-tense tendons outstanding on his neck as he drew the blade across it, he finished shaving.

His mirror was too small to look at his face all at once as close as shaving demanded. Once his second pass, sideways along the grain of his face, was done, and he wiped the shaving soap from his cheeks and earlobes, he pulled back to see himself directly.

Perhaps the beard had served a purpose after all, he reflected. His cheeks had grown gaunt and his neck thin as a plucked cockerel's. Skin pale and smooth now, there was no hiding the tolls hunger and tiredness had taken on him.

Ready and more awake, he returned to the hospital for more of the same, as after the cannonades, the sunrise call to prayer rose up and throughout Erzurum.

The next letter that arrived for Denniston was nothing more than a fragment. A page, or maybe pages, had been shed like moulting feathers as it travelled out to Erzurum. It arrived wrapped not in an envelope but an illustrated copy of *The Spectator*, and began and ended abruptly.

—Spirits! Imagine it!

I had known Miss Evelyn to be of a radical temperament but, I had thought, in a modest and moderate sort of way. I had even quietly admired her for her way of speaking out in favour of sex, in particular whenever some gentleman or other began to talk of what a woman is or ought to be in this world: 'How should they know so well?' she would ask, 'they who have never lived as women?'

This, I had not expected.

Her Church is that of the Spiritualists, she has told me, as if confiding some small girlish secret. So while we share faith in a Christian God, we differ in the ways we see the world He has made. For she holds the belief that death is not simply the place a soul goes to wait for the Return of the Lord, but rather is dynamic as life itself: a place where souls become spirits, to learn and act and grow, and by so doing come closer to God, and by the outreaching of communers among the living, impart knowledge and Revelation to those they've left behind!

I hardly know what I think of it all. Though I can see in it some great comfort – and I see it, indeed, in the shining of her dark eyes when she speaks of these spirits and of her Faith – it seems too great a departure from all that's established, even for myself: one raised to quiet belief in the cause of Dissent. But I was raised also to hold personal faith and communion with God as more important by far than the strictures of Church in England or Church in Rome. So ought I not to accept her personal revelation, as it applies to her, and keep my own faith close to my chest? I find it difficult to make myself do so, but perhaps the shock will pass.

She believes, she says, not in a Heaven or Hell, but in an afterlife that seems alien to me, in near-direct contradiction with scripture. 'And though worms destroy this body, yet in my flesh shall I see God'; how so then, if there's to be no bodily resurrection? If, indeed, as Miss Evelyn would attest, there is no need for one, as the afterlife is a hierarchy and journey of spirits, all tending in timeless time towards paradise?

I'm afraid my prose has gotten ragged. You must forgive me, but I am shaken. I had considered Miss Evelyn a friend, but now feel I don't quite know her: as if I'd seen her always through a curtain of gauze and come to love her friendship through it; yet only now has the curtain drawn up, and I find what's behind it unfamiliar after all. It is a strange feeling; a lurch in the heart of me.

But it is of little import, I suppose, for I'll soon be leaving Edinburgh and the Carmichaels behind for a time, and returning once more to Manchester for December and Advent.

Yet I also hear tell of something that might please you somewhat: though I'll pass the rest of winter in Manchester, come summer I'll be found in Glasgow.

Until then I pray for—

It was hectic, as Miss Guthrie's letters went. But in amongst its chaos of clauses and cluttered thoughts, Denniston clung to one phrase like a castaway to his flotsam raft:

'Come summer I'll be found in Glasgow.'

Night had drawn in outside the doctors' lodging, but inside was warm, filled with the golden light of lamps and candles, and the red murmur of the stove. And in that night, and in that strange letter, that single phrase gave Denniston more hope than he felt quite decent in holding. He grinned as he read, and gripped tight to the paper, until the feeling recoiled and collapsed, felt only fleetingly, too fragile to last. Where would he be come summer?

The foundations of Turkish command were failing, as the heart of its empire at Istanbul grew weaker with each passing day. To him it seemed a tragedy, like watching a sickness move through a body that had once been healthy, while all its doctors could do was apportion it weeks more, days more, and after that, nothing.

He turned through the pages of The Spectator, to see if it would afford him more knowledge than rumour and gossip had given him. What it said of Istanbul – always 'Constantinople' in the English papers – it said as if a coming decline were as brute and incidental a fact as the weather, inconvenient but not of consequence: 'With disaster will always come great discontent…'

But what, then, of Erzurum, barely afloat on a sea of small disasters? That it would fall eventually was an unspoken but certain thing. It was only a question of when, and whether the fall would begin from within, or from without – today or tomorrow.

Tomorrow and tomorrow and tomorrow, Denniston thought. Summer was too far away to bear thinking on, in the depths of a winter night. Better to ask what would become of him by break of spring. Better still to think nothing at all, and act instead, in the moment. It was all he had done so far. He told himself that, in dire times, it was all that worked.

He gently folded the letter and went to his luggage; to the tin biscuit box Vashin had found him to keep his correspondence in. He stashed it away with the others, then went to his shaving kit for a pair of scissors. He sat once more on the rug, laying out the pages of the illustrated Spectator like a fan of cards. Slowly, Denniston began to cut the pages into images.

Grey shaded plates of Indian elephants, newly delivered to the zoo; clean-shaven sailors coming into port at Liverpool; the end of an Indian famine that Denniston had not even known had begun; and stories of Russian forces encircling hungry Plevna, and of Mukhtar Pasha's second severe defeat at the battle of Deve Boyun, and of discontent brewing in 'Constantinople'.

That night he papered a corner of the room with the illustrated plates, making almost a kind of shrine to decoration and detail, in amongst the spartan interior of their lodging. There was only brief amusement from the others before they began to help. They knew it too: better to do than to stop, think, and feel.

Walker papered, quick and meticulous, while Kincaid whistled and snipped up the pictures with his own pair of small scissors, used to keep his thick red beard relatively in check.

Guppie slept through the hurricane of activity. He had taken to sleeping most all of the time he wasn't directly called on duty, and coughing wetly as he slept. It was hard to stay lively around him, Denniston found, when they spoke – as if Guppie's very presence had a clammy leeching effect. He was growing sick again, Denniston feared. Or perhaps Guppie had never stopped being sick, and only hid it at times better than others?

Chapter 12

After days of cannonades and assaults another silence fell across the plain round Erzurum. Snow fell too, as if it was what muffled the noise of artillery, the ardour of men towards violence.

Duty on the fortifications may have slowed to a sleepwalk once more, as the battle again became a waiting game, but in the hospital the Stafford House doctors were never short of work. Like flotsam washes up on a nearby beach, more and more each day after some great shipwreck, wounded men washed into the hospital.

The rate of arrivals was greater by far than that of departures. Some convalesced, some even to satisfaction, but for every life the hospital saved so many more were lost. Every doctor by now knew well enough the quickest route from the hospital to the Muslim cemetery on the city's eastern edge. They'd had cause, too, to learn of a smaller graveyard on a flank of the hill, where Christians and Jews were permitted burial. It was walled in on all sides with shoddy brick and crumbling stucco so that above it hung only a closed-off square of sky, and below the ground was hard, and growing harder with every cold new day.

They were understaffed, more so than they had been to begin with. They had lost a *jarra bashi* to a fever that showed warning signs of typhoid.

Guppie's cough had worsened too. It hacked out, distinctive and familiar across the hospital wards, as Denniston went about his work. This time it carried on, stretching out til it was almost irritating, each sound knocking into Denniston's thoughts and upsetting them, over and over.

He focused on cleaning gut for sutures, cleaning his needles, with alcohol and a furrowed brow.

Guppie's coughing ended only when his breath ran too short. It turned to wheezing; rattling gasps that, unconscious, Denniston's mind still strained to hear.

'There now, Guppie… There now…'

Voices floated across the ward. Denniston didn't look up, turning instead to the wound in need of stitching.

'There's no sense in this, now, is there? You'll work yourself into the ground.'

'I don't…want to be a bother.'

'You're not. You wouldn't be.'

'I only need a moment.'

'You need a few days, that's all. Just until this cough stops. Then you'll be good as new and back to work in no time.'

'I shouldn't...'

'Guppie... Be a good chap and get home with you. Get some rest.'

'You'll be fine?'

'We'll be fine.'

Lips pursed in concentration, Denniston listened, but did not look up. It seemed to him there was no time; not until night had fallen, and the lamps were lit, and he walked not home but to the home of the colonel, Emin Bey: the man he'd taken on as his first private case.

He wondered if, soon, the remaining six healthy doctors might have to take on Guppie as another. Physician heal thyself, he thought – if only it were so simple.

'I feel I can trust a man more when I can see his face,' Emin Bey mused as he sat up on a divan, using scraps of flat bread to pick morsels from a dish of brown beans cooked with garlic. He ate daintily for a man with such big hands, scarred knuckles and powder-burnt fingers. His wounded arm was held close to his chest. 'I am consider putting it out as a decree. All men in my command shall be clean-shaven until I say otherwise. There's no fighting to be had, and slim rations – they need something to distract them. Perhaps that's it...'

Denniston listened, sitting similarly, and quietly stroked the rough-smooth surface of his own chin, shaved clean that morning. Bashfully, he considered his own part in the idea.

'A surgeon in particular,' Emin Bey grinned, showing tobacco-stained front teeth beneath a waxed heavy moustache. 'If his face is smooth and clean, then I feel I can trust him more. The cleanness of his hands and the precision of them. Yourself, for example, Denniston *hekim*. See? Not a cut upon you, and yet your face is smooth as a boy's! You see, I look on a face such as yours and feel I can trust in its honesty, and also your skill as a surgeon...'

They spoke together in French, as they always did: a second language for both of them, but as good a middle-ground as they shared.

Emin Bey leaned forward over the law table they shared in his quarters. Held between his big fingers, the tiny cup of silt-thick black coffee seemed almost ridiculous.

'I know by experience that your ability is sound,' he said, looking at Denniston, disarmingly direct. 'But it's a different thing to have faith, no? So, when I say that I have faith in your honesty, you will know I do not say so lightly. And when I ask you something that might test it..? Again, I do not do so lightly.'

Emin Bey gestured downward with an incline of his head. Denniston's gaze followed, to the clean white sling that held Emin Bey's half-shattered left arm. The doctor tried to keep his face placid, impassive, but a flicker of foreboding still came in at the brow, or perhaps the corner of the lip.

Emin Bey's next words were sterner. 'Tell me truthfully, Denniston *hekim*. My arm...' Perhaps it was not sternness after all, but a touch of fear. 'Please, when will I use it again?'

Denniston thought for only a moment. What policy was there but honesty now? 'Truthfully, *effendi*? You will not. The bone is shattered. It will not mend. The injury is stable, I've seen to that, but still, the wound is not—... I worry for it...'

Emin Bey looked down in silence. He refilled his cup with coffee, and tilted in several new spoons of sugar. 'The wound is not...what?' he asked almost casually.

'Not quite clean,' Denniston admitted. 'Not safe. Not as it is now.'

'What would you do with it? In Europe?'

'In Europe...I would have removed it, just below the shoulder. Then and there, at the time I first met you. That sort of operation, and in bad conditions...I would not do it lightly. But it would stop the danger.'

'You are aware that the Prophet forbids this..?'

'With all due respect, I am aware that drinking is also forbidden.'

'This is true.'

'It will kill you, your arm. You will be whole in Heaven, but I think your men would rather have you here a while longer...'

'Heaven? I think it's unlikely I shall see the Garden, Denniston *hekim*. I have too much familiarity with forbidden things already, as you said.'

'Then live. Go on where you are needed. I knew a *pasha*, in Istanbul, who had undergone a similar operation. I imagine his reasons were similar. You fear that you shan't enter Heaven? Then live long enough to earn it, *effendi*.'

Within three days, every man under Emin Bey's command was clean-shaven, or close enough to it to keep within their colonel's decree. The barbers, butchers, dentists, tailors, and drapers of Erzurum – all those with shears and tools sharp enough to cut loose a beard or trim clear a moustache – were busy once more after the drab and slow days that war had brought to the city. Their shops were full of grumbling soldiers with hunger in their hollow cheeks, and sleepless nights hanging round their eyes.

After, the shops fell empty again, their scissors blunted, their razors and filleting knives whetted til their edges had been worn concave as a soldier's yataghan. But for a time, the barracks and earthworks were manned by soldiers who looked unconscionably young – nearly vulnerable, Denniston thought, of the ones he saw.

Each day that passed in silence, broken only by the bass of tentative artillery, the threat of renewed assaults on the walls grew closer. There was talk in the hospital, the barracks, and the hollowed-out houses where off-duty soldiers gathered to smoke their cigarettes, made sacred by scarcity. There was talk in the hospital, between the cots and beds, and through the curtain-screens that divided ward from ward and ward from theatre.

The Russians had been taking on reinforcements from the East, so the rumours said. The Russian force had grown into a horde, ready to trample the walls and earthworks to dust with the sheer weight and number of their high, thick boots. The Russians were awaiting some new cannon, whose mouth yawned half as wide as Erzurum's greatest gate. And Melikov or Gukasov, Heimann or Lazarian – or any number of other commanders, whose names Erzurum used interchangeably, like curses, never quite knowing which was responsible for what new offence – were rubbing their kid-gloved hands together, gleeful over whatever new device they'd dreamed up to fell the city walls or else get behind them.

More than this, Kars had finally fallen, after holding out since May.

With no knowing when the next attack might come, or with how much force, all of Erzurum lived by fits and starts. In fits, townsfolk and soldiers, and men and women, worked side by side to shore up the walls, trenches and earthworks. In starts they fell slack, into waiting and doubting, like muscles cramp and weaken when too much has been asked of them for too long.

The doctors slept little. Beyond their usual night shifts, a new night shift had started at home. Guppie's condition had worsened. He ran a high fever, and it seemed to tire and break him, so much he could do nothing but lie in bed. And by turns the other doctors sat up beside him, reading, silently smoking.

'Minnie..!' Guppie had taken to crying out in his sleep. 'Lotte!'

Sitting by his bedside, Denniston tried to write, but this new turn of delirium in Guppie made it hard. It was not the noise that bothered him now. His irritation at it had melted away into sympathy. Rather, it caused Denniston to remember the things he would rather not.

How Nellie, his sister, had borne the fever that he himself had suffered, both of them children at the time. Typhoid fever was the first name of an illness that Denniston ever learnt, when their family's doctor looked at the rose blotches over his body; put a hearing-tube to his chest and poked at his stiff swollen gut, and pronounced his diagnosis. But Denniston's fever had broken. With the kind of optimism only children can muster and truly believe in, he'd told Nellie that hers would too, in time. 'Just look at me,' he'd said, 'I'm fit as a fiddle now, aren't I?' For a week, her little fingers had scrabbled at the bedclothes as she muttered and called out to her father, her brothers, and would not rise. And then she fell still; fell asleep and would not wake.

Sitting vigil over Guppie, Denniston could do nothing but watch, and wait; remember, and vainly hope.

James

My dear Miss Guthrie,

Grim times have come to Erzurum, and times grow worse every day. The sky is dense, flat, and grey as an old tin cup, and has seen all manner of awfulness happen under it of late. Not the bloody business of fighting, or anything sharp and shocking like that, but things more quietly dreadful. Funerals, failures of medicine and compassion, the slow wasting of this city as the blockade around it tightens. I think we will be fully encircled soon; I know I keep on saying it, but it seems truer each time.

I spend little time outside now, cooped up always in hospital or at home, but it makes it worse now that there's so little sign of sunshine. All this I talk of, and presided over by the broad grey sky, hanging over us like a pall.

We lost Guppie since my last letter to you. A night ago, in fact, so it still feels fresh and not quite real.

Typhoid, I think, and the others seem to agree. First he stopped his work, which meant more for the rest of us, though none would begrudge him. We only wanted him to be well again, and for his own sakes more than ours. He required care though, so we slept even less than before, and during all our waking hours we got thorny and sulky, sullen as sleepwalkers. He was almost improving, though, until only very recently. And then all Friday night we stayed up by his bedside, one by one, as he rambled about home and names of people we did not know but who were clearly very dear to him.

He died in Kincaid's shift. A bold and quite savage looking man, as I may have mentioned, but still, when we woke, we found Guppie gone and Kincaid in tears.

For my part, I felt quite paralysed. How useless I was. How guilty too, for though I'd put in effort, and hope, and good will, I felt it had all too late.

So, we worked through the morning, but focus was difficult to come by – I think it was the same for us all. The best thing, we decided, would be to bury the body before the opportunity slipped away. We sent out Vashin to ask what arrangements could be made, and we got together a congregation for that evening.

In the little Christian graveyard on the hillside, there were nine of us in all: we doctors, an American missionary and his wife, and one Mr. Zohrab, a sharp-bearded consul to Britain from up-town who had turned out for the occasion. I suppose we've been so hard at work that many aspects of town life in Erzurum still come as a surprise to us: I couldn't tell you who commands the garrison, and until now did not know Erzurum had a consulate at all.

Zohrab handed us a grimy Union Flag and we draped it over the coffin we'd had clapped together for Guppie. The missionary, Mr. Baker, gave his 'dust to dust,' all very sonorous and sweet while we dug as deep a hole as we could in the stony hard cold ground – not quite six feet, I'm sure, but there came a point where our tools were no more use, and the dirt would yield no more.

Featherston let go the first handful of earth, over the coffin when we'd lowered it. It fluttered and spread, all black dust and small stones, over the Union Flag, and the smaller grimier shape of Guppie's armband: brown canvas and a red crescent.

There were seven of us, all surgeons under the Red Crescent, all engaged in the same sort of work, and all living under the same roof, though we kept different hours. And differently constituted as we were, all having our disagreements and partings of opinion, we always had a purpose and situation in common, binding us together with mutual sympathy. We helped each other and laboured together and laughed and rested together. And now there are six of us instead.

I don't know who said it first, but soon we were all repeating it, almost like it was a joke we all found too funny to give over to silence. 'Who's next then? Whose turn next?'

I've tried turning to the books you sent me for solace. I read them in the most earnest and comprehensive way, but I regret to say they did nothing to ease my heart. Neither Bible nor Psalms. I understand and almost envy your faith and confidence. I've said so before and I'll say it now. To you they must be a great comfort. But I only felt a kind of selfishness.

Rather, I couldn't stop thinking of Guppie's family – the names he called out in his sleep, I suppose – and the shock that they'll now receive. Every death is like that to someone, though. In some small part of the world, in some small way, and to someone, it's an earthquake, a hurricane, changing utterly what it doesn't destroy.

Perhaps that's the reason for my ill-feeling in reading into religion. Your books give me the means to ease my heart and mind. Yet with the few other books I have – of medicine, anatomy, etc. – I can pretend to be like Atlas, holding earth and sky together. Why turn to medicine, except to stop widows becoming widows, mothers from losing sons? But by God, sometimes it's hard even to pretend…

I ought to stop. I apologise for my black mood, and probably my ill humour.

I hope to have better tidings to tell you in letters to come – honestly, Miss Guthrie, I do.

Until then I remain

Yours very sincerely,

James Denniston

Guppie was among the first but not the last. It was as if in death his symptoms scattered, and the typhoid fever that took him cropped and multiplied like weeds in each corner of the city.

In the hospital it ran rampant. Those who came in wounded would change their healing wounds for sickness in a matter of days: coughing first, and weakness, then blooms like sudden awful roses under their pale and feverish skin. Some died early on, choking in their delirious sleep as they bled from the nose. Denniston found a few each morning, moustaches caked muddy-red, eyes swollen and skin waxy. Knowing what comes next, he wondered if they weren't the lucky ones.

Shouting and coughing rang staccato through the rooms, and might have echoed if not for the crowding. Others muttered in their sleep. Where Guppie called out English names and English words, these men garbled their own native languages in fevered confusion, til the wards sounded like Babel.

Denniston murmured too, walking between the beds and cots and heaps of bedding. 'Look for tender livers, spleens, swollen and sensitive. Abscesses to the abdomen and violent blushes there too…'

He remembered Guppie, and the family he would not be returning to, the names he'd called out in his delirium. He recalled his sister. For their sakes, he had tried to tell himself, he would make things better, day by day, making whatever difference he could. But as soon as he began to work, he slipped into the cold that, until now, had been a blessing. Confronted by the sheer numbers of the sick – 'an epidemic,' someone had said – hard facts bred hard necessities.

'Those ones,' he continued, pacing. 'Those are the ones we can do nothing for. Bleeding in the intestines. Infection comes after that. Make sure they're comfortable, but otherwise focus on the others.'

Casson walked beside him, talking under him, translating for a retinue of *jarra bashi*s that followed behind. Somehow they'd concluded he was an expert, but no doubt that came with no small sneer in Casson's translation: *already got sick with it, this one, so I suppose he ought to know.* True, Denniston had had more experience, first-hand and in study, of typhoid fever than most, but an expert..? Denniston did not feel he was an expert in anything – fully prepared for anything – least of all this.

'There'll be seizures too,' said Denniston. 'Don't restrain them or interfere. You'll do more harm than good that way. Put something soft under their head if they've fallen. Clear space. Be sure there's nothing about that they'll hurt themselves on. Just clear space, if you can. Clear—'

Denniston's words choked into nothing, then a gurgling desperate laugh. He saw the hospital as it was, so far from how it ought to be. Patients three to a bed, and others propped against the plaster-cracked walls; a muddle of bed-pans, dishes, implements, rags all stained with sweat. Flies circled like buzzards do, alive even in winter, crowded into the fever-heat of the hospital.

'There's no space,' he croaked. 'None.' The cold manner had lifted a moment, and what lay beneath was awful.

'Denniston?' The voice was distant; hard to say now to whom it belonged. 'Denniston, are you quite well? Sit down. Just...sit down a moment.'

The world cramped and flushed. It blurred through Denniston's eyelashes as they fell halfway shut. He was too aware of his skin, as if he was mummified in it, trapped in it. Mixed cold and beading sweat; the dryness of his mouth.

'Just a moment. Sit down.'

'Damn it, sit him down. Make him—... I don't know! You heard the man, make sure he doesn't hurt himself!'

He was staring through the teeth of something – no, down a tunnel and into light... A blue-black darkness. Voices he couldn't understand. A feeling of something having slipped his grasp. Things came clear in slow and difficult swells of knowing, then slipped back into something that wasn't quite sleep.

'—A walk then.' That was Pinkerton's voice. 'Short. A constitutional, out in the snow, then back beside the stove – just to sit for a while. Lord knows we've all earned that much, haven't we?'

He had lost time. Consciousness too, Denniston thought. The hospital swam then stilled in his vision. He identified it first not by sight, but by the smells and sounds. The coughing, moaning, muttering, and intermittent thunder of outbursts, outcries – they were all the same from before the darkness fell on him. They would be the same whether he was here or not.

'How's that sound?' Pinkerton was speaking still. 'James?'

Denniston forced himself to focus as best he could. '...Where?' he managed to say.

The hospital was too warm. Every fevered body threw out what seemed like waves of heat. And yet Denniston was swaddled up in two coarse blankets, wrapped to the jaw, and still he found himself shivering.

'Out of here for a start,' said Pinkerton.

'Our work... Our shifts...'

'Mm.' Pinkerton was looking down, packing the stubby bowl of his pipe.

'Worried we'll be missed? For today perhaps you might be, but not nearly so much as if you – well, if you proved unable to come back tomorrow, or the day after, or the day after that. Do you understand?'

Tomorrow and tomorrow and tomorrow, thought Denniston...That line had a tidal pull, almost dragging him backward into his thoughts, away from his shuddering cold-sweating body and sudden-aching bones. He resisted, shaking his head and focusing on the chill and the soreness of staying awake.

'It's not typhoid,' he said quickly. It seemed important to explain that much. 'Can't be. Had it before. I'd know. Immune, now.'

'...I never said it was, James. Don't worry over it.'

'It took her. Took her instead of me.'

'James? James, come back.'

The world dilated. The pull was no longer a tide but more like gravity itself, distorting things so they ceased to make sense. Dry mouth; swollen eyes. He knew that much. But there were men around him whose names he couldn't place, doing things he couldn't comprehend, just on the horizons of his vision. There were beds and he bent down beside them. Their mouths moved but he couldn't understand the words. There was a pattern to where they walked and when – like flies, flies circling, up lazy against the cracked plaster ceiling...

'James? Listen to me, I'm here. James.'

Denniston started from himself again. Pinkerton had reached out to touch his balled-tight fist with two gentle fingers. Denniston told himself to breathe.

'Shall we go?' Pinkerton asked softly. 'It's alright if we don't. If you don't feel strong enough, it's alright. But it might do you good...'

Denniston nodded weakly and Pinkerton helped him to his feet.

'Best to bring the blankets,' said the older doctor, giving Denniston his arm to lean on.

They walked between the clamouring beds and rows of bedless patients against the walls, out into the steely sunlight, where snow compacted underfoot. It was easier to breathe, Denniston found, now that the air was thinner, crisper, cleaner.

'Where to now, do I hear you ask?' Pinkerton spoke in mellow tones, his pace genial and easy. 'As I see it, in a place like this, there's only two ways to walk: up or down. Today? Today, I fear the hike up might kill us both. Down it is, then.'

Pinkerton gave a curt bark of laughter, then made chewing noises as he lit his pipe with a match. He began to lead their way through the walled yards and street-sections that surrounded the hospital, then out into a broad main causeway.

Here the snow was muddy, soot-stained, but at least covered the filthy gutters that ran down each side of the road. Listless women sat veiled in doorways and shopfronts sat boarded closed. An ass trembled up the way past them, a man gripping its rope tether, helping it pull a covered cart. They struggled, though the way the sheet over it sagged suggested the goods-cart was all but empty. Man and beast both seemed made entirely of ribs, all bones showing through fragile skin, like those of a plucked bird.

'They're hungry now,' Pinkerton mused. 'I fancy we all are. There are stores, of course, in a fort town like this, but kept locked tight to withstand a siege… Seems counter-intuitive to me, though: if you're hungry when the siege starts, how much worse will it get as it goes on?'

Dogs, charcoal-coated and skinny as lightning, peered wild-eyed from alley entrances and what might have once been courtyard gardens. They trotted half-tame, in the open of the street. It didn't bear thinking about what they'd been eating to survive. Yet survive they had, almost flourishing, multiplying, while Erzurum chewed itself into starvation, surrounded by the Russians' awful patience.

The doctors came eventually to one of the city's inner rings of walls. The tiered old fortifications weren't regular, squares and stars, as in Europe. Nor did they even bear comparison to the walls of the one part-crumbled castle Denniston had seen once in Pollok, near Paisley. Rather, they meandered round the city, perimeters within perimeters, following its topography – aimless shapes, like the outer membrane of a cell seen under optics.

No patrols ran along these walls. There was nowhere atop them to walk, being only like a garden wall, but a little taller, a little thicker and more rugged. Instead, the two doctors found one of the intermittent stubs of tower that cropped along the fortifications, and climbed the fifteen steep steps to the top, where they stood on smarting legs, leaning against the crenellations. Their breath was hard now, and sour with hunger. Any other time, Denniston might have made the walk without complaint. Now he felt weaker, older than he was, aged in the past few hours.

The city outstripped the wall and the base of the tower for a while ahead. Flat-roofed houses huddled together as if for warmth, thin cracks between them the only available view down into the street. Some wore crowns of crenellations like the wall and watch-tower. Some hosted rickety chairs, or else figures made small by the distance, drubbing their laundry, collecting pails of snow for meltwater, beating dust from sheets and rugs. All went about their business, as they always had and, with luck, always would, even in the shadow of encirclement, siege, starvation.

There was one more small swathe of wall beyond this one, and then another thin stripe of cityscape, and finally the thick outer wall. Beyond lay the churned up snow and rough-turned dirt of the earthworks: a grey maze of barricades, trenches, and dug-outs, where once the city outskirts had been.

After that, the featureless white out-fanning of the plains stretched northward. Whatever skirmishes had torn up the land, and whatever fields and pastures had been left empty and fallow there, the snow had long since covered them.

'Look.' Pinkerton pointed out in that direction, across the plain and into a blot of shapes straggled across the northern horizon. 'Here's our city, beneath and behind us. Over yonder, that's theirs. Canvas and hides and fur and strong drink for warmth, and waiting just as we are.' He paused to tap a clump of ashes from his pipe, before sticking the stem straight back into his mouth. 'Fancy I'd take our bare little house over a tent any day. I know which city I'd rather defend...'

Denniston pulled the blanket tight around his shoulders. The shivering had let up somewhat, and his head felt clearer for looking out through the clarity of the day. The sounds of Erzurum around and below them helped too. Yet he dreaded looking down at the earthworks. Another assault and he'd be down there again, in the dirt and the smoke, the blood and black powder, marled together into a constant din.

'Casson's full of rumours, you know...' Denniston began. 'He listens to the patients, the soldiers, when they talk. Understands them in his sly sort of way. He says it's the birthday of some Russian Grand Duke or other very soon. A general, maybe; tomorrow, maybe, or else the day after, or the day after that. That's when they'll come across the plain again, he says. Just for the occasion of it. Another try at the walls...'

'Do you think they'll manage it?' Pinkerton chewed at his pipe-stem.

'Hard to say. I've not seen the fortifications in a while now.'

'You've seen the hospital though...'

'Aye,' Denniston agreed darkly. 'And every man I've seen in it is a man missing from the defences...'

'Our own army, growing larger with every passing day.'

'Aye. And there's the rub...'

'Mm. Do you think it'll be tomorrow, then?'

'Not certain I know what I think anymore. But God, I hope not... I can't be like this when they come. I can't. None of us can. One slip or lapse – an inch less effort or focus – and then..?' Denniston turned his face to the wind and blew out a puff of air, as if snuffing a candle. 'It's not typhoid,' he repeated. 'Just tiredness. I just need some time.'

'We're all tired, James. I don't imagine any of us can quite recall not being...'

Denniston tried. He thought back, searching his memory for a time before Erzurum. It was more difficult than it ought to have been. It seemed his whole life had been black sour bread and tar-dark coffee – meagre greasy mutton on what could be considered very good days. The nights were no longer for sleeping in, and he felt they never had been otherwise. It was hard to think himself into the mindset of who he'd been before the siege.

All that his memory gave him, as he tried so hard to ransack its records, was a single instance: a gas-lit room with a shining smooth wood floor, springy like live-wood under his feet. He recalled a dress of green velvet, dark and slightly waving hair – a night in Greenock; a face he'd not dared hope to see again; a conversation about dancing.

I'm afraid I don't know how...

Then what ever shall you do at a dance, Doctor Denniston?

Look a loner or a fool, I fancy.

And what if you were to have a teacher?

There was no illness to speak of. It was neither typhoid, nor the flu that had been spreading through the Stafford House Committee hospital. Yet Denniston still suffered symptoms, even if there seemed to be no scientifically sensible cause.

There was a panic that rose slowly but would suddenly overtake him, staggering his breath and shattering any sentence he might try to utter before he could let it go. There were night-sweats and bad dreams, when he had the luxury of sleeping at all. He remembered faces in awful clarity, and struggled groping through his memory for names to fit to them. And every time he tried to recall, he failed. The guilt came after that, thick as tar but icy-cold.

It confined him to quarters. He couldn't leave; daylight itself, or the open sky, seemed things too fearful to bear. In the course of three days, he wrote three letters. All but one of them, he burnt in the stove, all the better to forget what he had said in them.

Dimly, Denniston noted the other doctors in their comings and goings. They would slip in and out of sight, reading to him by his bedside, or else speaking to him like they might to a startled animal – and he would realise he had been shaking, thrashing, muttering, or had gotten into such a state of fright that he had been afraid to breathe.

But there were times too when things were almost clear. Denniston would hear them, then, speaking amongst themselves as they sat about the stove, half-shadowed in its red glow. They spoke about him, mostly. He could make that out, even if it was hard to match the voices he heard to the names that he'd once known.

'There's nothing whatever the matter with him. Some women's sickness is all.'

'A kind of hysteria, then?'

'As I said, nothing whatever seriously the matter…'

'And yet he's confined to his bed. Unable to speak, unable to bear daylight, or be of much use to anyone – and when we could use him so very badly now? That seems serious enough to me.'

'Hm. I've seen the same thing in the soldiers, you know? Sometimes. The ones just out of the fighting. Same wild eyes, same restless shaking.'

'Are they struck mute too?'

'Not that I could understand if they weren't, but I think, sometimes, yes… As if it hollows them out: doing what they must do… Perhaps the same thing happened to James.'

'Are you a philosopher, Pinkerton, or a mere grubby sawbones like the rest of us?'

'I think a good doctor can be a bit of both. Ought to be, perhaps…'

Denniston hardly cared what they said about him. Worse was how little they said of Guppie, as if the poor corpse in the paltry grave on the hillside were already forgotten.

Necessity made it a short convalescence. As the others had said, they could use a man like him. They had lost Guppie, lost *jarra bashi*s, and could not afford to have a pair of skilled hands out of action for long – certainly not in the wake of what was to come.

There came a second full assault. There had been talk of it for a long time now, but still Erzurum was unprepared. In one bloody night, the Russians broke through the earthworks and into the outer fortifications, past the sole purview of soldiers and into the city itself, and the lives of its citizens. The Russian forces fought for a foothold, and found it in Erzurum's crowded Aziziye district, ill-fated into strategic importance by its closeness to a fort. In the morning, there were dead and wounded from both sides, littering the streets, and the fort was in Russian hands.

Once more, the Stafford House hospital reeked of blood, as injury heaped upon illness. Weak in the knees and pale of face, short of breath with a cough that seemed to wax with the waning of his former nervous illness, Denniston washed, dressed, and returned to his duties. The spirit of the work, however, was different.

He'd come to Erzurum with a full-hearted feeling, that every patient he treated was a person deserving care and every comfort and push towards recovery he could possibly give them. Yet he'd lost it somewhere – in the trenches, and the overpacked hospital, where the lucky shared beds, and others lived out their last hours on the cold floor.

Something in his own brief sickness, or else in Guppie's passing, had helped him find that initial instinct again. The cold into which his thoughts had sunk had broken for good, and it left behind a more human warmth.

Casson and Walker swept through the hospital, assisted each by their own train of *jarra bashi*s, like brisk winds sweeping leaves in their wake.

Denniston, however, moved slower but inexorable, straight and clear as the shafts of sunlight that cast through the hospital windows. He was always clean, always careful, always speaking, quiet and calmly, of good and hopeful things.

Chapter 13

He was in her arms and dying. The couch was already soaked dark with blood. More came every moment, though she couldn't tell from where. Everywhere, it seemed. His greatcoat was wet, hot and cloying to the touch. She couldn't staunch it; couldn't make his breath come regular.

'Don't!' she rasped. Her voice was tired and raw; she'd screamed when he came home. 'Don't you dare..!'

But nothing would help. Not hot tears or shuddering embraces, and no amount of desperate words. Still, she wept and groaned. Sometimes the noises she made came out like his name. 'Hasan..? Hasan!' But mostly they'd turned animal.

He had been so brave, her brother Hasan. Always, for the both of them, he had been brave, older than her, keeping her safe. She had idolised him, as a child, after their father had died. Perhaps she idolised him still. She kept the image inside her of Hasan as he had been. A dark-haired boy with a wood-axe, a shade of badly grown hair on his upper lip and chin, brows that met in the middle. A boy brandishing the axe they used to split firewood, shouting 'No! No, you can't have her!' at the man who'd offered a bride-price for her, even before her blood had come. But that image was part of the problem now. Here was her brother, a grown man in body, but in her mind still a boy, and dying young.

He seemed so afraid. Roving eyes, searching and begging for the help she couldn't give him. The beginning of a cry started in his chest. He grit his teeth and it fell silent before it could start. His shoulders stopped shaking. He was in her arms and dead.

She allowed herself one long howl. Not even a sob anymore. But this home was not her home. It belonged to a stranger. She knelt upon their kindness. She had let her brother bleed on their hearthrug, when he'd said that he was cold. For the sake of all that, she gathered herself up; made herself quiet and decent.

Yet through the walls of this house she heard moaning and crying, and felt it like it was her own. It sounded all through the neighbourhood, through every street and building: sounds like the screams of foxes mating in the night; sometimes, still, the crack of a rifle being fired.

The soldiers had come in the night to Aziziye. Those yet alive lived only because they had fled, she thought. No time to take valuables, no time to think or consider, they had all been pushed from their homes and thrust upon the charity of strangers, further into the city. It was shameful, she thought. It was not enough that the Russians had made them run; they had forced them to go begging too.

It had been close to dawn that the survivors of the fighting had come stumbling back from Aziziye – from trying to hold the Russians back. And her brother had been among them, dropping red into the snow til it looked like he was trailing petals – like they scattered at weddings.

Now he was with God.

That was simple, clear, almost comforting. It was more mercy than was given to those left behind.

'What will you do now?' her host asked: a widow, head wrapped in a black scarf; some cousin of their mother's who had offered bread and vinegar pickles to her as soon as she arrived. The salt, she'd said, would calm her nerves. But now the widow spoke, she hardly heard. 'Nene?'

'I'm sorry..?' She shook her head; pawed at her eyes with the heels of her hands.

'I said, what will you do now?'

'I don't know...'

'It's good that he found you. Before.'

'Is it..?' Nene frowned. 'I don't know...'

'You've lost a lot, child. It changes things. Yanks the rug from under you. It takes time to find your footing again, after...'

But she didn't want to find her damn footing. She didn't want bread, or vinegar pickles, or calm nerves. She wanted to bury her brother, or better, she wanted him back. She wanted her brother back, her home back. She wanted his blood off her hands, off her cheeks, off her clothes. And she wanted the men who had done this to him dead.

They gathered by the well that morning, the citizens of Aziziye. Scores of feet troubled the snow into mud. Scores of shoulders jostled. Scores of lungs seemed to hold their breath.

One by one, some among them got up and onto the wall of the well, balancing against its bucket-winch. An elder, who said it had been in God's hands, and they must all pull together now to do what they can with what's left to them. A muezzin, who said that the matter was in God's hands from now on, and only through Him would the siege be lifted, and the kuffār be driven back. Others stepped up and told the rest what they had lost.

Everyone had lost a father, a brother, a son in the fight to defend the fort and the streets around it. For all that sacrifice, still they'd failed.

Nene stood in the crowd, leaning on the barrel of her brother's long rifle. She had spent the morning drubbing the worst of the blood from her brother's greatcoat, and wore it now. It was warm – a good coat, if ragged in places – and served as a reminder. So did the dull stains she couldn't quite wash out.

This talk bothered her. It stuck in her throat and stung in her ears til she had to say something. She shouldered through the crowd, not knowing what she was doing, or quite what words she'd use. But she felt it, there, in the pit of her belly: a heavy impatience that wouldn't be silent. It led her to the well. It carried her up to stand on its wall.

'We accept this, do we? We forget what we've lost, and we try again?' Her voice cracked, then held firm. 'Do we wait meekly? The Russians won't! They'll come again. We'll make new homes til the next attack, and then they'll take those too!

'You men – when a wolf worries your flocks, or a fox frights your chickens, do you sit meekly? You women – when a man makes to touch your clothes or speaks ill of your family, do you sit meekly? No! Show them you're meek and they'll take more and more.

'We've all of us lost things we can't buy back or rebuild. And fighting won't bring back the ones we've lost. But it will give them justice! And it will win back our homes! And it will show the ones who drove us out that we are not to be crossed!'

There was shouting in the crowd now. There was colour in their cheeks. There were hands in the air.

'What do you do when a wolf worries your flocks?' Nene Hatun shouted. 'You take up your rifle and shoot the damn wolf!'

Chapter 14

James

My dear Miss Guthrie,

We have our work cut out for us now. We contended with rampant disease, fleas, deteriorating conditions in this sewerless city, and our overcrowded English hospital. Add to that burden new patients from the recent Russian assault on one of the outermost neighbourhoods of the city. Worse still was the effort of the Turks, the following night, to take back their homes and the fort from out of Russian hands.

No official sally was made – not in the sense of soldiers acting under officers' orders. Rather, the citizens of the neighbourhood in question, Aziziye, took up whatever arms they could for the purpose: tools, sickles, hoes, axes, knives from the kitchen, the occasional musket, shotgun, or rifle. With those, and numbers alone, they stormed the fort, breaking down its doors with torches and axes. I've heard of almost nothing but this story for the last day or two. It's already become quite the folk-legend – all the more so for the fact that it has a heroine. Most tellings vary one way or another, but none leave out Nene Hatun: a girl armed with her slain brother's rifle and a hatchet, who was first through the breach in the doors…

To the Turks I fancy it comes all as a victory to rally behind. No Russians were spared, backed into the fort they were so eager to claim. To the Turks, I fancy that's part of the story's appeal. But to me it seems a downward step for the whole city towards savagery. And in battle, as in the hospital beds, the line between citizen and soldier grows ever more blurred. If the Russians do take the city eventually, and they know that Erzurum's civilians gave their soldiers no quarter, what reason should they have to show mercy in return?

We have the same bullet-wounds as before. Dreadful broad deep things, shattering bones etc., making terrible holes on entry, and worse still on their egress from the body. And that is for those lucky enough to have the bullets leave them at all. Some remain inside, causing swelling and putrefaction in the tissues concerned. This is the work of the wide conical German-made rounds the Russians seem mostly to fire, which do their jobs awfully well – we 'English Hekims', as the Turks call us, must every day endeavour to do ours better.

Shells, too. The casing and charge of artillery rounds is one problem, but quite another is the tendency they have to turn everything close to their impact into a weapon: daggers of flying splintered wood, shards of hot stone and broken metal. Worse is that they are indiscriminate. A Russian rifleman may aim for a man armed also with a rifle, but a Russian shell will fall where it will, and hurt and kill fighters and civilians both. A shell may strike a marketplace, a house, just as easily as a barracks building, a section of earthworks, a fort.

Such injuries as these, though, we have a good deal of experience with by now. But the fighting in this most recent assault was at closer quarters than any we've known so far – at point and push of bayonet, as I think the awful phrase goes.

They're simpler wounds, in their way: less ragged than those made by bullet or shell, but they have a more sinister character. Perhaps it comes from the knowledge that these wounds were dealt not impersonally, from a distance, but by men who could see the whites of one another's eyes, and would each have done the same or worse to the other given the chance.

In dealing with this new influx of injured patients, differences are beginning to emerge between myself and my Stafford House colleagues.

They will dart about, pragmatic in choosing those to whom they'll minister, and to what extent. To those with the best chance of recovery, they'll tend first and most vehemently, but will move on quickly, once they've done what's required – and only what's required. Each patient is a case to them: a number among numbers, and the numbers, I admit, are great. Overtasked as we are, they try to tend to the whole hospital at once.

I try to work more slowly, doing all that can be done for a patient at the time, then doing the same for the next. It is that simple, but has led to arguments.

Only yesterday I started with one patient requiring quite an extensive operation, having taken the thrust of a bayonet to the abdomen. Kincaid said, exasperated: might it not be best to treat first of all the patients who require the least effort to be comfortable and likely to recover? I asked why that should mean they're any more deserving of care than this unfortunate soldier. And I went on with the operation with one assistant to help, steady and unhurried, as if this first patient were the only one I'd deal with for the day. And at the time, in a sense, I found it helped to let myself believe he was: my sole focus and complete intent.

I should mention, the patient in question looks likely to make a full recovery, and shall soon be back to his post.

On another occasion, Casson made a remark on my insistence upon total cleanliness between each patient. How I use carbolic to wash myself and my implements, or else I boil the latter in water if I can't get carbolic. I replied that I find it helps to reduce risk and rates of infection in my patients, and that perhaps he should try it for himself. He said, tightly: 'A gentleman's hands are always clean.'

That, I admit, drove me close to losing my temper. Here, on the far side of the world, I encountered it too: the same stubborn high-blown attitude that I'd found in the practices of the beastly doctors I'd been so loathe to work under in Glasgow. Pride above pragmatism; precedent over progress. Just what I hoped to leave behind, I had found in one of my colleagues. But Casson and I have gone, since the journey to Erzurum, from friendship to scarcely seeing eye to eye on any matter. I think we both have the other's respect, more so than we ever did while we still liked one another, but at times, for me, it's strained. I find myself contributing to conversations of his just to contradict him, and by his manner around me, I think he feels just as pettily.

Still, I am doing good work, and must only keep on.

In the meantime, I have something in mind that I've been turning over for a fair while now. I've said it before, and no doubt will often have to say it again, but I'm ill-versed in the formalities and proprieties of this sort of thing. The terms of our correspondence – my first with a lady, I'm not bashful to admit – are unfamiliar ground to me, though it's easy enough to confide in you, and a great comfort to hear back.

I'm going to venture and ask if I may not address you in my letters by your Christian name? It seems so formal and distant to address you as I do, seeing that I now consider you one of the few real friends I have.

But perhaps I presume too much. I shan't attempt to refer to you any differently until I get your reply, and express permission, whether that be in a matter of days, or weeks, or months. I never can predict the patterns of the post, and they become more irregular every day. We rely upon our man Vashin for that, and with every one he takes through the blockade, I worry that it might be the last he carries – or the last that I write.

May that day not come too soon.

Meanwhile I am yours

Very sincerely,

James Denniston

The table in the British consulate was laid more richly than any of the doctors had seen since Istanbul.

There were green and purple olives, knotty-braided pastries filled with crumbling cheese and minced meat, and two thick sauces – one orange and tasting of smoke and sweet carrots; one beetroot-purple and richly earthy in flavour – to be scooped up with soft flat breads. There were salty pickles of radish, cucumber, and carrot, and Denniston fell upon them in particular with abandon. How long had it been since he'd last had fruit or vegetables, or seen evidence of any other delicate growing thing?

But there was an agitation in it, too. Here he was, eating well, as a guest of Mr. Zohrab, the British consul in Erzurum, and yet all the way to the grand house that made up the consulate, half-starved townsfolk lined the streets. He'd been pulled from his duties at the hospital to eat a meal more lavish by far than most of the city could hope to see in their lives. It was difficult not to feel guilty.

'You flatter me, gentlemen,' Zohrab smiled neatly. 'Truly, that you were able to allow even so small a lapse in your duties, and accept my hospitality? It is a tremendous pleasure, and a *great* privilege, gentlemen. A *great* pleasure.'

He spoke warmly, smooth as running honey, and in perfect English. But despite his title and mastery of the tongue, he was, in his looks and name, at least half a Turk: dark-haired and trim-bearded, with olive-purple circles round his clever brown eyes. Yet his manners, dress, and speech were all the very measure of an English gentleman – more English and Englishman even than Casson, who bristled with subtle shows around Zohrab, as if their similarity put them in competition. In truth, hard work and hard living had muted Casson's gentility, while Turkish blood and Turkish surroundings had only emphasised Zohrab's.

'So small a lapse in our duty?' Casson smiled in reply. 'I'm sure our duties will forgive us this much. After all, to err is human.'

'And to refuse good food and wine, when there's so little of either about?' Kincaid blustered in, tilting down his throat another gulp of Bulgarian red. 'Inexcusable!' His tongue flickered round his lips and he raise a hand to smooth his beard.

'More's the point,' Denniston clipped, 'we have our *jarra bashi*s and have trained them well. They do good work now, even without oversight. At least for a time.' He said it as much to convince himself, however, as the others.

A servant in butler's black entered the dining room with a broad bowl in hand: a bed of somthing smooth, creamy, centered around a well of steaming tender stewed and spiced mutton. Denniston recalled that Barrington-Kennet had liked to be served *a la turc*, by lads in bright red jackets and huge loose trousers. By contrast, Zohrab preferred Western service. It seemed both men looked in the Orient for whatever was most novel to them.

They set to their food. Walker and Featherston were silent, deeply focused on eating, even halfway through this fourth course. Denniston looked on from across the rectangular hardwood table. He couldn't help but feel their intensity had only a little to do with their hunger faced with the feast before them. Each glanced up between every mouthful, stealing glimpses of the two women seated at the table with them.

One was Zohrab's wife: a pale Englishwoman, thin-faced and chestnut haired, diving into the conversation with incisive snatches of wisdom whenever the matters of politics or international relations were raised. The other young woman was either his daughter or ward – none had the courage to ask which – and she was small, compact, with what might have been Zohrab's dark hair and lashes, and lucent eyes. Together they were the first women of European dress and manners any of the doctors had seen in months; the first they had seen without a veil of some kind, and much less spoken to in something you'd call conversation.

Denniston hardly begrudged his colleagues their staring. He was nervous, however, feeling constantly that he was about to be caught out in some lapse of character, some misdemeanour, whether here in polite society, or for his absence from the hospital. Watching the others, he recalled what the agent of the Stafford House Committee had told them in Trabzon. He had advised them, 'learn from the soldiers you tend to…eat whenever you can, whatever you can,' for one never knows when the day will come that nothing but coffee passes your lips.

'I'm glad,' Zohrab glowed, 'truly, gentleman, I am heartened!'

'As if it was not kind enough,' Mrs. Zohrab said, 'helping the wounded of Erzurum. Rather, you are leaving it improved; leaving the lives of its people, improved; indeed, leaving skilled and well-taught men to carry on your legacy.'

'Commendable,' the younger woman agreed with a smile.

'I only regret,' Zohrab continued, 'that we met under such circumstances as we did.' He shook his head. 'Your friend and colleague, Doctor Guppie, was it? Terrible. A true tragedy. You had and have still my tenderest condolences…'

Everything Zohrab said, Denniston observed, had the air of being rehearsed. He seemed the sort of man who played out conversations with himself and his shaving mirror each morning.

'It only makes one wonder, however,' Zohrab said, 'quite why it took us so long to finally become acquainted – and, as I said, under such unfortunate circumstances.'

'We arrived in the midst of a battle,' said Denniston. 'We found ourselves quite busy ever since.'

'Of course, of course… But are we not all subjects of Her Majesty the Queen? Long may she reign, of course. I only meant that, in such a place as this, where we are rare as pearls, would we not do well to be friends?'

'Oh certainly!' Walker said, eagerly, after hastily swallowing.

'Without a doubt,' Casson agreed. 'You know of course that if you have any complaints – medical or otherwise – you may call on us. As friends.'

'Splendid. Quite splendid. For I fear, gentlemen, the dark times are only just beginning. I have, as consul, certain channels of intelligence, and through them, I have heard unfortunate news…'

'I must say,' said Casson, 'I'm not certain I can remember getting any other sort since coming here.'

'It concerns Kars, gentlemen. Kars has fallen. A rout en masse from the city, with only Hami Pasha left behind, with 10,000 men for defence – you can imagine how that bore up against Melikov and Lazarev's next assault…'

'We had heard rumours,' Pinkerton said carefully, 'but the hospital is always full of them. A man abed can do nothing much more than talk, can he?'

'There's yet more,' said Zohrab, with a dramatic rise of his perfect eyebrows. 'Mukhtar Pasha is yet in retreat – *tactical* retreat, you understand – and with 30,000 men. His retreat leads this way!'

Denniston frowned. 'Through miles on miles of snow and cold? Men already half-dead from frostbite and the fighting at Kars, and he intends to march them through a blockade? That's—…' Madness, he had been about to say. But he noted the stares from around the table, and his talk tailed into a sigh.

'Agreed,' said Kincaid, as if intuiting what Denniston had failed to say. It was a surprise, to Denniston; a moment of warmth, to be supported so. 'I don't envy the soldiers under him, and I don't look forward to clearing up the mess he's made of them…'

'Ah,' said Zohrab. 'There you cut to the heart of the matter. Mukhtar Pasha will no doubt fall back to Erzurum itself. It's not certain, of course – in war so little is – but if one thing might encourage his men to cut through such *hardships* as they'll endure in the attempt, it's the hope of strong walls and reinforcements to join with. Erzurum's weak garrison and Mukhtar Pasha's broken *ordu* will become one stronger army. And perhaps, with winter on our side and not that of the Russians – fancy that! – Erzurum will yet bear up against what's to come!'

Zohrab spoke now with all the excitement of an inveterate gossip. That's all this was to him. As a diplomat, this war would not touch Zohrab, Denniston realised; he was glad only of the front-row seat he had from which to watch it all unfold.

'That supposes,' Casson said, 'that Mukhtar Pasha ever makes it so far as Erzurum.'

There was a moment's deep silence. Zohrab eventually broke it, neutrally: 'There are those who would call such a plan unwise, yes. But that is speculation. All war, gentleman, is speculation, and "full of false alarms," yes? What is certain, though, is that you shall be very well occupied if he does arrive, and with what remains of his forces… But, ah!'

The butler returned from out of mind, pouring each man another glass of wine, and each woman another half.

'Enough of dark times and grave news,' Zohrab continued. 'Tell me of home, gentlemen! Do you write letters back?'

Denniston and Casson both looked up, each at the other, then looked down embarrassed. It was as if they both remembered the way they'd used to sit, as companions, writing letters together on the way to Erzurum, with the scratching of their pens, each to a different recipient, as all the conversation they needed.

Zohrab carried on. 'I'm sure you must, I'm sure you must! I find them indispensable in times such as these. But is it not difficult to find a means to send them?'

'Difficult, yes,' said Denniston. 'But not so much as you'd think.'

'We have a man for that – Vashin, a Circassian,' Casson said, 'who's so far proved cunning in the extreme with getting our post through and back to us.'

'A Circassian, you say? No wonder then – a wily people – and willing to do nearly anything if only it will spite some Russian somewhere. But I have a solution you may find more *reliable*. In so benighted a part of the country as this, untouched by telegraph, my position necessitates that I have a diplomatic courier, weekly from here to Trabzon, and thence on to Istanbul. After that? Why, wherever you might like! Wherever your correspondence might be addressed.'

Denniston began to smile. His cheeks were creased and lined and gaunt, and the smile was warm across them as he began to understand Zohrab's offer.

'Tell me, gentlemen,' Zohrab said, 'shall I have him carry your letters also? It would be no trouble, no trouble at all.'

'I think,' said Casson, 'that we should all like that very much.'

'Pinkerton?' Denniston asked as they walked the short way back to the hospital. Snow lay uneven on the ground. On the roofs around them, it sat in frozen drifts.

'Yes?'

'What did he mean? Mr. Zohrab, by what he said about Vashin.'

'About his being Circassian, you mean?'

'About why he should want to work for us over the Russians. Armenians, Anatolian Greeks, Georgians, Persians – it seems anyone who's not a Turk in these parts has little love for the Ottomans. Not even the Turks seem happy as they could be with rule from Istanbul. Why should the Circassians be different?'

'They have less love still for the Russians,' Pinkerton answered. 'Fresher wounds and deeper grudges, I suppose.'

'Go on...'

'Your little book of maps,' said Pinkerton. 'Recent, is it?'

'Current enough.'

'Well then. On any of its pages, in any of its charts, can you point to a "Circassia"?'

'Can't say I've looked,' Denniston admitted.

'I've saved you time then. Don't try, you won't find it. Come now, Denniston, I know I'm full of dusty airs and what must seem ancient history to you, but this is recent, man! It was in the papers for Christ's sakes.'

'There was a war, then?'

'At first, yes. For a long time. Since before even I was born, I think. How old are you, Denniston?'

'Twenty-three.'

'You'd have been a child, then. I suppose our man Vashin would have been, too. God but it makes one feel old… But it ended in a massacre, long, slow, deliberate, drawn out. The Tsar annexed Circassia, but the locals wouldn't settle down. So the Tsar built forts, and the locals attacked them. And the Tsar built roads to move his troops, and the locals attacked them too. And the Tsar burnt the forests that surrounded the roads, so the locals would have nowhere to hide. And the Tsar burnt the villages, even up into the mountains, so the locals would have nowhere to live. Whole tribes were killed. And then some clever bastard in Moscow decided that it would be much easier to think of Circassia as part of Russia now if only the Circassians were just *gone*. They moved them.'

'By force?'

'By force. Into Turkey, mostly. If you're going to live under an Empire, I suppose, better to make it one that at least shares your faith.'

'So when Zohrab said he shouldn't be surprised if Vashin has no small amount of spite stored up for the Russians…'

'He's a diplomat. He was being diplomatic.'

'He means Vashin hates them.'

'Can you deny he'd have his reasons?'

'Not for one minute.'

Agnes

Dear Doctor Denniston,

That is, I am only a little apologetic to say, what I will continue to call you for the time being; I hope you will continue in good faith to call me Miss Guthrie and nothing shorter. You must think me a terrible prude, but I assure you that prudery has nothing to do with it. Rather think of it as an exercise in propriety and decorum between two correspondents such as we are: a matter of which you profess to know little. So perhaps consider this gentle rebuttal also an education, and let us agree to say no more of it, as friends, mutually considered.

While I am in the vein of rebuttals, rejections, and otherwise being stubborn and disappointing, I should address a compliment you paid in a recent letter. You suggested that I am exceptional by the standards of my sex in being more 'natural', that is to say more 'genuine', and less given to dissembling. I know that you are not perhaps accustomed to paying compliments, and think yourself lacking in art in that line; this, however, seem to me particularly artless. Any praise anyone might pay that drags down all women to elevate me is praise I'd sooner go without; in truth, it's no compliment to me at all, but rather an insult from which I'm excepted. Regarding compliments, doctor Denniston, I suggest you continue your practice.

I do hope, though, that does not all seem too brusque, in particular as a way in which to start a letter. It sounds as if you have had quite the time of it in recent days, and for that I am deeply sorry. For your friend Guppie in particular, let me offer my condolences; I never knew him but he seemed of a good and honest heart, and I trust he is with God now, as reward for all his goodness. To a man such as yourself, I know that might be but small consolation, so to you I will simply add that I am very sorry for the loss. Now the true apologies must begin, for I have yet more festivities with which to bore you. I only hope they shall prove a comfort and a diversion, rather than adding salt to the wound of your current austerity.

Once more in Manchester, and with Advent fast approaching, the mood is turning toward liveliness. Cold and brisk though the days are growing, my evenings have kept me warm through dancing and hearty company. You often fret, in your letters, over what a hedonist I must think you for taking brandy, or tobacco, or any other small comfort, but I think you are a veritable stylite – monk-like – by comparison to myself. Here am I, while you face your difficulties and privations, enjoying myself so thoroughly. I was, last night, at the Mckies'. For such an affair they had a very grand room, ceilings dripping with crystal, but only one big beetle-black piano for music. Its back was open, like wings to better speed its music to our ears, but all the same, the number of guests meant that conversation and the sound of ringing classes quite overbore the songs. Yet we did not go without dancing; I fancy we dance just as eagerly and with equal ease in Manchester as in Greenock – yourself and your uncertain steps excepted, though I am sure they are nothing a few more lessons from a patient teacher could not fix. But the piano's music was half-drowned by the shuffle and fall of our footwork, so we danced almost solely to our own massed tempo: thud, slip, shuffle, steady as a metronome.

You will not think me too liberal with my attentions, but I had perhaps half a dozen dances and with half as many partners. Among them were the two younger Mckies. One has begun preparations for going into the cloth, and the other has gained himself a commission in one regiment of horse or another – I don't recall which, though the cut of the uniform stands out in my mind, and I daresay I could describe it. For all their new duties, or the discipline you might expect in a pastor, both proved hard to extricate from the punch, and later, the champagne. Indeed, in the case of the latter, the military Mckie attempted some French manner of opening the bottle; he used the edge of his drawn sabre! A terrible mess, however, and a waste of champagne was the main result. I danced with neither after that, but turned my attentions instead to one young Mr. Arrol.

He is a cool breeze next to the hot bluster of the other two. And I am thankful that he holds and considers himself as significantly less of a bravado than the Mckie men, each of whom – whether in clergy black or cavalry pink – speak to a lady in such a way as to let her know two things: how highly they estimate their own sway over and knowledge of her sex, and how little they truly know of either. Arrol, for his part, works with the Chronicle, and a little here and there as well with some bureau for taxation, or something in that line; so he is full of fascinating conversation, from all corners of the world, without needing to so much as mention himself: this is, I find, unusual in the extreme amongst gentlemen of his age.

There was mention of talk in Her Majesty's government of the war you're involved in, and whether Britain herself shall also be involved before long. Before I quite knew it, I found that I had started to justify the possibility of our Christian nation coming to the Turk's aid, if only it might limit the kind of suffering your letters have depicted. This is an about-turn in my previous opinions, as I'm sure you will note; no doubt you shall view it as a personal victory, and it is one I will grant ungrudging. For I think you have been correct all along: it is at the heart of Christian doctrine to put the limitation of suffering, and improvement in the lots of others, above our own interests; and what do we learn from the Good Samaritan, but that this Christian duty does not extend only to those with whom we share a creed, but must be granted to all humanity, regardless of origin?

By that point, though, I had even had a little champagne, and must say that conversation turned somewhat less serious as the night drew on and the collection pails were passed round. So you see, for me to live as gaily as I am lucky enough to do, and yet to condemn your taking tobacco or 'hot grog' sometimes, would be a matter of beams and motes, would it not? I would first have to remove the impediment from my own eye before presuming to say what I see in yours.

Indeed, I think the contrast in our pleasures makes me empathise somewhat more. And sometimes I will admit that I fret for your safety. It is a Sunday today, so indeed, I think I shall pray for it, and give today over to higher matters, and so make amends for my hedonism. But what of your Sundays, I find myself wondering. In Erzurum, I suppose they pass quite like any other day.

Until I hear from you again

Sincerely yours,
Miss Agnes Guthrie

Even Fridays, which were the closest the Muslims kept to a Sabbath, passed much like any other day. Perhaps the calls from minarets, and the shows of prayer were more vehement, more sincere. But for Denniston, Friday and Sunday, Sabbath and workday, passed all in much the same way.

The day had darkened long ago, as he took coffee in the home of a private case: an official in the upper city, whose wife had fallen sick with a fever. Now he hurried home, between the banked townhouses that sat round the city's hilltop, following the winding road that led the fastest route down and to his lodging.

There were painted facades here, and tiles that glinted with colour like jewels as he passed by with his lamp. Even European styles of building sat amongst the Oriental. Many were designed that way, like Zohrab's consulate, while more still were veneered, to fit some fashion that had come and gone.

As Denniston's journey led downward, however, they gave way to rougher clusters of apartment buildings of two or three storeys, staircases built into their sides, cracked wooden shutters on their small rare windows. Their roofs were flat, caked with snow, and skinny trails of smoke climbed up from the fuel-starved stoves within.

The winding path grew straight and broadened, flanked on either side by brimming open gutters. From off its course split narrow alleys, in which sewer and sidestreet, as terms, became indistinct.

Denniston considered the letter he'd received. Perhaps he had not expected permission, but he had not prepared himself for rejection either – it seemed a small thing, after all, to ask to use a Christian name on occasion. In a letter filled with the names of other men, it felt bruising, embarrassing to him. Boorish though the others might have been, they had the advantage over him: they were in England, while he was far away. What did it matter? he tried to tell himself. Hadn't Miss Guthrie said, in that same letter, that they were friends? As a friend, ought he not to be happy for her, as she seemed happy in her life? Friendship, after all, is a fine thing in itself. He tried to feel more grateful than wounded.

As he walked, and thought, Denniston passed from the parts of the city somehow still well-fed, and down to the homes of the hungry. Empty shops with boarded fronts lined the street; here and there, the ruins left by a shell-fall.

Dogs trotted down the street and lazed in the shadows. There seemed to be more now than there had been even weeks before: creatures with more ribs, more teeth, more bones to their rangy flesh than any healthy animal ought to have. One, motley-furred and with torn ears, followed him for a time. It seemed less to be begging and more like a wolf, stalking its prey.

Denniston felt the sturdy shape of his revolver in the pocket of his fur coat. He had not gone out of doors without it; not since Istanbul. Still it was yet unused, but its weight had become more of a comfort than ever he'd first expected.

He was close to home now. He skipped over a gutter full of something that might have reeked had it not been frozen solid. The snow had slurried and grown treacherous underfoot. But he too had grown used to those perils. And what were they compared with the threat of shell, starvation, siege?

A voice barked out from the shade of a doorway.

Denniston's step faltered. His thoughts stopped, abrupt. He tensed in apprehension as he turned towards the sound. The words might have been Turkish, or else some cousin language. In either case, he couldn't understand them, but the tone made him tense.

A man's shape followed the sound, shuffling from the shadows, still speaking. His head was uncovered despite the cold; his hair was cut short, his face dark as leather, and lined at the eyes and mouth. When he spoke, Denniston saw he was all but toothless, gumming and spitting the words of his language as if every one tasted worse than the last. He was stooped, hunched. There was barely enough of him to cover his bones, let alone fill the billows of his homespun clothes. Yet he brandished a knotted dark wood stick.

Denniston raised his hands, backing away as the man advanced. 'I meant no offence,' he said, slow and clear as he could. The words felt useless, even as he spoke them. Why should this man know English? Even if he did, why should he have cause to listen?

Denniston's voice had shaken. The man quickened his step, still spitting words, angrier by the moment. He'd scented weakness, and closed in on it.

Denniston veered back, clumsy, arms still held out empty. He tried to retreat homewards, but was loathe to show the man his back.

In a moment, the man had leapt forward. A wild lunge; a flailing strike.

Denniston raised his arms, flinching, to cover his head and shoulders. Three blows rained down on his forearms, striking hard even through the padding of his coat. No way to reach for his pocket and the pistol without exposing his head to the flurry.

'Help!' Denniston found himself yelping.

Strike after strike after strike… He flailed at the man's stick, trying to fend it off. It knocked painful off one gloved hand, hitting bone.

Shouting voices rounded a corner. They broke out and over the wizened man's curses. Running footsteps, then the sound of a scrap and scuffle. The assault had stopped. Denniston lowered his defences.

Two uniformed men and one woman had fought the other man to the filthy ground. The men bent back his arms, striking at his hands and shoulders til he crumpled, dropping the stick. The woman crouched to pick it up, raising it over her head. As Denniston watched, she struck the poor man blow after blow on the legs and back. He curled into a ball, like a dried and dead spider – silent through the beating, giving out not even a whimper.

'What are you doing!?' Denniston shouted. 'Stop! Stop it, I said!'

The men went still, turning to look at Denniston with confusion in their faces. '*Effendi*?' They knew him, or else knew the band round his arm.

'Can't you see the poor devil's half-mad? Half-dead with hunger? Stop it! Stop right now!'

The woman scowled and dropped the stick. At her feet, the ragged man lay in a heap, shuddering but silent.

The soldiers perhaps had not understood Denniston's words, but they understood his tone. They bowed their heads, but their faces were still uncertain. '*Hekim effendi*,' they murmured. '*Afedersin... Afedersiniz...*'

'Enough of that,' Denniston sighed, moving to the injured man's side. 'He'll need help, same as any of the rest of you.' He crouched to haul the man to his feet, bruised arms and shoulders complaining as he lifted. 'Well? Don't just stand there, help me then!'

Murmuring still, the three bent to pick up the man, carrying him once more uphill. With them, Denniston went not homeward, but back to the hospital again.

What was it that Miss Guthrie had said of the Good Samaritan in her letter? Denniston wondered if this, at least, might have impressed her. What had he done now, if not turn the other cheek?

James

My dear Miss Guthrie,

Far from boring me, or making me bitter, I love to hear the small details of your life. In truth, every bit of comfort or company you enjoy is very heartening to hear about. It's good to remember there is some of both still left in the world, when I myself see so little of either recently. Not even the complaints of my hungry belly at hearing of your adventures in cookery can undermine the pleasure I take in them – indeed, I could stand to hear more, for reading of good food is still a comfort when you live in its absolute absence.

You ask often enough for more from me – more 'colour' – but I'm afraid I'm a poor writer, and have only dun and tan to paint with. No crystal-dripping ceilings to talk of here; I suppose the icicles hanging from roof lintels are the nearest I come to that.

Still, I tell you all the news I know, and all the trivia I can recall, and I hope that suffices to keep you satisfied. But I wonder, would you like to have a description of a day here as we spend it? One of those less eventful, less dramatic, but perhaps still of interest? Very well, I'll give you one, if you'll forgive a round unvarnished tale.

To begin with there is generally a good deal of frost in the morning. These days the air is fiercely cold and you hardly dare touch any piece of metal without gloves or first breathing on it a while, for fear of getting stuck. If I sit down to breakfast, I will always look on my spoon with a measure of distrust for this very reason!

But despite the cold, I will tend to go directly from my bed and outside, to break the ice that's formed on the water-trough, and to give myself a good brisk soaking. It's a discomfort that's become absolutely necessary to comfort in the long-run, I think, for you never saw such a place as this for fleas. The hospital being a hotbed for them, they're the bane of every ordinary day, and a persistent terror to us all.

Some time around sunrise we'll have breakfast. Our man Vashin cooks passably well, though I'm sure he cannot compare with you – however, the supplies he has to work with are sad indeed, so generally breakfast is a matter of barley gruel, and something black and steaming in a chipped mug: cocoa, coffee, beef tea, one ceases to see any difference after a while. A smoke after that is a touch of luxury that most of us still enjoy.

After that, off to the hospital for a morning of hard work. Overseeing the jarra bashis in dressing cases and helping with the harder ones; operating where necessary, which in the wake of the recently renewed fighting is far from uncommon; and otherwise looking after the comfort of all our charges. I say that this is our morning's work, but often it'll last till six in the afternoon or later. Then onto our private patients.

I have one colonel, Emin Bey, who was struck badly by a bullet – made in Germany, fired by Russians, on Turkish soil, and so making for a truly cosmopolitan war. He suffers awfully but stoically through the shattering of his arm. In Europe I'd have had it off in a moment, to ensure there'd be no more danger from the wound – he has no hope of using the arm again, so it serves no purpose, after all. But his religion forbids any mutilation of the body, for I think the idea is that, to enter Heaven, one must be not only holy in spirit, but also whole in body.

(Pinkerton mentions that Christians too once had such worries. For, after all, what sort of sorry affair would the Resurrection be if the Lord raised everyone up but found them in bits and pieces? He said that they quickly changed this doctrine once they realised how impractical and unfair it'd be, forbidding the downright unlucky their citizenship in the Kingdom of Heaven. That sort of faith – that bows to practical compassion, and values life as much

as what comes after – I can understand and hold by, but this blind faith is at once admirable and abhorrent to me. But forgive me, I think my humour's grown a bit black of late, and I find interest where I can.)

But speaking of practical compassion, Emin Bey has just recently bowed to mine, and agreed to let me operate. And I'm glad of this, for he seems a fair and well-minded officer – a thing rare in any army, I think – so it would be a shame not to save him if I can.

I also have a number of townspeople I tend to. One notable Ottoman official's wife suffers very badly from typhoid fever, yet at first he'd not let me speak directly to her, let alone lift her veils for an examination. In a pidgin of French and the patchwork Turkish I've developed through my time here, I convinced him of my professionalism and was allowed a very cursory examination. Perhaps an interview might be better, so that she herself can tell me her troubles – next time I shall grit my teeth and bring along Casson as translator, and see if I can speak with her more frankly. No doubt his Turkish would also be useful in making the matter clear to her husband: his wife may lose some face by the standards of his customs, but it is that, I think, or lose his wife entirely, and to any decent man that ought to be no choice at all.

But you see, though we're on the side of the Turks, their customs are as often among our foes as Russians, fleas, disease, and cold. We do what we can, though, with what we're given.

Dinner is nearly invariably soup, made from a conglomeration of whatever we can get. About once a week Vashin might secure for us – from some market connection or other – a cut of greasy mutton. Though at home I'd scarce feed such meat to dogs, here we've all come to view it as a delicacy, and our mouths water at the thought. Otherwise, there is an ubiquitous kind of black bread, tough and dry, with a strong tendency to sourness. Tea or cocoa follows, with all of us huddled round the little stove in our lodgings, as we smoke pipes or cigarettes. When we talk it is mostly about things practical and immediately relevant: how might we get the most heat out of the least possible fuel, for instance?

We vary our evenings by writing or reading our letters. I confess, I often read yours back to myself, and find insight or interest I had previously missed each time. Such is the way, I fancy, with reading back Shakespeare, or any other good book, and I have so little reading material besides what you have sent me.

Sometimes there is also a tot of grog before bed. As you've said, we take our luxury where we can, often while chuckling at the minor depravities this place has sunk us into. What, we ask, would teetotallers say? We need only ask Featherston for the answer, for he numbers among them, and so not among ours as we nurse our grog. Even so, none of us abstains from the conversations that result. The grog warms us and seems to make us think of home, so we fall into talk of what we remember, and what we'd like to do when we get back there.

Casson is engaged to be married and, we hope, shall be, once he returns to England. Walker, like myself, hopes that his experiences in Erzurum might grant him enough of a name to fund a formal doctorate. Kincaid is married, and with a second child on the way.

Pinkerton has a comfortable retirement awaiting him, but said he would not be comfortable in it if he had not done some work like this beforehand – he is a man of faith, much like yours I think, and very devoted to the doing of good deeds. A fine fellow, and one whose companionship I find gratifying and educational, for he is one who talks of what he knows, not so that you might know that he knows it, but rather because he has such passion and wisdom in him that it overflows. He does not subject you to his expositions; rather, he shares of himself, which I fancy is the whole point of this venture, to his mind.

But after all that it's to bed with us – all but those still at the hospital, minding the night-time shift. Usually I sleep very soundly, not for great comfort, but rather for sheer exhaustion. And then, the next day, if I am fortunate, the cycle will begin anew – it's in upsets to it, or events of note, that my chiefest worries are to be found.

Meanwhile I am yours

Very sincerely,

James Denniston

Agnes

Dear Doctor Denniston,

I can scarcely imagine how it must be to find oneself in such a sorry situation regarding food; less still, to know that it will likely worsen before it improves. However, I'm glad to hear that reading of good food, and of my own adventures in the kitchen, comforts you more than it pains you.

I have been making a good deal of progress in these matters, you will be happy to know. At first this might have been the legacy of that young and radical woman Miss Evelyn Carmichael – she who would sooner have all in her household know the baking of bread, rather than go hungry in waiting for a servant to make it or buy it – but I find I have an acceptable head for it in and of myself, and my hand is becoming well turned to the work as well.

I have had much success with glazed buns, full of ginger and candied peel, and also with a sticky brown sugar cake crowned with patterned slices of softened apple. Cakes and breads for the most part so far, but I have also impressed upon our old cook in Manchester to teach me the makings of roasted meats, boiled poultry, hare and such like, and on my insistence we make good progress and some very fine feasts into the bargain. Certainly, my mother and father have no complaints now; any suggestion they might have made as to the propriety of a lady spending her time elbow-deep in dough has since disappeared thanks to the fruits of my labours. I fancy that their displeasure, however, might have proved more persistent had I turned out to have no talent for this sort of work.

Currently I am considering whether I might buy myself a book on the subject, so that I might learn on my own initiative. Relying on our cook has carried me so far – and of course she was very glad to help me, as it meant I would also be helping her, and sharing her work – but I have always regarded self-education highly, and as a means of gathering wisdom or skill, there is none that I enjoy more. So, a book, I think.

My father, indeed, has quite come round to this new interest of mine. He supposes that, between Godliness and artfulness, I am becoming quite the perfect figure of what a woman ought to be. If Miss Evelyn Carmichael was the start of this undertaking, she shall not be the end; were I to follow her example entirely, I fancy I would abandon this line of education immediately for sheer bloody-minded objection to a man's approving of it.

It has made me wonder, however: being that I have grown to value your opinion, in certain areas, quite highly, I am curious as to whether you have some established idea on the subject. What, to your mind, would make up the ideal traits in a woman? I trust you are a good judge of many things, if not all, and I look forward to having your answer.

Until I hear from you again

Sincerely yours,

Miss Agnes Guthrie

It was unconventional for surgery to be undertaken in a private home, rather than in theatre. Emin Bey, however, had insisted. If this was the point on which they would compromise – the price they paid for the colonel's permission to operate at all – then, Denniston reasoned, compromise they would have to.

A time had been arranged, and on that Wednesday afternoon, Denniston and Kincaid arrived at the townhouse where Emin Bey was quartered. In their hands they carried cases and bags for the tools they would need. On his shoulder, rolled up, Kincaid carried a clean sheet; if Emin Bey insisted this would be done in his quarters, at least they could leave those quarters unmarred by the undertaking.

It all took on the air of ritual. This was comforting to Denniston, but more importantly, comforting to Emin Bey. It was part of Denniston's common practice now, to treat any medical procedure as a personal engagement. And the colonel and he had, over several such visits as this, become something like friends.

The arrangement began like any of the other visits. Denniston and Emin Bey sat easy around the colonel's low table, on cushions, and drank silt-thick sweet black coffee. Denniston had had enough practice at drinking it now that he was beginning to almost like it this way – at least enough not to miss taking it with milk.

Kincaid seemed uneasy, however. He was a good man to work with in matters of surgery: strong but gentle, and with a soothing voice. But perhaps he had expected surgery and nothing more besides. This preamble left him uncertain – nervous. And when his nerves were up, Kincaid overspoke:

'If he's coming, you know – Mukhtar Pasha – I suppose he'll be heading up a column of half-dead men. Walking wounded.' Kincaid drained another cup of coffee. 'We'll be stuffed then. Working like dogs, dawn til dusk til dawn. We've not got enough beds for all our cases as it stands now. How'll we fit them all, is what I want to know?'

He knew only English, however, and the few words of Turkish that all the doctors had mastered. In truth, Denniston was thankful Emin Bey wouldn't get the truth of Kincaid's words. Instead, Denniston translated, mellowing what was said as he went.

'My colleague is concerned about the wounded Mukhtar Pasha will bring,' Denniston said in French. 'Particularly if they have to fight a battle to get through to Erzurum. Will they?'

'Kars is to the east,' said Emin Bey. 'So are the Russians. The south and north as well. I think there will either be a battle, or Mukhtar Pasha will have to do something very clever to slip free of one.'

'My colleague,' said Denniston, 'is uncertain we'll have enough space for the men that come with Mukhtar Pasha – enough beds, or supplies.'

'With any luck they will have been able to bring some of their own. This was a tactical retreat, not a complete rout. I trust the *pasha* won't have left his orta's ambulance supplies behind in a panic.' Emin Bey gave a small snort of laughter. It seemed more nervous than earnest, however. 'But perhaps there are more buildings that could be requisitioned; more beds I could muster up from somewhere. If I'm able to help you, I shall...'

'Thank you,' said Denniston. 'So far as I see it, it's only a matter of doing the best we can. I'm confident that will be enough. But I shall bear your promise in mind.' He was glad that they would be saving Emin Bey's life then – or preserving it for a time longer. Not only for his own sake, or for their friendship, but for how useful his friendship might be. Denniston turned, then, to Kincaid, and changed once more into English. 'We'll give what extra effort we can. Clear whatever cases can be cleared. We may be able to get some help from Emin Bey down the line, but that'll come all to nothing if we're not ready to take advantage.'

'That could take days,' said Kincaid. 'We'll be run off our feet...'

'Better a little of that now then, than more than we can handle later. I fancy we'll work longer hours, nights, whatever we can. I certainly shall. Anyone who wants to join me, join me.'

Kincaid only nodded, grimly.

They traded coffee for brandy. Emin Bey had set aside a bottle.

'The real stuff,' he explained, as the cork squeaked from its neck. 'Charentais, reserve, aged in Limousin oak…' He passed the bottle under his nose, sniffed, and sighed happily, then poured three glasses.

The doctors took only small polite sips. It seemed at least to settle Kincaid's nerves, though for Denniston it left only a bitterness in his mouth that persisted as they continued, alongside notes of hazelnuts and orange peel.

Emin Bey drank more as the doctors cleared a table, laid down the sheet, and cleaned their instruments. The colonel had gone pale and silent, Denniston observed. His teeth were gritted tight. They granted him a nip of ether, to add to the haze of brandy.

As they lay him down on the table and opened his shirt on one side, removing the dressings on his wound, Denniston wondered: had Emin Bey insisted this operation be done in private for comfort? Or had it been to save his men from seeing him pale, scared, beginning to shake?

That night Denniston returned home late. He had been to the hospital, straight from tending to Emin Bey, and worked there til long after nightfall. His words in the face of Mukhtar Pasha's arrival had not been bluster; he intended to act on them, and see them through, to the letter. It had left him bone-tired, however.

He sat up in a corner of the room the doctors shared. His bedding was beneath him, and a tallow candle burned beside – once he had not been able to stand the reek of tallow, but in recent weeks he'd grown used to it. But more than just the place where he bedded down each night, he had made this corner his own, in what small ways he could.

The walls of the house's ground floor were all pasted up still, with news pages, and the gaudy wrappers of tobacco pouches, the labels of coffee or tea tins. But in this corner, the decoration was thicker. An elephant reared on its hind-legs beside Denniston's head. By his left elbow was a Japanese man, ankle to throat in tattoos that overlapped like foliage in a thicket.

His battered and wartorn suitcase served as a kind of nightstand. On it sat the Bible and Psalter that Agnes had sent. His two thin medical texts sat on top, more thoroughly thumbed, more recently consulted.

He wished he'd owned more books to bring. He'd always found Shakespeare clever and comforting. His brother had always wondered how he could read it as he did – to him it was always so opaque, so foreign. But

Denniston had told him, even as he was almost still a child, that it wasn't so much a matter of trying to translate as if it were a foreign tongue that could be altered directly into plain sense. The strangeness in the poetry and the prose was part of what Denniston enjoyed. He would let it wash over him, knowing that simplification would neuter most of what made it beautiful. And when, sometimes, a phrase stood out, that made clear and perfect sense, it would be all the more special, and stick in his mind, like a burr caught on a coat-sleeve.

But all he had brought with him from Shakespeare was the handful of lines that had stuck in such a way. Things being what they are, the most part of his reading material comprised the bundle of letters he had in a biscuit tin, kept beneath his pillow – all from Agnes, and still none from home. His mother, he supposed, had not accepted his apology. He wondered if she ever would.

Denniston had intended to write that night, and respond to Agnes' most recent letter. Instead he found himself reading it, only reading it, over and over, too tired to do much more. It was not because any element of it gave him particular pleasure – not like those phrases from Shakespeare, though some parts of her letters came close – but rather the process itself was a comfort. He clung to it, in these uncertain times, like a castaway clings on the open ocean, to the driftwood that keeps him afloat.

Days passed in a sleepwalk of activity before he found the time and the energy, both together, to respond. And then it was with trepidation at what Agnes had asked him. What would be the traits he would look up to most in a lady? It would not be possible, in his reply, to be both honest and entirely proper, when the traits he most admired were found all together in her.

James

My dear Miss Guthrie,
You ask what I respect in the character of a lady, but you know that I'd hardly judge myself any kind of expect in the matter. Of late, after all, I've met so few. Yet, thanks to the education you've given me, I think I'm just expert enough in this vein to know I'm neither brave nor stupid enough to tell any lady what I think she ought to be.

But as you ask, and I trust you are too fair a person to set up such a question as a trap, I fancy we are talking not of what 'should be' but what 'ideally, might'. Moreover, we are writing in confidence. Even so, let me say first, that I'd forswear instantly anything I say that might cause offence, if you'd only give me the chance to do so. I hope I shall not have to, but this is tender ground: telling anyone how to perfect themselves can so often be a way of tacitly telling them where they are lacking. And that is not at all my intention, with you – of this I want you to be assured.

Simple to say, my ideal in a lady would have in abundance the traits where I fall short. With all you've said of your progress in the arts, and with the paucity of my current way of living, the first thing I can think of now is that she might cook well. I mean so that I might learn from her, and we might share the work of it. Or perhaps it's only my hunger makes me say as much – it feels such a long time since I had anything besides black bread and mutton.

I think also she might have an ear towards music – perhaps even a skill for it – and so make up for my untrained senses and lack of well trained taste. I like music well enough, but know little more than to ask if you might know this song, or that, and go only by the titles, for I cannot sing them back to you. There is one that Kincaid sometimes sings, for instance, that is sadder and sweeter than most of his more regular airs, and I find it makes me wish for home more than almost anything else. But in this instance I don't know even a title to go by…

If she could dance, I wish she might teach me. If she was well-read and versed in languages, I would be proud if even a smudge of her brilliance wore off onto me. If she was pious, perhaps it might make me a better Christian, or at least a better man…

But I'm suddenly aware that all this sounds very selfish: wishing for a lady better than me, so that I might live up to her, or else be made better by her. It only serves to confirm that what we speak of is fantasy after all, for I fancy such a woman would never stoop to have me in the first place.

For the time being I will only say, Miss Guthrie, that it occurs to me now have very sufficient you are in all the traits and more besides. I hope that you will let me say so?

Until I hear from you again
I am yours very sincerely,
James Denniston

Chapter 15

The bandages were heavy, caked and filthy, round his head. The splint on his arm had gotten damp – water maybe, or something oozing from the wound it braced – and then in the night the whole dressing had frozen. At first the flesh felt blazing-cold, then swollen, stinging, heavy. After the heaviness, there was nothing. From elbow to wrist, Murad's arm was numb – something seen more than felt.

That morning he'd tried to remove the dressing, but found the fingers on his other hand were too clumsy with cold to get a good grip. For a moment Murad had considered his bayonet: he could use that to peel it away. But the arm was numb, after all. How would he feel if he made a mess of it? Pierced the skin and started to cut at himself, not cut himself free from the frozen wrapping? Best not to, he decided.

It was in God's hands now. The rest of the day was in the hands of Mukhtar Pasha. It seemed he'd passed from the hands of one to the other and back again, over and over, since June. Kizil-Tepe, Kars, and then the retreat from Kars. Perhaps he ought to be thankful that his unit had been chosen to run rather than hold with Hami Pasha. But closing in on Erzurum now, it felt vain and stupid to hope for anything much. Survival maybe? But chances were slim, and his arm was frozen, and his rifle had been taken from him because he could not use it with just one arm, and no man in his column seemed much better off. So hoping for survival was foolish. Murad would hate to arrive in the Garden disappointed.

Ahead, the horizon was torn and and stirred up. They had marched this way – the whole division – travelling fast to Kars to relieve it. They'd failed at Kars, come back perhaps to fail at Erzurum, and to Murad's eyes the plain around the city now looked nothing like it had before. Black and brown tents blistered all round this side of the city, like mushrooms after rain. Smoke rose up in creepers and pillars. Erzurum rose up dark and blasted from a mess of trenches and shattered outskirts, and the Russians formed a crescent around it.

The *pasha* had split his forces. Some went south, far enough off as to be below the horizon, out of view of any but Russian outriders. They were the lucky ones. Lucky from the start, because they still had their health, their bodies were whole. They had the grenadiers, the Kurdish cavalry, the bashibazouks that had not deserted when they realised that an army in retreat won no loot. In the column with Murad, every man looked alike, and every man looked different. Weapons taken; given to those who could still fight. Limbs taken by battle, spirits broken by battle, bodies cold as the grave already from the forced march back from Kars.

Their officers barely tried to keep them in marching order as they moved across the plain. They straggled, stained with blood, some on crutches and hobbling behind, now the carts that carried them had been given to the first column. They moved wide, in shallow ranks, covering their side of the landscape. A 'screening force' – that was the word used among the officers. 'Suicide,' was the one the soldiers used. 'Suicide' or 'sacrifice.'

And yet Murad was calm. And yet he couldn't think why. Everything seemed inevitable now. Everything seemed like it always had been.

Somewhere in the line there were gunshots now. Screaming echoed along their loose formation, turning to talk, and murmuring, and rumours.

'Outriders,' a soldier muttered, a few men down. A man with bandages thick beneath his cap. 'Testing us at the edges. Hope our boys give 'em hell for it.'

'Hell…' another said. 'That's where we're all headed, idiot.'

'And after, Heaven…'

A boy stumbled, a few men to Murad's left, and lost his stomach, vomiting into the snow.

Still, Murad was calm. Every soul shall taste of death – wasn't that what the imam had said, in his town? Every soul shall taste of death, and each at his appointed time.

A trumpet sounded out across the plain. An officer was speak through a brass cone.

'Brothers! Among us are men from many nations, but we march and we fight on this day – this same day – together, and under the same flag. Among us are men of many faiths and—…' The voice cracked.

The trumpet sounded again. Others picked up its note.

'Brothers..? I'm going to say a prayer. I'll pray for us all, and ask you do the same. Pray now, all of you – each in your own tongue, and to your own God, but pray, brothers…'

A shout followed, all through the line. Some men called on God. Most were only shouting.

They began to run, not for the city, but straight for the Russian line. Their tents, their trenches, their long-guns.

'Hell? Hell!' came a voice, between sounds like distant thunder. Shells. Murad knew that by now. For some, memory made battle worse. But Murad had gone numb to that as well. 'Hell! If that's where we're headed, let's drag them with us! Boys, brothers, to hell!'

Murad ran. His legs felt light. He had in his hand a sword-bayonet. He didn't mind his arm so much now, when there was so much else to feel. He didn't much mind the bandages over his eye, or the holes in his right boot, or how they let the snow in. There were footfalls all around him. There was a storm, brewing around him. There was shouting, a charge, no hope but this.

Then the ground burst open ahead of him. As if through gauze, Murad saw a man's neck punched inward, and the back of his head cave out. Red mist hung on the air a moment, and then was gone.

A pit had been dug suddenly. It didn't make sense, flat ground one second, and now a pit ahead of him. And it was filled with meat and smoke, and red-black snakes, slick and awful. A man screamed silently in it, face pale in all the red darkness.

Hell. Was that it? Hell opening up in front of him?

Murad's calm had melted. Beneath it, a writhing fear.

Chapter 16

It wasn't a battle but a massacre. Denniston had seen none of the fighting - he had too much work to watch from the hilltop, as some others had - but he'd since seen nothing but its aftermath, and heard of nothing else.

There were hundreds more crammed into the hospital than days ago. Paths a foot wide led between wounded men, dying men, propped against each other, shoulder to shoulder. There was no room for stretchers or gurneys, and more work than Denniston could bear to think of, except one case at a time. As to what could really be done for most of them - the dying - the answer lay mostly in comfort. In the Stafford House Committee hospital, there was none of that left to give.

These were the soldiers who had been fortunate; saved by Mukhtar Pasha's brutal gambit. Depending on who was telling the tale, it was either a tactical masterstroke, or a crime against mercy and one's fellow man. The *pasha* had played those already sick and wounded from Kars and the retreat as his pawns. He sent them direct into the Russian lines, driving them towards the encampment of tents and trenches and stocked up supplies. The Russian command had panicked, focusing almost all its strength on crushing this desperate assault. They had fought and died like rats in a barrel, fighting mad to get out, while the healthy half of Mukhtar Pasha's force had come from the south, surging into the city, resisted only by scouts and stray artillery.

No doubt the officers yet living were celebrating the blow this had dealt to the Russians, and at the cost of nothing that was not already good as lost. No doubt the soldiers yet living, and garrisoned now in Erzurum's citadel, were telling tales and singing the praises of their brothers, who had fought and given the last of their strength to shore up poor faltering Erzurum. But Denniston didn't believe any among them would have changed places with those who'd charged and died on the plain - not for any amount of glory or glorious death.

As a boy, he might have admired them, or praised Mukhtar Pasha's pragmatism. Now he was sickened and enraged, but fast becoming too inured to these facts of war to feel anything for the bigger picture. He saved the whole of his heart for his patients. Do the best you can for the living, he told himself; limit suffering, sustain survival. That was all he could do, and all the rest was silence.

He ministered to a case of frostbite. The man was unconscious, delirious from pain and sickness. He was young – younger even than Denniston – such that he would have called him a boy, if it weren't for the things he'd endured. The toes on both his feet were black and white with cold. The frost would take them off, and less cleanly, less safely, if Denniston did not first. Ordinarily, he'd give the patient a choice, as he had given Emin Bey. But this patient was past words, as so many others were. And this choice was no choice at all.

Denniston set to work, all clean instruments and set stiff jaw. That was the look they'd all worn, since the first of Mukhtar Pasha's men arrived. The doctors' faces had turned pale as they tried not show they were close to panic. For days they'd barely slept – scarce done anything but work between these walls – and still there was more work to be done, far than they had prepared for.

Outside they were burying the dead. The hack and thud of mattock and pick struck rhythmic out through the air, reaching Dennniston through the hospital windows and sounding dully through the walls.

Kincaid and Featherston worked with a team of *jarra bashi*s and soldiers to crack the tiles of the courtyard and get at the ground beneath. The tiles had been pretty once, in locked patterns of leaves and opening flowers, blue and white and green. Since then, hundreds on hundreds of boots and what must have been thousands of men had come and gone over them, tramping mud, scuffing the faces of the flowers. Breaking them was no great loss now, compared with the necessity to be rid of the corpses – so many now that the hospital seemed more a factory for producing them than a place given over to keeping the living alive.

For all that Mukhtar Pasha's arrival was meant to have swelled Erzurum's strength, it seemed to have done far more to swell the ground beneath it. The Muslim cemetery was already dangerously full, bulging with mass graves that rose like kurgans from the stones around them. Impromptu graveyards sprung up around the city, in overturned gardens and dirt-paved streets.

Here in the courtyard they could not dig deep; the ground was too hard from the chill. Beneath the snow and the tiles, it was frozen into black iron, and picks seemed only to dent it. You could sweat for hours and make only the barest impression – enough perhaps for three men, lain awkwardly, each on top of the other. There was no dignity in death here. Perhaps there was no dignity in death at all.

Those waiting to be buried lay stacked up like logs beside the broken tiles. Cremation seemed logical, but even if the Muslims' faith would allow it, they had no fuel to keep both pyres and the stoves in the hospital burning. In warmer times, Denniston would have worried at the contamination the piled corpses could spread, into the nearby hospital, urging other living patients to join them. But in the cold, the world and the corpses all but froze solid. Left over night, the snow covered them til they were almost easy to forget. The reek of decay was muted and meek. And yet dogs howled in the nights, boasting of their full bellies. In a city of shallow and open graves, the feral dogs of the city feasted, while Erzurum itself began to starve.

At least winter had killed the last of the flies.

Agnes

My Dear Doctor Denniston,

There are countless books of conduct that will do for telling a young woman what she must or must not do, and I think I may even have read one or two among them. And surely I recall some rule underscoring the impropriety of a young woman writing anyone a letter from her sickbed or convalescent chamber.

However, being that you, I'm sure, are well-used to far worse – and being that I am already exchanging letters with a young gentleman without his having first sought my father's express and explicit permission – what is one more regulation overlooked between us? It does not do to think how many I have passed over already.

I've taken ill with some form of pox. Our own doctor says it's little enough to worry about, though more usual in children than in adults. His only recommended treatment is bedrest and isolation, and in truth his prescription is my only complaint in the matter. Could this malady not have chosen a more considerate time of year to strike than this, when the social calendar is thick and full as it might ever be, Advent being on its way?

I'll not bore you with talk of my symptoms; I imagine that you would rather hear of anything besides more sickness and medicine. Suffice to say they are much like a flue, except with the addition of a few more unsightly tells that – quietly and chiding myself somewhat for vanity – would most likely prevent me from wanting to go out and face company again, even if the option were open to me.

So I think you will understand when I say that I'm quite miserable, quite lonely at present in my quarantine. Yet, as ever, I can turn to you and feel at least the beginnings of a returning smile. Indeed, perhaps there is also a small frisson of childish glee in writing in contravention of decorum, and that may be part of the charm I feel at work on me even now. It is good to exchange words with someone, even from so far away, who thinks me so 'sufficient' – or even surpassingly sufficient – in spite of my looking currently like a badly plucked bird.

I only worry that, being as I am confined to my own company for how catching my condition can be, this pox will find some way to saturate the paper on which I write, and so add another malady to the menagerie of them you keep at the hospital in Erzurum. Worse, I fear it might prove infectious to you too! Call it a foolish woman's worry if you will – and I know that, at least in any voiced manner, you will not, which is why I invite you to do so in the first instance – but remembered that I have had the benefits of an education quite different from your own, and what I know of matters medical comes almost solely from you, and your letters. So, the concern seems a real one to me.

Confined to my bed, I have at least had a chance – or rather, a total paucity of other options – to give a really good reading to the Shakespeare you gave to me. Perhaps if I am laid low for long enough, I shall even be forced to begin On The Origin Of Species!

Until I hear from you again

Sincerely yours,

Miss Agnes Guthrie

Denniston lost track of the times he'd wash his hands each day, til the carbolic left them stiff and dry and smooth as paper. But his body suffered, growing skinny, going otherwise unwashed. His beard grew and his eyes hollowed.

Like carbolic, or like the razor scraping away stubble, recent days had left him raw. Everything seemed to affect him more, perhaps from lack of sleep, or overwork, or from simple saturation of experience. He could scarce lose a patient without feeling a sob start in his throat, thick and shameful. Not the sickness of the mind that had overcome him before, but rather a human attachment, and a feeling of personal loss as it was severed.

But the deliveries of Zohrab's diplomatic courier always lifted his spirits. If his fragility made loss a wrenching thing, it turned happiness into joy, and joy into short-lived ecstasy.

Now he smoked beside the stove in their lodgings, wearing his coat despite the fire's feeble warmth. The emotions he felt swung between both poles.

At first an aching fear. Agnes was ill. Erzurum and the hospital had taken enough from him already. If her condition was serious, it would be more than he could bear, trusting her whole health to the hands of another doctor, and one he didn't know.

But the fear became a worry, and grew milder as he read.

Chickenpox or the like, he thought. That was all. By the time she began to fret over whether the letters itself might transmit the disease, Denniston had begun to chuckle. The sound reached deep into him as Pinkerton looked up from the room's far side, where he sat, reading and smoking his pipe, raising one eyebrow. Denniston started to laugh, loud and wracking, til every sound came almost like a sob.

December 1877

Chapter 17

Consul Zohrab was leaving Erzurum under a diplomat's white flag. The courtyard had been shovelled clean of snow but already was filling with trunks, cases, round pinewood boxes. Most leaving with him, hauled out by soldiers and servants, but some yet were arriving by the hour.

His wife oversaw the removal, the loading of the carts. She stood in grey skirts, grey shawl, bodice, gloves, dove-coloured amidst the ashen snow.

Zohrab himself stood under the Western styled portico of the big house that had served as consulate. His clothes were neat as ever but dark, a white tie round his neck and white kerchief glinting from a breast pocket.

Boots tidemarked with snow, Casson and Denniston came into the courtyard, trudging white into the black frozen dirt. They came in silence, as they often did when forced into situations where they could not talk of work. An awkwardness still hung between them, as it had since arrival in Erzurum.

Denniston looked about the courtyard, at the furniture and gathering carts. Here were the first signs, he thought; the first rats fleeing the sinking ship. He had known this day would come, somewhere inside his imaginings, but it made it no easier to think what it might mean to lose the consul's courier.

Zohrab beckoned them over with a solemn wave. 'Gentlemen,' he nodded. 'When you remember our friendship, I shan't have you remember me as remiss. I'm glad we have this chance to say our goodbyes.'

'It's been a pleasure, sir,' said Casson, extending a hand to meet Zohrab's in a vigorous handshake, though both men's gloves made it clumsy.

'Quite the same to you, doctor. Quite the same to you both.'

Casson was gaunt now, as they all were; dark round the eyes, with patches of scraggy beard grown through round his once well groomed moustache. Yet he somehow retained an air of grace, effortlessly, in all his dealings – or rather, almost all, for Denniston could not put from his mind that he'd seen so collected and gracious a man lose his patience, his temper, and half his mind once.

Still, next to him, in his coat of mismatched pelts, with his haphazard tenacious growth of stubble and thin persistent cough, Denniston felt every bit the bandit and the bear. The niceties required for situations like this grew harder to call up with each passing day. All his emotional labour and more, he spent on his patients. The rest seemed increasingly false and needless by comparison. Perhaps it showed in his face: a flatness, or a twist of distaste.

'It wasn't you asked to meet us then?' Denniston said. 'You'd not call us all the way uphill, from work, just for that.'

Zohrab's face stiffened briefly. His eyes flashed hard as Denniston broke decorum. Then the smile returned, much like Casson's: a smile that is a kind of mask and also a kind of shield. It was a gesture Denniston had never mastered.

'Indeed,' Zohrab acknowledged. 'The summons came not from me, but my successor – from the man who's to live here now.'

'Not a new consul?' said Casson.

'Some captain, then. An officer,' said Denniston. 'One of Mukhtar Pasha's men?'

'Pushing you from office…' Casson scoffed. 'I wonder that anyone stands for it!'

Zohrab held out both palms, placating the doctors. 'You misunderstand me, truly, it's nothing so coarse as all that. My departure is my choice. I merely offered up my lodgings to someone who might continue to make good use of them.'

His choice, Denniston thought; forced by none but the Russians beyond the walls.

'There is no place for a diplomat during a siege, after all,' Zohrab continued. 'One might say that in war is to be found the chiefest failure of my profession. And in the making of peace once more? Well, that is my victory from the ashes. But for the time being, I think a siege is what we shall have on our hands very shortly. Once the Russian lines close and the city and the city is truly surrounded, why, I'd be the same as any other man within these walls – only somewhat less useful! Cut off from communications, and from the rest of the world? My work would cease entirely.'

'We each have our talents, and our tasks,' said Casson. 'We use them as best we can, where best we can. Am I correct?'

Denniston nodded, held silent a moment, then began: 'Who's this new man then? The one who's to live here now.'

'I'll admit, I don't know him by name. A Turkish official, I think, from Istanbul, but he's come with the *pasha* – or to help the *pasha* at any rate – and with a retinue of his own. He's brought doctors, I think. Finally, some reinforcements that benefit you, yes? At any rate, it seems he has an interest in such matters – and in your work… I suppose that's why he's asked to see you.'

'That bodes very well,' smiled Casson.

'Or very poorly…' Denniston said.

'We ought to make haste and see which then. Better not to keep this official waiting. He's in your study?'

'My former study,' Zohrab said.

Casson shook his hand once more and the doctors left along the portico.

'Gentlemen?' Zohrab's voice echoed along behind them. 'Doctors, one more thing! I have safe passage – I'm sure you can imagine – likely I'm the last who'll have it away from these walls in a long while. Two days, boys – you've two days to decide! None would think the less of you! If any among you should wish to accompany me, no man alive would think the less!'

His voice followed them through the consulate's doors, and then was cut off as they closed.

'Boys,' sniffed Denniston, incredulous. 'Is that what we are now? Boys playing a game, flocked up and sent home once the fun's over.'

'He's only doing us a favour,' Casson replied. 'Or trying to. Inviting us to get out while the going remains good, and before the real work begins. Can you blame him?'

'I could blame myself if I accepted. Before, we were a great help. We're soon to be a dire necessity, once the city seals up, begins to starve. Sanitation's bad enough already, but in a siege it'll be the first thing to go, and who knows what epidemics will start up in its absence.'

'And the cold… I tell you, the prices I've already seen asked for fuel…'

'A winter-long siege,' said Denniston.

'Can't say it sounds well.'

Inside was all shadows and the scent of new-flown dust. It would be all but a sin to light candles or lamps now in daylight hours, with supplies soon to be so scarce. Footsteps moved in unseen rooms overhead and all around, heavy booted, dragging and repositioning. It was a ghost of the warm fine-furnished house they'd come to, for a formal dinner in the midst of an encircled city.

Denniston and Casson moved through the atrium, past shrouded objects, bleached shapes on the walls where pictures had hung. Mounting the stairs they came onto a landing: another European touch to the building that had been a British consulate. They found their way to the study door in the near-dark and knocked.

A moment passed. Dust danced in the light from the high small windows. For a moment, Denniston's mind wandered back to the *seraskeriat* in Istanbul; then to the room where he'd waited to see Barrington-Kennet, only to find himself invited to dinner before he would be invited to the front. There was something familiar in this pause and this place.

'Come in.'

The study was a deal more spartan than Denniston remembered, as they entered. The lean sadness of an almost-empty bookcase stood to one side.

The bleak colour of the limewashed walls, and the semi-circular window gave the whole space a cold feeling. The dust moved like snow.

'You'll excuse my hospitality, sirs, not to mention the state of this place. It's between two owners, you understand, and each with quite different tastes. Nonetheless, Denniston *hekim*, welcome.' There was a familiar smile in that voice. 'Though I believe you asked that I call you James?'

Behind the low bare desk, silhouetted against the cool light from the window, stood Aydin Vefyk Pashazada: the 'interpreter' from the *seraskeriat*; the man who had recommended him to the Stafford House Committee, what seemed so long ago. He was dressed not quite in Ottoman blue and crimson, but in darkenings and deepenings of those colours. As before his attire was not quite a uniform, nor quite the suit of a civilian; not quite European or Oriental, but borrowing from and blending the two into something chameleonic. For all he complained of it, the state of the office suited him, with his understated clothes, his bare and neat accent, his trim dark beard and olive hands, folded careful on the desk in front of him.

Strange, Denniston thought, how it seemed so unsurprising. He had almost known it would happen this way, standing outside on the landing – as if it had happened already.

Aydin Vefyk gestured elegantly. 'I'd be pleased if you'd both sit.'

Almost on command, the doctors sat in two low waiting chairs, before the desk. Through the window behind it, cold sun slanted onto their faces.

'Aydin,' Deniston acknowledged, feeling shabbier than ever in the official's bone-bare study, and confronted with his immaculate dress, his immaculate manner. 'You don't have the look of a man who's just journeyed through one hell and landed right in another.'

'We all have our rituals, James. Things we do to keep sight of our true selves. You write letters, shave…though not so recently it seems. For my part? I keep order.'

'I'm to take it that you two are acquainted then,' Casson cut in.

'We met in Istanbul, yes,' said Aydin Vefyk.

'I have this man to thank for sending me here,' Denniston said. 'He saved me from myself when I'd hoped to go to Kars.'

Casson's eyebrows rose, as disbelief gave way to acceptance. 'I owe you my share of gratitude then, sir. Doctor Denniston is…an effective colleague. We're glad of him.'

Denniston's cheeks burnt hot beneath the itch of his beard. It was the first praise Casson had ever given him, more striking still for its stumbling understatement.

'Aydin Vefyk Pashazada,' Denniston began, hurrying to fill what might so easily have become a stunned silence. 'Let me introduce Doctor Thomas Casson.'

'A pleasure, sirs, to meet one of you, and see the other again,' said Aydin Vefyk, quickly. 'But you'll excuse me if I curtail the niceties and cut to the heart of the matter. Those are the sort of times we find ourselves in, I'm afraid. I have asked you here to speak to you not as gentlemen, or friends, but as professionals: the English *hekims* talked about among the soldiery and their superiors both. Being in the business of listening to such talk, I've heard a good deal about your work. It's on that I wish to speak to you.

'I fear my lines of intelligence might stay open only a while longer beyond these walls, and after that I shall have to consign myself to being as God to a much smaller world… But for now, I still know the movements of our enemy. Heimann has thinned his force from a flanking one to a true encirclement, so we have on our hands a siege. And in a city besieged, your enemies multiply – soldiers and artillery, yes, but famine, disease, and strife from within…'

'We've been duelling with those enemies since our arrival, sir,' said Casson with a confident smile. 'We're well acquainted by now.'

Vefyk was not smiling. 'Your confidence is heartening,' he said, coldly, 'but things will get worse, of that I can assure you. These aren't foes we can beat; only hold back as best we can, and pray the Russians are worse affected. For the soldiery, this war will become a waiting game. For you, the work is only just beginning.'

'You'll forgive me for asking after Istanbul,' ventured Denniston, 'but is this work to be for the soldiery? Or for their superiors, officials, and secretaries?'

'Why, for every man and woman in this city, of course. For the good of the empire, the service of His Imperial Majesty the Sultan. Certainly, illness does not distinguish between civilian and soldier, *nefer* or officer. I imagine you'll treat them all alike. But I'm under no illusions, James. Whether or not we can hold Erzurum, if this war is to be won beyond the limits of this battle, it cannot be done without fighting men. It cannot be done if the empire has no red blood yet in her veins. That means the many, not the few. Do you take my meaning?'

If the *pasha*s are stubborn old goats, that's the man who keeps them from the cabbage patch – those had been Barrington-Kennet's words, when asked about Aydin Vefyk Pashazada. Denniston recalled them well, and saw that they held true. There was relief in that, and comfort. He grinned, showing teeth stark white through his brown beard.

'I take your meaning,' he said.

'You'll have assistance,' Vefyk continued, more warmly now. 'I've seen to that. It's come to my attention that you've been left understaffed.' He said the word as cordially; as if he were not talking about Guppie, and the death of a friend, but as simple an inconvenience as finding one has packed for a picnic and failed to make enough sandwiches. 'I've brought relief.'

'New doctors?' said Casson.

'Westerners, like yourselves mostly. They will report to the hospital in die course. As will you, I think; I've taken up enough of your time already, and it is becoming increasingly valuable. But there's one more matter I wish to discuss. You're currently housed towards the outer walls, near Çaykara Caddesi, correct?'

Vefyk had long ago proved that what he knew far exceeded Denniston's patience for asking how he'd come by it. Casson only nodded, a dumbfounded look on his face.

'Would somewhere closer to the hospital – to your work – be more agreeable, do you think? More practical? Certainly it would save time in transit.'

'Just how is it you have that kind of sway?' Casson breathed in disbelief. 'First, the things you know… Now, that you have leave to push anyone from their home to house us..?'

'You have somewhere in mind?' Denniston asked.

'No-one else need be pushed from their home, Casson *hekim*, rest assured. Consul Zohrab had a family to house: wife, daughter, staff. I myself am more solitary by nature. This has left the consulate with a number of empty rooms. Indeed, if you look from some of their windows, your hospital is all but in view. I've installed our new surgeons here already. I hope you will follow their example, as they no doubt shall follow yours in days to come. For now, good day, doctors – we are all busy men.'

'Busy,' Doctor Charles Ryan muttered. 'Anyone with eyes can see that "busy" hardly begins to cover it!'

He'd come to the hospital in the early morning, only the day after the meeting with Aydin Vefyk. He was the kind of man to whom roguishness came naturally, and came off somehow as acceptable. Somehow both rugged and well-turned out, every ounce of scruff gave the tacit impression that it was there for a reason – that Ryan had carefully cultivated it, to better illustrate that he was every bit the adventurer. With a dust-coloured slouch hat held earnest over his breast, his overcoat and jacket already off and shirtsleeves already rolled up, he was almost rugged. His manners, however, were starched and crisp, creased only by a smile that could have been sympathetic or sly depending on the light and the angle. His accent was Australian.

'I know that surgeons, like officers, can get territorial if you give them the time and half a chance,' he continued, talking earnestly to Denniston as if they'd known each other all their lives. 'I've met enough of both to know it, I tell you. Pride's well and good, but when it comes in the way of progress? No, spit on that – when the stakes are high, the stakes are best shared. Knowing that's what separates good officers from bad. Doctors too...' Ryan gave a wry smile. 'I've heard you're a good one, Denniston. Care to prove me right?'

Denniston looked up from the array of instruments he was cleaning. He'd half-listened, attention split between Ryan and the pot of melted snow before him, diluted with carbolic, meticulously measured our, for it was rationed now. All the same, he could tell that Ryan spoke well. Words, however, had become less and less important to Denniston of late, with letters the sole exception.

'Good?' he said, furrowing his brow as he measured the word. 'More hands, that's good. What d'you have in the way of experience?'

'I studied at Melbourne and then Edinburgh, if that's what you want to know...' Ryan hesitated, like a man who has stumbled once and thrown off his whole stride. Perhaps he was stunned that all his charm had seemed to have no impact.

'It's not,' said Denniston. 'I meant experience, of these conditions, or anything close. No amount of schooling prepares you for that, I can tell you. You came here from Istanbul, with Vefyk?'

'And before that, from Lovcha,' said Ryan, a tough of swagger and confidence returning. Plevna, the Grivitsa redoubt, Plevna again...' He looked up to the ceiling, nonchalant, as he counted the names off on his fingers. 'Manned an ambulance in all that. Left the redoubt as one of the last, two broke-legged soldiers on the back of my horse. Had my taste of siege at Plevna, if that's what you're asking.'

'That's closer to the mark, yes. Can you speak for the others?'

'Idris, yes. None too sure about Morisot, but I reckon he's a good sort.'

'You're welcome then. All of you.' Denniston was becoming distracted again. 'So long as you start immediately, that is.'

'On your mark, sir,' Ryan grinned.

'Hands first, and implements and all. Get clean and get started. Carbolic, alcohol, things for boiling them – you'll find them here, and I want you to leave them here when you're done with them, am I clear?'

'As crystal.'

'Quick as you can then. Day's yet young.'

For a moment, Ryan looked taken aback. Something, his face suggested, had gone counter to his expectations. But his small smile quickly returned.

'For myself, I reckon I'm a pretty good judge of character,' he said as he set to cleaning. 'I'm glad I judged you right. It's a pleasure to work under you, Doctor Denniston.'

'You're not under me,' Denniston said, as he finished his own cleaning, and strode towards one of the side-rooms given over to surgery. 'You're with me. No time for orders; better you have initiative. I only hope your colleagues do too, or else can come by some quickly.'

The other new doctors he met in the course of the day, but hardly more than in passing, like ships in the night, as they went about their labours. Only Ryan had stopped to introduce himself, while Idris and Morisot went straight to their work, insinuating themselves into the constant rhythm of the hospital without ceremony.

Denniston couldn't decide who that fact favoured more: them, or Ryan. A dim tired part of his mind thought he'd get to know them in due course. For now, there was simply too much to keep them separate, and too little time for introductions.

Once more, despite reinforcements, the hospital was understaffed. Sickness had slipped in again among the *jarra bashi*s – the ones who had worked with the dead, attempting to bury them, for the most part – this time in what could have been typhus or dysentery. Too weak to work, they'd joined the hospital's patients, and become cases themselves.

As the day went on, Featherston was absent too. He had slipped away, it seemed, in his characteristic quiet, like a queen-cat expecting kittens. That night, the original doctors found him stumbling back to bed, from the frozen journey outside to get to the latrine.

'Sick,' was all he said, by way of explanation. 'I'm sorry. I shouldn't have… I'm sorry.'

His shirt was open, his chest dripping with sweat while his shoulders and hands shook. Between the buttons open over his torso, patches of fevered rash showed angry on his skin.

'Get to bed, Featherston,' said Pinkerton gently. 'Back to bed. We'll sit up with you, won't we?'

The doctors dined together, looking over occasionally at Featherston's bed. This was their last night in the house towards the walls. For some it was their last night together, for they quietly agreed Featherston would have to leave with Zohrab – laid low by what was likely typhus, he would either go with the consul, or die in Erzurum.

'It's a special occasion, then,' said Walker. 'A farewell party.'

'Not that we've anything to mark it by,' said Kincaid. 'Food's the same, cold's the same…'

'Food is better than we'll get soon,' said Vashin, defensively. He had cooked them a thin broth of mutton-bones, and got them black bread and potatoes. 'These bones have meat on them. If you know the premium they would fetch in the markets soon…' He sighed, wistfully.

'It's not that we're not grateful,' said Denniston. 'It's hungry work, all this. Hunger's enough to make you thankful for what you can get.'

'At least we'll have a change of scene soon enough,' said Pinkerton. 'A house on the hill. We're moving up in the world, gentlemen!'

They laughed at that, some more than others.

Snow fell outside. It was already late. Most went to bed, agreeing to watch Featherston in shifts, two hours at a time. Casson and Denniston took on the first watch.

They sat round Feartherston by the light of a tallow lamp. It reeked out a familiar stench, but they were both nearly immune by now and huddled to the small glow as if could warm them. Already the cold of night was creeping in through the plastered walls, the cracks between floor, jamb, and door.

Casson was never one to volunteer so eagerly for such work; less still after Denniston had done so, and it became clear they'd be sharing a shift. Already that put something in the atmosphere between them: a kind of strange anticipation, so far as Denniston felt it, as if both had plans for the other, and no clue how to enact them. But words always came easier to Casson.

'I'm going to do it,' he said, the closest to shy that Denniston had ever heard him. 'Leave, that is, with Zohrab. I expect you'll want to give me something of a ribbing for it, or else persuade me to stay. Something about duty; responsibility to those whose needs are greater than our own. You always were full of that, James – more than me, I have to admit. I misjudged you on that, didn't I? Calling you nothing but a mercenary. I'm sorry for that, and a deal else besides...'

Denniston was quiet, stunned. It almost hurt: the thought of staying on without him.

'Well?' Casson continued, resuming some of his old sharpness. 'I'm here, aren't I? You can start your lecture.'

'No...' Denniston said softly.

'No?'

'No, Tom... I think we're past that point. Each of us. Both of us.'

'Doctor James Denniston, past the point of duty... Well, I nev—...' Casson stopped himself and sighed. 'I'm sorry. I don't mean to mock. It's a habit I've been meaning to break for long enough.'

'You're right though, I suppose. In a way. Grand ideas are well and good, but we've been working so much with the facts it's hard to keep them in sight – make them work for you. Heroism, ideals...'

'Beats them out of you, doesn't it?

'Hetty..?' Featherston began to mumble in his sleep, then his voice cracked almost into a cry. 'Hetty, I'm sorry. I won't—! I won't be—!'

'Easy now, there's a good lad...' Casson cooed to him as Denniston mopped his feverish brow.

'Vefyk was right,' Denniston continued. 'He usually is, but...I think the only honest duty all this leaves you with is duty to yourself. Things you need to do to keep sight of yourself – keeping feeling you are who you're meant to be.'

'Might well be... I never marked you down for a philosopher, Denniston.'

'Nor did I, but it's not philosophy, is it? It's real, every minute of every day. You're doing the best you can, here, or you're not, and having to live with what that makes you.' Denniston tailed off.

'That's your lecture then? That I'm less than who I ought to be?'

'No. I just mean that I don't blame you. That's all I should have said. You've done right by yourself, and I've done right by me. We've both tried to be good men.'

'I think that's been my problem...' Casson gave a sad kind of laugh, one note and then gone. 'We've rowed over that, fought over it, almost come to blows over it – you and me. Different roads to the same destination, and we got so damned caught up in whose was the quickest or smoothest.'

'If we were bad men – lazier men – d'you think we might've been friends?'

Casson smiled, just as sad as his laugh had been, but didn't answer. They were silent for a time, until Casson finally spoke again.

'You're a letter writing man. We both are. If you're wondering why, then I think you ought to understand. Don't know who your letters go to, but no-one's as happy as I've seen you with a new letter when it's only from their mother. For me, it's been too long, and letters aren't enough. I miss home. I miss the ones waiting for me. That's where my duty is, maybe. I've...perhaps I've been a good doctor, a good man, but I've been a very poor fiancé. I want to stop. Go home. Start being a good husband instead.'

Once, Denniston might have had more to say: cruel things, accusations, arguments of the kind he used to play out each morning in front of his shaving mirror, in case they came of use. But now it only seemed that Casson had been brave enough to do something Denniston himself had longed to do, every night in this place: go home, stop needing the letters; talk to Agnes, and dare to hope...

'I can't begrudge you that,' said Denniston. 'Not for one moment.'

James

My Dear Miss Guthrie,

I am sorry to hear of your sickness. I hope that, by the time this reaches you, you'll be well recovered, for I'm sure it's nothing more than a bit of discomfort in the short-term, and in the long shall all be forgotten. Still, my hopes are with you, and of course, as a professional, I can assure you that you will be well again in time for Christmas. Perhaps you'll spare me some more of your own hopes as well. I may yet need them.

There's quite a sickness going round here since the Russians closed the ring around us and the siege began in earnest. Issues of the bowel and stomach, mainly, and getting towards epidemic in scale, but at least there's no more fighting now – only waiting, as we sit and see who General Winter starves out first.

You'll be curious, if we're under siege, as to how this letter's reached you at all, I expect. The siege has thrown up chances and opportunities on this side of the walls as well as without them. We have all done our best to seize them, in our own particular ways.

Zohrab, the British consul here, is taking his leave, and with him shall go our last round of official post, to Istanbul, and thence to you. Going under a white flag, he's invited any of us who'd accept to go with him in safety, and get away while the going's good. So with him shall go Featherston, who has fallen too ill with typhus to stay on, and Casson, who wants simply to go home. After our differences and disagreements, perhaps I wish I could begrudge him that, but I cannot – I would be a liar if I were to say that I didn't miss home and those I hope await me there.

For my part I shall stay. Home will wait, and the only part of me that shall leave with the consul is this letter.

In Zohrab's leaving though, we have gained a superior setting. The consulate is empty now. I being nearer the hospital than our current lodgings, has been offered to us and we've now crowded in to fill it. We are lodged up in the big house with peers old and new, for the reinforcements from Kars and Istanbul brought new medics also: a number of jarra bashis but also some Europeans, and one full-fledged surgeon of Turkish origin.

A doctor Morisot, for instance, has taken his lodgings in a small room off the lower front hallway. He is a Frenchman, small of stature and quite festively built despite the hardships and hunger that he and the others must have been through. His dark hair is neat across his head, but the whiskers under his chin and round his jaw have gotten unkempt, giving him the look of either a billy-goat, or one who, finding himself without a scarf in winter, has attempted to grow one.

Another notable is Doctor Idris. He is a proud Ottoman in all ways, and a military surgeon since long before any of us first served under the Red Crescent. Before his departure, Casson made the mistake early on of talking to Idris in officious and impatient Turkish, ordering him around as he would with a common jarra bashi. But Idris is no mere assistant, and made it known quite vehemently from that moment forward. He stared down our Doctor Casson, hissing some choice words in Turkish that – even had I understood them – I don't think I could repeat to you. Consequently, we have all been more respectful since, and deservedly so, for he's a very competent healer from what I've seen: quite the surgeon with battlefield wounds, etc., and he seems not to sleep at all. Rather, he works, prays, and smokes, and sometimes is seen to eat, though not as often as mortal men ought to.

Then there is Doctor Charles Ryan. At first I thought he might have been a straight Englishman. He has a definite air of the traveller and so I marked the veer of his accent little, thinking that time abroad might have altered it from the Queen's. In fact he's come to us from Australia, and is further from home than any among us. He has neither seen nor heard from home in years, such that his high spirits quite put one's own homesickness in perspective. He is perhaps a year or two older than I am, but no more, and seems to have seen far more of the world than any of us: Melbourne, Edinburgh, France and Austria, the Balkans, and all through Turkey to Erzurum. He is one for journeys more than destinations, I think, and tackles all things in life – whether obstacle or objective – with equal vigour and enthusiasm.

He has taken up residence in a chamber no bigger than a briefcase, but with a long balcony attached, for he says he likes to walk when sleep fails him, even in the cold.

I've done quite the opposite and claimed for myself a sitting room, with fireplace – though mostly empty and cold – and bureau desk, all in very Western taste save the Turkish styled couch I bed down upon. No windows, and yet the nights have grown so chill of late that I'm happy to sacrifice light for warmth. Being unable to see into the world outside, I can almost imagine myself in some London garret, thinking how pleasant it would be to fill all these beautiful shelves with books where currently they stand empty save for my pitiful-small collection. (On the subject of which, please do write to me of any passages in Shakespeare, or ideas in Darwin, that particularly strike you! I am very glad to hear you are reading one, and may yet read the latter.)

That is, until duty calls once more, and I must out and away from my imaginings, exiting onto the streets, not of London or Glasgow or Manchester, but Erzurum once more.

Until I hear from you again
I am yours very sincerely,
James Denniston

Chapter 18

It goes beyond clean hands,' Denniston grunted, kicking the blade of the shovel into the ground with one heavy-booted foot. 'Cleanliness has to do with surroundings. Environments. If your hands and tools are clean…' The shovel bit again. '…But your patients are convalescing packed together like potted meat…' Another dig at the iron-hard ground. '…And the environment itself is…' A grunt. '…Unsatisfactory. Unsanitary..?'

'Typhus,' concluded Walker, digging too. 'Jail fever. Cholera. Whatever you're contending with, and whatever you want to call it, where conditions are close and unclean, it'll get in and get out of hand.'

'When it comes to epidemics,' explained Denniston, 'prevention will always be more effective than treatment.'

They laboured together under a grey sky, clearing snow from the black ground and clearing wreckage and rubble. A short stone's throw from the hospital courtyard, shells had fallen weeks back, caving in a house and blasting its small yard to raw earth. At the time it had seemed a tragedy, but Walker had since seen in it an opportunity.

They worked, with Ryan and three soldiers on loan from Emin Bey's command, to expose and open the ground and dig latrines. Not glamorous, certainly, but to Denniston it seemed a stroke of genius: the area was far enough from the hospital and from other houses not to put them at risk, and downhill from the nearest well, so as not to corrupt its water.

'I don't see…' said Ryan, between hacks of his mattock, '…what that has to do with digging latrine pits.' He was one for doing whatever work was required, but Denniston had discovered there was nothing that could stop his affable complaints while he did so.

'For a man who's spent so much time among soldiers…' said Denniston.

'For such an accomplished battlefield surgeon!' Walker chipped in.

'…You seem to have learnt very little from them,' Denniston concluded. 'A man in Trabzon once told me: learn from your patients. And what's among the first things a soldier learns on the job?'

'Don't shit where you eat or sleep,' said Walker, grinning.

'Don't know that I'd have put it like that, but yes,' Denniston said. 'Closed graves, well-dug and positioned latrines, clean instruments and bodies and sheets and dressings – that's all prevention.'

'Ever wonder why these things don't break out in civilised places? Sewers and sanitation,' said Walker. 'No cholera or typhus or the like in London since Bazalgette, Newgate and Houndsditch excepted…'

'But being where we are now,' said Denniston, 'We do what we can with what we have. So, Charles – digging. Latrines and graves. It saves us work down the line, and saves lives, as much as taking out a bullet or stitching a wound.'

Cases of typhoid had died down and typhus took their place, alongside dysentery and cholera. The latter illnesses had spread like fire through heather in high summer and weakened the city's citizens and garrison to the point at which the walls were manned by skeleton crews and the streets and markets like those of a ghost-town. Perhaps all that prevented the Russians from noting this, and pressing another assault against Erzurum's disadvantage, was the fact that they were equally stricken, and worse affected by the recent heavy snows.

The first days of December became a matter of digging work and boiling bedding to kill lice and germs alike. The most skilled doctors worked like *jarra bashi*s, digging pits for the dead and pits for the waste of the living and covering both.

All this struggled against the current of what was fast becoming an array of epidemics. Denniston was only left wondering at his luck to not be affected yet, and asking himself: how much faster might these plagues have spread if not for the work they had done?

Agnes

My dear Doctor Denniston,

As you find my talk of good food, good cheer, and good company more heartening than torturous, I would have like to tell you of Christmas in Manchester. Life, however, is always full of compromise, and one cannot have one thing without giving up another. So, I have had to write to you now, earlier in Advent, for I think it would be better that you at least have a letter to read on Christmas, than have one arrive, talking of Christmas, after the fact. At this time of year it is easy, after all, to feel quite lonely.

I doubt you'll be going to church, and presume indeed you've not so much as looked at one since you crossed the Bosporus, with the sad exception of funerals. In light of this, please do not be surprised that my first port of call, beside making sure you know you are thought of and prayed for, is to swat any first smolderings of heathenry in you as they spark up. I hope you might at least say a prayer on the day, if not for the usual reasons one might at Christmas, then at least for my peace of mind. In turn I assure you there is at least one person in Britain who will be praying, too, for your comfort and safe return.

This does not go to say that Christmas, and the time leading to it, shall be all prayer and penitence for me and mine; we are not so puritanical as you might paint us. For one thing I shall be tempering the spiritual with the secular, and trying my hand at a steamed plum pudding, with figs and other fruits, and a not unconcerning amount of brandy also called for. As a medical man perhaps you can tell me: is it possible to become drunk by eating alone? For that, I fear is the only possible outcome of my pudding. Though it would make the renewed company of the boorish Mckie brothers – due to be visiting with us on Christmas – a little easier to bear, would it not?

Tell me, do you still receive no letters beside my own? Surely this must be more the fault of the post than your mother or friends. I will be writing a number of shorter Christmas greetings to other acquaintances over the coming days, your mother among them. Perhaps I should enquire as to whether she writes you at all? Of course I shan't; I hardly know her and would not want to seem as if I have an undue interest in her son; but it is a curious matter. For now I will simply leave unquestioned the miracles that continue to deliver my own letters to you, in spite of all adversity.

I only wish you might slip back to England so easily for the occasion. Your dancing might still leave something to be desired – indeed it may have grown worse, for do you not say, often, how far you feel to have fallen from civilisation? – but at least I would have one interesting person with whom to converse. And by the sound of your repast of late, you could not but be delighted by my efforts in the kitchen, whatever fruit they might bear.

But of course, I ought not to to entertain hopeless hopes, and save instead my strength for wishing you a safe return. You will come back in time, of that I'm sure, but I see for now why you stay; it's as noble a thing as it is a difficult one, certainly.

For now let me enclose a picture. You asked for one some time ago, and I scoffed at the idea then, as you had been so careless with the first. While it came back into your possession, with the return of your luggage, I think another is the least I can offer you – perhaps it will bring thoughts of home, as at this time of year those are more indispensable than ever. I hope it will give you some comfort.

A very merry Christmas to you, Doctor Denniston. God bless you and keep you.

Until I hear from you again
Sincerely yours,
Miss Agnes Guthrie

Christmas was coming to Erzurum.

For most of the city it passed by only as another snowy day amidst dozens more just like it. The walls were a prison now as much as they were protection. Behind them, time was measured out in terms of hunger, prayer, disease. Whether working, sleeping, eating – the latter two, never quite enough – everything became a matter of waiting. Why should Advent be any different?

For the doctors there were no days off to be had; no letting up in the pace of their duties, or the numbers in need of their help. There were few new injuries, but old wounds still festered on and needed care. Draining an excess of fluid in a wound, or excising infected tissue, became for Denniston novelties in what was otherwise the monotony of treating sickness. Most days, it felt like trying to hold back the tide. For every sick man, woman, or child that became stable or left the hospital in good health, new invalids took their place, stricken with typhus, dysentery, chills and a staggering diversity of fevers and fits.

Still, in the old consulate, the doctors settled in, and all but Idris made preparations for Christmas. They could not rest during this time, but between their turns at the hospital, they each tried their hands with equal diligence at making their loaned house as merry as they were able.

One night they sat about the kitchen table, shrouded in the shadows from one stubby candle. Quickly their discussions of Christmas had turned serious as anything else in their profession.

'The consul is gone,' said Vashin, leaning against one whitewashed wall and casting a deep shadow along it. 'Not his stores, though.'

'Indeed,' Vefyk put in from the head of the table. 'I should think we have one of the best-stocked pantries in the city at our disposal.'

Denniston reflected that perhaps he ought to have felt guilty at this fact: that they were hoarding such luxuries as spice and flour and currants, rather than sharing them amongst the townsfolk. But what would hardly dent Erzurum's overall hunger would make a true feast for the nine men living in this house. It was easy to quash the guilt, and hard not to look forward to what ignoring it would grant them. Agnes' most recent letter had put a hunger in him for at least a taste of what she would be enjoying over Christmas.

'We'll have a plum pudding then,' said Denniston. 'We've got the odds and ends for it, I'm sure.'

'Of course we shall!'

'We'll have to!'

The Englishmen – and honorary Englishmen, Ryan and Denniston – around the table broke into a babble of agreement. Morisot, Idris, Vashin and Vefyk hung back, in a mixture of confusion and bemusement at the passion of their peers.

'Now does anyone know how to go about making one?' said Walker.

'...not as such,' Kincaid admitted.

'There's someone I might ask for a recipe,' said Denniston. 'Not that I'd get it back in time.'

'So that accounts for what we don't know,' Walker said. 'How about what we do?'

'You...steam it?' Denniston began, more certain than he felt. 'Fruit, suet, eggs.'

'Steam it?' Walker echoed.

'Yes. In a cloth – a sheet or a shirt or something.'

'Well, I've got a spare,' Walker volunteered.

'What about plums?' asked Morisot, quizzically. 'Where do they enter the equation?'

'I'm not sure,' Denniston admitted. 'Figs, currants, I know about those, but I don't know about plums. I don't think they go in at all.'

'Then why is it called a plum pudding if it has no plums?'

'That, Morisot, is a mystery lost to the ages,' said Kincaid.

'Maybe Pinkerton's old enough to know,' Walker joked.

'Maybe you're old enough to mind your manners,' said Pinkerton, chewing the stem of his pipe.

'We'll find a way,' Denniston concluded. 'We'll do our best with what we have, as we've always done before. We only need a plan of action.'

'Not to derail your plot, gents,' said Ryan, with a grin. 'But I was walking in the garden the other day – clears the head you know, a quick constitutional – all gone to seed, or buried in snow, or dried up by now... But I'd swear, as I was walking, I saw the darnedest thing. A stubborn old turkey, crimson wattles and all, just daring me to catch it...'

'A turkey?' Denniston wondered aloud.

'Perhaps Zohrab's cook had bought it before the siege?' offered Zohrab. 'She might have been saving it for just this occasion.'

'For Christmas?'

'Well then, it's fate was sealed for the start, wasn't it?' said Ryan, puffing out his chest. 'If someone's to get the old devil, I'll bloody well volunteer!'

Together, in the coming days, they hashed together a plan, and stockpiled a bounty of things collectively reckoned to be relevant. They had flour, eggs of questionable antiquity, brandy, a tallowy mounding of mutton drippings gathered up over time, and a few handfuls of currants black and small and hard as beetles. All that would do for Denniston's pudding, he decided. They had also a sack of potatoes, and more dripping in which took cook them.

Walker donated a linen shirt to cut to measure by way of muslin for the pudding. Idris diligently washed the currants. Kincaid whisked the eggs so vigorously it seemed as though he were trying to beat the dubious freshness from them, sweat standing out on his ruddy brow.

On Christmas Eve, Denniston spent the evening elbow deep not in

Turks but dough, kneading the flour, eggs, and all into a confused mass. The others stood by, coming and going, offering solemn and expert-sounding advice but no assistance beside the generous helpings of tobacco ash they dropped into the mixture as they leaned over it.

Ryan found his cavalry sabre and set off into the garden, 'to hunt a turkey,' he said. As the linen sack of pudding steamed slowly in a pot above the stove, Ryan sat that night, drinking brandy, muttering to himself, and plucking the bird over which he'd triumphed so valiantly.

The others checked in, as if too excited to sleep, over the course of that night. By turns they watched over the cooking pudding, careful as with a patient.

James

My dear Miss Guthrie,

I fear this letter may turn out to be my last, at least for a while. To its merit, however, I think it'll be a good and long one. So much has happened in these past weeks, and I've had a Christmas of sorts, though a far from normal one. It has not perhaps been restful – still work carries on in the hospital – but we have had for ourselves at least a little leisure, and I have found the time to make this letter contain all that it ought to.

Say what you will of the Russians. I fancy that, with all the work and trouble they've caused me, I myself have plenty to say in that line. But say at least that they're Christians, and have not stooped to such a level that they utterly ignore Christian charity and mercy. For Christmas we've been granted an amnesty of sorts, to send out letters with impunity, though I don't doubt every one will be pawed over by some officer of intelligence, combed for military secrets before being sent on its way. Still, I have this small kindness to thank for your letter, which to our surprise, simply arrived, as post ought to, with no intervention from Vashin required. I imagine you, too, shall have it to thank for mine.

Your Christmas I'm sure was a very festive and tasteful affair, even if the company left something to be desired. I have every hope that you found at least a kernel of good conversation in amongst it all, and every faith in your plum pudding. I had not previously thought your culinary talents to be in the plum pudding line, but would dearly have loved to be shown how wrong I was to doubt it. After all, with so much brandy involved in its construction, how could anyone help but be carried away in its quality? (To answer your question, I must say that my medical talents are not much in the plum pudding line either. However, I believe some of the alcohol may be brought off in the cooking, while just enough remains to keep such heathens as myself happy.)

We made valiant culinary efforts of our own, though mostly to be praised in their enthusiasm and steadfastness than their quality. We had a turkey cooked to the best of our collected abilities, and potatoes, and fried bread with mutton drippings, and all took turns in contributing to our 'feast' while off-shift.

We also had a pudding – or rather, a pudding of sorts… I spent the better part of an afternoon churning and kneading the great mass of dough destined to become this pudding. It steamed the whole night, wrapped in cloth very capably and so on, when the time came to serve it, it looked much like it had when I still had my fists sunk into it: a massy pallid bolus of matter, crusted and crowned here and there with dark studs of currant.

The whole thing was such a grand team effort that I think we were all too much afraid of offending each other to naysay its quality. We all made appropriate noises and congratulated each other on it as we braved second and third helpings of the lead-dense monstrosity. Quietly though, I thought on what I wouldn't give for a serving of your own pudding, no doubt superior by orders of magnitude.

The triumph of all our proceedings though were the cases of champagne Ryan somehow sniffed out from beneath the consulate. Perhaps Zohrab had been saving them for some truly special dignitaries, or else for celebrating the city's liberation. But we doctors, much like soldiers, know from experience that it's better to celebrate what you have today than to save it for an uncertain tomorrow. So champagne fuelled our merrymaking, and most of all for Ryan, I think.

He proposed attempting something he had always wished to try: what he called the 'hussar's method' of opening a bottle of champagne. 'Have you know I rode with the cavalry in the Balkans, when I wasn't riding with the ambulance! I ought to know a thing or two about how to swing a sword by now, damned if I don't!' I think the whole thing went about as well as the similar feat your young Mr. Mckie tried to pull off at that Manchester party you mentioned.

Not for the first time in the last few days, Ryan drew out his sword – usually worn so dangling and dandyish low that I sometimes think he ought to have a little wheel attacked to the end of his scabbard to save it dragging on the ground - and fairly decapitated one of the innocent bottles. As tends to be the way with decapitations, the contents fairly volcanoed up the stump of the bottle's neck, and to our wide-eyed astonishment, Ryan clamped his mouth round the break and drank the overflow til the bottle was empty. Better that than waste it, perhaps, but I shan't recount to you the kind of stories he began to tell after.

Meanwhile, I myself was happy enough just to have your letter and your picture. I received no other post, but that's become almost a standing tradition by this point, and I see no reason or way that it should change now. For me at least having word from you made our repeated toasts 'to the honour of absent friends' all the more poignant.

However, it cannot all be making merry with me, can it? Featherston left us to save his health and will with any luck get back his health with time, but now our man Vashin has fallen ill too, and was unable to join or assist in our festivities. He's by now become quite a member of the strange family we've assembled, and so I thought it a shame he should not be at our table. But the sick don't get a day's reprieve from their symptoms even on Christmas – except perhaps for the cases of miracles – and so we got little reprieve either.

There still remains much to be done in the hospital, but mostly it's aiding the sick now, rather than the wounded. Ryan seems to be of the mind that this demeans him, much preferring the gallantry of surgery, but not in such a way as would see him do anything but excellent work. I think he only complains to hear the sound of his own voice. I am pleased, all in all, with the work of each new 'reinforcement' we've had, but I do still wonder how we'll get on, ultimately, without Casson and Featherston.

I worry particularly, when it seems that we're all passing in and out of the hands of sickness ourselves as regularly as we have so far. The jarra bashis are affected particularly badly, and many have only added to the graves they worked so hard to dig. With most of the cases in the hospital still very grave, we will likely be more than busy for a time. Perhaps a reprieve from the pleasant distraction of letters might even be a blessing in disguise – though one I'm loathe to accept.

I wonder sometimes: what would the man I was at the start of this year think of he could only see me now, drawing towards it close?

'How thin you've got!' he might say to me. 'How thick your beard has grown! Are you sure you are quite taking care of yourself?'

To which I suppose I would say, 'You see, I have so many others to take care of...' Or something to that effect.

Regardless, I am getting quite ridiculous now, I think, and ought to close. Let me do so, however, by saying that you cannot imagine the solace your friendship, this Christmas or in recent months, has granted me, Miss Guthrie. Thank you, and a very merry Christmas to you and yours.

Until I hear from you again

I am yours very sincerely,

James Denniston

Chapter 19

He had grown so thin. Such brittle limbs, every step felt like it would break him. Or perhaps that was the tiredness. How long now without sleep? No matter, when he simply had no time.

Things were a cold and colourless blur now. Boil up sugarwater for the cases of typhus and dysentery, feed it to them for hours, one tiny frustrating sip at a time. Mop brows and change and clean soiled bedding. Only to be pulled from work by a hand on his shoulder.

'Another,' said Pinkerton, leading him out into the yard.

Another funeral. Dirt falling over a familiar face. No coffins anymore. No telling if it was Walker or Kincaid or Ryan anymore. Only another death.

How many had died? Nameless multitudes, doctors as much as patients. Had any of them had names to begin with, or deserved them to begin with, and in death did they gain them or lose them? Denniston only knew that every death meant more work for the rest, and there was no time to waste. Back to work, always back to work. When had he last eaten? When had he last had time to sleep?

Denniston woke with a start. For a moment it seemed his body had forgotten how to breathe. He gasped, wrenching a painful intake of air as his lungs tried to remember.

'A dream…' he managed. 'Only a dream…'

The same dream as before, however, and every night recently. They had plagued him of late, always something in the same vein: no time to sleep between helping patients and attending the funerals of friends, nor any time to eat. In each dream he seemed to find himself in a worse way – more worn down, closer to starving. And every day, in the waking world, left him a little worse off too.

Denniston fumbled in the dark, lighting first a lucifer match, and then a tallow candle. He checked his pocketwatch, wound up the previous night and laid on the table beside the low couch he used for a bed. It was still before dawn. But he was awake now, and might as well be about his business.

He began as he always did these days. Slipping the biscuit tin of letters from out of his suitcase, kept under the couch, he brought out a stiff blue-grey photograph. It showed a woman, sitting in a sober and stiff-backed black dress, high in the neck, but with a pair of pretty slippers half-shown peeking out from under its skirts – silk perhaps, and probably blue, though the colourless print made it hard to tell. Wisps and slight waves of dark hair teased round her ears, and the sharp lines of her jaw. Her eyes were large, and dark, and firm, staring the viewer or the camera down in what might look much like daring or defiance. In a neat and familiar hand, the print was signed on the back:

For Doctor James Denniston
And the eyes of no-one else!
With the kind regard of
Miss Agnes Guthrie,
8th of December, 1877

A sound echoed down the corridor outside. It was a moan, ragged round the edges: Vashin, delirious with his fever. Whether it was the same illness that had struck down Guppie, or that had affected Featherston, it was hard to say and hardly mattered. Either the Circassian would recover, now he had taken ill, or he would not. Until his fate was known for certain, they would make him comfortable as they could. It was all they could do.

But without his work, the consulate grew dim each night as the doctors rationed candles and fuel – both things that Vashin had used to procure for them, from whatever connections he had in Erzurum's markets. The food they ate was poorer too, and the corridors and landings gathered dust.

By the light of his single candle, Denniston dressed in shirtsleeves and trousers, a kind of fleece-lined jacket of sheepskin that Vashin had acquired for him, before putting on his coat. He combed irritable fingers through his haphazard growth of beard. There was no time to be rid of it. There was too much, otherwise, to be done.

He went to Vashin first. It would cost nothing to do what he could for those closest by. But Vashin, by then, was sleeping sound once more, though sweat stood out on his brow, and a rash lay angry on his ashen sunken skin.

Denniston took the Circassian's chamberpot and made the long route through the consulate and into the garden. The back door would have been quicker, but he was loathe to risk contaminating the kitchen to get to it. Instead he took the front door, and walked out, boots croaking against the snow, to dispose of the waste a safe way from the house, in the garden latrine that lay behind a screen of tall bare-branched poplars.

From there he went to the water pump across the barren garden, washed the chamberpot, and, taking the paper-wrapped cake of carbolic soap he carried from inside his jacket pocket, washed his hands as well.

After a trip to the kitchen to get a clay jug, and a walk back to the pump, Denniston returned to Vashin's small room with a jug of sugared water and a clean pot to put under the Circassian's bed. With a cloth he mopped Vashin's brow, as the sick man gave out another small whimper.

Perhaps, Denniston reflected, he too was plagued with bad dreams.

On to the hospital, then, via the kitchen, where he took a heel of black bread to eat on the short journey.

The city he walked through was ghostly empty, streets thick with snow and chased with grey dawn mist. Dogs whined always in the distance. Somewhere a baby began to cry. It was strange, Denniston thought, to be reminded that there could still be children in a place such as this, at times such as those that had taken hold of Erzurum.

This was the nature of the siege, and of every day they endured now: a silence, broken sometimes by sound, and rarely for the better. No distant thunder of artillery now, or the nearer explosions of shells; only tireless, tiring, restless work, dream-plagued sleep. Sometimes there would be food, but only enough to remind him that he had been hungry all this while. Sometimes there would come a sound – the squall of a child, the wailing of mourners or else of the sick, the faint tired song of the call to prayer – but mostly it was silence. There were no letters anymore to break it, and little in the way of conversation.

There were fewer of them able to work now, and fewer still able to work to the fullness of their abilities. Exhaustion and hunger had taken their toll. Denniston knew he'd just as likely find some sleepless doctor already at the hospital as he would be the first to arrive for an hour or two. He'd begrudge neither, and take surprise in neither. There was no routine any longer; only what one could do, from day to day, and what one simply could not.

But even when Denniston's body forced him to rest, his mind would not be still. He found himself writing, on increasingly poor scraps of paper, with pens of ever-decreasing quality. Walker at least had shown him how to make ink from rubbing alcohol and soot, gathered from the insides of lamps and stoves and chimneys, so he need not worry about its scarcity. He counted such small mercies where he could.

Though there was no longer any post, certainly, some of what he wrote could be called letters, for all they went unsent. Many of them began with that same phrase, 'My dear Miss Guthrie'. It had grown familiar by now, and comforting for it. He found it ordered his thoughts like no other preamble quite could.

But what came after was often a messy mixture of his thoughts and a writing up of his cases. He reported dryly on the figures and facts of each casualty and convalescence: the small dramas and tragedies that formed the texture of his days now. It felt like a great indulgence, taking notes this way, thinking they might one day be of use in the writing of a thesis or article to The Lancet. A strange indulgence, then, in hoping for any kind of future at all.

Denniston arrived at the hospital. The courtyard was covered with snow, but mounds stood out above its surface, where graves had been opened, filled, and closed as best they could be. Inside, he stoked the stoves that kept the crowded wards warm, and checked the wadding that closed the windows against draughts. As ever, he washed his hands, and began his rounds.

It was New Year's Eve, Ryan told him later, but there was nothing else to mark it as such.

The work and rhythms of Denniston's life took on such a monotony that only his writing stood out – without it his memories merged and became indistinct. In the closing dark of the year, he wrote into the silence of the siege. December passed, and January began.

January 1878

Chapter 20

James

I feel the world has grown smaller around me. I fancy that's the point of a siege: to make one's enemy feel that their defences have become a trap, shrinking in on them, tighter every day.

In my case, everything is a matter of walls. The city walls, the walls of the hospital, the walls of my windowless bedroom... I cannot remember the last time I was not walled in by something, and with that feeling comes a kind of helplessness. I have so few options open to me – so few choices to be made that are any kind of choice at all.

I fancy it's the same for everyone, run ragged by poverty of choice.

Mukhtar Pasha had summoned Denniston that morning. 'Granted an audience,' were the tightly rehearsed English words used by the young Turkish ensign sent to retrieve him. But its courtesy felt like a threat, and Denniston had known that there was no real option to refuse.

Armed men had walked him through the streets of Erzurum, and inside the high fort where Erzurum's command made its headquarters. Soon, as he had in Istanbul, he stood before the desk of a *pasha*, with Aydin Vefyk nearby as interpreter. But unlike the *pasha* in Istanbul, Mukhtar Pasha was dressed more for the field than the parade ground. In dark blue uniform and winter overcoat, he was a kindly looking old man, fine-arched brows and glorious white beard, but his stare was unerring, unnerving, and Denniston found it hard to meet his eyes for long.

'The *pasha* asks how many of his fighting men you have, at present, in your charge? And the *pasha* asks how many of them, by your estimate, might recover and return to their posts eventually? What of the ones who might do so within the week? Can you make it so?'

Vefyk relayed the *pasha*'s words, unsmiling and professional. In the consulate, he and Denniston almost considered one another as friends. Here, it seemed, friendship did not suit the task at hand, for there was no sign of it in Vefyk's face now.

'We English *hekims* all keep our own records,' Denniston said. 'For my part, I've been consulting the others'. Collating them to get to some kind of established figure.'

'What figure is that?'

'At an estimate, I'd think we have 12,000 in our care. I can't talk for other hospitals in the city.'

'You need not. They will talk for themselves in due course. Of those 12,000, how many are soldiers and how many civilians?'

'Honestly, I couldn't say. I'd have to look into my notes, and even then...'

Mukhtar Pasha raised an eyebrow. Denniston looked away rather than brave his stare.

'...Even then,' Denniston continued carefully, 'the numbers are fluid. What I tell you today could be nonsense by tomorrow. Between inpatients, death and desertion, so many come and go...'

'Desertion?' Vefyk echoed, voice hard.

'Only from the hospital! A turn of phrase, that's all. The civilians are prone to discharging themselves, early as they can, sure that nothing pressing is the matter with them. We can't very well hold then and keep them against their will. I think...' Denniston sighed. 'What I think is that the siege has them counting the days they have left with their families, in their own homes. They don't know how many more they'll have. Can you blame them for valuing that?'

Neither Mukhtar Pasha nor Vefyk answered. Instead Vefyk continued his line of questions: 'And the soldiers?'

'Some of them are keen to keep to their beds for as long as they can. Glad of the rest, I think. Others insist like the civilians do – up and off from their beds, back to their posts and duties, as soon as you look away.'

'That is *all* you mean by desertion?'

'Quite everything.'

'Thank you, Denniston *hekim*.' Mukhtar Pasha conferred with Vefyk a moment before he continued his translation. 'Rations are the *pasha*'s next order of inquiry. What do you grant the sick? Are those soon to return to active duty permitted more, or better, than the other convalescents?'

'Our supplies are provided courtesy of the Stafford House Committee,' Denniston began, coldly, sensing the direction of the conversation now. 'Bought and paid for and transported by charity money, from donors overseas.'

'The *pasha* did not ask where your supplies come from. His questions was clear: to whom do they go?'

'Whether medical supplies, rations, or time and effort, we afford each man, woman, and child whatever we can, and to whatever extent will best help their recovery.'

Mukhtar Pasha listened to Vefyk's translation with eyes closed, face soft and thoughtful. Then he responded in Turkish. Already Denniston felt that he knew what was coming. It had gotten into him as a feeling that was not quite dread or anger, but caught somewhere between the two.

'The *pasha* states quite clearly, Erzurum is suffering and will soon starve if there is not order. In his wisdom and experience, he requests that you grant no more from your stores to those who cannot recover, or will not do so in due course.'

There it was: the spark that changed all to an anger that Denniston could not keep from his voice. 'You mean starve anyone less than useful?'

'This war will be won or lost by fighters, James… There are those who will die, regardless of what effort or supplies to expend on them, correct?'

'And they became worthless the moment they had the bad luck of getting hurt, is that it? While carrying out his orders, and the orders of men like him? This is the thanks they get.'

'The situation in Erzurum is *desperate*, and growing worse. There are no easy decisions in war, James. Those decisions still have to be made.'

'With all due respect, Aydin,' Denniston said, fighting to keep his voice even, 'the Stafford House Committee is not under the *pasha*'s command. We are an independent charitable organisation, privately supplied. In short, sirs, the disposition of our own stores is not military business. It is Committee business. Medical business. And the matter ends there.'

'You have your orders, doctor.'

'My orders are to keep your people in good health.' Denniston fell into a cold quiet rage. His hands trembled, wringing against each other. 'Will you excuse me? I've got duties to return to.'

As he left, and the anger went from a shapeless passion to something clear enough to think about, Denniston realised: it was not the awful order he'd been given that angered him so, but rather its logic. Had he not always argued for necessity, against Casson and men like Casson? Logic made of Mukhtar Pasha's orders a necessity, but ethics made them impossible. What reconciliation could there ever be between the two?

The next grey morning, more soldiers came to the hospital. As they had been before, they were armed, a squad six ragged but able-bodied men, with requests that went beyond treatment.

Their boots tramped snow slurry across the hospital floors. Three had newer breech-loading rifles, British or German made. One had a musket, a muzzle-loader, long and heavy. Another, shouting as he entered, and with red stitching on his sleeves, carried a service revolver. Behind him stood a thickset Turk who carried nothing but a wood-axe. The eager look in the eyes of the last scared Denniston more than any of those armed with guns.

The shouting continued. The soldier with the pistol had it lowered, but out of its holster, in quiet warning. The *jarra bashi*s that, moments ago, had been hurrying between the beds froze still. Some even made themselves small, hiding down by the bunks and cots they'd been tending to.

Denniston's stomach sank. The soldier was making demands – that much was clear, even if he could not understand the precise words – and after yesterday's conversation with Mukhtar Pasha and Aydin Vefyk, Denniston thought he knew whose orders these men were acting on.

The orders, however, were not what he'd expected. First, the fittest men among the hospital patients began to stir, rising from their beds to stumble out and into the cold of the courtyard. Outside, the bawl of a well-drilled voice shouted them into rank and file, as if for inspection.

'Idris?' Denniston called. 'Doctor Idris?' Without Casson the Turkish doctor was his best hope for an interpreter.

Idris appeared at his elbow, hurrying from where he had paused, halfway across the ward.

'What's he saying?' Denniston asked.

'He asks for any man able to stand. Any who can hold a weapon. They must report immediately. Go to their units.'

'My God...' Denniston had feared for the crippled, the critical cases among his patients, and what it would mean if Mukhtar Pasha's men came to round them up. This, in its way, might be worse. 'Stop it! Stop this at once!'

Denniston stormed between empty cots and rows of bedding on the floor where patients once had lain. He stopped a few strides from the soldier with the pistol, staring and seething.

'These men are under our care,' he hissed. Idris was beside him, translating, in calmer tones than Denniston could bring himself to use. 'They've not been discharged! They are not ready to go back to their duties, no matter how you press them. Do you hear me?'

Now, even those farther from recovery were beginning to stir. Those weak with typhoid fever and the wasting of typhus got from their bedding. Others still held back, sheets clutched tight around themselves as they stared with frightened eyes at the soldiers. Civilians crowded together, frantically whispering. Somewhere, Denniston heard a woman begin to weep.

'It'll kill them, do you understand?' Denniston hissed.

But the soldier with the pistol had brought it up and levelled it with Denniston's forehead. He felt the aim of its muzzle like a fingertip pressed mocking into his face. Casson had held the butt of a gun out to him once. Never before had he had the mouth of one aimed at him. His skin felt cold. His heart beat out a frantic din in his chest.

'They're no use to you. If they were we'd have sent them back already!' Denniston said, quietly now, forcing calm into his voice as he raised his empty hands to the height of his eyes.

A rifleman discharged a shot nearby, up into the air. It sounded out deafening through the ward, ringing in Denniston's ears. Plaster dust drifted down from the ceiling where the warning shot had struck. It settled in Denniston's hair and on his fast-blinking eyelashes.

'Listen to me…' he all but whispered. 'You wouldn't dare shoot me. You wouldn't. Who'll fish bullets out of you and your friends if you put one in me, you bastard… Tell Mukhtar Pasha—…'

The pistol moved from Denniston to aim itself off into the room. For an awful moment, Denniston saw where it was pointed. Then another shot was fired. In a cot nearby, one of the soldiers who'd lingered spasmed once – a brief twitch of the limbs – and then fell still as blood pooled out from a wound in his neck, to stain his bedclothes red.

Denniston had been right. They wouldn't shoot the doctors – they wouldn't dare – but the patients were expendable. Those who wouldn't come were as good as deserters already.

Denniston was shaking as he tried to speak and found no more words would come. No more objections. He was pale and sweating now; felt sick and starved both at once. With both shots still ringing in his ears he slumped down onto an empty bed and sat for a time, helpless.

When Ryan walked over, he sat a few minutes at first, in silence before he finally spoke. 'It doesn't get easier,' he said, 'being around violence like that. Killing, war in general…'

'I'd been around killing,' Denniston said, lamely. 'Artillery and assaults… I thought I'd seen it all.'

'Hot blood, that. This was cold. That's what's shook you.'

Denniston's shoulders gave another perfunctory shake.

'There's no shame in that,' said Ryan.

A full half of the wards were empty now. The soldiers, and even some of the civilians, had filed out, then been ushered out, then, at last, dragged by their comrades into the snow. Denniston had done nothing.

'It's not that…' he said.

'What then?' Ryan asked.

'It's what I'm wondering… I'm asking myself if they didn't do us a favour. Saving us the hard choice by making it for us. Have you seen our stores recently? We couldn't have—… Not for all of them…'

'War's all monstrous deeds and bastards of choices, James. This one's not on you. Whatever's planned for those men, it's not on you. You did what you could…'

James

Of the ragged regiments Mukhtar Pasha put together, half were ordered to the northmost gate, half to the southwestern.

I picture them lined up in rags, some with rifles, muskets, pistols, a sabre; others less lucky, armed only with a knife, or given an improvised pike, or cavalry lance but no mount. None of them ready for battle, or for another of Mukhtar Pasha's now-signature mad dashes. He intended not a pitched battle but a tooth-and-nail escape; a divided force's two parts acting decoy each for the other.

What a waste, I thought, when he had lost so much, and spent so much of his manpower, acting out the same gambit to get into the city. And entertained the same image in my mind as I had when I saw Zohrab emptying the consulate, making ready to leave: of rats fleeing a sinking ship, braving the waters rather than face the wreck.

The Turkish artillery began, shells sowing whatever chaos they couldn't amongst the Russian investments. In two columns the sallies charged out. I didn't see, but I can imagine them: two gouts of infantry and spindly starved horses, fewer in number than could be counted on both hands. Ragged uniforms where there was any uniform at all. A cap here, perhaps, or a flag brandished there. Running to their deaths by way of running for their lives.

Divided in number, they must have divided the Russian resistance, surprised it into indecision. The besieging ring buckled, and for a time it broke as the straggle of Turks fought mad as dogs to get clear.

To the North they were worse than decimated. For us left behind in the city, there is no knowing how few survived, and how many of them might have been captured. But they were the gambit given in return for bloody success in the southwest. That column ruptured the Russian line and shot through. From what I heard, Mukhtar Pasha himself led their charge. So, a monster then, but one monstrously brave.

Whether they will return with reinforcements or only make good their escape, and carry word to Istanbul of our state here at Erzurum, I do not know. However much I disapprove of the Pasha's methods of triage, I know that I have fewer patients to care for now, and so can care more thoroughly. Our supplies are less stretched, and so little is needed to hold these walls against a winter-weakened foe, that I suppose this was Mukhtar Pasha's intent: leave Erzurum empty so her walls might hold out the longer.

If by the realisation of some dim hope relief from the west arrives in weeks to come – whether from Istanbul, or European involvement in this war – then who knows how the Battle of Erzurum may yet end. But for now, half the flesh has gone from Erzurum's bones and what remains is a shadow.

I cannot dwell on what happened beyond these walls, and what the survivors will now face in a winter like this. Those men are beyond my help now, and I try not to consider them. Though I can't help but consider: of the men in my care, how many, too, are beyond my help? What use in forestalling the inevitable?

I do not know if this is destined to be a letter, a case-study, or only a fragment — a note to be swept aside and forgotten. When letters cannot be sent, and case-studies may never be completed, and when loose papers might burn to nothing in the blast of some haphazard shell, there hardly seems any point. But I find it calms me. And I think that, in the face of uncertainty, there will always be a strange instinct to record.

Chapter 21

James

My dear Agnes,

This letter shan't be sent. I don't know if this is a permanent state of affairs or whether eventually I shall have the chance to send it off. I think maybe that, looking back on it by then, I shall be too ashamed of it to do so. But for now I write to you for comfort, and so shall call you Agnes for comfort too. What difference does it make at this point? Nothing seems to make a very great difference, in the grand scheme of things.

I've been considering my motivations in getting into this mess. That is, I've been looking rather more darkly on them than in the past. I suppose I had thought of this enterprise as an investment of time. I hoped to make returns on it – a salary at least more acceptable than I'd get at home. I have that, but how little else, really?

I had, for instance, my retainer from the SHC, but since the siege lines closed that of course has not come through. And even if I had those funds, the barest of provisions have fairly tripled in price of late. Dark bricks of bread, beef tea, tobacco, and little else. It wouldn't surprise me if their prices rise again before the siege is done with.

I am living from savings now. I fancy we all are. And money does not go far at all, no matter how much one spends. How little or how much, it makes no difference, one cannot keep fed either way.

My private patients receive me with a habitual solemnity I've grown used to by now. The men, whose faces at least are uncovered, are gaunt in the cheek, sad round the gums. But when I visit, they still offer me black coffee, cigarettes, and something to eat even if nothing in the line of great heartiness or luxury.

Given how kind this city still is to us, we doctors still attempt to give back as best we can. We've begun a subscription – a hat passed round at week's end – whereby we all give what we can to provide whatever we may for the families of our hospital cases. But increasingly our hatful affords less and less, for of course we have no more money than anyone else left in this damned city.

A small family of American missionaries – I think I mentioned them before – have taken similar duties on themselves. God only knows why they, too, have stayed, but they clothe the needy, feed the hungry, while the patriarch among their number speaks in a preacher's trembling tones about the mercy of God, the dignity of humble and even arduous living, and the glory of His kingdom. All very Christian of them, and I'm sure you would approve.

But this is all what I hear and nothing more. I have not seen them since we laid poor Guppie to rest. Mostly I know of them from how Ryan sings the praises of the youngest among them: a lady he calls Miss Nocholson, and fancies to be quite a fine-looking lady, when he is not expressing his concerns about her delicacy, and all-round ill fit to this line of work, or these hard circumstances.

At this point my opinion differs from his, though. It seems to me that anyone at all who has fixed themselves in this city and not fled when they could is steadfast beyond the human norm. That is, they deserve as much respect for their fortitude as they do pity or concern for what's proved it. This grit is to be found amongst fairly every soldier still in Erzurum. They are determined to fight to the last cartridge, they say, or else the last man standing. But those who've stayed in Erzurum determined to alleviate suffering as best they can are no less dedicated or stalwart, whether they might be a young female with an American mission, or a civilian volunteered as a wound-dresser, or what have you…

As to fighting to the last cartridge though, I fancy there is very little fight left to be had. No cartridges, you see, or very few to spare – supplies of ammunition are almost as low as stocks of food, though not dwindling quite so quickly.

With Mukhtar Pasha gone Erzurum has again a new commander left behind in his stead. I've not met him, but Aydin Vefyk has sketched his character in brief: a younger man, a Kurd, named Ismail Pasha, quite frustrated that promotion to command of a whole city's garrison has left him in command of so few, and able to do so little.

There is no fighting, of course, any more. Clearly the intention of the Russians is no longer to take the city by force. After how dear it cost them to take Aziziye, and how much dearer it cost them to lose it again, one can scarcely blame them. I suppose they must also have been fairly battered by Mukhtar Pasha's gallant retreat. In any case, their main weapons are now cold and starvation, and they are both double-edged swords, for I fancy they hurt the Russians as badly as they do us. They have the worst of the cold; we, the worst of the hunger. And in both camps, sickness, I imagine, is rife.

There are fewer cases to care for in our hospital now, but also fewer doctors to care for them. Morisot has already taken ill, not with the first signs of the fever but with dysentery, and it's a good deal of work just to bring him enough water that he retains even a little of it. Ryan works on but he's faring poorly as well, weak and tired and absent-minded, finding it hard to eat when there is food to be eaten at all. Moreover, another two of our jarra bashis are bedbound in the hospital with pneumonia and typhoid respectively.

What time I might better spend sleeping is useless at any rate. I will always be tired, and always sleep poorly, regardless. So, instead I find myself taking notes, writing letters, to you, or to no-one but the fires of the kitchen stove. But as I said, it calms my nerves and collects my thoughts. And perhaps they will one day come in useful, for medical records when I come home – a doctor's thesis? That last idea seems so far-off as to be laughable now, belonging to a world entirely separate from the one that owns me now.

But until I return to that world
I am yours very sincerely,
James Denniston

The weather had grown colder. One night passed and by morning it seemed the whole world had frozen solid. Twenty-five cases of frostbite came up from the fortifications and to the Stafford House Committee hospital. They were the lucky ones, Denniston reflected grimly.

One patient had found another that morning, in visiting the latrine-pits in the shell-blasted ruins downhill from the hospital. He had all but frozen solid, joints locked into an undignified statue as he crouched over the uncovered pit. Denniston had seen the body, with icicles in its beard and frost like a rheum over its open eyes.

He spent that morning outdoors and shivering, in sheepskin jacket and fur coat, strips of cloth wrapped round his legs, over the trousers and boots, up to the knee.

He found what wood he could among the wreckage and set to sheltering the latrines: walls for them, and a clapped-together little roof to keep off the snow. It might not help very much, but if it helped a little it was better than nothing.

But he found himself worrying that this was now his response to seeing a dead man: one entrusted to his care, and who had died such a pointless and ignominious death. He remembered finding the aftermath of the skirmish, and the mess of corpses on the way to Erzurum. It had struck him so hard he wondered if he would ever be the same. Now, however, he saw death daily, and carried on, busying himself as he had before. If any proof was needed that he was not the same, and would not ever be, then was that not it?

Like immersing oneself in a tub of ice-cold water, he thought; at first it's a shrill and unbearable feeling. Then it burns dully in the flesh, and gets into the joints. In time, though, the body accepts it, and in resignation turns cold and insensible as well. Denniston had become numb in ways he was not before.

Yesterday he attended the funeral of two *jarra bashis*. Typhus took them, or the cold, or the sheer malnourished misery of this place – it hardly mattered which now. All he felt was that, perhaps, it was a waste. What difference did it make to the living or the dead to dig holes and say words for corpses? The snow would do the burying for them, given time, and the cold at least would stop corruption spreading from their death. So what difference did it make, except to waste time that might be better spent?

Spending time, Denniston found, was his chiefest solace now. He could not stand to have any spare; could not stand to be idle. Faced with a man frozen to death, he nailed together boards for a latrine-shelter. Faced with the option of sleeping, he would so much rather write. Faced with a lull in hospital work, he would wash his hands, and wish his instruments, and wash his hands again. It was as if he could not stop moving, for fear that he too would freeze.

That night Denniston took care of Ryan, sitting by the Australian's bedside rather than go to bed himself. His reasons in part were practical: he found that if he lay down at night, his chest would feel thick inside, and his breath would start to rattle. Better, he decided, to be upright, and be of what use he could.

'Your fits have stopped,' said Denniston, a book open and unread on his lap.

'Have they?' Ryan joked. 'I hadn't noticed.'

'It's not a lot, but it's something. A sign the worst of it's over with.'

'Makes me a more charming conversationalist, I reckon.' Ryan turned slightly over in bed, onto his side, towards Denniston. He winced at the movement, but only briefly. 'What was it then? Always easier to say, isn't it, after the fact.'

'Probably typhus. Statistics would support that, there's so much of it going around.'

Ryan grimaced. 'It's another story for the old oeuvre, I suppose. I, Charles Ryan, survived the typhus epidemic of Erzurum, 1877-1878… I can see myself boring some pretty young thing with it now.'

'Not your most glamorous story, is it?'

'Defying death? There's always a certain je ne sais quoi in that, isn't there? I'd call that glamour. Man's always drawn to what the grave touches but doesn't quite claim…'

'What's that meant to mean?'

'Couldn't say, but it sounds good, doesn't it? Romantic.'

Ryan had more than proved himself as a raconteur in recent weeks. Bedbound, between his previous fits of delirium, he talked more than ever. Whether his stories were true or not, he told them with such panache it hardly mattered, such that it was hard not to take almost as much joy in listening to them as he did in telling them.

Riverside skirmishes at Plevna. Outrunning a wing of Russian lancers on the road to Erzurum. Daring and steel-nerved battlefield operations, and officers who sprung up from their finished surgery to lead their men ever onward. Kohl-lined eyes peering out from beneath diaphanous veils and the wives of other men Ryan could've sworn he caught looking at him, with the beginnings of desire aglimmer in their gazes.

That was the usual matter of his stories, but that night he told another.

'You know, James… Coming from Istanbul to Erzurum, we heard some pretty tall tales. People always tell tales about what's waiting for them wherever they're travelling. Always far better than what you've got now, or far far worse.'

'I take it Erzurum was the latter?'

'You could say that. We'd heard the city was already surrounded – doomed to a long siege and starvation. Reckon that news wasn't far off the mark, only early.'

'Or prophetic.'

Ryan laughed, then clutched at his chest as the laughter turned to coughing. 'We heard of citizens with broomsticks and table-legs, hunting pieces for the best equipped, and holding off half the Russian army, too. Routing the Rus from the streets of their neighbourhoods. No sooner had the Russians made any headway than the brave people of Erzurum would kick them back out into the snow. That's what we heard. Left you wondering how the siege could've started at all with every man, woman, and child so brave… But you don't poke holes in a good story.'

'You hardly need to,' said Denniston. 'We heard the same stories inside the walls. Fancy there's some truth in those at least.'

'But what we also heard is what we were on our way to relieve. Us doctors, I mean. We were the replacements, or so we were told, for a hospital staffed by dead men. That we were stepping into their shoes. Shelling, illness, stray gunfire, cold and hunger – we heard you and the rest from the SHC were already six feet under. I've got to admit, James, I'm glad those rumours turned out untrue.'

'More true than I'd like,' said Denniston, thinking of Guppie, a foreigner in the tiny Christian graveyard on the hillside. 'But thank you all the same.'

February 1878

Chapter 22

James

My dear Mother,

I am sorry to have sent no letters since Istanbul. The post, since, has been very bad, and I fancy that perhaps that accounts for why I've heard nothing of you either. Or perhaps you, like me, have been waiting for the right words to come to you – words with which to make things right – and found that they will not come. So, as I haven't those words, I'm making do.

Christmas has come and passed. I didn't write then, though I thought to do so. We doctors – my colleagues and I – made the best of it though. I fixed a pudding, kneading dough and stuffing it with currants, but I fancy you would have scowled at me and shown me how to do it right. The results were not ideal. But we had a turkey as well, and a merry time of things, all considered, and I wished very much that you might be enjoying the same, and would be in good company at Christmas.

There have since been some nasty ailments going around. The city suffers quite badly, but I fancy that's why I'm here. If I weren't willing to suffer some privation to that end that what would have been the point in coming out at all? I think suffering through typhoid fever that autumn, so many years ago, has stood me in good stead here – I'm spared the bother of it, and am up about and bonny as a daisy, and can instead tend to those less fortunate.

I hope to say that I shall continue down that path. Very well, fighting-fit, and working hard though sleeping little. But of course it is in higher hands than mine whether that proves true. I know that you will at least have wishes and prayers both to that effect. Know in turn that I have all the same wishes for you at home.

To tell it true I don't know when I shall be back, or under what circumstances. Spring or summer perhaps. But in either case, Ma, I look forward to it immensely. Only, do not worry for me too much in the meantime. I don't wish to be the cause of more upset than I already have. Surround yourself with good people, live well, and think of me sometimes fondly.

Until then I am yours with love,

James

The month was young but already proved cruel. While Ryan convalesced, and had improved enough to walk about, and do what work he could, Pinkerton had taken his place in sickness. Now it was by his bedside that Denniston sat each night. No-one else would. Too tired, they said, or else too busy, or too sick or recently sick.

Pinkerton said far less than Ryan had on his sickbed. He only lay on his back, breathing faster and shorter than any sleeping man ought to, as Denniston watched, and feared.

The illness had taken him suddenly, first with pallor and violent shivers, then with wet coughing that stained his handkerchief pink. He wheezed and gasped, and was quickly too short of breath to stand.

It was too sudden, Denniston thought. If they had known better, or there had been more warning, they might have treated him, and what he suffered now might have been easier, or at least less worrying.

Pinkerton strained upright in bed, back spasming straight. He bent in on himself, coughing, and the strain of his spine as he hacked and gasped only showed how thin he'd become beneath his nightshirt and longjohns.

'Easy now... Easy there...' Denniston muttered under his breath, knowing he was not heard. Useless, he thought; useless, all of this.

Pinkerton was confused, even when conscious. Mostly he scarcely seemed to know where he was, or to whom he was speaking. He knew that he was sick, but seemed unconcerned, almost blissful. It was only the shows of pain that went across his face as he coughed, and clutched a hand to his side now, that suggested differently.

When he fell back against his bed, sweat stood out profuse on his brow. Denniston leaned forward with a cloth. The least he could do was clean that, and give what comfort he could. He wouldn't have his friend sweat through a fever untended, and leave the sweat to worsen his chills.

Pinkerton's eyes screwed tight as Denniston mopped his brow. Then they snapped open. His face contorted for a moment, beneath the wild over-growth of his sideburns and new-grown stubble. But past the spasm of pain, his mouth moved into a smile, and his eyes seemed to focus.

'James..?'

'Yes,' said Denniston, eager to the point of desperation. He was recognised. It was a sign perhaps; the first tell of Pinkerton's improvement. 'Yes, that's me. I'm here. I've been here, helping...'

'Of course you are,' Pinkerton rasped. 'Of course.'

'Can I do anything? How do you feel? Are you thirsty? Cold?'

'I am old, James. You know full well...'

'You're younger than your years. You know that!' Denniston's voice pitched up, cracking. Pinkerton's eyes had closed and it terrified him to see the older man slipping from consciousness again. 'I saw you pull a bloody cart through two feet of snow! You walked me through the streets while I was mad, damn it, and you made me sane again! You'll be fine, just you see. Just you see…'

But Pinkerton's face had gone slack once more, and his breathing resumed its panting. The smile, however, stayed on his face, til that too slackened and was lost.

Pinkerton did not wake. Two days later, he died, quietly, with closed eyes.

James

My dear Agnes,

Do you know, I heard tell of a western diplomat – French, I think – who slipped in and out of the city recently. I heard that in his entourage he brought a few bundles of letters that had been held at Istanbul. None came to me, however, and I was not able to corner him and slip a letter of my own into his pocket for the sending.

A pity, but not an unexpected one.

Agnes, I don't know what else to say. We've had illness among the doctors, you know that. We lost Guppie, Ryan and Morisot took ill but have recovered, and I wish the same for Featherston, though don't know now how he fares. But Pinkerton, too, was among the sick, and is now among the dead. It pains me to say so. He had always been very kind, to me and all others.

No one else who knew him could attend the funeral. At times like this, I suppose it's a wonder we found time to have one at all. It was only myself and Mr. Nicholson, the missionary, who's taken on the duty of giving rites to any Christian dead at Erzurum. I said nothing, and even his rites were threadbare. Slush on the ground in place of snow, and a grey misery of rain to fall on our hatless heads as we bowed them, and gave Pinkerton into the earth.

Perhaps I ought to have said something. I don't know what, then, I could have said. I was overwhelmed and still am, and guilty that his loss should have struck me harder than any other we've suffered of late, for I'm far from a stranger to death by now.

What's done is done, though, and the only words set down for him will be the ones I give you now.

Pinkerton was a fount, of wisdom and of knowledge, seemingly on all things he saw in the world. A simple walk by his side always became an opportunity for learning. Like as not he would point something out in minutes and begin to tell you its history, its provenance, how it came to be the way it was and why it was the way it is. How he knew so much about so much I'll never begin to know. He put it down to age, but I would sooner attribute it to a keen eye, a good memory, and a fond love for how much wonder there is to be found in the world.

He was a fount of kindness too though, to me and to others. God only knows that I have had my own dark hours in recent times, but it was Pinkerton – so often – that picked me up, dusted me off, and set me on my feet once more. He never patronised, but helped one toward one's own repair. I fancy I learnt a good deal from him about what there is to doctoring besides surgery, diagnosis, and treatment. Perhaps I did not learn enough though. Could I have been more effective with him? I'll never know, and perhaps always regret the fact.

I know so little of his life beyond Erzurum. He was, I think, the only son his parents had. His father was a doctor in India, but beyond that I know nothing of him. I don't know to whom I should give news of his passing, or how much it might shock them. Once again, compared with Pinkerton, I'm quite mired in how little I know. But the thought is so familiar it's almost a comfort now.

The price of all things here has gotten ruinously dear. Death seems the only exception, though it taxes those left behind harshly enough. I am nearly bankrupt just from the buying of bread – a horrible compounding of straw and Indian corn – but somehow beer and tobacco continues to appear. Surely you'll find me an awfully sensual person for it, but I must admit that both are very great comforts to one who has so few others left.

In recent days, the lines have begun to open. Russian parties come to and fro, under flags of truce, asking for surrender. Though it must seem a very attractive prospect for weary starving Erzurum, it's not an offer we've taken as yet. But with these emissaries come news, and mostly it's of Turkish defeat, no doubt to dampen our spirits. Hami Pasha's last garrison at Kars has fallen, though I think that news has been overdue for a long time now. So too the fortress at Oltu has fallen, and so on, and similar tales of defeat. The sultan has offered a truce to Russia, encouraged by Britain, and yet the Russian armies continue pressing westward, and the forces round Erzurum remain. No news of Mukhtar Pasha though, in all this talk of defeat.

I wonder, in light of this, how much longer Erzurum will resist Russian offers. After all, a truce has been called, and holding out longer looks like futility. I don't know how the Turks can look at the prospect of peace dangled before them and not long to seize it. For myself, I long for the day when the days when the roads and gates and lines of communication open once more. I feel quite selfish for doing so, but feel so terribly alone that it's impossible to quash my hopes.

To peace then, and springtime, and kinder days to come, and a chance to send this letter maybe…

Until then I am yours

Very sincerely,

James Denniston

The following night, Denniston returned from the hospital and from his private cases. He found the consulate quiet. It was not late yet, only just evening, but the big house was filled with the incomplete silence of patients in sickbeds, wood and plaster both shifting in the descending cold. Otherwise, the silence was an empty one. Denniston was first back.

He walked the hall as dust danced in the light of the sunset. Then he proceeded off into the ground-floor corridor that led to the former sitting-room he'd claimed as his own.

His footsteps clapped slow down the passage as he passed the room that had been Pinkerton's. The door had been locked shut since they'd removed the body. Denniston had not been certain if he intended to keep it shut up until Pinkerton's effects could be passed on to his people, or if it was only because a sense of stillness seemed fitting. But now the door was ajar and motion sounded inside. He reached into his coat-pocket to touch the grip of his revolver, eased open the door, and stepped inside.

Vashin was within, bothering over the drawers, the open suitcase under the window-sill, the pillow-covers and hanging spare suit. His head snapped round to hear Denniston enter. A fraction of a second later, he fairly jumped from his skin in delayed surprise.

'Vashin?' Denniston said, uncertain. 'What are you doing up? And in here?'

'Cleaning, *effendi*!' Vashin bowed his head convulsively, like a deep repeating nod. 'Only cleaning.'

'You're improved then. Up and cleaning dutifully. I'd thought you still unfit for much more than bedrest...'

'Much improved.' Vashin gave another bow of his head, sharp as if he were ducking something Denniston had thrown at him. 'It's good to be busy, *effendi*. I keep busy.'

Despite Vashin's eager smile and insistences, a sheen of sweat and a swarthy blush showed on his face. His eyes were feverish, and he wore only his night-shirt, bare feet cold against the floorboards. Could this be some new fit of delirium, Denniston wondered, brought on by Vashin's sickness? Perhaps, but the man was holding onto something – trying to hide it in the folds of his shift.

'In your hand,' Denniston observed, gently. 'You have something there. Would you show it to me?'

'Nothing, *effendi*, nothing at all.' Vashin fumbled the thing against his clothes, as if searching for a pocket to hide it in.

Denniston took a step closer, one hand still in his coat pocket. His heart began to pound and its beat sounded loud in his ears. In Vashin's eyes was the look of a desperate man. Denniston shared his nerves now, just below his suspicion and disappointment. 'Please, Vashin, I'm sure it's nothing.

Only show me, so I know…'

Vashin made a whining sound in the back of his closed mouth. He extended his hand and opened it, shaking, to show the contents: a few crumpled leaves of paper money, creased like a vine leaf around something circular, and made from smooth-buffed metal. It was a pocketwatch. Pinkerton's initials stood out on the age-worn brass.

'I'm sorry, *effendi*,' Vashin whispered. 'So sorry…'

'How long?' Denniston hissed coldly. 'How long have you been here and playing the patient while you were up and stealing from the rest of us?'

'Never from you, Denniston *effendi*! Never from the others!'

'Just Pinkerton then? So it's graverobbing, is it? Only without getting dirt under your fingernails! Vashin, look at me!'

'…so sorry.' Vashin's English began to break. 'We are starving… All starving… Only to feed, *effendi* – only please to feed us living now!'

Denniston's pity eclipsed his rage. Perhaps he lacked the energy now to be truly angry, and mercy came more easily. He'd seen heinous things done by men, inspired by a place and a time such as this – worse things by far, and for worse reasons.

'Please, Vashin,' he said evenly. 'Stay here. I'll be back shortly.'

'Please…' Vashin echoed, mutely. His face was shining with sweat now. And that was how Denniston left him, taking the key from the inner side of the door and locking it behind him.

He paced in the kitchen for a time, still in his coat as he considered the matter. The anger had passed but it pained him still. Vashin had wronged them, broken their trust, and ought to face some kind of justice. But he had left Vashin in a room with a window unlocked. He might return and find Pinkerton's room empty, but in a fortress-city under siege, where would Vashin go, with night falling and in nothing but his night-shirt?

'Damn it…' Denniston muttered, hands working by themselves to boil water over the dung-burning stove with which to make beef tea. 'Damn it to hell, but I wish he hadn't…'

Things could have been so much simpler if Vashin had only acted differently. Or perhaps if Denniston had come home later, more in line with routine, and not found him…

He would wait for Ryan, or Kincaid, or any other able-bodied man to arrive home. Then they would be better equipped to deal with Vashin, and the matter could be put behind them.

Kincaid was first back. Denniston ambushed him in the hallway immediately, telling him in a barrage of hurried words what had happened.

'God but that's worth a beating…' Kincaid muttered, colour high in his cheeks. 'You hold him, I'll administer a kicking, and then he's out on his ear. Nothing more to do with us.'

'No.' Denniston shook his head. 'It's not that simple.'

'Isn't it? Sounded simple enough to me!'

'He wronged us, yes, personally. But there's been a crime committed too. I fancy he ought to face some kind of trial for that. After all he's done for us, doesn't he deserve that much?'

In truth, perhaps Denniston simply wanted the decision out of his hands. The matter of Vashin conflicted him too much to think clearly.

Kincaid grumbled but agreed, and together they unlocked Pinkerton's room. Vashin was still there, sitting dejected and with hanging head on Pinkerton's bed. They marched the Circassian to his room, thrust a coat over his shoulders, boots onto his feet, and were off through the dark streets, and to the fort where Erzurum's *seraskeriat* was headquartered. If there was to be justice, after all, what power remained in Erzurum but the military to administer it?

The *seraskeriat* at least seemed not to sleep, but to work at a constant sleepwalk. A tired-eyed desk-officer directed them through dark and low-ceilinged passages to another desk in another office, where a grey-haired and hollow cheeked Turk peered at them over a pair of half-moon spectacles.

He asked a question in Turkish. Denniston realised he had brought no one to interpret. Vashin, however, began to speak quickly, plaintively. Denniston had half-expected the stream of Turkish to be an alibi, but by the desk-officer's expression, and eventual response, it seemed instead to be a full confession.

'He stole from you?' said the officer, in careful English.

'Yes,' Denniston answered; no sense going into the nuances of the case if his words wouldn't be understood.

'And you caught him?'

'Yes.'

'What you want done?'

'I'm sorry..?'

'The thief – what it is you want done to him?'

Denniston was taken aback. Vashin eyed him, not pleading any longer, but only expectant. 'Maybe a…fortnight? In prison?' Denniston sputtered out. 'Two weeks, no more.'

'*İnşallah*,' the officer shrugged. He rose from his desk, straightened up and stretched, his back popping like wood on a fire. 'Follow, please.'

The two doctors and their charge followed, and their journey tended downward, under the fort and into the heart of the hill on which Erzurum was built. They could not have walked for long, but in so short a space of time Denniston already felt they were miles from fresh air or the light of the sun. Here, the walls were slick with condensation, the ceilings dripped, and the air was cold as ice. Denniston felt the atmosphere, thick in his lungs, like an urge to wetly cough.

THE WAR: A STREET IN ERZEROUM.
FROM A SKETCH BY ONE OF OUR SPECIAL ART

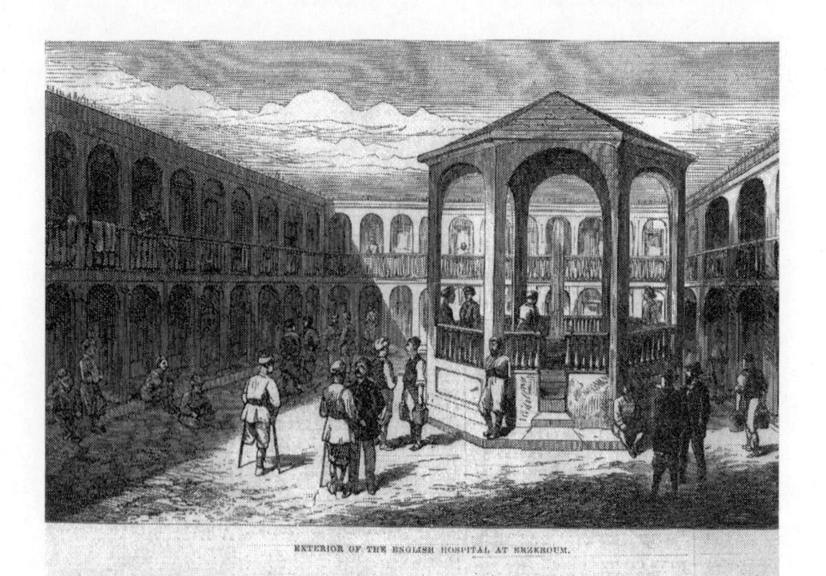

EXTERIOR OF THE ENGLISH HOSPITAL AT ERZEROUM.

The desk-officer spoke to a bald-headed jailer, who guided them down a long oubliette of a corridor. The two Turks spoke amongst themselves for a moment, outside an iron-studded door.

This place was a dungeon, not a prison, and belonged more to the depths beneath some castle than a modern fortress. The atmosphere was close and leeching, and already Denniston wondered if it was worse than Vashin deserved.

And yet the jailer grabbed Vashin by the arm, unlocked the door, and thrust him through. And for the second time that day, Denniston watched as Vashin disappeared, behind lock and key.

The next day, visiting Emin Bey as had become routine now, Denniston asked the old colonel for a favour. They spoke in their customary French. Perhaps their grasp of the language had not improved, but they had grown better at understanding one another, through their regular talks, and an ease had come between them, from that or from the tacit acknowledgement that Denniston had saved the colonel's life in removing his arm.

'You know you need only ask,' Emin Bey answered as he stirred sugar into his coffee.

'Last night,' Denniston began, 'I found a man had wronged me, and I had him imprisoned.'

Emin Bey drew in a sharp take of breath through his pursed lips.

'I presume you have seen the prisons here, then,' said Denniston. 'They were miserable, wet, and cold. The man I sent there was ill.'

'Well enough to get into trouble, it seems.'

'Yes, but sick enough that the sentence I gave might kill him. I did not consider it. And besides, that I gave a sentence at all..? It bothers me. It was hardly a trial, barely justice. A joke. I only hope this kind of mockery of a fair hearing is particular to Erzurum recently – not commonplace in this country.'

Emin Bey did not answer that unspoken question. 'You would have me ask for him released then?'

'I would. It doesn't seem right, to have a man die slowly for the theft of twelve lira. Moreover, the man in question was…a friend, I suppose. he deserved better.'

'Denniston *hekim*!' Emin Bey grinned, clapping one hand to his uniformed chest, as he might once have clapped both hands together. 'These last months have been a poor time for heroes, and yet you find a way, *mashallah*!'

'I do not think I deserve that much praise, sir.'

'Truly? You treat all men like your brothers, and now you treat even the man who has wronged you with mercy. Very Christian, I think… It deserves to be noted and remembered. But, ah! That reminds me.'

Emin Bey rose and surged across the room, to a cabinet, from which he removed a small box. He moved over to Denniston and bowed, offering it with one open hand.

'For what you did in service to me. A gift for a good man,' said Emin Bey solemnly. 'Only a small token, but I hope you will accept...'

Denniston took the box with uncertain hands and opened it. Inside was a silver-chased girdle, hung about with little cameos: stars and crescents that jingled like bells as he lifted it between his fingers. A fine and pretty thing, of fair workmanship, it fairly dumbfounded him.

'Consider it, please, a memento of this place, Denniston *hekim*. Only a trifle, but it was made here, and bought here. It should serve to remind you of Erzurum, if ever you want to be reminded. There is an English word for this, I think..?'

'A keepsake, perhaps?'

'Yes. A keepsake. A gift from myself to you...and perhaps a gift for a lady, too, when you return home?' Emin Bey gave a roguish smile, looking more like Ryan for a moment than himself.

Denniston began to blush, closed the trinket back into the box, and thrust it into his lap, before changing the subject, red-faced. 'You will see what can be done, then? For the man in the prison.'

'Only tell me his name, and it shall be done.'

'Vashin,' said Denniston. But already he was growing absent-minded, considering what the girdle might look like, trim and bright against the black fabric of Agnes Guthrie's waist...

'What would you have me do with him then, after I've had him released?'

'I don't mind. Let him go on his way, I suppose. What you will, so long as doesn't come back to me.'

Chapter 23

On the 8th of February, Ismail Pasha watched as the Sultan's red flag and white crescent flew for the last time above the citadel, and as he watched, it was lowered. First it stayed at half-pole, in mourning for what was lost. Later it would descend entirely, be taken from the pole. Replaced, Ismail thought bitterly. Soon the tsar's colours would take its place.

They met in the northern square at midday, overlooked by the mosque, its arched windows, its rows of pollard poplar trees, and its skinny grey minaret. Ismail supposed it was something to be thankful for, that the minaret still stood, so close to the walls on the Russian's strongest side.

The men on both sides were arrayed for battle rather than ceremony. There was no flash or thunder left in either army after winter and the siege. Ismail Pasha looked at his boys, lining the sides of the plaza. These were the ones still healthy when Mukhtar Pasha made his second retreat. Now the remains of the Erzurum garrison were ragged, in dull colours and faded caps, exhausted even by standing attention, to watch the Russians come.

But the Russians were no better off. No, the *pasha* corrected himself – not Russians, most of them, but Georgians, Armenians, but all in Muscovite green and heavy winter furs. They were a ragged lot, but held their heads high, and marched to a mocking cacophony of brass instruments, throbbing drums, blaring bugles. The overhead sun shone on their boots. Victory had given them leave to polish them, it seemed.

Still, as parades go, it was a somber one.

Ismail Pasha stood before the poplar trees, on the steps of the mosque and waited as the Russians filed in, rank on square on rank into the plaza. It was nothing short of a show of force, he decided: a demonstration that he ought to be thankful for this armistice and a bloodless peace. Perhaps it was true. Ismail Pasha was no longer afraid, but Mukhtar Pasha had told him once, 'of fear and shame, shame has the sharper teeth.' Those teeth had already begun to gnaw at him.

Another screech of bugles sounded across the plaza, announcing the general before he came. They had at least sent Melikov, Ismail observed. If they had sent so small a man as Lazarian or Heimann instead, why, Ismail Pasha should have been sorely tempted to fall on his sword rather than surrender it.

Count General Mikhail Tarielovich Loris-Melikov, at least, was a man one could surrender to in good enough conscience. Or rather, he seemed it.

Riding between the ranks of his men on a white horse, in well-kept bright white overcoat, braided and with two rows of gleaming buttons, he was almost enough to distract from the bony hobble of his horse, the frostbite in the faces and hands of his men.

Ismail Pasha watched him dismount. Another storm of noise came flatulent from that infernal brassband as he the general found his footing, hitched his swordbelt up from the disarray it had gotten into, and strode towards the mosque's steps, and towards the poplars and the *pasha*. He kept his hand on the gilt handle of his sabre, smugly. A proud smile glinted between the hedgerows of Melikov's muttonchops – an absurd and European fashion, Ismail Pasha thought; here is a Prince of Armenia who thinks he is a Count in Moscow who in turn longs to be a factory-owner in France. Quite absurd.

Ismail Pasha bowed his head so the general would not see his bitter scowl, or how his eyes had begun to sting. With steady hands, he unsheathed his kılıç, and passed the sword hilt-first to Melikov.

The general stood for a moment, not taking the sword. To his bitter shame, Ismail realised, he was being made to wait.

'I do not know you…' Melikov said, in smooth Turkish. 'I had hoped to accept Ahmed Mukhtar Pasha's sword today, but again he's fled, has he not? Are the dispatches true? Is he already called *Gazi* at court? "Victorious"… And for what, I wonder? Running?'

'For twice outmanoeuvring you,' Ismail Pasha said, looking up with a smile.

'I would sooner congratulate the man who holds his ground.' Melikov said, and took the *pasha*'s sword. He looked down its dramatically curved blade for a moment, sighting down its length as if down the barrel of a rifle.

Ismail Pasha's breath caught. Here he waited for the gesture that would grant him back his honour, or send him away in disgrace greater than he'd already suffered.

He all but sighed as Melikov return the sword. Hilt-first, he passed it back into the *pasha*'s hands. 'You may keep your colours, so long as ours replace them,' he said. 'You will march beyond the borders of this province, under arms and with honour intact, and from there march where you will.'

Ismail Pasha told himself, sheathing his sword again, neatly as he could: I will not shed a tear. But already they were beginning to ache at the corners of his eyes.

'I am less disappointed in you than I had thought to be, sir,' said Melikov. 'Will two days be agreeable to you?'

'Very agreeable. Thank you, Melikov *effendi*. May I commend you, that God has given you victory.'

Chapter 24

James

My dear Agnes,
It has been two days since the formal surrender, and today we watched the Turks go. A sad sight, and one that moved me more than I had expected.

These were men who, if treated properly, I knew to be capable of anything in the way of fighting and bravery, and more than capable of enjoying all kinds of hardship. Hunger, however, had rendered them miserable; illness too, and the slow gnawing of intolerably poor conditions. They had fought for this city – doubtless they all knew many who had died for it too – and yet here they were ordered out of it.

Aydin Vefyk told me, when we met at the kitchen table to say our farewells, that many of the officers had got together and offered, wretched as they were, to defy the powers in Istanbul, and the truce, and to fight for Ismail Pasha to the last. They offered, said Vefyk, on behalf of their men, and the honour of their regiments, even if the honour of the Sultan himself would not permit it.

But the pasha, he said, has been so thoroughly broken and downcast since Erzurum formally accepted terms that he merely shook his head, sadly, and said, no – no, this cannot go on.

The Russians came in quite the parade, but the Turks left in a sorry and very quiet state by comparison. A long and no doubt sad road is ahead of them before they reach friendly ground. We're told that the armistice involves any number of little towns along the way, and even as far afield as the Danube basin, and all are held by the tsar's forces. They will have to pass plenty of them, and it seems these surrendered towns will remain in Russian hands until the poor Turks pay out some fabulous ransom for each in turn – so the garrison from Erzurum will have plenty of ready reminders of what they left behind.

Other than news, Aydin Vefyk's farewell contained little that was personable. It's not that we have fallen out so much that, really, I never knew the man. He has always been an enigma, and I feel his profession has obliged him at times to seem a friend. I am glad of those times, though, and the opportunities they have presented me.

'I'm sure we shall hear from one another again,' was his final note in our talk. 'God has sent stranger chances both our ways, after all.'

Since then, the Russians have begun to crowd into all the forts and guard houses in the city, manning the walls much as the Turks did before. Oddly, little has changed, except that church-bells now ring between the calls to prayer, woodsmoke rises from hearth-chimneys again. And – I suppose it must be admitted – this new batch of soldiers do a fair bit more in the way of drinking than those that came before.

Guiltily, I am grateful to them. Not for ridding me of my charges or putting me out of work, the hospital being all but empty now and feeling emptier still for the contrast. But for bringing with them letters, and opening up the roads once more so I might send mine!

I received one of yours the day before yesterday. In amongst all this melancholy – the defeatist and defeated air of this whole place – I think I've never known a more welcome sight. For all the little sermons, and all the interest in my spiritual welfare that your letters contain, I might easily mistake your intentions as being more toward conversion than comfort. At Christmas you seemed particularly concerned as to the state of my faith. It's as though you've taken me on as your personal mission, believing me to be a confirmed atheist. At least in that your opinion differs from my mother's – you at least reckon I am worth saving, while she, I think, reckons my soul to be entirely lost. I wonder, in your case, to what extent my liking for Darwin's work is to blame for your low opinion of my spiritual health?

I assure you, though, I have my own beliefs and opinions, and none of them absolutely exclude the existence of a Higher Power. While I am anything but orthodox, I don't suppose you are either – only, you are far better at expressing yourself and your convictions than me.

Not only are you fond of argument, you make of pugnacity a kind of art! Please do not take this as anything but a compliment, for I truly do mean it as praise. Indeed, it was something which first impressed me when we met originally. I only regret that I can't boast the same abilities, You know what a great bear I am with words, grumbling and bumbling in all my manners. Still, I promise you I will try to express my opinions on this matter to you one day, even if only for the pleasure of having you lay them low.

For now, thank God – see? I can do that as well as the next man, though whether you take it to be piety or blasphemy is another matter – we are not prisoners of the Russians, nor even really doctors for them. Time being, we are guests of a sort, and nothing less than simple Englishmen, Scotsmen, and so on. And while our Russian hosts have their share of offensive behaviours, I believe they are trying to be hospitable, and to treat us and the townsfolk in something like a friendly manner. Needless to say, some among the townsfolk are less inclined to return that courtesy, so tensions between them and the occupiers keep the days in Erzurum interesting.

I look very much forward to sending this missive, and receiving more of yours. Peace is sweet and the post is, I have come to believe, a miracle all in itself.

Until I hear from you again though
I remain yours very sincerely,
James Denniston

With time, Denniston thought, one ought to become inured to the prestige of other, reputedly greater men. Rank ought not to sway him – not for exposure to such men, though he had known a few now, but for living so close in proximity to the frailty of all men, great or small. Great men die of dysentery just as other men do, and are no less in need of brandy or ether to see them through injury and surgery. Some men are great in and of themselves – virtuous, honourable, intelligent or wise, whether by talent or practice – but such men occur as often among men of no rank or station as they do among men born to nobility, wealth, or influence.

All this Denniston knew – or told himself he knew – and yet he still felt a giddiness in sharing a room with General Heimann. Here, in the neglected ambassadorial suite of a once very fine Western-styled hotel – the only one of its kind in Erzurum – was the man who had encircled and besieged Erzurum. Here was the man who had ordered the artillery fire and assaults that had plagued the city and filled the hospitals in recent months; the man who had closed the city up tight while typhus, typhoid, and cholera thrived inside its walls. That is, until Melikov swept west from Kars to accept the city's surrender, and claim Heimann's victory. But in his wake, General Vasily Heimann was left behind, while Melikov continued his victory parade towards Istanbul.

A pair of brushed and polished aides de camp in pine green jackets and shining high boots poured black tea for Denniston and Ryan from a good china teapot. All very European, Denniston thought; an effort had been made to put himself and Ryan at ease.

Heimann raised cup and saucer to the height of his gold-edged collar. To the doctors seated across from him, at a high square table, he uttered what could almost have been a toast:

'Good monsieurs, I thank you for accepting my hospitality. Humble as it may be in such a time as this, and after all the city has endured, I assure you, Erzurum is on the mend. Brought into the Empire, perhaps it will even be brought into the modern age, given time!'

He spoke in perfect French. Setting down his cup, and the saucer too, he slapped a white-gloved hand onto his white trousered red-ribboned thigh: a deliberate attempt at British joviality.

Contrived, Denniston thought, as it would be if he and the other European doctors threw out as many wallahs and inshallahs as did their

Turkish patients. The giddiness he had felt passed quickly in Heimann's presence. Thick pointed moustaches, gold braid and brilliant white officer's dress – but he was still only a man, and one with sagging jowls and tired lids round his twinkling eyes. More's the point, as Denniston had told Ryan when they received the invitation to this audience the day before, clearly Heimann did not want only to thank them for their service against him. He wanted something from them; they need only wait and see what.

'After what we endured in Erzurum – and for myself at Kars,' Ryan began, with a sly smile at the mention of enduring Melikov's siege at Kars alongside Heimann's here, 'all this is far from humble. Truly.' He gestured round them at the moulded coving that edged the ceiling, the dripping crystals of the small gas-lit chandelier; at the tall windows and green-gold curtains that lined one side of the room, and most of all the flames that roared warm in the fireplace. 'We've not had so much as real tea in months, general.'

'We are grateful for that much,' said Denniston, feeling he should contribute, though Ryan was the more confident talker, and the more fluent speaker of French.

'Well deserved, certainly! Of course, of course, it's very well deserved. I've heard of your exploits and your efforts, monsieurs, and I hope you will not think it mere flattery when I say that your hospital – as a rock of steadfast service and modern thinking in a raging sea – is a legend in the making!'

For all his protests, it seemed nothing but flattery to Denniston. Ryan and the general exchanged pleasantries for as long as it took for their cups to empty. Quickly, the aides cleared away the china and replaced the tea-service with a set of fine small glasses: the sort the Turks used for their silty black coffee.

'If you've been without tea, *monsieurs*, then I suppose it has been longer still since you last had good French brandy.' Heimann grinned a gracious grin beneath his copious moustaches.

'You might be surprised, general,' Denniston said, feeling, for once, quite sly himself as he remembered Emin Bey's bottle of reserve. 'If I've had any luxury recently, it's been good French brandy.'

Ryan looked askance at Denniston, surprised for only a moment, before he caught himself and was gracious once more. 'Of course, we've had a lot of bad stuff from nowhere in particular as well! I, for on, shouldn't say no to a reminder as to what quality tastes like.'

Brandy was poured, red-amber in the little glasses. Quickly it was drunk – tasting to Denniston of plum pudding and expensive carpentry – and two more rounds came after. Each time, Heimann gave a toast in earnest, rising to his feet and lifting his glass toward the ceiling.

'*Monsieurs*, if you please, to our Turkish hosts, and their continued health. May the past not divide us! … If you please now, to the faith we share; to Christians in heathen lands! … To you, my guests, to your health, and the health of your families. *Za vas*!'

All the while, Denniston exchanged glances with Ryan, between the rise and fall of glasses, the quench and lingering burn of brandy. Whatever Heimann's offer was – whatever his demand might be – it would come soon. He had dazzled them with luxury and plied them with alcohol, flattering all the while. He beat about the bush for only so long.

'Now, between gentlemen – for of course, *monsieurs*, you are educated men; gentlemen, of course – I have a request to make of you. A small favour, in which I hope you will see a chance for mutual benefit…'

Heimann set down his empty brandy glass. It was not refilled. Carefully, Denniston sipped at the contents of his own third pouring.

'I would look *favourably* on it, *monsieurs,*' Heimann continued seriously, 'if you would do me the great honour of – how can I say this? – coming to some arrangement with me regarding your lodgings.'

Denniston wished he would talk in straight lines. Heimann, however, seemed a man who took pride in his equivocation – the kind to confuse wordiness with wisdom, and who could complicate even serious matters just by talking about them.

'Your lodgings, you understand, and mine,' Heimann finished, smiling.

'General?' Denniston ventured. 'I'm not sure I do.'

'Understand?'

'Quite.'

Heimann's smile faltered. 'Allow me to explain. Currently, myself and my staff are lodged here, and find that while adequate it is a poor match to our needs. As gentlemen, of course, you understand that a gentleman has needs. You would, certainly, be provided for very well in return. I would see to it myself that you are well housed after you relocate…'

'General, it's not luxury we want,' said Ryan affably. 'The thing with our present home is that you can fairly toss a stone from it to the hospital. You ought to know a thing or two about the strategic importance of *positioning*, after all.'

'*Monsieurs,* I reiterate: you would be provided for to your preference, and with the utmost *consideration*!'

'We have our preference, general,' said Denniston. 'It lies with our duties and our cases. I would not want to neglect them for the time it might take to relocate. The hospital has known quite enough in the way of disruptions recently.'

'The battle is over,' Heimann said curtly. 'The war soon will be. What work do you have left to do?'

'Your war is over,' Ryan corrected. 'Ours is against older and stronger enemies than you. Their names are sickness and suffering, and their efforts don't let up just because people have stopped shooting at each other, thank you very much.'

In that moment, Denniston was proud of him and of his words – even of himself.

'Then, *monsieurs*,' said Heimann, still with strange eagerness in his voice, 'I shall wish you good evening. I look forward to resuming our talks soon. After all, a hard-won bargain is always the sweeter in the end, no? I only need make it sweet enough to benefit us both. Look at Erzurum herself. She is a prime example. Everything has its price, monsieurs, one only needs to offer it, and at the right time.'

James

My dear Agnes,
The general of the Russian forces now occupying Erzurum has gotten the belief into his head that our house is the finest in Erzurum – or at least the finest of sufficient size for himself and his staff. As such, he has been quite restless over bargaining us out of it.

We held out for perhaps just under a week before General Heimann's offers finally overcame us. A poor innings held against the Russians, by comparison with our Turkish compatriots perhaps, but I think the terms of our surrender were more favourable by far:

Brandy, two crates; champagne, one; and a good deal of vodka. A turkey and a side of beef, and promises of near-infinite potatoes; some salted fish, the quality of which Heimann vouched for very insistently, but regarding which we are less sure. On top of this, a box of forty good cigars, plenty of loose tobacco, and of course new accommodation: a place still only a short while from the hospital – a point on which we would not be budged – and with a hutch of laying chickens outside.

A squad of soldiers in green jackets and beige overcoats marched upon the consulate the morning after we accepted terms. Grunting and barking at each other in Russian, they negotiated the migration of our furniture and affects out into the courtyard and then five streets across the city.

Strange once more to see the consulate crowded round with soldiers-turned-stevedores, and the space outside filled with the building's gutted contents, just as it had been when Zohrab prepared to leave it behind. There was my bureau desk, for instance, with its feet stained dark in the yard-slurry and snow, a draw hanging out of its side half-open, like the mouth of a panting dog. There was my suitcase, strapped to its desktop. And I admit, I was caught on hooks all through the move for fear the locked door or the case might somehow burst open, scattering my papers and case-writing and letters all to the winds and the snowmelt and the high probability of rain. They held firm, however, but I fussed over them all the same, chattering to the soldiers in French quite broken up with nerves as they hauled my things through the streets, as roughly as if they were escorting a criminal.

Doctor Idris treated the whole matter with some distrust and the Russians themselves with more. He insisted on carrying his own weight, as if he felt the Russians would sooner confiscate his affects and take him into custody for the mere fact of being a Turk than they would offer him the same service they offered us. Old as he is, and small in stature, he thankfully has an ant-like strength and the stubborn long-suffering patience of a mule, which is more than I could say for our Russian help.

That brief drama done with, though, we are installed now, and starting to get settled in.

Our new surroundings are quite à la Turc when compared with the Western comforts of the consulate: a small yard with the promised chickens and turkey, and a little blue-tiled fountain appended onto an edge of the building, still bubbling away quite cheerfully for all this city has been through of late. Being some ways downhill from the hospital now though, and therefore downwater of its latrines, I am reluctant to use the water for anything very much, and would prefer to go to the hospital proper for use of its pump.

It is, all in all, two storeys high, with the topmost smaller than the lower, and yet with a terraced roof leading out from it, hung over with wooden beams and climbing vines. Though the terrace is grubby with neglect from the long winter, and though I doubt we'll get much use from it while the days are still bitter-cold, I fancy it would be very pretty in warmer weather.

I wonder, then: shall we be here still when the clime turns kinder, and spring comes properly in? I don't know whether we have any obligation beyond the Hippocratic to remain, now that we are no longer directly serving the Turks. We have our contracts to the SHC, of course, for I think another month, and perhaps we ought to report to some other hospital for that duration. But for now we are comfortable here, and no communications have come to that effect.

We have far fewer cases now, and many of those with any chance of recovery are well on their way towards it. In any case, we are no longer starving, and there is wood now in our stoves. The chill we suffered through has made my chest quite fussy, and I find myself coughing at night, but I think it's nothing that won't be fixed soon enough. After all, the worst of winter's rages are over now, and our new home is very warm.

Regardless, the siege is up, and the contract that still hangs over Kincaid and Walker and I will end shortly as well. If peace holds between England and the Russians I might even be home in six weeks or so. But from the way the Russians talk, who knows what might happen. Ever uncertainty keeps us alert.

Until then I am yours, Very sincerely,
James Denniston

Their letters were quite confused by now. Agnes' came in bundles from Istanbul and Bayburt, and holding stations along the way, and from dates scattered all through the last two months. It made conversing by letter hard, but Denniston still took great joy in them – greater still for how long he'd gone without.

He did not try to order them. Their disarray became part of the charm these batches of new letters had. He would pick one at random when he sat down to write, and respond to it. Too long he'd been forced towards order in all aspects of his life; order or failure, order or death. It was good to be permitted some chaos now.

His new room was larger than the last, and with a great low bed, softer by far than he'd grown used to. Patterned rugs lay on the ground and the corners between wall and ceiling sloped in pleasing fashion, not in sharp angles but curves toward panels of fragrant wood that mirrored the floorboards below. A lamp of etched and pierceworked brass hung down in the room's middle. Another similar lamp sat on the desk he had brought from the consulate.

Starkest difference of all, this room had a window and cushioned window-seat. It looked out from the second floor, downhill across Erzurum: terrace roofs, winter trees, muddy streets, fortifications and then the swathe of mud that marked the earthworks, gone now to neglect. But outward from that was a plain, empty now of the Russian host, and in spring likely to be grown over with grass once more. On clear days, one could even glimpse the shapes of mountains, showing out in the misty distance.

Denniston sat at his desk, as he had in Istanbul before, and for the first time in quite some time indeed, he discovered he was calm. Cool sunlight slanted through the window and fell sideways onto his desktop. His days had enough work in them now to feel worthwhile, but not so much as to wear on him. He was fulfilled and at peace.

Agnes had not told him to stop using her Christian name in letters, though neither had she given express permission. It had been tacitly given, however, for she signed off her letters the same way. It seemed a small thing to be so pleased about, but Denniston was pleased all the same, knowing as he did what it signified: esteem, trust, and progress between them. Whether as friends or more, it hardly mattered. Whether Agnes chose, in the long of things, to give him friendship or love, Denniston was determined to treasure either.

That, too, was part of his peace: certainty in uncertainty, and comfort in himself.

Agnes

Dear James,
Picture my bureau quite scattered with letters, my paper-knife nearly blunt from the opening of them, and the drawers of my desk quite overflowing; all this is because I have taken it upon myself to put all your correspondence into some kind of sequence. Your letters come in such an odd chronology now, released and written all at different times and many fragmentary or else entirely undated, that it is more than just one woman's job to order and apprehend them all. Of course, however, I try as best I can.

Such tales and dramatics they contain, and recounted in a very satisfactory way throughout your most recent letters that it seems my calls for 'colour' went well-heeded. Some of them seem such tall stories that I've half a mind to test you on their verity in person when some months have elapsed; I would first need to see you again, however, and you say yourself you do not know when that might be. I hope it might be sooner than never, but in the meantime I think I shall want my collection of correspondences in good order all the same: a story like yours ought not to be done the disservice of being told any way but from beginning to end.

There are to be considered, though, your latest and most hopeful estimates: a matter of months, half a dozen weeks, and then all this might be over. It's a queer thought to entertain; I have known you as Doctor James Denniston of Erzurum much longer now than I had as James Denniston of Greenock or Glasgow. From what you have said, your former selves might hardly recognise you were they to meet you now – I wonder if I should know you better, being that I have been conversing with your current self all this long and wintry while. I have never met this new man in person, of course, but I do look forward to doing so.

Little news from beyond Istanbul makes it so far as Manchester. In the absence of your letters, until recently it was all too easy to imagine the worst of all cases. I heard only of the Turkish retreat, and do you know it came upon me as a very motley sort of feeling, of both dread and hope, and not only because I had been so fixed in opinion regarding this war at its onset: that the Russians ought to be victorious, as quickly and absolutely as they may. Rather, it struck me that I knew, on receiving that news, that I would hear from you again soon or not at all.

To hear that you are kept kindly enough, as a very merry sort of prisoner, is, as such, a relief to me. There is, however, much talk of war in the papers here, after Great Britain so firmly interceded on behalf of the Turks in prompting this truce: many, mostly young men, are spoiling for Britain to bring force to their demands on Russia, and come to the aid of Turkey. France, after all, is similarly filled with threats of involvement in the whole affair.

I wonder if your pride, or perhaps what you might term your more 'mercenary' sensibilities, might prefer a longer war, and an extension on your contract with the Stafford House Committee? But I worry what it might mean, should the papers and the rumours prove true, and the war spark up once more, larger than it was before.

Until I hear from you again

Sincerely yours,

Miss Agnes Guthrie

James

My dear Miss Guthrie,

For my part I worry what peace might mean. Of course it would mean a homecoming in a matter of weeks, and I cannot deny that this a heartwarming prospect, at least for certain parts of my character. But for others there is some small amount of dread to the idea.

Should I come home so soon then my plans for the present and future are quite unsettled. Here the future is uncertain, but my role in it is quite assured. Home, however, I haven't the slimmest idea of what I shall do to keep myself occupied or, more notably, employed – I've had enough of starvation and austerity for one lifetime, I think, and should like to be more comfortable, financially, in days to come. But on the other hand, I'm afraid that this little adventure – as you so glamorously term it – has quite aroused a roving propensity in me, and so I imagine I'll find it very difficult to settle down to the quiet and humdrum way of things again. As in all things, I fancy I shall have to come to some manner of compromise.

For now, however, I carry on into all this uncertainty, and keep my head up over it. 'Sufficient unto the day is the evil thereof,' etc.

The evils of the day, in this instance, comprise mostly in a house full of Russians. By day and by some turns at night the hospital keeps us busy, but most evenings we're press-ganged into playing hosts for hordes of notables and dandies in officer's whites, spurs clicking and with sabres hung rakishly low, clattering against their boots and so on...

For them, our new home has become quite the favourite rendezvous. It's due in no small part, I think, to how affable an entertainer our Doctor Ryan is, and how much he seems to enjoy gambling with and taking such great sums of money from the packs of local princes and counts that prowl Erzurum now.

Do you know, I don't think I've met a single commissioned officer who didn't have at least one other title to his name, and yet so few among them seem any more noble spirited than the commoner folk I've lived among all my life. Titles, I suppose, come very cheap in this part of the world, and so I'm not surprised they do so little to make their bearers any richer in virtue.

In any case, they crowd to the door and in a great effusive rush of good humour and apparent amiability, surge into our little house as if it were the still-besieged city and our front door a breach in the walls. To their credit, they make small gifts to us – sweetmeats, chocolates, tea – which I have given up claiming we do not deserve. And to their shame they remain long into the night, making loud and slurring toasts in Russian, and on second thought in French for our personal benefit, so we might not feel left out. For my part, I'd sooner be left out of it entirely, but Walker, Kincaid, and Ryan feel differently.

To this end we are rarely without friends, but I fear it's less for our personal merit and jolly society, and more for the case of excellent Irish whiskey that General Heimann lately sent down to us from his headquarters at our old house.

At least our guests are among the better behaved Russians abroad now in Erzurum. Not all are so cordial, towards us or the city's peace in general. Last night Ryan and I had a great row with some of our neighbours. A house next to ours has a few line officers I think for inmates and, to put it shortly, they managed to blow themselves up!

By the means of their own pigheaded stupidity and greed, some of them, after no small amount of whatever intoxicants they could get their hands on, had begun tearing up surplus cartridges for the gunpowder inside. These charges, you understand, are mostly for the older style of small arms still used among some of their regiments, but others were reserved for artillery pieces, and so had quite the kick to them.

Seeing that peace has been bought in Erzurum, I suppose they thought to sell on the powder and shot, as they would have no further need for them personally. But no doubt some idiot among them saw nothing amiss in smoking while they did so, until of course a grain of powder caught light, and all the rest went up as well.

The result was fire-crews all through the night, and panic in the streets. heir whole house went up, and our own got such a shake we were all sure that we'd found ourselves in the midst of another cannonade, as if the war had started over again. I don't doubt many of the Turks felt similarly and were very alarmed indeed. I was blown nearly clean out of my bed and I think the same must've been true of my colleagues, for we were all up and awake in moments, shouting over the ringing in our ears about what had happened and what might be done.

We at once set out to help however we could, in a flurry of, I must admit, blasphemies and curses, hurrying into the smoking rubble that had been the house next door. Four were found badly hurt, whom we pulled away and stabilized til they could be brought to the hospital. Three, I have only a little pity in saying, were dead when we found them.

It was strange, after this change of times and pace in our lives, to be thrown into the same excitement as flocked to us during the days of the siege; to have shrapnel and powderburns in the hospital once more. But beyond such small upsets, recent times progress much in the same routine style – not quiet by the standards of Greenock, perhaps, but all in relative calm.

Of course in the meantime

I am yours very sincerely,

James Denniston

March 1878

Chapter 25

Denniston had never been a full-fledged doctor in peacetime or on home soil. At the Greenock infirmary he had been an assistant – a *jarra bashi* by any other name – and at Glasgow he had been a student. But Erzurum had made him a surgeon, and one of the foremost doctors in the city's highest performing hospital. Indeed, at times, he had very nearly been the only doctor at work in that hospital, when illness and evacuation had taken so many others from their work.

War, and its tireless manufacturing of wounded men and of sickness, had given him the opportunity that, in Greenock, Glasgow, Edinburgh, or Manchester, he would have had to buy, whether through bribes and references, or a family pedigree. Being that he had neither money, nor a highly placed family name, it would have meant a glorified apprenticeship at the hands of an older doctor, still clinging to older views and less effective methods. Erzurum had given him his own practice, his own patients, and taught him the duty a doctor ought to feel towards both.

The siege, however, was over. Slowly, the hospital was trickling empty. Even the epidemics had loosened their grip on the city. In these quieter times, Denniston fancied that the difference between doctor's work here and at home was lessening too. His cases had grown simpler: consulting hours in the hospital, and private visits to homes, families, individuals, whom he came to know as people as well as patients.

In the mornings and through to the afternoon he would go out into the city. Crisp air, raw skies white as laundered bed-linens – these things helped his breathing, laboured as it had been of late. On these rounds, he would see to civilians. There were some he visited on the way.

A baker, with a persistent ulcer on his gum and an ache in his teeth, was his first port of call. The baker, a Georgian, finished setting the fires of his ovens just as Denniston passed, filling his plaster-and-brick home with subtle-scented smoke and the stronger aroma of baking bread. Denniston examined and advised him to treat the ulcer with a bicarbonate of soda poultice to relieve the pain until it subsided. The baker gifted him a ring of warm chewy bread for his effort, crusted with dark-toasted sesame seeds, and from there, Denniston carried on.

The hospital had become a kind of consulting clinic in recent weeks, where civilians and the Russian rank-and-file could wait in line to be seen and voice their concerns and complaints. Kincaid, Ryan and Denniston alternated between seeing the walk-ins, dousing tensions in the queues between the onetime enemies – now turned occupiers and occupied – and tending to the hospital's longer stays and persistent cases. Walker, Morisot, and Ryan all up now from their sickbeds, they each of them went about their work at whatever pace suited them best – their days permitted that now.

After Denniston's consulting hours he'd see to more private cases: Russian officers, and Turkish civilians not rich enough to leave Erzurum entirely after its occupation. With the Russians he took tea and brandy; with the Turks, tobacco and coffee as he saw to their maladies, eased their minds, assured them they were jumping at shows, not coming on sick, or else would soon be well again.

Little in the way of money changed hands in Erzurum these days, except at the gamblings tables of the Russians. Denniston asked none for his treatment, but often went home paid all the same, in meat and eggs, beer and coffee and tea, sometimes a plucked chicken. From the Russians, most of all, his services gained him clemency, favours owed, in what was still essentially captivity, in a city most civilly held hostage.

On that night, the ninth of March, Denniston wended his way home, meandering through the upper city's snare of streets, case by case. The weather had grown cool rather than cold of late. He no longer needed his great motley fur coat, and travelled once more in his hat and threadbare longsuffering jacket, with the same unused revolver still snug and tight in its pocket.

At the Stafford House Committee doctors' new lodgings, a letter waited for him. It was short, abrupt, full of worry and hope, and began with his Christian name. It was dated from the tenth of February, and had wandered all this time before reaching him.

He read it, sitting at the window-seat of his room, smiling til his cold-chapped cheeks felt stiff and stretched. She had cared for him; feared for him; called him not 'Doctor' but 'James'.

Dear James,

You have said I will not hear from you again for some time, and talk of closed lines, encirclement, ongoing sieges; this silence, I tell myself, I can bear, but I wonder now if this is a lie. I could endure it if I knew that it would resolve; knew certainly that you would write to me again and tell me all is well. But your last letters – 'last,' a damnable word – are already so full of loss. Death in your part of the world already seems so indiscriminate, whether by shill or shot or sickness…

I fear for you, quite unbearably. It's difficult to form words. I sleep badly now, and so my waking hours are hazy, like dough stretched thin to make bread, and nothing seems very clear. Even in my own life, the most regular things seem all unsurety. So you see, the fear enters everything.

I do not know if this letter will ever reach you. All the same I am sending it on the strange, slim chance that you might get it some day, and know not so much that I pray and fret over your safety, but that I have all this time been very glad for your correspondence – indeed, for your companionship. I thank God that we met. My only sadness and my only fear is that we shall only have met twice, and never again thereafter.

James, you are a good man, a kind man, and one I am proud to have known, to an extent that surprises none more than myself. My hopes are with you, for however much or little they might be worth.

Until I hear from you again
I am yours very sincerely,
Agnes Guthrie

The letter's corners were creased now from how tight he had held it. Suddenly his whole feeling on the letter became bashful. It was more intimate than any she'd sent since or before – more open and raw than he felt quite right in looking at. Could it be that she had sent it without thinking, and regretted it now? He wanted to reread it, yet felt that he could not. Instead he folded it tight and stashed it in the biscuit tin where he kept his other letters, buried beneath the others, at the hidden bottom of the stack.

At least in letters she'd sent after, the form of address had remained the same: *Dear James.*

James

My dear Agnes,

Just last night I received a letter dating from more than a month ago. And as with all your letters, I need not tell you how very welcome it was. You were in rather gloomy spirits at the time. And this, for me, is conflicting. I do not know if I should be deeply sorry to have put you through such a miserable time, or whether I should be deeply flattered that you found yourself feeling so intensely on my account. I hope it's not too presumptuous to say that, currently, I am both. Bashfully, I must admit, that I am humbled, pained, and pleased, all to a measureless degree, and one my words certainly are not fit to fathom.

Of course, it's all to no end. You have heard, since, that I am still very much all right, and that is what matters. Certainly I am not dead, in so far as my own medical opinion is to be trusted. But if you should prefer that I forget the letters you sent in your worries – or even destroy any trace of it – I shall do so without hesitating. I know better than any that worrying, and times of duress can make us say things we would not otherwise wish to say. It is up to you, as ever; and as ever, I'll endeavour to respect your wishes and ideas of propriety.

If this letter, though, was due to some news you heard, I think we have some wretched sensationalist in the press to be blame. Ryan, for instance, mentioned rumours that the SHC surgeons had died to a man before Mukhtar Pasha's relief came. And I have also heard of a correspondent to some paper or other at Bayburt, who telegraphed home that every doctor sent out to Erzurum had died there, or very soon would do, and published this news without a shred of proof to reinforce it. Certainly, telegraphs from Istanbul were sent some small time later, saying what rubbish those reports were, but not before the tabloids in England had leapt on the news and printed it.

Still, it did not always seem appropriate that we hope for so much luck as we have all had in surviving, relatively hale and healthy. Others were not so lucky, and I'd not have Guppie or Pinkerton forgotten.

And if you have any embarrassment over the matters you put down in that February letter, I feel I should say – if it is any help – that I was not always in high spirits myself. But when those darker moments came, it wasn't with the sorts of thoughts you'd approve that I consoled myself – thoughts as to faith and salvation and God's will and that I was doing it – but rather I took solace in thoughts of home, and friends, and family, and you.

We doctors made many toasts over the course of the siege, though sometimes only with water or beef tea, or coffee. It was a way, I think, of airing our hopes; turning them into wishes and discovering that we shared them, all of us, and that somehow perhaps this might make them more solid. On almost every given night, the last toast was in honour of 'wives and sweethearts', and every time I must say that I smiled in secret to myself, and thought silently of you, and took from those thoughts whatever strength I could.

Make of that what you will, or ask me only to make of it no more, and I shall, without question. But for now, please know that I'm yet alive and well, and I think you have had more of a hand in that than I can ever properly express, or you will ever truly know.

For now I am yours
Very Sincerely,
James Denniston

Chapter 26

A telegram came. The Russians had only just begun to set up Erzurum's first telegraph office, but it was not yet complete. This message came by wire to Bayburt, and the Turkish remnant headquarters set up there. To Erzurum, though, it came as post, by way of a mounted courier with a little printed card stashed in his sack full of mail.

It was Kincaid that received it that afternoon, but for all the rest of the day he kept quiet. It was only that night that he gave out the news, at the table in their lodgings that served for both dinner, drinking, and the card games of Ryan, Kincaid, Walker, and whatever Russian guests they had for the evening.

'They say we'll be allowed to leave.' Four vodkas had slurred Kincaid's voice, and loosed his lips.

'Who does?' Walker asked.

'The Committee. The SHC.'

'Contract's up,' said Walker. 'I'm not surprised.'

'But that's the thing. Contract or no, they're ordering us out.'

'Funny word to use then,' said Denniston. '"Allowed".'

'All British doctors allowed to leave. Stop.' Kincaid quoted mechanically. 'SHC hospital to be left to local authority. Stop.'

'Left to local authority just means left behind,' Denniston muttered. 'Why phrase it as permission to leave – like it's an honour? – why phrase it like that when it sounds more like dereliction of duty?'

'Ah,' said one Russian, stroking his moustaches in a way no doubt meant to warn them he intended to let them in on some great military secret, and expected their awe and gratitude. 'Ahh, you see, now... Word from Europe. The world at large! It's assured, gentlemen – that is, I have it on good authority, most assuredly...'

His name, if Denniston recalled correctly, was Colonel Roman Stepanovich Shuvalov. He remembered only because he had twice had to ward this man away from the hospital's supplies of white spirits and rubbing alcohols. But from Ryan he knew a little more of the man: that he was unusual among Russian officers in the sense that he had no title of his own save what courtesy granted him. He was, or so he had confided to Ryan, the third son of one Count Shuvalov in Saint Petersburg – but of course this meant little more to most Russians than that they ought to call him 'sir'. It afforded him command of a small unit, and the dubious honour, ungranted to many of his peers, of leading his men in the line of battle. For this last accolade, he bore a shrapnel scar, just close to the left edge of his hairline. Moreover, Ryan had excised a misfired bullet from his side not two weeks back, and so, it seemed, earned the right to mock him.

'What is it you're so assured of, Shuvalov?' Ryan said, with a dramatic sigh. 'Always so full of secrets, man. I'd suggest you go into intelligence, if not for some pretty significant deficits in that department.'

Shuvalov puffed out his chest and continued. 'I have it from the mouth of Brigadier Anatoly Ilyich, and on his sworn word. Austria, gentlemen... Austria has declared war on the Russian Empire!' He paused for a response that he seemed to find disappointing: not a gasp among his audience. 'What's more!' He continued with renewed bluster. 'England has declared itself for Austria! ... Or was it the other way around? I forget, I'm afraid, but regardless, it seems inevitable. We shall all,' he said sadly, 'find ourselves on opposite sides of a war soon enough.'

'I admit,' Dennison began, taking a measured sip of brandy, 'I don't quite know where the SHC would stand if that were true.'

'And I assure you, doctor, it is!' said Shuvalov.

'Well then, if war has been declared,' Denniston declined to correct himself, with the secret smile of a sober man speaking to one more drunk by far. 'Britons we might be, but we didn't ship out here on Britain's behalf, did we?'

'The Committee's neutral,' said Walker. 'That's the official stance. Medical aid, not military support.'

'And what of your *unofficial* stance, doctors?' said Shuvalov, clearly thinking himself very sly. 'And what of it when France joins the fray and declares for Russia, hm?'

'My stance..?' Denniston said, quivering, faltering. He didn't know. Some part of him would use whatever skills he had against the Russians – would go back to that at a moment's notice, as he had for the Turks. He was invested in their cause now, and Shuvalov had done nothing to coax him towards the Russian one. But peace was sweet. He'd had a taste, and was not ready to leave it behind – not with his contract all but over, and home very nearly in sight.

'*Your* stance,' Ryan cut in, rescuing them all, 'will be far too shaky to see you to quarters if you drink any more tonight, colonel. Let me show you out. One more for the road, and then I'll walk you – least I could do, of course. I have, I'm pretty sure, a hipflask somewhere... Maybe that could tempt you away and to bed?'

James

My dear Agnes,

We have been asked from the city by the SHC – not pressingly, not active immediately, but the 'allowance' has been given us. Perhaps the reason is simple: Erzurum's occupation, and the coming close of our contracts. Or else perhaps it's pre-emptive, the Committee knowing, as no-one else seems to know for certain, that we stand on the eve of war. That is, war renewed between Turks and Russians, but newly broken out as well by interventions on both sides by France and Austria and Great Britain.

Whether these tales are confirmed or turn out to be little more than distorted rumours, I don't doubt they will be very much passé by the time this letter reaches you. All the same, perhaps you will find it interesting to hear what I hear, as I hear it, and so get something of an insight into our experiences here at Erzurum. That is, after all, something you often say would please you.

Talk of war between Britain and Russia has lit a fire under much of what I do now in Erzurum, and much of what goes on in the city at large – as if the whole town were a kettle and everything in it had started to simmer.

Much as I help Russian soldiers and Turkish civilians alike, I think there are things said by both about me behind my back, each muttering over my treating the other. The Russians though have less trust of we British and Commonwealth doctors than do the Turks, whose respect we have spent longer already in earning. This is particularly true of the rank and file Russians. Every street corner seems a-gaggle with footsoldiery. With no duties to better divert them, they loiter, and mutter as I pass. Ryan, Kincaid, and Walker talk of similar experiences. Half the city knows by now where each of us has come from, and is hasty enough to presume we are all patriotic to the point of being enemies now – and all for nothing but rumours!

This makes little change to our routines, though. Indeed, we don't have time to let it affect our days, for the call to leave – whenever it might be realised – has given us work aplenty, mostly in the form of accounting, inventorying, and otherwise and in all ways making surveys of our deeds here. Truly though, I think this is one of the cruelest duties I've done for the SHC's sakes: trying vainly but as best I can to make out my accounts and cases for the Committee.

Requisitions and acquisitions; orders and imports and personal costs; what of our supplies has been wasted, and what has seen fair use. The price racks up and up into numbers that, in honesty, inspire a kind of miserable vertigo – surely more than any one person could pay, and yet still the figures do not seem nearly proportionate to the damage done to Erzurum and its families. The figures are both too much, and not nearly enough.

This would be the case whether war hung over us or not. As it does, the only change is that, when we doctors take walks, we take them outside the citadel's walls; within them, the atmosphere has grown too heady to allow for any calm.

Beyond the walls, there were of course battles, and the ravages left by a besieging army. The land is marked by that: suburbs torched into skeletons, or more disturbingly, suburbs left empty and abandoned. The ground is torn up and pitted with earthworks, caved in since by rain. Here and there, a great pit dug by a falling shell.

But for all this, spring is having its say as well in the wide surrounds of the city. Shoots break through the much-abused earth, and the land is freckled and flattered with sprigs of green. Fields plundered by Russians and by the winter are again full of diligent Turks, bent to the task of making their land fruitful again, sowing new grain.

For all the shadow cast by war, the future here seems mostly bright. Perhaps that's the thing with dark times – that, after they are passed, everything seems lighter for the comparison. So I hope this trend might continue, and whatever the result of these rumours, I will see you again soon.

Until then I remain yours

Very sincerely,

James Denniston

The day was brighter than any of them could remember. Again the skies were blue, and a soft wind blew through the ruined land and weed-grown fields that surrounded the outskirts of Erzurum, beyond the citadel walls.

Denniston had suggested the walk, and took Ryan and Kincaid with him. 'A constitutional' was the phrase he'd used, though it reminded him sorely of Pinkerton as soon as he had uttered it; of the walk they took together in the snow, a blanket round Denniston's shoulders as they slowly ceased their shaking.

They left out of the city's western gate, the same one they had entered through on first arriving in Erzurum. At first the ground was wasteland, too churned into mud by the feet and hooves and wheels of that first pressing Turkish retreat into the city, and too cracked by ice and snow to be anything else. But the road that had once passed under that gate resumed a ways beyond the walls, and they followed it into trails and tracks that wound between hamlets and farmhouses, just now being reclaimed in the wake of the siege.

The Russian presence was sparser here, but not entirely absent. As the three doctors came upon a clutch of houses and outbuildings, they saw a pack of infantrymen, standing and squatting in the country-buildings' shade.

The doctors stopped still. The soldiers, in their tan and pine-green uniforms, were watching an old bent Turk's efforts to fix one of the cottages. Amongst themselves, they laughed as he struggled to repair its shattered roof.

Animals, Denniston thought. Idleness had turned them savage. But his small spark of anger turned to apprehension. The Russians had seen them and their attentions had changed.

'Bloody hell...' Kincaid muttered, as the pointing and murmuring began. Soon it turned to guffaws and laughter. 'He's coming over. The big lad – of course it'd be the big lad...'

The largest of the soldiers, barrel-chested and thick-legged, crossed the stretch of weed-strewn grass between his pack and the doctors. Denniston's jaw set tight as he watched the big man approach Ryan, bending his knees to equal their heights.

Still, Ryan angled his chin up, and looked down his nose at the other man. His whole posture was a study in calm superiority, uncowed by what would surely have made Denniston himself feel very much unmanned.

The Russian grinned, baring his teeth in Ryan's face. A snort of laughter, and still he got no rise from Ryan.

'Wonder if he has something to say?' Ryan said in measured English, not taking his eyes off the Russian's. 'If you're content to make faces, man, I'd sooner you did it further from mine...'

Then the big Russian scowled, face twisting into a leer. He began to shout, inches from Ryan's face, flecking his cheeks with spittle.

Ryan did not balk. He stood firm, but if he felt anything like Denniston did, perhaps it was because his knees had locked and his guts had clenched, and the sudden outburst had frozen him.

The rest was a blur.

A fist lashed out – Ryan's or the Russian's – but it was Ryan's face that came away bloody. Red streamed from a break in the skin of his scalp, but already Ryan was laying into the bigger man, fists whirling as the Russian bore up against the assault, buckling in under punches and wrapping his arms bearlike around the smaller man.

Kincaid joined the fray, wresting the soldier away from Ryan.

No sooner had he joined than the whole scene was a storm of fists and struggling limbs and raised voices. Denniston was in amongst it all – had lost himself in it, thinking not of himself but his friends.

A sudden sharp glint thrust the brawl into stunned silence and stillness. One of the Russians had drawn a heavy curved sabre.

'Bastard!' Ryan spat through bloody teeth, and went immediately to his own swordbelt. He loosed a few inches of steel before halting. The Russians had gone immediately for their own sidearms: swords and pistols, waving and levelling them.

It came over Denniston as a kind of helpless calm. He would not be going home. Here was where it would end, and by pointless accident – same as by shell or sickness.

A shot rang out across the landscape, deafening for a moment.

It doesn't hurt, was Denniston's first thought. There was no pain.

But the shot had been fired skywards. The captain of the Russian pack had fired, begun to shout the others into line, as he whipped Ryan's original aggressor to the ground with the butt of his pistol.

The fear came all at once as soon as Denniston realised he was safe. It was a sickening wave of relief, desperate and overwhelming as the urge to vomit. His vision swam. But through his hazy eyes he saw the officer turn to a figure, still astride another's chest and laying into them with blow after blow.

It was Kincaid. Under battered cheeks and blossoming bruises, there were the bright eyes and the fierce red beard. Nearby another Russian lay on the ground, close to the one he had flattened prone and pinned with the weight of his body. The other Russian rolled in dirt, whimpering. As Denniston watched, the whimpers became a howl – an animal sound, more like a hungry child than a grown man. He was cupping a trembling hand tight to the side of his skull, blood seeping out from his tight grip all the same.

Kincaid came to a stumbling stand, backing away from the chastened soldiers. His body heaved, his breathing panted. A rage had come over him, and now begun to pass. From his bloody mouth and bruised lips he spat a chunk of something shapeless and gristly. It was an ear.

Denniston turned and retched into the grass.

'Doctors,' the captain warned them in French. 'I suggest you go.'

They ran the first hundred yards back to the city gate. After that they walked in stunned silence.

What happened had shaken them, but worse for Denniston was seeing what hid inside Kincaid: a merciless savagery woken by hot blood. What else, he wondered, could a man like that do when provoked?

Days later, they had sat in the hospital's cleared out courtyard, no sign any longer of the corpses beneath the ground. A sudden merciless rain had fallen that morning, pockmarking the dust, then turning it to mud. They'd buffed and polished their boots the night before, but all for nothing now: they were grimed halfway to the knees, trousers tucked into their boots in military fashion. And the cane-thin Russian photographer, demanding their photograph for some newspaper back in Saint Petersburg, had caught every inch of their sorry state.

When a copy of the exposure came through, developed and printed, the doctors sat round the kitchen table in their lodgings, eyeing it, incredulous.

'We look a band of brigands!' Ryan cried, despairing.

The young Australian had taken such time pomading his bronze hair, starching his white collar, combing his whiskers that his surprise at least seemed well-warranted. But as to the rest, surely they'd known that even their best efforts would be in vain?

'You say that as if it's news,' Walker scoffed.

Dark and youthful once, his recent illness had left his complexion greyed and sullen in a way that showed, somehow, even in the pewter and silver and patina-green of the photograph. The shimmer and smile, at least, had not gone from his eyes, but it was something that showed only in motion. The photographer had not been able to capture it as they all sat unnaturally still, waiting for the chemicals in his little cloaked box to take.

They all hunched in over the copy, where it lay on the long low table in their house's downstairs room. A jostling and uneasy knot of elbows had formed around it, as each doctor tried to recognise themselves.

Ryan looked quite the man of action with his hussar's moustaches and a sabre leaning jaunty against one knee. He was the only one able to keep up a smile for as long as the Russian photojournalist took in fussing with his camera.

By contrast, the older Doctor Idris was all but scowling, straight through the surface of the picture and at the viewer themselves. A red Turkish cap sat straight and correct on his head. Deep lines furrowed his face.

Walker, too, had kept on his hat, similar to Idris' own: a Turkish thing, given him as a souvenir by one grateful patient, but he wore it aslant. In the finished photograph, his face was confused and blurred into many faces by how many times his expression had shifted during the exposure.

'I look a bloody ghost!' he said. 'All blurred together, nothing where it ought to be.'

Morisot was fortunate enough to be working with cases as the others ogled the picture. He avoided seeing his own likeness now, but there he still sat in the photograph, stout and unkempt about the jaw and chin. Of all the buttons on his waistcoat, only one stood any chance at closing over his jolly paunch. Even in the stillness of the photograph, it seemed engaged in a valiant struggle, fit to burst at any moment.

'Won't presume to speak for us all,' Denniston began, 'but I don't think I'll be asking for a copy to send home…'

In the image, he was sat just a little off from its centre, dark round the eyes and with a gauntness to his cheeks that not even a full beard could hide. A brigand indeed, he thought, wondering if Agnes would recognise him even if he did send a copy.

'Asked for or not,' said Ryan, 'this picture'll be bandied about Saint

Petersburg in whatever papers'll have it, within the bloody week.'

Walked chuckled. 'At least they'll see what a bloody job of work it's been, dealing with their lads. The age it's put on us all!'

The others bantered around him, but Denniston fixated more on something absent from the photograph. Kincaid was not present. For his part in the scrap outside the city walls, he'd been discharged on grounds of conduct unbecoming. Given the choice of a quiet return to Istanbul or the drawn-out mockery of a court-martial, he'd chosen the former, and been sent down like a schoolboy in modest disgrace. And for what? Defending himself, his colleagues, his friends. That was the conclusion Denniston had come to in the intervening days. The horror of Kincaid's act had passed, just as any horror of the visceral always must for a doctor. Instead, as a doctor should, Denniston looked to the cause, if not the cure.

It was easy to forget sometimes, given the comparative luxury of their lodgings and living, but such things served as a hard reminder. They were each of them prisoners, or else part of the spoils of war the Russians had won in occupying Erzurum. If this was how they were dealt with as allies-under-armistice, how might they be treated if Britain joined the war?

They would become prisoners in practice then, and lose what lenience they had.

It was in that week that the telegraph office was completed, set up at an empty shop in Aziziye, close to the walls.

In theory it was opened to the public, but in practice it was there for the benefit of the Russian command: Heimann and his staff. In between their uses of it, Russian officers of the lower sort crowded outside it, for the locals had little use for such devices. It was behind these gaggles of officers that Denniston and Walker waited, and waited, outside the office in the fragile sun.

'There's only one thing stops it being overrun by 'em,' said Walker. 'Counts and all, sending home to their diamond-dripping mothers for the fifth time this week.'

'And what's that?' Denniston asked.

Walker gestured around them at the muddy streets and pockmarked plaster of the neighbourhood; the boarded windows and smoke-scorched roofs, down towards the city's outer walls, and the small mounding of hill where there sat the fort the Russians had failed to hold.

'All this,' he said with a cattish smile. 'Aziziye itself.'

'They can take the city itself,' said Denniston. 'They can sit at the top of the hill and look down and say "that's ours", but when it comes to Aziziye…'

'Tried taking it once already and look where that landed them.'

'They're trying to take it now. Just not with gun and bayonet, but telegraph offices and cafes and all the rest…'

'A lighter touch,' said Walker. 'A heavy hand got them slaughtered. Scalped, I heard…'

Heavy hand or light touch, iron fist or velvet glove, the result was the same: the Russians were not welcome here in Aziziye. Those who came did so in force. The counts and all that Walker had mentioned, marching down to send a telegram with a full squad's escort. Even then it was not without the odd instance of a thrown stone, hisses and jeers sent down from the neighbourhood's blind rooftops. The Russians might have breached the walls in siege and took the fort here, but clearer in the Turkish memory was the night that they had retaken it. Even in defeat, it made them brave.

There were, thankfully, fewer officers today and no escorts. Only a young man in uniform dictating in nervous Russian to an operator; only the occasional correspondent for foreign papers, and aids to some embassy or other. Siege lifted, press and diplomats began to flood the city once more. Denniston wondered if, in time, Zohrab would return with them.

With the diplomats, and correspondents, and the telegram, the world was becoming smaller, and Erzurum becoming more a part of it. Like a web drawn across the Earth, Denniston reflected, from country to country and city to town, pulling everything it touched nearer together, in nexus of lines, words, news and economic reports, and all of it tied up tight by wires. Here, in the telegraph office, was a place where one could touch the world all at once through this web. Strange then, how claustrophobic it felt inside.

In the gloom and drifting dust and lamplight, behind windows still barricaded from both sunshine and street view, Denniston sent his own words through that web. He sent to Greenock and to Manchester, to his mother and to Agnes Guthrie, both with the same message.

MARCH 31ST STOP
HAVE BEEN ORDERED FROM THE CITY STOP
THOUGHT BEST TO SAY BY FASTEST MEANS STOP
HORSES ARE PROMISED STOP
WILL RIDE TO TRABZON THEN ON TO ISTANBUL STOP
ADDRESS ALL LETTERS THERE COURTESY OF SHC STOP
WILL WRITE AT LENGTH SOON STOP

April 1878

Chapter 27

Walker and Denniston rode from Erzurum to Trabzon. The roads were clearer. Snow still capped the mountains as they passed them, but it no longer logged the passes or covered the roads. Streams and rivers flowed fierce in their banks.

They kept up a good pace. They were used to long work now, and little sleep, and rough conditions to rest in. They were used to eating hard rations and being thankful for even the smallest luxuries. They were, Denniston felt, more hardy and worldly men than they had been when they entered Erzurum. And yet, for that, leaving Erzurum felt strange: a mixture of homecoming joy and homesick sorrow. The winter he'd spent in Erzurum had attached him to the place, and in turn it had done more to develop him than any number of years spent elsewhere in the world.

Ryan had joined them. Though not of the Stafford House Committee, but rather a true freelancer, he had no more reason now to stay in Erzurum than they had. He would, he had said, seek his fortunes along with them – he'd been fortunate enough in their company so far, after all.

Morisot and Idris, meanwhile, remained in Erzurum, one perhaps just as happy to help the Russians as the other was insistent on staying with the Turks.

But Denniston, Walker, and Ryan passed swift through Trabzon, then by boat once more to Istanbul, and almost straight from the Fatih harbour to the Stafford House Committee Headquarters. After the hardships of the road – bearable at the time, but far from preferable – calling on Barrington-Kennet seemed all but a necessity: a guarantee of good food and warm hospitality.

'Denniston! And Doctor Walker too! And I see you've brought a guest!' The powerfully built Englishman greeted them, in the headquarters sitting room. 'No no, you needn't stand on my behalf, man! If anything it's me should be doffing my hat with a nod at you, doctor. I assure you, it's not every night I have the pleasure to dine with a personage so celebrated in the papers – yes, yes, even the decent ones! Well, their margins at any rate, but I tell you, Denniston – of those margins you are quite the hero! Well now, stand up, stand up, come along, come in, I've—... Well of course I'll ask, have you dined?'

Denniston rose, feeling almost fragile under the barrage of robustness that comprised Barrington-Kennet's company after all this time. He shook his head in answer. 'We came straight from the docks, luggage and all I'm afraid.'

'You'll forgive me, I wasn't expecting you tonight, so I've laid on nothing special but… Well, I always make a point to have more prepared than I'll need for dining alone. Leaves one room to hope, you know?'

'We've been on the road some time, sir,' Ryan put in, already ingratiating himself to Barrington-Kennet. 'I'm sure comparison will make your hospitality seem very fine indeed.'

Barrington-Kennet stormed over to the Australian and looked him close in the face for a moment.

'Doctor Charles Ryan, sir. At your service. I was at Erzurum with these fine gentlemen, and wouldn't stay on without them.'

'Ryan…' Barrington-Kennet chewed the name over. 'I've heard of you too, I think. Plevna, was it?'

'Plevna,' Ryan nodded.

'Hmph. Another hero then. Truly, I'm spoilt tonight!' He clapped both hands over Ryan's shoulders, such that Denniston flinched at the suddenness of it. With a single note of boisterous laughter, Barrington-Kennet barked that he was glad to meet Ryan, and led them through to the dining room.

For a man so full of bluster – that trademark pride in which aristocrats by default are soaked from birth – Barrington-Kennet was, as ever, self-deprecating. For a man who claimed to have made no special preparations for guests, his dining table was heavily laden and glittered with silverware.

There were diamonds of pastry-like bread, baked golden with cheese. There was an orange herb-sprinkled soup that tasted dizzyingly of both beef and what might have been cherries. A polished brass platter sat in the centre of the spread, where a formation of small golden-brown roast pigeons clustered around a pyramid of rice, jewelled with dashes of coloured spice, slim green slivers of chopped nuts, chestnuts, and shreds of meat. Thin-skinned pastries of meat and peppers were arranged on another smaller plate, and a thick stew of oven-blackened vegetables lay hot in a clay casserole beside it. Barrington-Kennet had even provided wine, though beyond its red colour, Denniston knew too little to say anything for its quality, good or bad.

They ate ravenously, warmed by wine, as the commissioner coaxed out details of the journey from Erzurum: a tale told piecemeal, between mouthfuls.

'…April just beginning as we left Erzurum, but if you believe it, mountains still thick with snow, no visible road whatever! Cliffs with beards of ice that must have been waterfalls once. All of it bound up and blocked up, congested with white, packed tight and silent, for you know what snow seems always to do to sound: a voice doesn't carry and sound never goes far, does it?'

Never usually one for speaking so much or so candidly, let alone telling tales, Denniston was in good company, among friends and avid listeners. Moreover, he was aided by wine.

'We had horses, asses, mules, changed in and out at rest-stops and all. Lost count of the times we had to snowshoe the poor beasts; rags round their ankles and wadding their hooves like clumsy great mittens… But I fancy it's always better to walk, however slow and wobbling, than to sink straight down and not move at all? Or to slip! By God, a slip in those mountains? That's as good as a death sentence!'

Barrington-Kennet lit and chewed his way through a cigar. He was still disarmingly young, vivid, rose-cheeked and fair; but by Denniston's reckoning there were lines round his eyes that had not been there before, and a kind of darkening to the irises themselves, like something within him cast a greater shadow than once it had. Neither did he remember the commissioner drinking nearly so much as he did that evening.

'I can only be grateful,' Denniston continued, 'that we'd better guides on the return. Cebrael – the one your man in Trabzon set us up with, outbound – was well and good, but he had us going across country, sleeping out of doors almost every night! These ones got us roofs, though I think that may have been in no small part due to our guides' manner more than their wisdom. Hulking great hillmen, bearded, and with rifles and pistols and axes. Two of them, but more than enough to keep the wolves at bay… Or, I fancy, enough to suggest to any shepherd or farmer that it might be easier on him to lend us an outhouse for the night, and perhaps some cheese and bread, than it would be for him not to do so.

'All told it seemed less of an adventure, though… Just something to sit patiently through and endure.'

'Well after the time we had in Erzurum…' said Walker after hastily swallowing a mouthful of food.

'I think pretty much the most excitement we had on the journey back,' said Ryan, 'was on that bloody boat back from Trabzon. Howled up the worst storm I've seen in years, partway along the coast. Whips of lashing rain and biting wind; all round us a howling like artillery shells, but it was all just wind and the grumbling of thunder! Denniston – I tell you, he's quite mad – spent the whole time on *deck*! Bloody *enjoying* it!'

'I've always been proud of my sea-legs, Charles.'

'And besides,' said Walker, 'he's not the madman who spurred his horse into a lather, running all the bloody way to Trabzon, soon as we saw it, shouting "THE SEA, THE SEA!" Quite mad, the both of them, I'd say…'

Barrington-Kennet listened, quieter than Denniston had ever known him to be. The journey, he said, was half done either way. Whether Britain kept on at peace or joined the Turks in this slog of a war would determine much. 'Another six months, gentlemen, or not. And you, Ryan, I'd gladly take on a man like you if the war carried on. If it does or not, that'll quite determine the direction of your travels, I imagine – homeward bound or east again… One ought to be prepared either way.'

Agnes

Dear James,
This letter comes to you by care of a post office in Southport, but much more so by care of a table by a window that depicts rather a pretty, broad, and tree-lined lane; although it is, at present, quite lashed with rain. It is leisure brings us here, and the generous hospitality of the Andersons, who live here in town for much of the year, but the weather has quite literally clouded over the hope of it feeling like a holiday.

I imagine though, that you might, at the time of my writing this, be having a far worse time of it, travelling from Erzurum to Istanbul once more. The weather sounded hardly clement on your inbound journey, after all, and I do not fancy your return will be much kinder. I bear this in mind when I have a little rain to suffer through; it makes me much more grateful for the mere fact of having a roof over my head.

In any case, Southport's character is very different from that of Manchester, and a change from the city's turpitude and society is, I think, a welcome rest.

The penalty I face, of course, is that I shan't receive your letters here, but that has a kind of pleasure built into it too: perhaps I shall have a few to look forward to when I return. Yours, I promise you, are the only lines of correspondence I do not gladly forego in spending a short time here. The season for it is done for now, and yet one still receives the occasional invitation; the matter of declining – or more rarely, accepting – takes up both ink and time I'd rather use otherwise.

'My dear Mrs. Eliot, How pleased I was to receive your invitation; I do so hope your mother is well, for I recall some infirmity of the stomach kept her from company when last you and I met; and oh, it pains me to own that in this instance I shall not be able to accept…' etcetera.

Then there are the letters of young Mr. Arrol also, who you may recall I spoke with at some short length while with the McKies… Pleasant a reprieve as his company was then, Mr. Arrol does seem to have inferred something not meant from my attentions, and I receive letters from him rather frequently. Some, I will grant, are interesting of themselves – or rather, in parts and aspects, here and there, they are interesting – but more and more in recent days they come across overfamiliar in ways I find unwarranted and hard to appreciate.

Still I comb through them for oddments of insight. Positioned as he is in his chosen work, he does sometimes hear news missing from the papers, and I eagerly read anything he may let slip about our nation's affairs overseas. With the possibility of war such an anxious and uncertain shadow over both Britain and Turkey, I should think you understand very well why I bear reading his letters. Otherwise, I assure you, I have no interest in the man as a suitor, and scarcely much more as anything other than an occasional acquaintance – it is only my ill and ironic fortune that has made him a useful one.

I hope you will let me know any news that you yourself might hear. I should like to know when we might expect you back on England's shores.

Until then I am yours,

Very sincerely,

Agnes Guthrie

So similar was the room he stayed in now to the meagre one he'd rented a world ago in the Hotel d'Angleterre, Denniston might well have woken in it and thought to himself: these last months have all been a dream. The bed was almost identical: the same hard couch backed against one rough-plastered grey-white wall. The desk was similar too, doddering geriatrically when he leaned upon it to write. The view, however, from its high slim slit of window was different; so too the position of this hotel.

It was a tall and skinny structure, crammed between the foreign embassies of the Pera district. Here Barrington-Kennet, on behalf of the Committee, had arranged and paid for his lodging, among the swaying flags and babbling diversity of speech. It was, the commissioner suggested, best that he stay close to the Committee headquarters, for a time might come when urgent talks must be had.

The hotel's common-room he found eye-smarting with pipe-smoke and thick with a taste of brandy that stuck in the throat on each inhalation. The main part of its ambiance, however, was how rich it was in murmurs. Even when Denniston failed to understand the languages spoken – German, Hungarian, Dutch, Italian, Russian – he fancied their subject to be almost always the same: War or peace, which was it to be? With whom, against whom? When, and for how long?

He supposed such talk had been rife in Istanbul all through its history, since it was Constantinople. It was, after all, a place where two worlds met – east and west – and in such a brushing as that there would always be friction. Such wonderings came upon him often. It was, he thought to himself half-happily, the legacy that Pinkerton had left him: a constant questioning that came with knowing that the past is always there, in the present, buried just beneath the surface of every modern day.

The main difference, though, between this hotel and the Hotel d'Angleterre, was not place or time, but perception. Food, room, the street outside – all of it seemed to Denniston close to the lap of luxury. Comparison, he thought, is a powerful thing. Here he was able to sleep through the night. Here he was warm and comfortable, and seldom hungry save just before mealtimes. And he had not, so far as he knew, felt the bite of a single flea since arriving back in Istanbul.

Between his commitments to the Committee, Denniston had the leisure to write, to read, receive letters, and to shave. He wrote to Agnes of his journey back to Istanbul, and here, at the edge of Asia and the gateway to Europe, they exchanged letters with a regularity that seemed the greatest luxury of all. He had even received one from his mother, at long last, which made his throat so thick he thought he must cry.

My dear James,
We both spoke some harsh words when last we met. I've had your letters in the meantime though, and had time to think it all over. All we said, I'll say was warranted, each by the other. You've said your sorries though and I'll say mine. I hope this letter will be enough for that.

There comes a time, I realise, when a mother must let her son go, and admit to herself she's no more say in his affairs but to advise and support. I fancy I tried to advise, but failed utterly in supporting. I'm sorry for that.

It does my heart good to hear you're well, James. Whatever you take it on yourself to do now, whenever you come home, you're still my only son – the last child left to me, and inheritor of all my love. This does a little to explain my anger and fear and how they manifested when first you said you'd set out for Turkey. But it does not forgive it – that falls to you.

Come home safe. Until then, I pray for you, and whether you know it or not, all you do, you do with my love.

Yours with great affection,
Janet Denniston

Beyond the foreign districts of Istanbul, however, the confusion of war was turning to renewed enthusiasm. Eating pastries once, in a Turkish coffee-house, Denniston understood little of the conversations that raged back and forth between the servers, but their passion was clear. He recognised the words for 'Russian' at least, and some unsavoury terms he'd heard Turkish soldiers shout in the grips of pain or fever.

The Turks, he gathered, saw themselves more as offended than wounded.

And that was an easy view to hold, here in the capital, so far from the front and the fighting. Denniston himself stood conflicted. Should the war go on then surely Britain must come to Turkey's aid, or watch her be picked apart inch by inch, and admit weakness to the French. If war were to break out anew, then neither France nor Britain could afford to let it become anything but a proxy – Britain fighting France through the Turks; France fighting Britain through the Russians, with Austria and others picking at the scraps of this newer and suddenly larger war.

Some part of Denniston half hoped for it, more to give the Russians pause for thought after all they'd done to the people of Turkey, the Circassians, the people of Erzurum... But more than that, he hoped the war might draw to a quick kind close with no more loss of land or blood. The twinned concepts of honour and valour had for him long since lost their lustre. Peace, however, held a higher sheen than ever.

Agnes

Dear James,
I am surprised that your friend Ryan knows his Xenophon, or at least is well enough acquainted with him to quote appropriately, even in such a small dosage. I must say it is quite the romantic image you paint for me, of the last leg of your journey: you travellers three, ten miles from the coast and Trebizond, and so eager to draw into sight of the ocean that you ate up those last leagues at a gallop; the wind in your hair and the taste of salt on the wind, more pronounced with every mile, etcetera. And Ryan, as that first glimpse of blue crept into the horizon, shouting in raptures as Xenophon's Greeks did:

'The sea! The sea!'

Even parts of your journey, I suppose, mirrored that of the Ten Thousand, from the oriental interior and towards the ocean. Ryan, however, seems the sort of man that, if he had read the Greek author, he would never let you go uninformed of it; I think that, rather, he would he would point out every little parallel he could muster, between your travels and the Anabasis, if only to let you know that, yes indeed, here is another thing on which he is an expert. So runs, at least, the impression of him I have from your letters.

The company I have kept has been less than enlightening by comparison, and I should fancy decidedly less exhilarating.

We have in fact taken on ourselves to return to Glasgow for a short while, and from there shall either be in Arran soon enough – a part of the world I have never seen but have heard is very beautiful, in particular if you are heartened by the sight of goats and sheep – or, and this ironically for you shall be elsewhere, we might find ourselves in Greenock.

Current company includes the Shortridges who I think you will recall from

Greenock, being that the younger Miss Shortridge was such a landmark of the local social environ – which is to say, in plainer terms, quite the gossip and an irremediable flirt.

For all the vulgarity of her conversation, however, she hears much, and even seems to know as much of your movements as I do from your regular letters! No doubt thanks to reports from your mother, it sounds that you are quite the talk of the town in Greenock – demonised at first for what was made out to be quite the runaway effort on your part, but now it seems you are lionised as a great hero and adventurer, at least so far as Greenockians go.

For this reason I should think that, if we are to go to Greenock in months to come, I shall be hearing double of you: once in your own words, and once again in everyone else's.

In either case, it looks at present very likely that I shall be in Scotland for the summer.

Until then I am yours,
Very sincerely,
Agnes Guthrie

Reading Agnes' letters, it amazed Denniston sometimes to be reminded of how well read she was. A swarm of psalms and psalters and verses buzzed in her head at all times, ready every moment to be remembered, plucked out of thin air, and applied where she thought them most relevant. Not only that though, but Classics too, and more frivolous novels, and even the Darwin that he himself had recommended her, and she herself had scoffed at.

What dazzled him all the more though, was how far she was from being humble regarding any of it: her education, the languages she spoke, who and what else she knew. In a woman with so much to say about Christian modesty, he might have found it hypocritical or ridiculous. Yet, Denniston supposed, she did not boast; rather, she would not let herself be underestimated. He was dimly aware that this might have seemed unbecoming in a woman, at least to another sort of man. He himself found a kind of quietly glittering thrill in it.

Quite uninvited to do so, and quite without any mention in the letter itself, she had enclosed not only the usual newspaper – local to wherever she might have been at the time – but also a photograph. Another! And there in its curve-cornered white card borders, she sat in stony grey and chalk white. Yet the grain of the picture made it all seem textured, strangely tactile, immediate, almost intimate.

Denniston wondered what colour her dress might have been. The photograph rendered it an inky liquid black, no detail or decal save its shape, and the line of medals, brooches, and buttons that serried across her breast, quite like the ornaments that lined the coats of the Georgians and Circassians he had met. He noted this, and wondered if it had been deliberate: an appeal towards the exotic, to stay in keeping with what must now be his orientalised tastes? In truth, his tastes had changed little, in food or company or otherwise. More and more, the orient made him long for the comfort and familiarity of home: safely drab, solid, stable; wholesome as porridge when sweetened with honey.

At his desk, poised to reply, he thought perhaps he might ask her. Had she meant to impress him? To what extent did his opinion matter to her, and to what end? If to impress was her goal, she had attained it long ago. Quickly though, he grew too shy of this thought to express it.

What colour was the dress? He might ask that instead. But even that seemed too deep a lunge into her confidences. It was as good as asking for leave to imagine her, rather than to be happy with the pictures she sent: the ways she had already permitted herself to be seen. So he did not ask that either.

Rather, Denniston thought of her. Or else more accurate to say, she was in his thoughts of other things: as he took coffee and walked the streets of Istanbul; as he met with Ryan to discuss as they always did the looming potential for war. Denniston found himself looking at the Australian as if coloured by Agnes' perceptions. Ryan was and always had been fascinating – a magnetic and contagious personality, as Casson had been. But where Denniston had once wished to emulate such men, and been disappointed in his own quietness, slowness to express wit, and the frankness that was his default, he found now that he had, at some point, stopped wishing in that way. He was happier in himself; that Agnes seemed happy to know him had helped in that.

In the passing war-simmer of those days, Denniston contrived to think in ways she might approve of, if only he would tell her that he'd done so. He took no pains to do as she'd wish; certainly not in ways that went against his own wants and nature. Only, he tried to be, for her, a better version of his own self – not perhaps his original self, but the better and bolder man into which Erzurum had shaped him.

How many men, he wondered, had the world's thousand thousand wars made cruel, or hard, or cold before him? For how long would war continue to make such men? For himself, war seemed to have stripped something away: walls from round his heart, a caul from over his eyes. On every street and in all avenues of life, he saw suffering, and felt it as his own. War had made him this way, and had made him, by necessity, kind. He tried to express it to Agnes thusly:

In easing the pain in others I can begin to ease the ache inside myself.

Perhaps this is a flaw in a modern physician: sentiment and attachment. But I rather think that it is something essential. This may not be what's meant by the proverb in Luke – something you're much fitter than I to interpret – but it's the way it resonates with me. 'Physician, heal thyself.'

One day, neither a Saturday nor a Sunday – for both were celebrated by Christians of one sort or another in this part of the world – Denniston took it on himself to ask about until he found his way to a church.

It was small, wide, low-domed, barely announcing itself above the houses that crowded against its stone outer walls. In all its Eastern Orthodoxy, it seemed unorthodox to him. How much stranger must it have seemed to Agnes, he wondered? But its spireless profile made it seem more like a home than any Scottish or English church he'd been in – welcoming; a building for living in.

He'd avoided busy times by design. He was not confident in the religion he was baptised into and could not remember the last time he had been at any kind of organised worship, besides funerals. He was less confident still in this new Eastern denomination's modes of praise, and didn't wish to be seen while he stumbled through attendance and prayer.

But in the morning light, outside the church, he heard singing from within. Greek, he supposed by the familiar medicinality of some words, though he couldn't be certain. He waited to enter until the singing had faded, but the sound of it lingered like incense inside, and set a tone in his mind.

A few columns on either side of the church divided it in three. Denniston walked down the left aisle, ending in a painted screen of images and icons. As he knelt, the Virgin and a dwarflike Child looked over his head, robed and swaddled in blue, red, and green, faded with age and dim with shadow. But after the physical part of the observance was done, the rest seemed out of reach and uncertain.

Things might have been easier between them if he and Agnes had always believed the same things. But while she could not do without faith, Denniston could not do away with a careful measure of doubt.

It was not so much a doubt in any higher power, he'd assured her in letters. Rather, it was a doubt in the power and purity of humans; a doubt in the kind of men who would look down their noses and decry something built on scientific proof, just because accepting it as part of God's plan would require a look inward: a flexibility in their faith. Such men had reacted to Galileo, to Darwin, and beyond, in the ways that history had shown. In light of that, it seemed to Denniston that the men who made up the churches of this world had done all they could to make a mystery of God. They distance themselves from the divine so that their flock would feel more distant still.

Here, alone now after morning service in this quiet church, built in the name of a sect that had no bearing on him, nor had ever tried for any, Denniston tried to find a faith that was more his own.

Wordlessly, echoing inside his own head, he gave thanks. He thanked whatever God might be for his life, and the closeness he had found to others while in Turkey – others with him every day, and others far away but friends nonetheless, the worlds-wise gap between them bridged by written words. He prayed for peace or else to be sent home, for both now meant the same thing.

There was little ritual to it beyond kneeling and closing his eyes, but in his way at least he'd tried once more to speak with God. And it was a comfort to know his faith needed no answer.

May 1878

Chapter 28

In a matter of days, the skies turned all to sunlight. The waters of the Golden Horn and the Bosporus showed blinding blue whenever one looked seaward. Martins returned to the city for springtime, babbling in the overhangs of Istanbul's roofs, and building new nests against the old city walls of Fatih, rising stone and solid amongst borders of lush green trees.

The streets meantime grew dust-choked with the traffic of feet and carts. It rose in clouds even to second-storey windows, and settled again only with the occasional flash shower of rain.

Walker had since taken himself home. His contract with the Stafford House Committee had been served and in so far as he was concerned there was no sense waiting longer than he was needed.

'All that's left,' he had said, 'is waiting. Maybe for something, but probably for nothing after all. I'm only saving myself time's the way I see it.' He flashed his smile for the last time. 'No hard feelings, I'm sure?'

'No hard feelings,' Denniston agreed.

He saw Walker off with Ryan, onto a steamer bound for Malta then back to Marseilles. Gulls fought for scraps and the leavings of fishermen at the docks and jetties. Together, Denniston and Ryan watched the steamer glint white as it caught the sun, grey as it dimmed to the distance, then it disappeared beyond the horizon, swallowed in faraway blue.

'Makes a man wonder, doesn't it...' Ryan said, jaunting his hat back onto his head from where he'd held it at his breast for respect all this while. 'How long before that's us, bound for France, England, wherever we want in all the world...'

'All the world but here,' said Denniston. 'Don't know that I ever stop wondering that.' His fingers fumbled as he tried to roll a cigarette.

'If I go past Malta, I fancy I might stop there. Enjoy some sunshine...' Ryan plucked the paper and tobacco pouch from Denniston's hands. With a smile and a few neat twitches of his fingers, he produced a perfect cigarette from what Denniston himself could never save, and popped it into the corner of his mouth. 'One for me...' He fashioned another, just as perfect, and handed it back with the pouch and papers. 'And one for you.'

Denniston slipped the end of the cigarette into his mouth and lit it with a lucifer match. He passed the box to Ryan, who took it, and did the same.

'Reckon that's it now, eh?' Ryan said, breathing out smoke in the sunshine. 'You and I are all that's left. Doctors Denniston and Ryan, journeying homeward, or bound once more for adventure – who can say? Either way, reckon that's worth drinking to…'

Ryan made it sound as though there were only two of them left, but for Denniston that point had come and gone with Walker. Ryan was a newcomer, and though he and Denniston had grown closer than Denniston ever had to Walker, their camaraderie and the things they had endured together did not run so deep, or so far back in time. Of those with whom Denniston had left for Trabzon six months ago, only Denniston now remained on Turkish soil – himself, and the two left under it. It was that thought that made him agree with Ryan.

'If anything's worth drinking to, I suppose that is.'

'But is it worth the walk? Don't know where I'd get a drink in these parts – good Muslims all…'

'I can stand it if you can, Charles.'

'I could bear it, but on a day like this? Why brave the dust and clouds… Why walk when you can float?'

For a few para they had an old Turk row them across the Golden Horn in his shallow little boat. It was nearing sunset when they arrived in Pera, and made towards the cram of embassies, Greek tabernas, and European restaurants where brandy and wine could be easily had.

They found a social club, its street-facing front hung thick with vines and its interior packed with foreigners. All the talk inside was of Üsküdar, across the Bosporus, its streets and alleys and squares all thronged with refugees from the east.

There was talk of a bearded Armenian – a priest, they said – who stood near the Galata Tower and shouted over each call to prayer that echoed through Pera: 'Remember Kars! Do not, my children, forget Kars! Have mercy, have mercy, and do not forget!' He had chosen his position well, for if he shouted loud enough, half the European embassies and hostelries in the district would hear him. His pleas would fall on Christian ears.

'It's not just aid they want,' Ryan commented as he nursed a misty-cold glass of raki. 'It's intervention. From Britain or France, for Russia or the Ottomans – makes no difference to them.'

'If it gets them their homes back…' said Denniston.

'Or gives a chance at retribution, maybe. God knows there's fault to find on either side. Makes no difference to them, so long as something changes.'

'I knew a man who'd have something to say to that…' said Denniston, thinking of Pinkerton, who had always held up knowledge of the past as if it could give one the gift of prophecy, foretelling the shape of things to come. 'Just don't know what he'd say to it.'

The next morning Denniston woke to a mouth dry as dust and textured like an ill-kept carpet. The taste of brandy lingered like medicine on his tongue.

In his hotel's common-room, he forced himself to humourlessly winkle out the contents from a blue-shelled soft-boiled egg, and deposit them into his mouth. The toast on his plate he tried also to eat, but found it rather too much like trying to chew and swallow expensive notepaper: formal telegrams, invitations to weddings and funerals. His head ached. Every movement he wrung from his unsteady body seemed to creak now, in a way that only he could hear.

But that night with Ryan had been perhaps the first in six months he had allowed himself absolute licence; permission to laugh, drink, smile, and enjoy the company of friends both old and new. He oughtn't to begrudge it himself, he decided. Hadn't he passed a spartan Christmas, and a New Year's Eve that went by all but unannounced and unremarked on? He was overdue some leisure.

He recalled part of the night now, after the brandy had set things blurring. He and Ryan had begun to ask around for who might have a set of chess men, having gotten it into their head that they ought to have one sort of game or another. There was no chess set to be found, but they had at least discovered other men who were also searching for a game, and were too drunk to be particular as to what sort. Ryan, he remembered, had invented spontaneously a complicated kind of recreation involving dice, a suit of cards, darts and dart-board, and a draconian system of forfeits.

They had grown loud, bawdy. Denniston had worried as to their conduct. Was it too much, in a city that by all rights ought to be mourning?

'By God, man!' A gentleman whose face he'd forgotten had slapped him on the back. 'The whole city – the whole of Turkey – is a keg of powder fit to go up! And you worry that our antics are – what? – too volatile?'

'Catharsis, James,' Ryan had grinned, guiding Denniston once more towards the dart-board for another ill-fated throw. 'The letting of the humours. The ancients knew it well enough – a little upset restores the balance within, eh?'

But the morning after that night, as Denniston sat alone in the crowded common-room, earnestly attempting to outstare his empty egg-shell and his cold toast, the hotel was rife with mutters. The city, too, would need a catharsis of its own, it seemed. Unrest and anxiety were breaking out across Istanbul like rashes among Christians and Muslims alike. In the night, words had been daubed in Russian on the walls of a *seraskeriat* in Üsküdar.

PAPA TSAR SAYS
THESE WALLS ARE MINE
ONLY GIVE ME TIME

Similar messages had been appearing across the city for days now. One, Denniston heard, had even been painted on a mosque.

ALEXANDER THE LIBERATOR SAYS
PLANT THE CROSS AGAIN

But the dissidents, the daubers of slogans and stirrers of unrest, were Turks, or so the rumours said. All their attempts were to shock the sultan and his court once more into action and away from armistice.

'And now one of them's gone and got himself shot too,' said one of the hotel tenants: an Englishman with a stout shaving-brush of a moustache.

'Magnifique,' muttered a Frenchman from behind a newspaper. 'Now they have a martyr to rally behind.'

'That…or good cause to stop playing silly buggers and let politics run its course.'

Denniston returned to his room to escape the rising ruckus. The streets outside, however, sounded no quieter. Beyond the usual sound of foot-traffic and mule-carts, something seemed to be simmering. Shouts broke through his window, more often and impassioned than ever before.

It was into the afternoon when the courier arrived. A neatly turned out young Turk, dressed smart in military blue with a red felt cap. The triple-knock he laid on Denniston's door was swift and officious, true to every aspect of his manner.

'Denniston *effendi*?' he asked, at rigid attention in the doorway.

Denniston squinted. Human voices felt all too loud by far to him now. He wetted his lips, though, and nodded.

'This is for you, please.'

The courier drew from a satchel a small package of crisp expensive yellow paper, patterned with a calligraphic cypher and tied round with red ribbon. After that the door was closed and the courier gone, prompt as his arrival.

Frowning, Denniston brought it to his small writing desk, turned it over once, twice, to find a way in. The package, however, seemed folded in such a way as to have no obvious means of unwrapping it. He took his shaving kit and laid one side of the paper cleanly open with the blade of his razor.

Inside was another sprucely folded bundle of fine cloth and crisp papers. First among them, however, was a stiff cream card, written in precise English.

Doctor Denniston,
The letter within and the tughra upon it have a significance that, I realise, will perhaps be lost on you.

Suffice to say, they symbolise that all this comes by the grace of His Imperial Majesty, The Sultan Abdülhamid II, Emperor of the Ottomans,

Caliph of the Faithful, and with His thanks and the blessings of God.

I believe at least that the significance of decorations is universal. It being my business to be well-informed, I feel confident in my knowledge that they were hard won and deserved, earnt in full through your service under the Red Crescent.

You have only to claim them. We shall meet where first we met, the day after tomorrow, and from there the rest is simple. I only advise you to groom and dress as well as you're able – we are in Istanbul now, after all, and no longer in the provinces.

Yours faithfully,
Aydin Vefyk Pashazada

Denniston's frown deepened. Opening the letter within – a series of pools and whorls and streaks of Turkish script, in lines and monograms, none legible to him – his steady hands began to shake.

Two days later, Denniston stood in the shade of the Fatih *seraskeriat*. He held a handkerchief to his mouth to shield his lungs from the dust. Cold or heat, dust or fog, they still found something to complain about, whatever the weather. Of all things, only sea air seemed to soothe them, but surrounded by wooden buildings, the tramp of feet and bustle of a market square, there was none to be found here.

'You are Doctor James Denniston?' a voice said in clipped English, from within the *seraskeriat* doorway.

'I am,' said Denniston, turning to the voice from where he'd leaned against the building's concrete wall.

It was a young man, head shaved to shining and face smooth and dark. He wore an ornate oriental jacket and loose trousers in sapphire blue, ending in slippers: servant's dress but fit for court more than for a war office. 'If you would follow, please. My master is waiting.'

'Aydin Vefyk?'

'He is waiting,' the youth repeated.

Denniston followed him through the familiar hallway, sparred with shafts of light that fell from the high windows. Today, the shade was welcome; a reprieve from the May heat. Today, the door at the corridor's far end was open, waiting to admit him.

Where the *pasha* had set before, the floor was opened out. The desk was pushed against the back wall, bathed in light from one high window, and it was draped ornate now with rich cloth, red and edged with emerald green. A box of dark lacquered wood, chased with brasswork, sat small on the altar the desk had become and Aydin Vefyk *Pasha*za stood to one side. At the room's far wall were a line of attendants, similarly dressed to the youth who had guided Denniston inside. In contrast to them were two Europeans, suited and groomed, and opposite, a clutch of uniformed braid-dripping *pasha*s, smoking compulsively, seated cross-legged on rows of plush cushions, looking all as if they had not slept in weeks.

'Denniston *hekim*,' Aydin Vefyk said, as he turned to greet Denniston with his old knowing smile. 'Your looks have improved.'

Denniston looked to the floor, bashfully. He had made an effort, as asked; had paid for his one grey suit to be cleaned, mended, pressed; had shaved his face smooth save for a trim moustache and neat pair of sideburns; had gone to a barber for a cut and tamed his wiry hair with pomade.

'I hope you weren't expecting too much ceremony,' said Aydin Vefyk. 'Suffice to say this is all still very official. Witnesses from court and corps so on. An official of appropriate rank to bestow the honours you all have earnt.' He nodded at the other two foreigners. 'Now gentlemen, if you would form a line, and kneel...'

An attendant hurried slipper-silent forwards to place a plush silk cushion on the ground before the altar.

Denniston knelt first and closed his eyes. A strange sense of apprehension – of initiation into things unknown to him – crossed his mind, as in the church when he had tried to pray. He felt Vefyk lay a hand upon his bowed head. He heard the words of Turkish come, recited high and clear, almost like a song.

When he rose, Vefyk gestured for him to step forward.

An attendant opened the box and took out a white band of cloth, bearing a bright red crescent, and bound it about his upper arm before turning back to the box.

'Denniston *hekim*,' said Vefyk. 'For service to His Imperial Majesty, The Sultan Abdülhamid II, Emperor of the Ottomans, Caliph of the Faithful, and to His people, here in the eyes of God and the people of Turkey, I do initiate you into these sacred orders...'

Beside the crescent, on Denniston's arm, Vefyk pinned the decorations, one by one. Enamel and silver, the sunlight gleamed on them, and fell warm upon his face.

'*Mashallah*,' the *pasha*s murmured, like a rising chant. '*Mashallah*...'

Chapter 29

James

My dear Agnes,

I am on the move again. Either this news will surprise you, or find you entirely unsurprised, given what a rover you must now think me, for all my excursions and so-called adventures.

I shipped out alone from Istanbul, and not without some small degree of regret or sadness at the parting, for in leaving the Golden Horn behind me, I felt some chapter of my life coming to a close – opportunities and things yet to be experienced, slipping through my fingers and away. But I may yet be back, so I fancy it's of less consequence than it felt at the time.

I write now from a steamer bound ultimately for the southern coast of France. No doubt though we are determined to stop at one place or another along the way. One part of me wishes we would not, however. Every night spent ashore and in port is another night before I see Great Britain again, and I find I'm eager to be home – or at least, once in France, send this letter off to go ahead of me.

Your own letters, meanwhile, address to the Stafford House Committee in London. They will know where to find me, better than I, at present, know ultimately where I'm bound.

My future movements will all depend on the question of peace and war as it stands in the East. Turkey and Russia both seemed quite undecided when last I saw them. All the populace of Istanbul seemed full of foment and energy, but in no one direction. Some cried for whatever peace could be secured, and at whatever cost, for fear of a continued Russian advance through Asia Minor. Others – refugees mostly, and those with families pushed from territory already under Russian occupation, or family lost in the fighting – call for the Sultan to reclaim what's been lost and push the Tsar back within his old borders.

But the fighting strength of Turkey is, I am informed by a friend whose business is to know these things and whose intelligence I trust, significantly weakened. Battles such as Erzurum have hobbled and wounded Turkey so much that there can be no further fighting without new foreign support. So, Turkey and Russia either will pause in their hostilities, or they will renew them, and send great waves through the world's tapestry of alliances and agreements, and drag all to war with them.

If that is the case, and war is declared, I imagine I shall at once be uprooted by it, and swept along as well. I shall at once go out again to Turkey. It is not so much that I feel it would be a shame to remain when so many young men of our nation are just now setting off to war, but more that it'd shame me not to assist them and the Turks alike. After all, I have some experience of such things now, and could be of use. I feel I might also owe it to the Turks themselves, and not only for reasons of sentiment. They have, after all, taken it on themselves to award me a pair of medals for service and courage, and I can't very well go off shirking and cowering on home soil after that – I have two little pieces of silver and enamel to live up to, now!

For the time being, I am sure only of the fact that my pen is awful and my writing worse. I will close now, for I ought not to force more reading upon you, and of such poor penmanship. But then again, I fancy it was always thus, and you've laboured so nobly through worse letters by far.

I imagine London will be where I write from next. Hopefully I shall have better tools to do so by then.

Until then I remain yours

Very sincerely,

James Denniston

Agnes

Dear James,

Some news does reach me here, you know. I make a point of reading the dailies, and each Sunday of reading any number of broadsheets after service, as if by putting together all their biases I might arrive at something resembling the truth. Which is to say that there is talk here too of Turkey's prospects; in papers and parlours across Britain that epithet from the Crimea has re-emerged as wavering wounded Turkey is called once more "the sick man of Europe". I think you will tire of all the conversation and questions very quickly once you arrive in London, being an eyewitness to the favourite topic for idle talk in this nation now.

But as to the rest of your letter, I hope you do not think that I shall let you get off so easily without further questioning of my own. Tell me of your decorations! I am not so unobservant as to be thrown off by the round substantial padding you gave that information, and indeed I think I shall not be at peace until you've told me more on the subject; of course you know this of me, and so I might rather believe this is some gambit of yours. You mentioned the matter so briefly I might almost think you tease me with it, as if to lead me into a line of conversation like a mule is led by a carrot on a string.

I picture medals of gold and enamel and bright red ribbons; yet I would much sooner you told me how wrong I am in my assumptions and instead describe to me the truth of them. How were they given to you? With great pomp? Decadent ceremony? Or little to none? On what grounds were they awarded? The mind runs immediately to the vast-turbaned sultan shown in the caricatures here, pinning them to your breast amidst attar-scented airs and throngs of veiled wives, odalisques, etcetera. But again let me say: I would prefer your story over my suppositions, and shall remain here, and hope it is forthcoming.

In any case, I would extend my congratulations by letter, but I think it may not, in fact, be unrealistic to hope I might do so personally soon enough. Where precisely, as you say, is uncertain: at Manchester, Glasgow, or Greenock, or perhaps by some chance, even London? I hold out a quiet hope, however, that it shall be Greenock, for what a funny thing it would be to see one another again, after all this time, in the same place that we last parted.

Until then I am yours,

Very sincerely,

Agnes Guthrie

James

My dear Agnes,

I had in fact hoped to slip under that line of questioning for fear of becoming too bashful, but I suppose, for that, it's better I write of it than face up to your queries in person. My medals I'm afraid came to me with disappointingly little pomp or circumstance. Rather than some airy courtyard of Topkapi Palace, picture a large room in some war office building, lined with tired-eyed smoking pashas.

The medals themselves seemed to be ones specifically for awarding to foreigners who had done some great service or other to the sultan. Alongside me there were two others – an Austrian correspondent of some sort, and a French diplomat – being decorated similarly. Things being what they are in Turkey at present, I shouldn't be surprised if this business of pinning medals onto the 'right sort' of foreigner wasn't also some means of currying favour with foreign powers and foreign publics also. 'The sick man of Europe', after all, finds himself in need of friends, and this sort of thing would reflect kindly on him in the papers and parlour talk of other nations.

I mentioned that I might be bashful, but I must say, it's not that I'm unproud of these medals. They're comely things, in silver and green enamel, gold and satin, deftly painted with the sultan's monogram and other than that all of stars and crescents. More than that they are a reminder that I did what I could, in service to the people of Erzurum. Quietly, I am proud that I got them not as a soldier, and not by deeds of arms, but by working to mend what war had broken. So, once I am over my apprehension, I hope to be able to bore you thoroughly, showing them off in days to come.

I've also got for you a small something: a kind of girdle, of silver and with dangling trinkets of all sorts from it. I'm no judge as to prettiness, and don't know whether it's something from which you would get much use, but it's a fine curiosity all the same, and made in Erzurum. This much should make it, at least, very distinct in English society, or else a fair little keepsake – or else a token of my gratitude for your own contributions to my time in Erzurum. I look forward to having your more informed opinion on it, though, for as I said, I'm no judge of good taste.

I am, meantime, in London, and so the chance to make good on all these hopes and promises of meetings might present itself very soon! I am confined for the time being, seeing to matters with the Stafford House Committee. I must have my accounts from Erzurum viewed and reviewed, and in turn get my back pay, but it's all frightfully boring compared with the adventures you've grown used to having me recount. But I hope I may yet, while I'm amongst Committee people, have the chance to meet and speak with Lord Blantyre himself and personally thank him for my experiences in the Orient. After all, without his setting up the Committee in the first place, I should still be the man I was when last I was in London.

Did you say that you expected to be in Glasgow in June? If so, and if I know where you are, can I hope to meet you there? I will be visiting at the time as well.

Until then, now that I am home again and in a so-called civilised country, I hope that you won't think it necessary to give up writing altogether. Perhaps you won't think it necessary to write so often, and if that's your judgement I'd never think to begrudge you it. I'd find myself missing your views on things, though. I can promise you now, in light of this, that I will continue to appreciate any time you choose to give me, in writing or in person, very much.

In the meantime I am

Yours very sincerely,

James Denniston

Agnes

Dear James,

I think I know a little of what was involved in the earning of your honours; as such I should say you have every right to take pride in them! What the done thing might be in regard to wearing them, though, I do not know – not outside of military dress, which of course gives gentlemen the excuse to dodge more sober evening wear for the sake of strutting about like peacocks, glittering with any medals, pins, and ribbons they might get their hands on. But perhaps the fact that you cannot wear them about makes your decorations more tasteful: they are secret distinctions, held humbly, and won not in brash war but through the promotion of peace and prevention of suffering. If I were to be asked, I think I should like a man recognised for such deeds far better than I would some sabre-swinging dandy.

For my part, we are in Chorlton, at Broadoak, once more for the Spring, and quite besieged by visitors, welcome and otherwise. Cheshire has come over very green already. Though misty in the mornings, I've come to like a walk before breakfast; not perhaps very far-ranging, but it is one of the few times in the day at present that I have any time to myself. Otherwise, all else is done in a gaggle between Miss Bancroft, Miss Marston, and Prudence, the Honeysetts' youngest, and all to the music of the former's sneezing and sniffing, for the airs of the countryside at this time of year do seem to bother her so.

In any case, in this gaggle as I so often am, I have had difficulty keeping my friends from hearing a little about you now and then. Having heard a little they were soon eager to learn much more, but of course I have been very restrained; they have been hardly more than drip-fed information, by and by, up to this point, for I know that being 'spoken of' would quite scare you to pieces! Still, they are very complimentary regarding how fortunate I am to have been privy to all I have been, and for myself I must say that, perhaps, I am at that.

You are correct in that June will find us in Glasgow, if all is according to plan. My affairs are at least more certain than yours, it seems. Yet if war and the Committee will allow, we have so many houseguests coming and going already that one more would be far from importunate. You see, I have also been sure to drip-feed my mother and father just enough information about a certain young gentleman that my mother has taken it on herself to invite you to visit with us at Broadoak – that is, if you should be in the vicinity. For myself, I quite welcome her suggestion.

Until then, however, you are direly mistaken if you think I should stop writing to you simply because the letters should not have so far to travel. It was not only to offer comfort and civilisation in harsh times and barbarous places that I first grew conversant with you, after all. In regard to my letters, sir, you may expect them until spoken words suffice.

In the meantime I am yours,

Very sincerely,

Agnes Guthrie

James

My dear Agnes,

I must thank your father and mother and you for your great kindness in asking me to visit you at Broadoak. I'm sure I needn't assure you how glad I'd be to accept the invitation, but at present cannot possibly. I will be leaving London tomorrow night and returning direct to Edinburgh. The train is booked, much as I wish I might stop on my journey north.

It's Lord Blantyre that has me travelling again, of course. I waited here, as you know, and lingered on longer than necessary in hope of seeing him and, for now, settling my business with the Stafford House Committee. I found today, however, that he has gone up to Scotland, and after I've followed him there I don't doubt I'll then have to come back here to Elsham Road to close this line of affairs. Very tiresome, all of it, I can tell you.

But let me not brush over the matter at hand: I am truly sorry at not being able to accept your mother's invitation. I hope I'll be able to catch you, at the latest, in Glasgow, but of course my plans are no nearer settlement now than before. And if war breaks out? Well..!

I must say though, the idea of such a visit fills me with far less trepidation than the thought that you have had me as the subject of conversations! Surrounded by as many young ladies as you lately have been, and discussing me, I think I should be quite frozen with fright, and no use to anyone, in the line of pleasant talk or otherwise. You have my character down quite correctly on that count – as ever, you are an excellent judge in that vein.

Still it is comforting to hear that I am not alone in having spoken of you in glowing terms on a few staggered occasions, for you have done the same.

It is all practice, I suppose – speaking of you to others and weathering the fret of being spoken of – for I'm afraid that in your actual company I might come across similarly cold and awkward all over again. You know, after all, that I am about as much a one for compliments or easy conversation as I am for dancing!

Time being, I hope to hear from you in Edinburgh. (It is very heartening to read you as you state so firmly that, yes, I shall!) I will be a guest of my brother and sister-in-law – also an Agnes, but a Denniston too – and so your letters will find me at 4 Greenhill Terrace.

Meanwhile please, for my sakes, thank your father and mother most kindly!

Until we meet I am yours

Very sincerely,

James Denniston

Agnes

Dear James,

I neither pretend nor desire to be very well loved by young men in general or in particular, and as such claim to have no great insight into the ways of masculine thought or behaviour. However, you will recall my interactions with the two McKie brothers in Manchester during advent, and Mister Arrol's misunderstanding thereafter. I think at least such exchanges have been, for me, educational on the subject of compliments. Namely, James, regarding compliments, I believe them to be only as good as the intention behind them; the character of the one giving them, and their actual esteem for their subject. Without this, finesse counts for nothing, and a compliment becomes a hollow and false thing; which is to say, a lie, and that is far worse than any measure of apparent clumsiness.

More than this, not all compliments may be framed as such. Indeed, any act of body or of language might be taken as complimentary, if they reflect the actor's fine character and respect for oneself. I think now that perhaps these might be the purest of compliments: those not meant to flatter, yet nonetheless somehow a shining influence on both parties, showing them to look well in its light. Those compliments, certainly, you are full of, and give out very often and generously.

All this goes to say that, in your last letter, and indeed most of your letters, your humbleness often does you credit; there is a point, however, where it also grants you less than you are due. Certainly if you draw the praise of others, for your good work and kind heart, that praise is true and well deserved. I advise you to accept it, rather than quailing at the thought. Honestly, to think you have endured cannonades and epidemics, winter and a Russian siege, yet still the talk of ladies over tea puts such a fright in you! I promise you, whatever is said, between milk and sugar and shortbread, it is all meant well.

It saddens me to hear you will be unable to accept our invitation for the time being. My mother and father, however, gratefully accept your apologies, and hope that in time you shall be able to take up the offer regardless – suffice to say, it is to be considered a standing one. For my part though, I would not begrudge you your absence: I know that you must do as you must, and see through your undertaking with the Committee before it can be concluded. I wonder, however, what your plans would be if the cloudy threat of war should dissipate and you should find yourself on home soil and at peace? What shape would your ideal take, and how does it compare with your actual plans? For of course you must have a plan of some kind – all your predictions and preparations cannot be pinned only on the opposite outcome, after all.

In the meantime I am yours,

Very sincerely,

Agnes Guthrie

James

My dear Agnes,

You'll recall my friend Doctor Charles Ryan, originally of Melbourne, but formerly of Plevna and Erzurum? He always had what one would call 'the gift of the gab' down to an art, and used it to great effect with our patients, both those recovering and those who we knew never would. To them it was a gift as well, bestowed very generously in every direction, and it helped also to cheer our spirits as we worked.

Casson was much alike, and had quite the knack in encouraging the loyalty and faith of his fellow men. But with Ryan, this talent came in just as effortlessly with women, whether the veiled wives of Turkish officials, or Western ladies. This brings me towards saying, of course, that he was ever one for compliments too, delivered artfully, and with a smile that seemed always to know more than it let on.

My point here is as follows. There were times when I wished I might have something of that manner, even if only to make me more at ease. I fear I am a bad conversationalist, and do not think that my adventures in the East have made my speech any the smoother. Indeed I'm worse still when overtaken by some worry or anxiety about how I'm perceived. Yet, by the standards you say you hold, it seems you might at least see this as a show of earnestness, and an absence of guile; whereas Ryan's complimentary manner was precisely the sort for which you have no time or heart to spare.

All the same, for all this, a part of me is glad of the circumstances under which we became properly acquainted. For it was not truly at the Carmichaels' in Glasgow that we came to know each other, but merely where we met. Rather, I think it was in Erzurum that we grew to know each other; in Erzurum where you were with me all the while, as light and warmth in the cold long night that place marks now in my life.

I hope I don't presume too much in saying so, Agnes. I wonder if you agree. In any case, I mean that I would have made a poorer impression by far if I had exchanged words with you first without the chance to consider and measure them, by means of pen and paper. These letters have helped me make a better impression than I might have, and I think your responses have helped make me a better man than I was.

There seems no likelihood of war now. How all that rumbling thunder I saw in Istanbul, and all the fervour the papers have thrown out here, has come to so little I do not know, and in truth my feelings are no clearer to me.

Let me explain, to you and to myself. I am relieved to be at peace now, whether only for a time, or for my whole life long. I have met with Lord Blantyre, finally, and found that he spoke highly of me – apparently Barrington-Kennet sent ahead by letter to do the same. In chasing Blantyre I have spent an abominable amount of time on trains from London to Edinburgh and back, but in doing so, have finally settled all my business with the SHC. I've been granted not only my backpay, but also some small reimbursement for all this travelling.

And yet, in being set free, I also feel quite cut loose. I'm exposed once more to my prospects, slim as they are, just as I was when we first began to exchange letters. So, more and more, things have come full circle, and things do not look much brighter for me now than they did back then. At least if war had broken out then I should have had some further chance of doing something to earn a reputation, and so settle anywhere with some chance of success. As things stand, I think Greenock is my only resource and I must fall back on it eventually.

But there is one thing in my future that's certain at least. I'll go for now to Glasgow, in part to see my old professors, and mine their connections for what advantage I can glean. But in the main, it is looking forward to seeing you that draws me that way.

Many thanks for the standing invitation. I look forward also to taking advantage of it whenever I can do so without being a burden.

Until we meet I am yours

Very sincerely,

James Denniston

June 1878

Chapter 30

Agnes

Dear James,
I understand your apprehension as to the state of your prospects on these shores. I remember well your unwillingness to serve under any doctor of the old school, whose methods and manner you would find personally abhorrent, and under whom you feel your own talent would chafe. You say that, without funds or reputation, you would be forced into such a servile situation for an uncertain length of time, and for little money.

Must I remind you, however, that you came to Erzurum in just such a state. With neither fame nor capital to your name, you were able to set yourself up as quite the hero there, and with a hospital almost of your own by the end of it! You need only find for yourself a new Erzurum – a place which will benefit from you as much as you will from it – and work as hard there as you did before. By will and sweat and skill, God willing, I have faith that what you want will follow.

Meantime, summer has set in here, and we find the Scottish sky as bright as well-buffed tin. A sunny day in Glasgow may be a strange, rare thing, but it's welcome indeed, and I find it fits my disposition very pleasantly. Even Mrs. Carmichael – of whom, if you have one abiding memory, it should be that she is ordinarily dour as grey serge – is come over with a mood to be outside and walking. This being a practise with which I have myself been quite taken of late, I am more than happy to instigate a daily constitutional. So, we promenade through the city, a loose line of pairs, and all in conversation, each day. And each time, James, I think to myself how it would be to walk with you, and talk with you, in such a way.

Will you join us soon? Are you yet in Glasgow, or have you gone already? Will you shortly return? Strange, but I don't think that even your time in Erzurum, in all its uncertainty, filled me with so many questions, each feeling more urgent than the last. When do you feel is a likely time for a visit? I should like to be able to expect you.

Until then I am yours,
Very sincerely,
Agnes Guthrie

James

My dear Agnes,

I was til lately in Glasgow, and there had the benefit of some discussions with those among my old professors for which I had some admiration. Some meetings were merely port and gentlemen's gossip. At others though, I was granted some very sound advice. I may have arrived upon a direction for my immediate future: I think I should like to deepen my studies. My experiences in Erzurum will, I believe, have given me an understanding of certain things medical that would be useful to the profession as a whole, after all.

Currently I am in Greenock, and have been staying at the Walkers' for some days, seeing other old friends, and notably, my dear mother. I do not think I need to say it, but she was incredulous and very pleased to have found me all in one piece. Not sufficiently pleased, though, to spare me six months' worth of scolding for going out to Turkey in the first instance, though!

If you are now in Glasgow, and at Crophill with the Carmichaels, I intend to arrive back in the city on Wednesday. If you are otherwise engaged I shall muster some patience, but perhaps I might do myself the pleasure of calling on you on Thursday? What might be the best time to find you in and able to receive company? I await your response eagerly.

Until then I am yours

Very sincerely,

James Denniston

Agnes

Dear James,

You are correct, and will find me at Crophill for the foreseeable future. We have grown accustomed to a walk at two in the afternoon, so I wonder if, perhaps, you might join us then?

Although we have been speaking together all these months, across land and ocean and all between, I think we shall still have a good deal to discuss together.

Do you know, I do not think I can remember the sound of your voice, I have grown so used to supplying some version of it in my head as I read your handwriting. I look forward to reacquainting myself with it. I look forward to Thursday very much.

Until then I am yours,

Very sincerely,

Agnes Guthrie

Afterword

James Denniston was awarded the Star of the Third Order of Osmanieh, and the Star of the Third Order of the Medjidie for his achievements in Erzurum.

He returned to the University of Glasgow and was awarded his MD. The cases he tended and the experiences he endured in Erzurum formed the backbone of his thesis. It is stored to this day in the university's archives.

He and Agnes Guthrie were married on the 9th of November 1880, at Broadoak, the Guthrie family home in Cheshire. They raised two sons and a daughter: Alexander Guthrie, William Cunningham, and Elizabeth.

They settled together in Dunoon, Scotland, where James set up in general practice. He eventually raised the funds to start a cottage hospital there, which remains part of Dunoon's health service even now.

By the age of 35, James's health was deteriorating due to a return of the pulmonary symptoms he first began to suffer in Erzurum. He resigned his commission in Dunoon and travelled south to Cheshire.

His illness, however, worsened, and obliged him to travel once more in search of a kinder climate. He became a ship's doctor and voyaged across the world, even reuniting with Charles Ryan in Melbourne.

Ryan himself was awarded the Fourth Order of the Medjidie, and the Third Order of Osmanieh for his service. At the outbreak of World War I in 1914, he was appointed assistant director of medical services for the Australian forces' 1st Division. In the Gallipoli campaign he worked against the same Ottoman Empire he had served almost forty years before.

James Denniston, however, died before he could see Europe teetering once more on the edge of war. He passed away on the 10th of April, 1895, aboard the SS *Tongarir.* He was buried at sea.

His children, however, continued his legacy, both in medicine and in the living of interesting lives.

William Cunningham Denniston and Elizabeth Denniston both followed in their father's footsteps, studying medicine.

His first son, Alexander 'Alastair' Guthrie Denniston, dedicated his life to serving his country in intelligence and decryption. During World War I he helped to found Room 40, which laid the foundations for what would, in time, become GCHQ. During World War II he set up and headed

Bletchley Park, working with mathematicians such as Alan Turing to break the Axis Enigma Code. The popular historical consensus is that their work in decrypting Axis communications shortened the war by two to four years. As to how many lives this foreshortening saved, the numbers are beyond counting.

To this day, Doctor James Denniston's descendants continue to work in medicine and charity.

The Red Crescent begun as an informal symbol: an inversion of the Ottoman flag, used by medical volunteers during the Russo-Turkish War of 1876-1878. It has since been adopted as the official symbol of humanitarian aid throughout 33 states in the Muslim world. Under the Red Crescent, in the present day, men and women still work as James Denniston did, to relieve suffering in a world still wracked by war.